ARC covers created in Canva

Cover Art/Title Page/Chapter Headers/Character Art/Map/Wheel of the Year: By Giulia Martini @julsiji

Interior Full-Page Illustration: By @pandyals_art

Alpha Readers: Chelsey Brand, Cynthia Brubaker, Jenn Trocine, Bethany Steadman

Dev/Copy/Line/Proof: Rachel Bunner of Rachel's Top Edits @rachels.top.edits

Contents

36. Also By M.A. Brown

M.A. Brown transports you to another world that's lush, vibrant, and brimming with lore. The characters are so intricately fleshed out and flawed you will be desperate for more when you turn the last page.
- *Stephanie Combs, author of, The Sun And Her Shadow*

In true M.A. Brown fashion, this lyrical and enigmatic book will make, break, and reshape you. A dark, sultry and irresistible read that will keep you turning pages late into the night.
- *Cynthia Brubaker, author of, Of Hearts and Hunters*

The Seventh Sister

By M.A. Brown

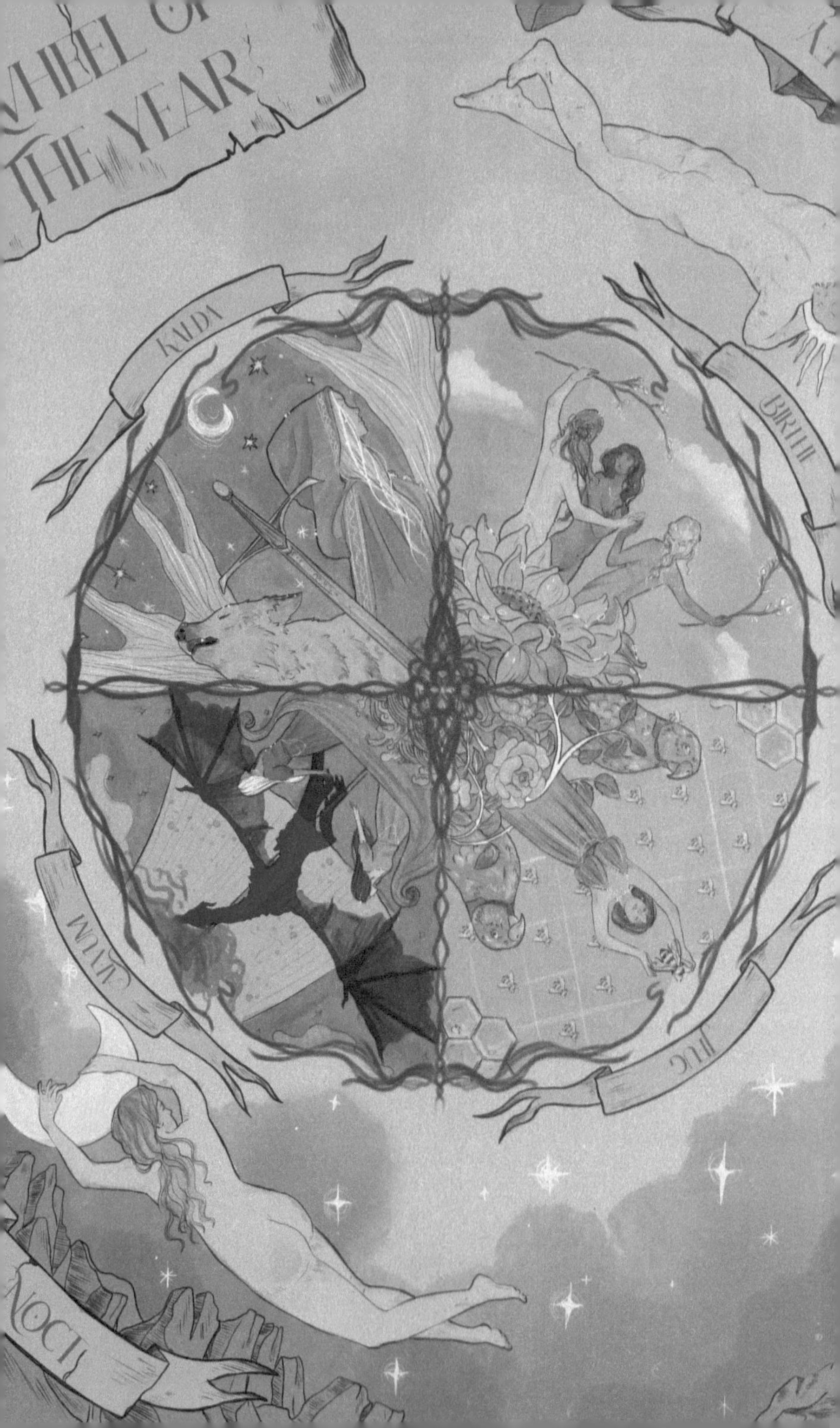

WHEEL OF
THE YEAR
KALDA
BIRTH
LUNA
LUG
NOCIS

XXXVIII
UMBRA

EMPHYREA
PONTONIUS GATE
BERTH
BLACKWOOD
UTHAR

DEAR READER,

I woke up from a dream several years ago with the beginning of this story in my head. Over the course of the following week, I poured six-ty-thousand words onto the page. I could not write this tale fast enough. And then the unthinkable happened. My computer crashed and all that work was lost. I was completely devastated. I proceed-ed to publish, not one, not two, but three stories before I decided it was finally time to come back to this world and write the story my heart was longing to tell. Never has something been so easy for me to work on, never has a world felt so vivid, or the characters in it so real. This story is so very near and dear to me, and I am so excited to relin-quish it to you so you can walk through Strattaria in Ertha's shoes.

As eager as I am for you to read this story, I would be remiss if I didn't take a moment to warn you, this tale will not be for everyone. It is quite a bit different, and darker than my other works. It is an adult fantasy and as such deals with more adult themes and is explicit, with graphic sex, language, and violence. There is attempted assault, assault, suicidal ideation and gore. There is mention and depictions of death and death of a parent. There are mentions of miscarriage off page, and a birth on page. If any of this is upsetting to you I'd advise that you proceed with caution.

Thank you so much for picking up this story, it means the world to me and I hope you enjoy journying with Ertha as much as I have.

Megan

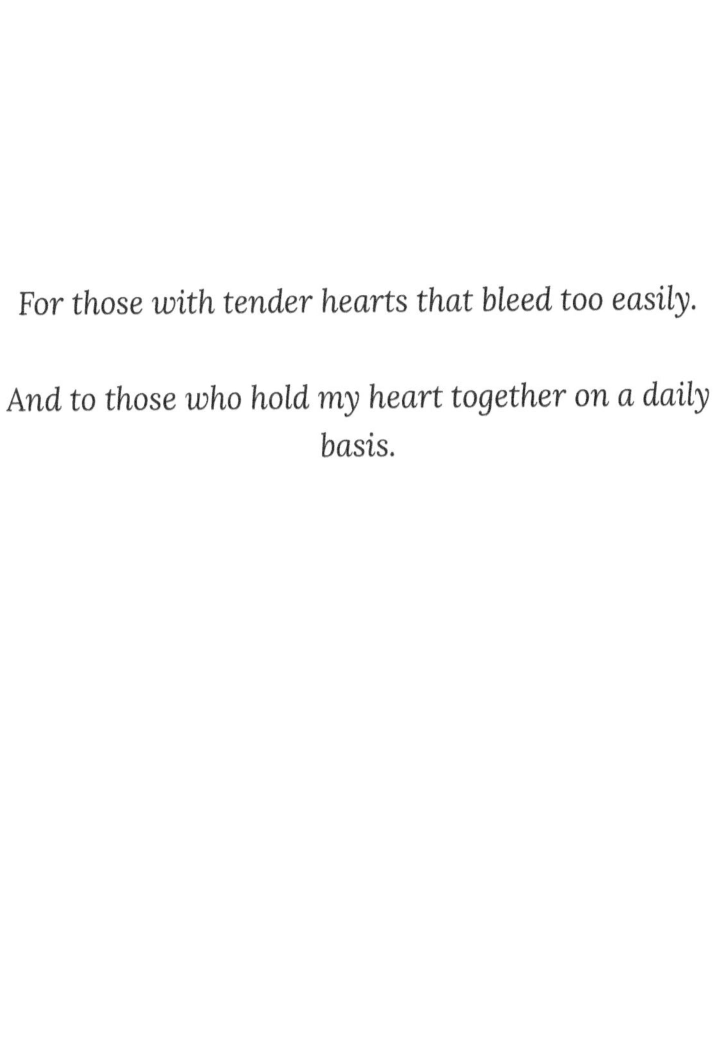

For those with tender hearts that bleed too easily.

And to those who hold my heart together on a daily basis.

Glossary

S TRATTARIA- THE EXISTENCE SPUN by the Emrys

Umbra- The hollow realm in the center of Strattaria and prison of the Niflym

Emphyrea- The realm of the Emrys suspended above the world they created

Dey- The period of time where Jyord treks across them Emphyrea with the Sun

Noct- The period of time when Melantha spins darkness and Selenyss treks across the Emphyrea with the moon

Kalda- The death of the year, marked by cold weather and dormant plants

Byrthe- The beginning or rebirth of the year

Jeug- The warmest part of the year

Aevum- The harvest season and time of the year where leaves begin to fall in preparation for kalda

Eklipsis- A celebration that takes place during the midpoint of kalda to celebrate the annual joining of Jyord and Selenyss

The Hunt- the Uthari marital ritual that takes place annually on Eklipsis

The Emrys

Imbola- Emrys of winds
Lugha- Emrys of grains and fruit
Edothea- Emrys of stone and soil
Ananasa- Emrys of fertility and childbirth
Yaganya- Crone Emrys; mother of all witches
Jyord- Emrys of the deys and sun
Melantha- Emrys of noct
Sidra- Daughter of the Crone
Orannus- Emrys of the ocean
Selenyss- Emrys of the moon
Inesmara- The Emrys of love
Agredmonya - The Red Lady, The Emrys of death
Wyrta- Emrys of luck and fortune
Taranya- Emrys of thunderstorms and lightning
Skai- Emrys of snow and blizzards

The Niflym

Terr- The most feared and suspected leader of the Niflym

A Guide to the Kingdoms

The Seven Kingdoms

VANYTH- VANYTH IS A marshy and moorland kingdom that lies in the west. Its people are peaceful and known for their pursuits in literature and art. They are the predominant exporters of food and grain in Strattaria, and as such, often fall prey to their raiding neighbors across the Yaenos Sea.

Uthar- Uthar is home to the Legendary Sons of Uthar. They sustain their kingdom by raiding the coasts and ships of other peoples. They have a massive navy due in large part to their proximity to the Blackwood, where they harvest lumber for their ships. There are many myths and stories told about the mysterious kingdom since few dare to visit it and those who do, don't often return, except traders, who, rumor has it, are never permitted to go farther than the docks.

Corvus- Corvus is an isolated kingdom resting near the top of the world. It is surrounded by the Celestial Mountains, a treacherous maze of ship-killing fjords, and the Impassable Cliffs of Drakonfell, making it one of the most secure kingdoms in all of Strattaria. They are well-known for their prodigious university, and it has been long rumored that their mastery of the alchemical craft surpasses all others.

Orybous- The Orybous Isles are an archipelago situated off the northern coast of Vanyth. The possession of the isles have long been disputed between three rival brotherhoods: the Ochrai, the Malichai, and the Leviathai. At present, there is a tentative peace between them. A high-ranking member from each brotherhood sits on a ruling council called the Triarii, who reside in an area of neutrality known as Triumvirate City.

Posidonia- Home of the Mer people, this kingdom spans much of the floor of the Yaenos and Leviathan Seas. They have land-based outposts for trading with the surface-dwelling kingdoms, including Posidonia's Gate. Their kingdom is split into two parts, Upper and Lower Posidonia, each ruled by a separate royal family.

Iliff- This icy kingdom, home of the Ilf kind, sits at the base of the world. The country is often considered by artists to be the most beautiful of all the kingdoms, famed for its Crystal Cliffs and Glacial Rivers. It is, however, also infamous for its seemingly endless war of succession between the clans, which is why its seat of power has been dubbed the Bloody Throne.

Enar- Home of the Great Grass Sea peoples. Enar sits just north of the kingdom of Uthar and has been one of the only kingdoms to keep Uthar from its shores. This is due in large part to the difficulty in traversing the Great Grass Sea and, of course, their Moltar Dragons, which have yet to be beaten in battle.

The Fallen Kingdoms

Lamya- Once known as the Witch Kingdom, the mountain stronghold of Lamya, built into the Yaganya mountain rage just south of the Celestial Mountains, has long since been abandoned due to the genocide of the witches.

Drakonfell- While not technically a fallen kingdom, the people of Drakonfell have not been seen for centuries, and all access to their lands on the roof of the world were cut off and are now impassable.

The Uncharted Lands

On the far side of Strattaria lay the uncharted lands. The existence of these lands is highly contested and cannot be confirmed due to the treacherous nature of the sea surrounding their theorized location, which is said to be so tumultuous that even the Mer can not traverse it.

Ertha- ER-thuh

Helima- HA-lee-muh

Fenris- FEN-riss

Ingemar-ing-GUH-mar

Kastor- KASS- tor

Huggin- H-OO-gin

Munnin- M-OO-nin

Rhapso- RAP-so

Thyra- Thigh-ruh

Otaden- OH-ta-den

The creation of Strattaria as it was whispered on the wind by the most holy Emrys Imbola to the prophet Zithusala.

IN THE BEGINNING, WE, the Emrys, were alone in the Emphyrea. We lived quite contentedly, drinking from the rivers of luminous aurora and sheltering in our villas against the slopes of the Emphyrean Mountains.

But planted and growing within each of us upon our divine conception was a unique power. Some of us could make light, some could shape stone. I could weave my will into the air, teasing it into a tempest.

Now, I love my siblings and friends, they are precious to me, but we can often be boastful creatures. And after aeons together, as it often does, our boastfulness gave way to envy and scorn, so it was decided that there would be a great demonstration to allow us to display our talents. Thus proving once and for all who was the strongest and most exceptional among us.

Our demonstrations spanned eras. My sister spun stone and soil in the void below us, crafting a near-perfect mirror image of the Emphyrea. Some blew life in the shape of flora across the barren surface, bleeding bounty into the desolate space. My betrothed filled the lowlands with deep waters and spilled into them a multitude of small species plucked from his imagination. And on it went. We spun our magics and molded things that crept and crawled, seasons and storms. We were truly enraptured with our creations; so beloved were they to us that we deemed the land worthy of a name and called it Strattaria.

While some of our powers were beautiful and revered, others were feared and disdained. Rather than creating and adding to our world, they destroyed. They brewed illnesses among our new creatures, they spread rot and pestilence. Out of fear, we were quick to deem those powers as lesser. We shunned those who wielded them as Niflym, meaning "those who are tainted." We soon dismissed them, turning our attention again to Strattaria and ignoring the Niflym, letting them slip from our minds. We focused instead on stretching our abilities, honing them and creating, painting our creation with beauty and wonder.

But little did we know, disparaging their treatment, one among the Niflym, Terr, began to gather others, riling them up in rebellion. But so absorbed in the marvel and mastery of our magic were we that we paid them no heed until it was too late. In a rage, Terr threatened our youngest, Sidra, the daughter of the Yaganya the Crone. In a panic, I used my powers of wind and air to fling all the Niflym from the Emphyrea. My sister, with her quick wit, drew up the soil and stone of the new realm of Strattaria and bid it to swallow the Niflym, trapping and sealing them inside an eternal prison of darkness. But in the last moment before I cast them out, out of spite or desperation, Terr grabbed the arm of the crone's daughter and dragged her down with him into the belly of the world, to a place we would come to call "the Umbra."

As her daughter slipped into Terr's grasp, Yaganya let out a heart-shattering wail that I can still feel even now as an echo in my bones. Before anyone could stop her, she dove from the Emphyrea after her beloved daughter, but she was too late. We watched in horror as she crashed into Strattaria just as its maw snapped shut. With her dying breaths, her power warped and twisted her form, growing it even as it broke, and formed a range of mountains upon the land. Her ribs fractured, and her power spilled forth, and from it crawled a writhing mass of beings, each in the image of the Crone, each with a glittering sliver of her magic within them.

As one, we wept for Yaganya and Sidra; our tears watered Strattaria, and rivers flowed. When at long last our sorrow was wrung out of us and we were left hollow in our grief, the six most powerful among us—their ranks solidified by our competitions—made a sacrifice and birthed from their cores creatures in their likenesses to keep the remnants of our fallen friend and sister company.

Two among us used their powers of light and crafted a radiant sphere of gilded fire and a pearlescent orb of argent radiance. In turn, they carry their inventions of light across the Emphyrea so all on our Strattaria can see and remember where it was they came from and what was lost in their birth. And even todey, we watch over our creations still, moving the sun and the moon, watering their fields, and blowing sweet breezes across the lands.

S ELENYSS TURNED AWAY THE face of her moon as the raucous tune from the adjacent tavern and the elicit moans of our friends filled the too still silence between me and the man who stood in the shadows guarding the alley's entrance. They'd been at it for some time, and Jasper and I had exhausted all the safe topics of conversation.

I was about to ask him if he'd read anything of note lately—not a conversation that would go very far, since the only readings the Priestesses believed were acceptable were religious and healing texts—when a whimper from the mouth of the alley drew my gaze. A small, shaggy dog with milky eyes and scabby, patched skin molting through its tufted coat limped around the corner, whining with every step.

"Oh, you poor dear." I crouched down and held out a hand.

"Careful, my lady. It may be rabid," Jasper cautioned from over my shoulder.

I laughed. "This sweet boy? I don't think so. He just has a bit of mange and an empty belly. Don't you, sweet thing?" The pup in question was already licking my outstretched fingers and nuzzling against my palm to beg for scraps and scratches.

"Is that not contagious? I wouldn't want someone as lovely as you to end up afflicted." My companion cleared his throat nervously.

I looked back over my shoulder at him. His face had paled considerably, and his eyes darted between my hand and the dog like he worried it might be hungry enough to start snacking on my flesh. "Jasper, are you afraid of dogs?"

He scoffed, but it felt entirely too exaggerated to be sincere. "No, of course not."

I smiled gently. "Don't worry. I'll protect you from this beastie."

He grumbled something unintelligible as I turned my attention back to my new four-legged companion, withdrawing a tin of salve from my pocket.

"There's a good boy," I crooned sweetly as I unscrewed the lid and slathered handfuls of the herbal concoction onto the mutt's affliction. The worst of it seemed to be concentrated on his hindquarters. "Rest easy. I'll fix you right up."

By the time I was done, his tail was thumping his thanks and his improved mood against the alley floor.

Jasper cleared his throat again. "For the—uh—patient." I turned to find him offering a fistful of jerked meat in his trembling fingers as he studiously avoided looking directly at the dog.

My eyes crinkled at the corners as I contained my mirth at seeing him so disconcerted by the presence of such a small beast, but fears were fears, and there was no helping them. I took the meat and tore it into smaller, bite-sized pieces. The pup snuffled gratefully as he gobbled down every last morsel.

"Alright, Ertha. Let's go." Helima's singsong voice ricocheted down the narrow walkway as she strode toward me, blooming from the shadows, straightening her too tight dress borrowed from the donations bin. I hadn't bothered changing out of my pale blue and white dedicates dress. I'd opted instead to just hide the pristine swaths of fabric under a dark cloak with a deep cowl. "It'll be deybreak soon, and we can't get caught out of bed once the sun is up."

I scratched the dog behind the ears one last time as I stood and nodded a goodbye to Jasper. Of all the friends of men who Helima had dallied with on these sneaky outings of ours, he was the first who'd been polite. And more than polite, he'd been kind. A true gentleman.

"Wait, will I see you again? I'll be back in town again before Eklipsis." His words were slightly slurred from the mulled drink he'd been nursing all noct, but they were also earnest and sweet and came attached to a smile that almost made me want to break my no-kissing rule.

I looked up at him demurely through my silver lashes. "We'll see." I rested a hand on his stubbled cheek in farewell, and he caught it up, turned his face, and pressed a kiss to my palm before he let it fall and faded back into the dark of the alley, summoned by the call of his friend just as I had been.

"Well, he was handsome." Helima giggled as we linked arms and slipped out onto the main road through the fishing village that knelt at the feet of the Selenyss Temple, where we were both currently supposed to be laid up, abed with women's troubles—at least, that's what I'd told the dedicate that morning when she'd summoned me with a knock on my cell door. "Tall too. Was he a good kisser? Because mine was an excellent kisser."

"Right, all you did was a bit of kissing." I nudged her teasingly. "And I didn't kiss him. You know my rule."

She was the bold one out of the pair of us. In all the years since I'd been sent to study at the temple, I'd never once thought of sneaking out until she had arrived from Orybous to be a kitchen helper a handful of years past, her red hair wild and her violet eyes feral and full of mischief. We'd been fast and fierce friends. Well, maybe I'd thought about it, but I'd certainly never acted on the impulse.

"I didn't say he wasn't excellent at other things too; he certainly knew his way around the under-side of a woman's skirt. And he had the biggest co—"

"Helima, language!" I scolded in feigned horror. "You can't enter the temple compound with a mouth like that."

Helima's lips curled into a ridiculous grin that was pure feline and made me love her all the more. "That's probably the least wicked thing I've done with my mouth all noct."

We dissolved into an effervescent fit of laughter that we tried to stifle behind our fingers, only settling when she unlinked our arms and pulled a twine-wrapped bundle from the pocket inside her cloak. "Happy name dey, Ertha."

I took it from her and hurriedly unwrapped the string and waxed linen cloth. In it lay a palm-sized, damson-colored cake stamped with the likeness of Selenyss.

"Oh, Helima, this is perfect. When did you find the time to bake it?" I breathed in the nostalgic scent of wine-soaked plums, decadent sugars, salacious spices, and fond childhood memories of sneaking similar delectables arranged atop gilded, towering trays on banquet tables with my sisters. "And where on Strattaria did you get the herbs?"

She shrugged. "You know, here and there. I might have made friends with a trader's son when we snuck out to that bonfire on the beach last jeug. Go ahead—try it."

"Alright, but you must have some too." I broke the cake in half and handed her a piece, careful not to spill the mince filling stuffed into the innermost layer.

We chewed in silence as we made the trek to the temple along the main road, savoring the confectionary magic Helima had wrought. She was too good to work in the kitchens of the temple for the rest of her deys—scrubbing pots, exclusively making the plainest dishes imaginable, and living in the darkness of noct, only seeing glimpses of stolen sunlight in passing.

"One more cycle of seasons until you can go home," she said as we licked our fingers clean, not willing to waste even a crumb. "Are you excited?"

Excited didn't even begin to cover it. There wasn't a word all-encompassing enough for the thrill I felt at the ticking down of deys. It had been so long since I'd seen my home. My family sent letters of course, but nothing could compare to the sounds of their voices or the feel of their loving arms. But I would miss Helima, which was why a plan had slowly been taking shape in my mind—I just needed to make sure it was what she wanted too.

"Would you come with me when I leave? There is a cooking academy there. I could write to my sister, Thyra. She could help secure you a scholarship?"

Our steps faltered as Helima threw her arms around my neck. "By the Emrys, Ertha, of course I'll come with you! I've been dreading the idea of you leaving me here all alone with these stodgy old priestesses. You really don't think your family will mind?"

"Not at all. There's already eight of us sisters; who's going to be bothered by one more?"

I wrapped my hand around hers and gave it a squeeze as we turned to crest the top of the small rise upon which the crystalline temple complex was built, watching over the fishing village at its feet like a goose minding her goslings. In the graying light of approaching dawn, I could just make out the silhouetted peaks of the Emphyrea spearing down through the canvas-white clouds that would soon be painted with Jyord's light now that Selenyss had set her moon aside, and I was beset with the memory of my arrival just over ten years ago. My governess and I had arrived late, our ship delayed at sea. As my feet had landed on the docks, Jyord's light had struck the temple, illuminating its glassy walls in an amber glow as warm as honey freshly stripped from the hive.

I smiled fondly at the reminiscence as Helima and I tiptoed around the back of the temple to the kitchen gate meant for deliveries. At this early hour and with dey dancing quickly over the horizon, hopefully there would not be many about, as all dedicates lived a nocturnal existence. By now, even the most scholarly or pious were long in their beds, with the exception of the High Priestess, who made rounds occasionally to make sure all was in order. But if the Emrys of fortune, Wyrta, smiled on us as she had every time before, we would not cross her path.

The gate groaned softly as I slid it open, in need of a good oiling, my ears pricked for any sound of approaching feet as we slipped through and shut it. The kitchen garden was almost eerie in the half light, like I was seeing it at the wrong angle, an image warped by irregular mirror glass. We quickly made for the breezeway connected to the courtyard, where we would separate—her to the servants' quarters and I to the dedicates'. There was admittedly little difference in their size and accommodation, the only exception being that the servants were allowed larger windows. Dedicates were meant to keep their eyes on Selenyss and their minds on their prayers, not on frivolities like the pattern of the waves or the rolling of the grasses in the breeze.

Helima and I embraced in farewell at the foot of the stairs on the far side of the courtyard, when a voice bloomed out of the darkness of a nearby arcade, followed by the stooped form of the High Priestess. "Ertha and Helima." The wizened woman wheezed into a handkerchief. "What in the Emrys' names are you doing roaming outside of your cells at this hour? The dawn bell tolled nearly an hour past."

An excuse, I had an excuse all preplanned in the event this happened—though, admittedly, a flimsy one—and I fumbled over it. "I-I needed a tea from the kitchens, Your Holiness. Ehm, women's troubles, you see..."

"An untruth. Your bleeding ceased three nocts ago." Damn clever woman. Of course she watched the launderette for my sheets and tracked my cycles. She wouldn't want anyone to accuse her of ill-keeping me if someone were to mar the purity of my maidenhead. "You've been sneaking out again, haven't you?" She pointed a crooked and angry finger at us. I glanced at Helima to see if the Priestess's knowledge of our comings and goings was news to her as it was to me, but Helima refused to meet my gaze and instead bowed her head in a sullen and cowed silence that seemed so unlike the woman she had been mere moments ago. "I've warned you, girl, that your whorish instincts will get you into trouble. To the kitchens with you. Wake the cook and tell her to give you ten sound lashes."

Horror twisted my organs like the tines of a fork twisting stringy meat. "No, please! No!" I grabbed the edge of Helima's sleeve to halt her retreat and drew her behind my back, placing myself firmly between her and the Priestess. "Please. It was my idea to leave the temple. Let me take the punishment for her."

"Bah." The Priestess spat on the dust-dried stones at her feet. "You should have thought of that before sneaking out. You know very well the punishment for rules that have been broken. Although you cannot be disciplined, you should have had the foresight to realize that our ordinances would apply to her."

I took a step closer; insistence driving my steps. I could not allow my friend to be subjected to such cruelty.

A bell tolled from below in the village, cutting through the still morning air like a strike of lightning on a sunny dey.

The Priestess's bushy eyebrows crawled up her folded forehead in undiluted shock. Her already ashen skin went waxy. "To your cell. Now, Ertha. Quickly. Helima, the kitchens—wake the cook. Warn her if she hasn't heard them already. She will tell you what they mean and what to do."

Helima reached out and squeezed my hand before she ran back the way we'd come.

"What? What is it? What is that bell?"

The villagers, out of respect for the temple inhabitants' lifestyles, refrained from ringing the hour—or at all—except on feast deys. I wracked my brain and could think of no feast they would be celebrating today. Something uncomfortable and wary churned in the hollow next to my quivering heart.

The Priestess did not answer as she flung herself toward the stairs that led to the battlements in a billow of white robes and the scrape of an ill-turned foot. Instead of heeding her demands with meekness as Helima had, I followed closely on her heels.

As we reached the top of the outer wall, the first rays of Jyord's sun burst red over the southern horizon and the stone around us—clear and veined in white—reflected it perfectly. I stared in awe at the bricks beneath my feet as they began to glow with such a brilliance, it seemed as though each crystal held a bit of Jyord's fire. But red—red was a poor omen indeed; I'd heard it from the fishmongers these past ten years. *Red sun in the morning, Jyord gives warning.* I thought that must have been the reason for the bell, but then I turned and saw them. A large ship anchored just outside the cove, surrounded by landing crafts, its figurehead carved in the likeness of a wolf, its banners black.

"It cannot be," I whispered, not quite believing my own eyes. "Priestess?" I turned to the hunched woman; her knuckles white as they gripped her prayer rope. Below me in the courtyard, I heard the scrambling of boot heels on cobbles followed by the bell of the sanctum tolling in response to the one in town. A chill crept like tapping spider legs down my back, weaving webs of unease around my spine.

The old woman turned her watery gaze on me, her pupils blown so wide, they nearly swallowed the green of her eyes. "The Sons of Uthar," she gasped.

Her long, gnarled fingers darted out and grabbed my arm. Uneven nails bit into my skin as she dragged me back the way we had come, but not before I caught sight of the plague of men in black armor swarming like an angry horde of ants out of their landing boats and onto shore.

I pulled in vain against her. "Wait, no. We must head directly to the village and help; there will be wounded."

But she ignored my protests and dug her nails deeper into my wrist. With surprising strength for one so old, she yanked me faster down the halls now filled with panic-faced dedicates in various stages of dress.

We reached my cell door, and she flung me inside. The toe of my boot caught on the lip of the floor stone, and I sprawled on the cold cobbles, my palms tearing and my knees screaming on impact.

"What do you think you are doing!" I shouted at her. Indignation swelled like a tide within me as I shoved myself to my knees.

She pulled a knife from somewhere in the folds of her robes and tossed it toward me. "They will kidnap you for ransom if they discover who you are. You had better use that before they can lay a finger on you. Do not let yourself be taken."

She spun around and slammed the door. The outer bolt groaned shut, rasping in its catchment with a horrible finality, locking me in. I scrambled to my feet and flung myself at the wooden door, pounding my fists.

I yelled after her, "Just let me help! Please let me out!" I wiggled the latch and rattled the door uselessly, my throat clenched in a strangling fist of fury and fear. Scalding tears welled in my eyes, blurring the heavy wood in front of me. "You can't just leave me here!"

But she could, and she did.

I SCREAMED UNTIL MY lungs shredded raw and the sounds of battle and the fear of being caught stilled my tongue to silence. The light from the slip of a window at the top of my wall grew from the soft hues of dawn to the gilded gossamer tones of early afternoon.

Think, I had to think. There had to be a way to open the Emrys-damned door. This was no time to let emotion get the better of me. I had to find a way out. A way to help.

My eyes landed on the knife etched in ancient runic symbols, the blade as long as my forearm, the hilt made of bleached white ivory. I'd seen it used—though rarely—in ceremonies that demanded a blood sacrifice. I snatched it up with fingers that trembled so fiercely, it seemed as though the blade hummed with a life of its own against my palm.

I turned and thrust it into the slight crack between the wall and the door, where I approximated the bolt to be, and putting all my body weight into it, I levered it up. Again and again until sweat broke out on my brow and my fingers ached from the scrape of the knife's handle, until I heard a crack like a breaking bone. I greedily gulped air as I pushed the door open and stumbled into the hall. Immediately, I regretted it. The coppery tang of blood stuffed my mouth like cotton until I wanted to wretch. The thready clash of metal on metal echoed distantly down the hall, snaring my attention and clearing my mind.

I hiked up my skirt and tied the knife to my thigh with the ribbons used to hold up my stockings, then I ducked back into my cell and grabbed the woven basket full of healing herbs and various other supplies that sat at the foot of my narrow bed. Without much more thought, I ran toward the stairs that lead to the main courtyard, toward the stench of blood.

My heart thrashed against my ribs, but I tried to focus on calming my breath the way my teachers had taught me to do when a healing became particularly complicated. All my miserable attempts at peaceful composure shattered the moment I reached the courtyard. Dedicates lay strewn about, their bodies contorted unnaturally, some missing limbs entirely. My stomach roiled as blood filled my slippers and saturated my hemline, creeping up like the grasping hand of Death trying to lay claim to my soul. The silence screamed that no one was alive; I didn't need to check the bodies to know their hearts lay still.

I cautiously peered into the shadowed mouths of the hollow hallways that lead off the main courtyard, looking for any lingering blood-hungry Sons before I slogged my way through the gore to the alleyway that led to the back of the temple, where the kitchens lay. A dim, flickering hope burned next to my heart and whispered, however irrationally, that Helima would be there in hiding.

I tried to block out the things that squished beneath my feet in the alley, the light dimmed by twin overhangs blocking out the rays of eerie, crimson sunlight. As I came to the other side, I pressed myself against the wall, and with one more breath to steady myself, I snuck a glance into the garden. Again, I didn't see any Sons. Perhaps they'd finished pillaging, or perhaps they were lurking elsewhere—either way, I silently thanked the Emrys that they did not bar my way. I ran quickly through the rows of knee-high planter boxes filled with an assortment of shrubby medicinal and cooking herbs. I usually found this part of the temple complex with its densely planted herbs perfuming the air to be the most soothing, but the raw edge of anxiety that gnawed along the vertebrae of my spine like a dog on a soupbone made it hard to feel anything except sharp, toothy, adrenaline-fueled focus.

My mouth gaped in a silent scream, and I smothered it with a bitten fist as I took in the entry to the kitchens. Sprawled across the cobblestone threshold lay Helima. Her auburn hair that spilled from under her head covering was matted nearly black with blood. I dropped to my knees, and my basket tumbled freely from my hand as I scooped her into my lap, carefully cradling her head.

"Helima. Oh Helima." I sobbed. I never should have let her leave my side.

I delved into myself, where the well of my Emrys-given gifts lay, the source of my healing abilities. In my mind's eye, I saw it: a crystalline-clear pool from which I could pull droplets of power. Like a drop of rain striking a puddle in reverse, first the ripples formed, and then the droplets sped through me to my fingertips. I had done this so often that it'd become second nature, and in a fraction of a heartbeat, the power slipped from my fingers and into Helima, looking for the source of her injuries. There were many, too many, and they had been there too long. The fire that was inside her, that was her, was little more than a floundering ember drowning in blood.

I pressed my forehead to hers and sent a silent prayer to the Emrys of death to ease her passing. I felt her brow furrow under mine, and her voice croaked, barely above a whisper, "Ertha?"

I lifted my head and stroked her brow. "Yes, dear friend, it's me. I'm here."

"Heed Her…" She gasped, her blood-stained hand clawing at her throat.

"It's okay, Helima. Rest now. Everything is okay." I brushed my fingers along her cheek.

Her eyes flung wide, unseeing and out of focus with this realm. "She says...you must balance—" Blood bubbled from the corner of her mouth as she gasped and sucked for air that wouldn't fill her lungs all the way "Balance...the scales...As above...so...below."

I held back a sob, I had been at many death beds; the things the dying saw or spoke of sometimes made little sense, but it didn't matter. What mattered was being there for them, witnessing them and their passing. It had never occurred to me, however, that I would be doing it for a friend, and so soon. My healing gifts scrambled frantically, pushing at the tips of my fingers to seep into her skin, but her body rejected it. She was too far gone to be pieced back together again. I pressed my quivering lips into a thin line, refusing to be anything but strong for her.

"Heed her...Ertha...She says...it is dire." Her breath pulled and gurgled as her lungs shook, dancing with death inside the cage of her ribs. "I love...you..."

Silver rimmed my eyes and blurred my vision. "And I you."

She smiled and feebly reached a hand for mine. I took her cold fingers and sang softly, the song of the dying from her native land.

"*Take the boat home*
Take the boat home
To the land beyond the seas
Take the fair boat
Take the fair boat
And kiss Orannus once for me."

Before I could finish, the light slipped from her violet eyes, leaving her gaze hollow and gray. I choked on the words of the song lodged like glass in my throat. I wanted to scream and rage at the Emrys, but it would be of no use. So instead, as I gently laid my friend back down and slid her eyes closed for the last time, I begged the Emrys, any who were listening, to let me save someone, anyone. If only I could use my powers to save just one life.

The temple was still, silent as a tomb, which was, after all, what it had become. I pressed a final kiss to Helima's forehead. Perhaps if I could make it to the village, there would be people alive there. I froze halfway between sitting and standing as I reached for my basket of supplies. From the corner of my eye, I swore I saw the flash of billowing red skirts just beyond the back gate. But how could that be? All the dedicates and people who lived within the walls wore white, and the Sons wore Umbra black. Maybe a villager? Unthinking, I tore down the path to the gate. It was usually locked by now, but it hung crumpled and half off its hinges—forced open by the Sons, no doubt.

The large grove of ancient trees behind the temple seemed foreboding, when, before, it had seemed full of wonder. The shadows between trunks seemed too dark and writhing despite the blaring sun. I veered left along the wall in the direction I had seen the skirt dash. If it had been a villager coming to the temple for healing or sanctuary, perhaps the Emrys had seen fit to answer my prayer. But it wasn't a villager whose leg I stumbled over as I passed a clump of vinterberry bushes; it was a bloodied Son of Uthar, his back pressed against the gleaming walls of the temple he and his kind had so disgracefully raided, his head hanging limply, the stab wound on his side leaking blood onto the sacred ground he'd desecrated.

Rage shook my hands in a trembling fury, and I cursed, a phrase better suited to the fishmonger I'd heard it from. An Emrys had answered my prayer alright, the trickster to be sure; no one else would have been so cruel.

I knelt next to the unconscious man and settled my basket beside me, knowing full well it would take more than herbs to heal him. And heal him I must despite his sins, because the greater sin would be to leave him, and that sin, I knew, could cost me everything; it could cost me the gifts of healing. The Emrys had granted it to me, and they could take it away for ignoring those in need. Healing was meant to be blind. I could feel the well of power inside me quiver. I could feel it shifting into my veins as though it were trying to jump from me of its own accord to heal the Son.

My fingers found the blood-slicked buckles of his noctmare-black leather breastplate, and I fumbled with them until they slipped loose. The one at his shoulder followed, and I managed to heave the piece of armor off his muscle-bulked torso. His head lolled to the side, deeply unconscious. I freed him of his wolf-shaped helm pounded out of black metal to reveal a surprisingly human face. Not that I'd expected the rumors to be true, that the Sons themselves were literal beasts; those were just bedtime tales to frighten children into behaving.

My former governess loved those tales. *"Behave, Highness, or a Son of Uthar may come howling in the noct and gobble you up with his fangs."* But the Sons of Uthar had come, and the reality was far worse than what I'd imagined as a child in my bed despite the fact, or maybe because of the fact that they were, after all, real flesh-and-blood men.

I rocked back on my heels and surveyed the man before me. He couldn't have been more than two to three years my senior. As far as I could see, the wound in his side was the only damage done to him aside from some raking marks along his forearm under the straps of his arm guards. Were they from Helima? Had she fought against him with all her meager strength? I probed the hole in his tunic under his left arm, ripping it wider so I could see the whole gash. Had she taken a knife to him and plunged it into the weakest point in his armor, hoping it might slow him so she could run? So she could live? How many lay dead in a sea of their own blood inside the temple because of this man? I swallowed the wrath blistering my throat. "*Healing is blind*," I had been so often reminded by my instructors. Healers exist to mend the broken, not to bestow judgment upon the fallen.

My power leapt from my fingers. It ached to explore the man's wound as I plunged them gently into the torn flesh. A sharp inhale was all the reaction he gave. I placed my free hand on his forehead and silenced his mind, dulling the pain. I wriggled my fingers further in, between his rib bones, until I could feel the deepest part of the damage: a slight, barely there nick to his heart. I closed my eyes and poured all my focus into the feeling of my fingers in his rent flesh. I envisioned the fibers of torn muscle pulling and knitting back together.

I slid my fingers back a hair again and again and continued to mend until there was nothing left but an angry gash where the knife had entered him. I placed my bloodied palm flat against his ribs over what remained. My hand glowed slightly, silver like the moon, and pulled those last threads of flesh together until even the gash was gone; it could not be said I did not do everything in my ability to save him.

My head spun as it so often did after an intense healing, and I slumped onto my backside into the blood-soiled dirt with an ungraceful *umph*.

"Well, what do we have here?"

I whipped my head up and spun to face a group of men on horseback. My stomach knotted, and I tried not to wretch at the sight of their black armor. I'd been so focused on healing that I hadn't heard them approach. The Priestess's last warning not to allow myself to be captured echoed across my bones and made me shiver.

"It looks like we've found ourselves a True Healer, Sons." The man's gruff, oil-slicked voice was as terrifying as the baying of hounds in a dark wood on a moonless noct as he glowered down at me. He was older, his long hair graying, and obviously high ranking by the way he held himself. Perhaps there was a slight chance he would think me inconsequential and I would be able to escape.

My eyes darted around, looking for any potential path to dash down if only I could scramble to my feet quickly enough. The Son on the horse to the elder man's right glowered down at me, and my spine stiffened as I dared to look at his eyes. They were nothing but hollow pits of pitch that rooted me to the soil. "A true prize indeed, Commander," he drawled, though he sounded slightly bored. "The Father will be pleased."

"Your name, girl," the Commander barked.

I took a breath, willing my voice not to wobble. "Fuck you." I spat at his horse's feet.

He laughed. They all laughed. Fury stoked to life in my ribcage like a hearth and welled in my eyes, but I dashed it away with the heel of my hand.

"The Commander asked for your name, girl," the hollow-eyed man growled. Everything about him screamed of otherness. His hair was shorn on either side of his head, and what was left in the center was braided back in thick ropes down to his waist in a bizarre style I had never seen either at court as a child or on those who made the pilgrimage to the temple on occasion. And the color of it—so black, it seemed to leech light from around him.

I suppressed a shudder and answered, keeping my chin held high. "My name is Ertha."

"And your family name, Ertha?" The way my name sounded in his mouth felt like maggots on my skin.

"I have none. I am merely a devotee of the temple," I lied, lowering my lids as I continued to try to plot a path of escape. The dark one had mentioned the Father, who I knew to be the king of Uthar. I couldn't let them take me, not to him, not anywhere.

The dark one sneered, "Odd for a devotee to be wearing a diadem, no?" The hair on the back of my neck stood on end. If he knew what it meant—gooseflesh rippled across my back and swept in waves around the rest of my body—I didn't want to consider what would happen.

My brain grappled for an explanation like fingers against the underside of a frozen lake. "I-I am the dedicated Maiden of the temple. The diadem is a symbol of my purity and commitment to the Emrys." I sent up a prayer to every Emrys I could think of that his knowledge when it came to the inner workings of the temples of Selenyss was lacking. The temples didn't keep dedicated Maidens, not anymore. To the best of my knowledge, only the temples dedicated to the Emrys of fertility and birth, Ananasa, still held with such traditions. But this untruth was the swiftest one I could come up with, and besides, I *was* a maiden still, so that fact could be verified if he were brutish enough to demand a midwife check, as I knew some did before marital vows could be spoken.

I held my breath as he was silent for several long moments.

"I was unaware that the Selenyss Temples still held to the old ways." His voice carried only the slightest hint of suspicion, and I took that as a success.

"Well, in Vanyth, they do," I affirmed with as much confidence as I could.

Thyra had once told me confidence could cover almost any sin, and right then, I prayed it truly could, for if they found out I was the seventh sister to the heir of the Vanithian crown, it would not only be *my* life in peril.

T HE COMMANDER BARKED ORDERS for the wounded man at my side to be loaded onto a cart along with a handful of other injured. "Put the Healer on there too so she can get to work on the wounded Sons."

My head jerked up, my eyes bursting wide with panic. "I-I can't. I have to stay." The words spilled out of my mouth without thought, and I cursed myself for the floundering naïvety of them.

The Commander sneered. "Silly girl, do you really think we would ever leave a treasure such as yourself behind?" A few of the men chuckled along with him. He threw his head back and roared with laughter, though I noted that the dark one did not. "No, Healer. We may not have found what we were after, but you are a more than sufficient replacement."

Rough hands grabbed me by the arms, yanked me to my feet, and shoved me toward the cart. I stumbled, catching myself on its edge. Wooden slivers dug into my already wounded palms, and I bit back tears.

One of my handlers laughed. "On ya get, swee'art."

He shoved me up, groping me unnecessarily as he did. I rounded on him as I settled myself on the edge of the small two-wheeled cart and spat in his eye.

"Oi! You bitch!" His hand connected with the side of my face so swiftly, I didn't see it coming. My vision swam, sparking with dark stars at the edges, and my ears rang.

The grizzled Commander trotted over and kicked the Son squarely in the jaw. "You Emrys-blinded fool! Do you have shit for brains? Didn't you hear me? That 'bitch' is just as valuable if not more so than what we came here for. The Father would have your head if any harm were to come to her, and that's only if you live through the punishment I'd inflict on you first."

The force of the blow had knocked the Son clean on his rump, and his mouth hung open, leaking blood from the corner as he gazed dazedly up at the Commander. "As ya say, sir."

The Commander growled, "Fenris, the Healer is in your charge until we give her to the Father."

The dark one, Fenris, rode over and nodded to the older man. "As you say, Ingemar, so shall it be done." He'd replied formally, but if I wasn't mistaken, there had been a double-edged note of sarcasm in his tone.

Ingemar muttered something that sounded an awful lot like, "Can't trust any of these Emrys-blessed imbeciles," followed by a fading string of curses as he rode to the head of the group that was already traipsing around the temple toward the main road back to the village.

I looked to Fenris and found his onyx eyes on me. A chill that felt an awful lot like a bad omen skittered across my skin.

"Better get healing." He nodded behind me to where the worst of the wounded lay.

I stuck out my chin more defiantly than I felt. "And if I don't?"

He shrugged, the picture of apathy, and fixed his gaze ahead as the cart lurched forward.

The foul man must have known I would heal them, because his dark eyes flicked toward me, and he smirked as I sighed and slid my way across the blood-slicked boards toward the first man. How Fenris and the one called Ingemar knew so much about True Healers was an unnerving mystery since, as far as I knew, I was the only one. My mother and eldest sister—Thyra, the heir to my father's throne—had spent much time querying every one of the seven courts and every tribe, including the Umbra-damned Uthari court, to see if they knew the location of another Healer or any text pertaining to the healing arts. Though, knowing all the rumors surrounding the Uthari, even if they had known something, they'd likely lied. That had been over ten years ago, and I wondered as

I delved into the man in front of me: if there had been a Healer in Uthar, were they still alive?

The whimpering cries of children pulled my attention as the procession of Sons marched down the main road through the village. My heart broke, its jagged pieces spearing me between the ribs as I surveyed the destruction. Bodies lay strewn everywhere. Small fires were being put out by battered old women. Children clung sobbing to their mothers' bloodied skirts as they held felled husbands. From the looks of it, no male over the age of ten had been left alive.

Rage simmered up, boiling over from the depths of my soul, spilling hot, angry tears that streamed down my cheeks as, one by one, my people ceased their cries, their eyes falling on me and the wagon as it lumbered by. I rubbed my tears away furiously with the heel of my hand. Then, with my thumb, pointer, and middle finger raised—the sign of the Emrys' blessing in Vanyth—I shot my arm into the air for all those left alive to see.

Silently, the villagers raise an arm in return, a farewell and a subtle act of defiance, a sign that we would not be broken. My rage was replaced with pride for my people, who, todey, had lost every-thing to these Umbra-spawned heathens but still held strong and united.

"Put your arm down, you foolish girl, before In-gemar sees," Fenris hissed through his teeth from where he sat astride his horse. "He may not be looking now, but if he turns, he will have every last one of these women and children slaughtered."

I glared and slowly lowered my arm; we were almost to the edge of town anyhow. I looked over the people one more time and nearly called out. On the edge of the crowd, a lady in a violently red dress knelt before a dead man and seemed to be whispering in his ear. Was she the woman who had been at the temple? Had she been there seeking help for the man she laid hands upon?

As if sensing my attention, she raised her eyes to meet mine. My breath stuck in my lungs, and I froze; her gaze struck me dumb. A loud hum-ming filled my ears, indistinct at first, but then the sound grew as I fought to look anywhere but at the woman's harshly beautiful face, until the noise clearly became the cawing of a raven. Its sound pierced me with ice, riddling my body with goosebumps, and Helima's last words echoed beneath the raven's cries. *"Balance the scales. As above, so below."*

The cart's wheel crashed over a large rock and flung me into the man I was supposed to be tending. My breath came in ragged gasps as I gulped down the salty sea air.

"Aren't you meant to be healing the man, not trying to seduce him?" Fenris's dry voice drawled mockingly. "Is it really necessary to be atop him like that? You'll give the men ideas."

Ignoring his crassness, I peered back to where the woman had been a moment before, but she was gone, as if she'd simply vanished. Perhaps I'd imagined her, an illusion brought on by the stress and exertion of healing, but the sick feeling that festered in the pit of my stomach made me certain I hadn't.

A moment later, we crested a dune and descended onto a beach.This stretch of shoreline was where the town often gathered for celebrations, as its distance from the town and the docks lessened the risk that either would catch fire. But it was also completely out of sight, which was what had made it such a convenient landing for the enemy.

The cart rolled to a halt in the sands, and I stumbled down from it, wincing as I put pressure on the slivers in my palms. I looked down at myself and noticed the ruin that was my dress. The blood on it had turned a horrible coppery brown, the fabric crusted and stiff. Then I raised my hands. They were caked with so much blood, I couldn't see a single patch of clean skin beneath them. The blood of my people, my friend, the blood of my enemies, all mingled together. My breath caught again, and the sand beneath my feet seemed to sway. I tried to suck in air, my breasts heaving like overworked smith's bellows; it still felt as if it wasn't enough. My throat ached as I spun around, looking for something, someone, anyone or anything that could help me. My eyes landed on the Uthari ship with its wolf head banners and its black wood hull, as if it had sailed straight from the darkest nether regions of the Umbra, and I heaved. The contents of my stomach spilled across the sand again and again until I was hollowed out.

My keeper and the Commander were occupied with the others as I reeled helplessly. Steps away, the waves crashed violently on the shore. I stumbled toward where they broke—punishing, frothy, and white against the sand—and flung myself down. I dug my hands into the gritty, frigid beach, hauled up handfuls, and began to scrub the layered-on blood from my arms, from my face. The salt stung my broken skin, but it was a distant prick of pain compared to the knife of grief lodged in my heart. I would have to tediously pull the grains out later lest they fester, since I couldn't heal myself. The oceanic water around me turned pink, and then it dawned on me: the waves could be my salvation. A few strides out to where the water dropped into the abyss, and I would be pulled under by the tide to drown. I would not be forced to suffer captivity and servitude to my enemies, to the men who had slaughtered my friend.

I stood and took the first slogging step. The waves crashed against me, pushing me back as if the Emrys of the sea, Orannus, was trying to tell me it was a poor idea, but I didn't listen.

An arm snaked around my waist suddenly and dragged me back. A voice hissed against the shell of my ear. "I don't think so, girl. I like my head on my shoulders, thank you very much." Fenris deposited me on my feet in the sand. "And if you go killing yourself on my watch, my head is precisely what the Father will demand."

I scowled up at him through seawater-drenched locks. "I'd love to see your head roll," I muttered.

"Don't kill yourself, and you just might live long enough to see all of our heads roll."

He grabbed my hand to pull me toward the landing boats getting ready to row to the ship anchored offshore. He'd held my fingers for only a heartbeat when he hissed and cast them away with a curse. His brow furrowed deeply as he glanced in disgust with his unholy eyes from his palm to me. Was I so repulsive that he couldn't touch my bare skin? Perhaps the Emrys had protected me from him and made it so this creature of a man, who looked as though the Umbra itself had spat him out, could do me no harm.

He growled and, in one smooth motion, swept me off my feet, cradled to his chest like a babe, trudging toward the waiting boat.

"Let me down! I can walk on my own!" I protested, thrashing in his grip.

He didn't answer and instead dumped me rather unceremoniously into a waiting craft, much to the amusement of the other men.

As he helped several of the other Sons heave the vessel into the waves, I huddled down against the hull to keep out of the biting grasp of Imbola's wind. Fenris's black boots thudded into the boat, and we embarked. I wholly regretted my dip in the sea as a chill breeze stole the warmth from my skin. By the time the oarsmen rowed us to the main ship, my skin was nothing but blue-hued, pimpled gooseflesh. I had to clench my jaw to keep my teeth from rattling together.

This time when Fenris scooped me up, I didn't protest. On surprisingly steady feet, he crossed the rolling skiff to where a plank had been lowered over the side of the vessel. He gracefully stepped up on it, and a moment later, we were hauled upward in nauseating fits and jerks.

Ingemar's lips curled in an unpleasant, near-predatory half smile as Fenris placed me before him on the deck in a sodden heap. "Welcome aboard, Healer. The Sons in need of your care are below deck in a rear room. I expect them all to be fit and mended by the time we reach Uthar. A little show of your abilities to prove your usefulness to the Father."

His unspoken words showed menacingly in his eyes as I trembled uncontrollably with cold. If I didn't prove my worth, I was as good as dead. Unless I brought up my royal heritage, which didn't seem like a wise idea, considering what the High Priestess had suggested.

I nodded curtly and unblinkingly held his gaze to show him I understood. Fenris clamped a hand on my shoulder, helped me to my feet, and steered me below.

Healing The Damned

T HE AMALGAMATED STENCH OF piss and blood stung my nostrils and pricked tears from my eyes. My sight blurred as my keeper roughly guided me down a narrow set of rickety stairs into the dank and damp hold packed with sweaty Sons. The smell alone would have been enough to make me wretch were my stomach not already devoid of its contents, and the roll of the ship certainly didn't help matters.

"Here." Fenris grunted and shoved a dented and rust-spotted tin cup full of fresh—well, fresh-ish—water at me, scooped from a bucket hooked onto the hold's wall at the bottom of the stairs. I could barely hear him over the din of the Sons' leering laughter and raucous conversation, as if they were in a tavern for ale and had not just slaughtered hundreds of innocent people for no discernible reason other than their vile nature to take rather than make, to destroy rather than cultivate. Well, I supposed it had not been for no reason; Ingemar had mentioned I was a substitute for something, something they hadn't found. What in the Emrys' names could it have been? There was nothing of noteworthy value in the temple. Though with kalda, the coldest part of the year, fast approaching, they could have just been after the town's ale stores for all I knew, the savage carrion beasts that they were.

I sipped from the water cup slowly, trying not to spill, not that a little water would have hurt the state of the ship. The floor bucked unkindly beneath my feet, and my fingers still trembled with chill. When I finished my drink, Fenris steered me by the arm through the main hold to the tune of whistles and lewd comments slung my way. He led me to a small room at the back of the ship, where the wounded lay in rows covered by rough-spun wool blankets.

There were five of them not including the one I'd healed outside the temple. Five of them could very nearly cause me to dry up, to use every last drop of healing power I possessed. Depending on the severity of their wounds and the duration of the trip, it might not be physically possible for me to heal them all before we made landfall.

I tried not to wring my hands in my filthy skirts as I turned to where Fenris had propped himself on a barrel by the door, the hilts of his twin swords visible over his lax shoulders, nonchalantly cleaning blood from under his nails with a dagger.

"How long?" I asked, my words weaker than I would have liked.

I didn't have to specify. "Deybreak."

I shuddered, and this time, it had nothing to do with the cold. I knelt by the first man, took his head in my hands, and carefully unraveled the rough bandage from around his face. I winced down at the wound; someone had stabbed out his right eye. It was an Emrys-damned miracle he'd survived the assault. Though, which Emrys looked after such reprehensible creatures was beyond me. A terrible, prickling voice, like the tap of a spider's leg on the inside of my skull, whispered that perhaps it hadn't been an Emrys at all, but their inverse, the Niflym. Dread scraped along my bones, and I cast the thought aside with a shudder.

I closed my eyes and delved into the Son with my abilities. Infection was already trying to take hold; whatever he'd been stabbed with had been contaminated by something nasty. I glanced up to find Fenris watching me carefully.

"I cannot regrow an eye."

"Don't think he'll mind." He shrugged apathetically, his black eyes wholly and unflinchingly fixed on me as he jerked his chin toward the soldier I worked on.

I didn't much care what the Son did or didn't mind; it wasn't he who held my life in his hands like a cat held a mouse. "And Ingemar, will he mind?"

Another shrug. Fenris was impossible to read with those soulless eyes. I shut him out, batting away my awareness of him like a fly. I let my eyelids flutter closed and again focused on the Son in need in front of me. Painstakingly, I burned away the infection that tried desperately to take root in his hollowed-out eye socket. I knitted the muscles and the flesh.

Time moved differently when I healed; the world melted, and it became just me and the threads of life in the void. A weaver in a dark room with nothing but her loom. Sometimes, a healing could feel like it took no time at all, and sometimes, it felt like it took an age. There was no telling how long it had been in actuality until I pulled myself back.

I gasped as I withdrew my hands from his head and collapsed hard onto my backside. For a moment, my mind reeled. Dazedly, I blinked, searching the room for the temple healers only to have the flashed memories of the gore from the morning blur my vision red. I gripped my skirts in white-knuckled fists, and the hilt of the High Priestess's blade I'd tucked there grazed my clenched fingers. It felt simultaneously like an aeon ago and a moment ago. I traced my fingers along it and glanced up to where Fenris was still perched. An emotion that went far deeper than anger seethed through my blood as he stared down at me, wicking all the light in the room until he looked like shadow given form.

For a heartbeat, I wanted to damn all my oaths to heal blindly to do no harm. I imagined it would be so easy to catch him unawares. A simple touch, and I could put him to sleep with my healing gifts. Putting people to sleep was second nature; I did it all the time so those under my care would not feel pain. Oh, but some despicable part of me that had teeth and barbs and scales wanted him to feel it. So perhaps I could make him just drowsy enough to slow him down, and then I could bury the knife in his black heart so he would know how this felt.

"I wouldn't if I were you, Healer."

The use of my title on his lips sent daggers down my spine. "Wouldn't what?" I tried to smile innocently, but I had a feeling it looked anything but.

His lips peeled back into a smirk. "Whatever murderous plan you're concocting. I've seen enough vengeance in people's eyes to know the look."

I let my fingers stray away from the blade and feigned indifference. "I imagine that's true, given your line of work."

He chuckled dryly. "You have no idea, Healer."

I looked down at my hands sullied in the blood of yet another Son. "I need a bucket of clean, soapy water, if such a thing can be found on this Emrys-forsaken vessel."

He nodded to a bucket at his feet. "I had it brought in while you were healing. Anything else, princess?"

He said "princess" mockingly, but it still made me flinch, though I hoped not noticeably as I tried to cover the movement by smoothing my hair away from my face and tucking it back under my veil.

"Soap?" I asked hopefully.

"Thought you might ask." His lip twitched into a smile that painted images across the canvas of my imagination of a wolf about to sink its teeth into his prey, and he held out a hand. In his nicked and scarred palm was a lumpy, brown clod. I stood, closed the gap between us, and snatched it from him quickly, as if he might change his mind, careful not to let our skin touch. I squatted down and scrubbed vigorously, relishing the pitchy tree tar scent as much as if it were the fancily scented soaps my sisters and queen mother adored.

The clod was filled with some sort of exfoliating grit, which I appreciated until I dragged it over the tender patches of my palm, where splinters were embedded. I'd nearly forgotten about them. I hissed in pain before biting my lip to squash the sound.

"What's wrong?" Fenris crouched down next to me and captured my hand. His nearly devoured mine whole. "You're injured," he said flatly. I was surprised he didn't pull back in disgust as he had before.

I tried to twist my wrist from his grasp, but his fingers threaded around it and made the motion futile. "It's nothing, just a few slivers. No need to worry about it."

He grunted rather than giving me a proper reply and jerked me to my feet. Then he drew a menacing blade from his hip. I could feel my pupils blow wide as they took in every inch of sharp-edged steel fisted in his hand.

"Please don't hurt me." I hated how tear-choked those words sounded as they fell from my quivering lip.

Fenris snorted. "Quit squirming. I'm just going to get the little bits out before they fester. So unless you can heal yourself, stay still so I don't miss and get your fingers instead."

He gripped my hand, and with clinical precision, deftly needled the intruding pieces of wood out of my flesh one by one. I winced, and a little gasp of pain slipped free from my parted lips as he pulled the last and largest. Blood welled up on my palm. From under his leather armor, he pulled a wide ribbon of pale lavender linen—perhaps a token from a lady love for luck, I wondered. *Though perhaps not,* I thought as he wound it carefully around my palm and tied both ends securely atop my hand. If it had been from a lover, using it on me seemed a dreadful waste.

I looked up at him and met his ebony eyes. They shuddered. For a split second, I imagined I saw normal eyes with irises of the deepest blue rather than pure black pools, but before I could blink, they seemed just as dark and eternal as they had before. My stomach swooped and dropped, as if I had been flung from a great height. I pulled my hand back much more forcefully than was probably necessary, turned my back on him with a muttered thanks thrown inelegantly over my shoulder, and knelt with my next patient—the man I'd meant to heal on the journey from the temple to the sea before becoming distracted by the anguish of my people. Emotions clogged my throat, each one vying for my attention and tears.

Out of the corner of my eye, I saw Fenris lean back against his barrel again, the picture of an indolent predator learning the patterns of its prey. I suppressed a shudder. Despite his kindness just a moment prior, I couldn't bring myself to forget what he was: a cold-blooded, murdering Son of Uthar. His help had likely been given less out of kindness and more out of duty to his Commander and the Father, since, for the time being, he was my keeper and had to ensure my safety under punishment of death.

I took a deep breath to purge my racing thoughts, closed my eyes, and focused again on the well inside me, drawing my gifts up and out to my fingertips.

"Do your fingers always glow silvery like that?"

Startled, I opened my eyes and stared at my hands. They looked as though they had been dipped in luminous liquid quicksilver, as they always did when I healed. I glanced at him sideways from under my lashes.

"Have you not seen a True Healer work before?" I asked rather than giving a direct answer, using the moment to pry for information. "You and the Commander seem to have an extensive amount of knowledge when it comes to Healers," I added when he didn't answer right away.

"I have," he confirmed as he rubbed his stubbled chin. The move snagged my attention, and I wondered if it was something he did when in thought or if it was a tell, a tick that let on that he'd lied. Though, this admittance contradicted what the Uthari had sent in reply to my mother so long ago, so perhaps it was the truth after all. "But I have never seen anything like that," he added, nodding to my still outstretched hands.

My brow furrowed; I didn't know what to say. I'd always assumed the manifestation of my abilities as light was a normal thing, and no one had contradicted me. Though, none of my teachers had met another True Healer either, just read about them.

I curled my fingers into my palms and stretched them back out again, willing them to shine brighter as I pushed more of my healing into them. "Perhaps I'm doing it wrong then," I mused aloud, and for a fleeting moment, I considered this captivity might be a blessing from the Emrys rather than a curse. Perhaps they meant for me to learn. "I look forward to meeting this Healer in the court so I may learn more about my gifts." I turned to him to confirm that the Healer he spoke of was still there.

Fenris's eyes grew deeper than pitch. "That won't be possible," he murmured darkly through ground teeth.

A stone's weight settled in my stomach, and I understood. "Oh," was all I could say.

"Better get back to healing." He looked meaningfully down at the man in front of me, as if warning me that my fate could be the same as my predecessors, like I might have missed that as a possibility.

I swallowed around my heart that had suddenly decided to take up residence in my throat, a bird roosted in the nest of emotions lodged there. "Yes, yes, you're right." I placed my hands on either side of the Son's head and began.

Time spun away from me as I healed the rest of the Sons. I drifted in formless black with nothing in my mind's eye but the light from my well of healing and the injuries at hand. A fractured skull, several brain bleeds, broken ribs, internal bleeding, lacerated organs, and a partially severed spine later, Fenris startled me back to reality with a shockingly gentle hand on my shoulder.

I blinked up at him, disoriented and unable to focus. Someone stood in shadow behind him.

"Well, well. How did the little Healer do?" I recognized the voice even as my eyes struggled to bring him into sharper relief. Ingemar.

I gestured blindly to the man I'd been working on. "This man's spine will need more healing. He is going to live however." The words felt raw as they clawed up my throat.

The Commander laughed. "Fucking Emrys, you're a strong one, aren't you? The Father will be pleased. Fenris, get her home and make her presentable. Tie her in a Emrys-damned bow so we can gift her to the Father!" He laughed again as he stomped from the room.

Fenris, at least I assumed it was Fenris, grabbed me under the arm and hauled me to my feet. His grip was strong but not rough as he led me back up through the now-empty vessel and out into the pink of dawn's light.

I blinked squirming black spots from my eyes. Fog blanketed the harbor laid out before us, churning in a light breeze coming in off the crashing sea. Hazy details of the city behind it speared through the morning mist. I tripped my way down the gang-plank—distantly grateful not to have to use that rickety hoist again—and onto the dock, that firm grip the only thing keeping me solidly on two feet.

"Welcome to Berth, Healer," Fenris whispered, his breath feverishly hot against the back of my veil.

I looked up past the fog-shrouded capital city of Uthar at the stone Fortress of the Father, where it loomed high on the cliffs, lording over the sprawling city that knelt subserviently before it. The ground beneath me swayed, the brush of my lashes against my cheeks was like a butterfly's kiss as the edges of the city before me folded in. I felt the slump of my body, and then there was nothing but the dark of my mind and silence.

THE CRACKLE OF A fire roaring in a hearth woke me. Weariness clung to my bones like lead as I struggled to push myself into a seated position. I was half buried in a plush of down blankets. Leather skins filled with hot water were curled carefully like sleeping animals at my sides and feet. Fresh bandages were wrapped in place of the lavender linen across my palm, and I'd been dressed in a clean shift. Embarrassment crept up my pale cheeks—I had last been with Fenris in the harbor; surely it would not have been he who had undressed me?

I looked around at a stark yet comfortable chamber. I had to be somewhere deep within the Fortress, where else would they put a prisoner? The floors, bedstead, and the wardrobe that sat across from it were all hewn of an ebony wood grown only in the Blackwood of Uthar. A settee and a low table sat in front of the fireplace to my left where an adjacent partition no doubt led to a bathing chamber. My second and most probable inclination was that a servant had dressed me. Some of the fire died in my face at this realization, though some embers remained since someone had still seen me nude—something that had not occurred since a scandalous swimming incident with my sisters in the weeks before my journey to the Selenyss Temple.

The woven rug that ran the length of the bed was a pleasant surprise as I swung my feet over the edge. A soft pair of woolen slippers waited for me as well. I slipped them on gratefully, they were only a bit too snug, and padded softly to the large entry door to the right of the sitting area. I gave a swift tug and, of course, found it locked. I supposed it could have been worse; this could have been a dank prison cell. I peered into the bathing chamber, where a large, copper tub took up most of the space, and into the closet, which turned out to be a privy. A reflecting glass sat perched in the corner of the dim room; the woman in it looked spectral with her long, silver-white hair unbound and her skin nearly translucent. I gasped and my hand fluttered, startled to my lips like a bird to its roost. When had I last seen myself? Instruments of vanity were not allowed at the temple beyond a simple wide-toothed wooden comb.

It must have been at home on the dey of my departure, before I had yet to fully hit puberty. My skin had been golden and my hair much shorter. My breasts and hips were far more ample than I'd envisioned them to be when dressing myself these past years. The youthful plumpness to my face was gone, replaced with the much starker lines of womanhood. My eyes as well, opalescent, nearly glowed in the dark as they always had, but now they looked far less mirthful. Though that particular transformation could have come in the past dey—or deys, depending on how long I'd slept.

I returned to the bedroom and poked around in the wardrobe; a handful of dresses my approximate size were hung neatly along with an array of slippers and boots. On a shelf above sat a small chest. I pulled it down and set it on the foot of the bed. I flipped open the lid to inspect the contents: my diadem, the bone-handled knife, a few other baubles odds, ends, and trinkets—not my own—also littered the box. I pulled out the diadem and ran my fingers along the crystals and moonstones, all braided into the silver wire. The diadem was as much a part of my being as my hands and feet. It had been gifted to me by my father, the king, on my fifth name dey, and I had worn it ever since. It was imbued with old magic to grow with the wearer, as were the diadems of my sisters. I'd always been curious about the trove of enchanted heirlooms my family had been gifted generations ago by a witch before their kind had been hunted into extinction. No one, however, had been willing to tell me that particular tale, or perhaps they didn't know it. Either way, I could no longer wear it. I couldn't chance anyone in the Uthari court recognizing it and deducing who I was. It was bad enough I was trapped here as a Healer, but as a royal hostage, the Father could force my father into all manner of wicked and unfair agreements with my life in the balance. As a Healer, I stood a chance of having some freedoms, and if I could figure out how, maybe I could even escape.

Carefully, I replaced the diadem and fingered the hilt of the dagger. It was curious that they'd left it in my possession—perhaps they'd assumed it was an instrument of healing and that there was no possible way for me to defend myself or assault someone with it. In that respect, they were partially correct. As a princess in the palace, I'd had guards and had only been instructed in the most basic means of defense, which is to say they taught me to scream and run for help. As a pupil in the temple, there had been no need for me to defend myself, as all who lived in service to Selenyss were well respected. The knife was next to useless to me unless I were to either be blessed with luck or decide to take my life as the Priestess had suggested. There had been that fleeting moment on the passing when the brutish beast of hate had bared its teeth within me and I'd wanted to use it, but that was so unlike me, and was against every oath of healing I'd taken, I shuddered now to think on it. I flipped the lid of the chest shut and replaced it in the wardrobe. I didn't want to look at it any longer.

A covered tray was perched on the table by the settee, and my stomach growled as soon as I set eyes on it. I cautiously sat and peeled away the cloth cover. I sighed contentedly as I took in the jerked meats, the lump of cheese, the crusty bread spread with creamy, yellow butter, and the stoneware mug covered with a small wooden lid. I greedily reached for the bread when it dawned on me that it may be poisoned with a sleeping draft or some sort of potion to make me compliant to my captors' wills. I reached into the well of my gifts and was momentarily shocked to find just how low it was. I had been so very near to drying out, a fate worse than death that would have left me little more than a husk, doomed to a half life of agony. I shuddered at the thought, then pulled up a single drop and threaded it into my fingers. I touched each piece of food in turn and then removed the lid from the mug and dipped in a single glowing finger to detect any poisons in much the same way I detected infection and injuries within a body. Thankfully, I found none.

The bread went first, more quickly than was strictly ladylike, followed by the meat and cheese in unison. When there was not a single crumb remaining, I snagged the mug and curled up on the settee with my feet tucked under me. I sniffed it, inhaling the soothing scents of lavender and mint. A sip of the lightly honeyed brew also revealed catmint, a touch of cinnamon, and the slightest pinch of woebegone—a spiky plant named for the ailment it cured. A powder made of its desiccated thorns had a near intoxicating effect in large doses. From rumors I'd gathered when I'd been young, it was often insufflated at late-noct parties, but in doses as small as this, it simply soothed the heart.

The brew was divine and also precisely the combination of herbs I would have recommended to a person suffering acute anxiety. Though I perhaps would have added some milky oat tops or lemon balm to add an extra layer of soothing, considering my anxiety was beyond acute. I did, however, appreciate the gesture and wondered who had been so thoughtful.

A key suddenly rasped in the locked door. I bolted upright so quickly that the mug shot out of my hands and shattered on the floor. The door creaked open, and a friendly seeming woman in her middle years gazed upon me softly like she was looking at a frightened doe. "Oh, ye poor lamb. I did no mean to frighten you! What are ye doin' out of bed!"

"I woke up," I muttered dumbly, intensely aware that this must have been the woman who'd dressed me. I moved to pick up the shards of mug.

"Ach, no. I can get those after, mistress." The woman came the rest of the way in, shutting the door with a soft snick behind her sweeping skirts.

I looked up from where I half crouched, fear coiled in my gut. *After.* After what? So I asked just that.

"After ye meet the Father, m'lady. Lord Fenris do send his apologies, but he will be meeting you there."

"He's a lord?" I was so stunned, the words sprang free before I could stop them. That man, who radiated otherness like some people emanated joy or regality, was a lord? I rose and sat dazedly back onto the settee. I would have been less surprised had she told me he was actually a creature masquerading in a man's skin. He far more closely resembled the legends of the Sons of Uthar I'd grown up on—men who could shift into bestial form and devour maidens for supper—than the Sons I'd healed. I turned to look over the settee's back, where the woman rummaged in the wardrobe, pulling things out and putting them back with a tsk or a disapproving hiss. "How did a Son become a lord?" In Vanyth, the knights and warriors held rank in court, but it was lesser than that of lords.

The woman just laughed, a low, velvety sort of laugh that I supposed some might consider sultry. And as she busied herself pulling things from the wardrobe, I imagined she was undoubtedly found quite attractive by many. Her skin was a rich, warm, color, her black hair was braided ornately so half of it was wound in a coronet around her head and the rest hung in curling wisps down to her low back, and her dress clung in all the right places, accentuating her voluptuous curves. She was the type of woman I'd always marveled at as a young girl in court, the kind that could turn heads and seemed to have an easy grace. She could have warmed the bed of any nobleman, and maybe, I flushed to think, she warmed Lord Fenris's bed.

"Lord Fenris do no be an ordinary Son, m'lady. I should know; I am keeper of his house."

She beckoned me over to stand by her, her arms full of garments plucked from the wardrobe, and I went obediently. It had been a long time since I'd been dressed by someone, but I knew the motions of it like a dance not performed in many years that still clung to the edge of memories.

"What do you mean he is no ordinary Son? And please call me Ertha, not 'my lady.' We both know I am a prisoner."

Her brow furrowed as she looked up from where she knelt to help me into a pair of green woolen stockings. She tied them with beautifully embroidered ribbons around my thighs. "I beg pardon, but ye are no quite a prisoner, m'lady. No while ye do be in m'lords custody. He will no allow ye to be treated so poorly. Though I do suppose ye are no here of yer own will." She sighed and looked at me sympathetically. "But there do be many in the court who do be here under similar circumstance, if ye catch my meaning."

She shimmied a long-sleeve, garden-green dress made of the same soft wool as the stockings over my shift, the bodice of it embroidered with silver vines and flowers. Was she implying she wasn't here of her own free will?

Before I could ask, she said, "If ye do wish it, I will call you Ertha, and ye do be able to use my given name, Munnin, as well."

"Thank you, Munnin," I murmured as she cinched the laces at the back of my dress and wrapped a long rope of pearls around my neck so it layered across the swell of my bosom. "Do you know why exactly I'm meeting with the Father?"

"M'lord did mention the issue of yer custody will be decided."

I blanched. "I thought you said I was in Fenris's custody."

She smiled in a way that might have been meant to be reassuring. "Ye do be now, as the Commander did charge him with yer care, but final say do remain with the Father. Now sit so I do be able to fix yer hair." She steered me back toward the settee by the fire and began brushing my hair with a boar-hair brush in long, soothing strokes.

"Whose care might I end up in then if not Fenris's?" If Fenris was my best option for freedom here in Uthar, then that also meant he was my best option for escape.

She hesitated, her steady brush strokes stuttering. "The Commander do be the next likely option.

He and Fenris do be on even footing with the Father. One do be his right hand and the other do be his left."

My breath caught against the sides of my lungs and floundered. The man had looked at me with such a predatory glint in his eyes. There was no doubt in my mind that I would not only lack any sort of freedom in his care, but also anything remotely resembling human decency. There would be no soothing herbal teas in his household unless they were the sort meant to remove someone's free will, the sort I'd delved my foods for before I'd risked eating.

"I shall pray to all the Emrys then that my custody remains with Fenris." The somewhat lesser of the two evils was by far more preferable.

"As will I." Munnin gently and deftly tugged at my hair, forming intricate, small braids along the sides of my head. From my brow back down the center, she braided the hair in one thick plait to just above the nape of my neck, where she wove in silver threads to hold the braids in place but allowed the rest of my hair to hang free down my back.

She held up a hand mirror for me to examine the style. I frowned slightly as I realized the look imitated Fenris's own hair but without shaving the sides of my head.

"Do you no care for it? I do no think we have time to change it before yer due before the Father." The look of concern she had for the work she'd done made my stomach twist, wrung by fists of guilt.

"No, it's lovely, Munnin. Thank you. It is just an unfamiliar style."

And as I thought about it, so was Fenris's and Munnin's coloring, and Munnin's accent. The native Uthari were a fair race, all sallow skinned and flaxen haired rather than olive and dark. I had initially been so put off by Fenris's general air that I hadn't paused to consider he wasn't Uthari at all. In my defense, I'd also been dragged from my home and witnessed many I cared for die, worst of all being Helima. My heart floundered for a few beats, tripping over itself and my grief. A storm of oncoming tears nettled the back of my eyes, and I blinked them away before Munnin could see.

"It do be a popular style where we hail from," she said as she helped me lace fur-lined buskin boots and wrapped me in a fur-lined cloak of a scarlet so deep that it was almost black.

She'd said *we*. "You and Fenris?" I asked.

"Aye, and me brother, Huggin. He do be the one escorting ye todey." Her eyes shone with a deep pride, one I knew well from speaking of my sisters.

"And where is it that you are from?" I pried as she handed me a pair of soft leather gloves to match the cloak and I slid them on.

She jerked and tugged at hems and skirts, making sure every stitch of my ensemble was in place. "We do come from the North, from Corvus."

"Corvus," I repeated, slightly stunned. I'd only met an emissary from the northern kingdom once, what felt like a lifetime ago. They had come to my father's court to negotiate a trade treaty. My father had offered one of my sister's hands in marriage, Veronya, who was three years my senior. She'd been little more than a child at the time; she hadn't even bled yet. The offer was politely declined. If

I recollected correctly, there had been a boy with the emissary, a nobleman's son perhaps, who was closer in age to my eldest sister, Thyra. The corners of my lips curled as I recalled the fit she'd had when she'd found out a boy her age had been attending the council and she hadn't. Try as I might, however, I could not remember much about the Corvusi's features beyond the shockingly blue eyes of the nobleman's son. I peered at Munnin closely, and sure enough, her eyes were a similar, if less brilliant, shade of blue. If blue eyes were the standard in Corvus, I wondered what affliction had caused Fenris's to be such a horrific hue. "How exactly did three Corvusi end up in Uthar?" I pried further, knowing I was pressing my luck.

As expected, she simply smiled at me, though there was more sorrow in the turn of her lips and the crinkle of her eyes than there should have been on a smiling face. "That, Ertha, do no be my tale to tell." And with that, she led me out of the room.

I lost track of the number of turns we'd made since exiting Fenris's private apartments. I'd counted six, not including the turn out of my chamber, all while Munnin chattered about this and that. Her brother, Huggin, led us along, his ham-sized hands never leaving the hilt of a lethal-looking dagger at his side. He was a head and shoulders taller than Munnin, who already stood quite a bit taller than I. The two of them shared the same complexion, eyes, and ebony hair. His was shorn around his ears like Fenris's, but rather than a long series of braids, his hair was simply in a high knot at the back. The similarities seemed to end with the siblings' appearances. Where Munnin talked relentlessly, all I had heard from Huggin was a grunt.

We passed through what Munnin called the lesser court, a grand chamber lined with tables and benches, where the lesser nobility assembled and held balls. The upper nobility, she informed me, met in a much larger, more elaborate hall several floors up, not far from Fenris's apartments, implying that Fenris himself was part of the upper nobility.

We exited the lesser court through a balcony door. No, not simply a balcony, a wide stone walk that ran around the Fortress's walls. I snuck a look over the edge of the parapet, and my stomach squirmed back for safety against my spine. The Fortress was carved partially into precipitous cliff-sides that overlooked the sprawling city of Berth. It was one of the things that made it nearly impenetrable. The main complex appeared to be split into two. One on each side of a chasm opposite the other. Swooping, intricately designed wrought iron bridges connected both halves like dangling bits of black lace strung up to dry. A raging waterfall poured over the back of the chasm and tumbled into a river deep in the bottom of the rock cleft. It spiraled its way through the city below, where much of the water was diverted into a network of canals, visible at this great height as silver threads. What wasn't diverted stretched its way out to the sea. From my vantage, I could see low walls and buildings scattered between either side of the Fortress along the cliff's top. If I recalled correctly from my lessons long ago, behind the Fortress was the dense forest known as the Blackwood, a deeply mysterious place rumored to host all manner of nasty beasties more terrible than the Sons. I shuddered to think what lay in its shadows.

"It do be somethin', don't it?" Munnin mused, following my gaze as it roamed the cliffs above, though she didn't specify what kind of something she thought it was, a marvel or a terror; her inflection gave no hints either.

I nodded. "Yes, it is...something."

Munnin kindly looped her arm through mine and steered me away from the wall and toward one of the iron bridges, where Huggin waited, hand still on his hilt—I doubted it strayed often. I balked as it became clear they intended to cross the arching, wrought pathway.

Munnin gave my arm a reassuring squeeze. "I do find it helps to look straight and not look down," she said in a conspiratorial tone that I might have found comforting under just about any other circumstance.

I swallowed the bile that rose in my throat. Heights were definitely not my favorite. I could handle small ones like the ladders in my father's royal library or the walls surrounding the lunar temple, as those had left me some kind of reassurance. The ladders had never been tall and, at worst, might have resulted in a small bone fracture if I fell. The temple walls were wide and sturdy, giving the impression of being on firm ground. This bridge, however, was suspended as if floating on a breeze from one side to the other, anchored on either end with nothing to support the middle.

I took my first tedious step and then forced myself to take another. The path was just wide enough for Munnin and me to walk abreast. I clung to her arm a little more firmly than I had before—just a smidge of pressure more and my nails would have bit through my gloves—and fixed my eyes on Huggin's broad shoulders ahead of us.

"How were these built?" My voice came out far more breathily than I had intended, half the sound snatched by Imbola's wind that seemed intent on teasing me.

"The legend do be that the Father did arrest a witch long ago. He did have her weave pathways with her magic before he did execute her."

"By the Emrys, why did she agree to do anything for him?" I gasped as a particularly strong buffet of wind seemed to sway the bridge beneath my boots. Munnin laid her free hand over mine, a slight but warm comfort.

Munnin shook her head morosely. "It do be said that he did promise her life if she did the task."

"He lied," I said flatly, my brow furrowed in fury. I couldn't believe I was moments from meeting such a fiend. It was unfathomable to me that his people didn't revolt. If my father committed such atrocities, even to a witch, the people would condemn him.

"Aye, he did." Her words were so softly spoken, I barely heard them, but they seemed to have the feel of intimate familiarity, and I wondered if it was a lie that kept her here as well.

Our feet hit a blessedly firm stone, and I let out a puffed breath of relief on the chill air. The moment, however, was short-lived as we entered the Fortress. We wound our way through dark stone halls to the richly carpeted antechamber of the throne room and found Ingemar waiting.

He was dressed not in armor but in dark gray breeches and a jerkin with the insignia of his rank embroidered onto the sleeve, belted over with his sword belt. His smile curdled my stomach as his lips curled into a malevolent and leering smile. "Lady Healer, so good to see you again." His words coated me in grime that felt suggestive and repugnant. "The Father and Mother are waiting." He grabbed me roughly from Munnin's arm, eliciting a sharp hiss from the woman. Huggin's knuckles turned white as they gripped the hilt of his sword. Ingemar smirked at them. "Stand down, curs. I'll protect the Healer from here." The way he said *protect* sounded more like *violate* when it fell from his mouth. It coated my insides with ice.

Munnin opened her mouth as if to protest, but Huggin placed a meaty hand on her shoulder, and she nodded to Ingemar, her expression tight with fury, her eyes full of worry. "We will check on ye after." She reached out and squeezed my hand one more time before letting go.

Ingemar chuckled, gripped me roughly by the back of the neck, and steered me toward the large, double blackwood doors that hung from thick, embossed iron hinges. They groaned open before us as we strode through at a clipped pace. The Commander's jagged nails dug into my neck more deeply with every step. I bit my lip to keep from crying out, even as I felt my skin sweat blood. I didn't want to give the bastard the satisfaction.

The throne room was surprisingly magnificent, sophisticated where I'd expected savage. From the long side wall, the sun beamed through arched, floor-to-ceiling, stained-glass windows that were beautiful somehow despite their lewd and gruesome depictions. Colors danced across the pristine, dark-tiled floor all the way to the raised dais, upon which sat two gruesomely large wrought iron thrones in front of a roaring hearth that spanned the full length of the platforms back. The effect, as I was sure it had been intended, was intimidating.

Fenris stood off to the right of the dais, dressed in smooth black that only further accentuated the otherness that rippled off him, as if he were a void that sucked all light into himself and churned it into shadow. The jerkin and breeches he wore were finely made, as were his leather boots. If it weren't for those coal eyes boring into me, I would not have recognized him as the man who had accompanied me on the ship yesterdey. Well, that and the swords belted across his back.

It dawned on me then how utterly vacant the throne room was—no milling courtiers vying to catch a glimpse of the Father's new prize or even any royal guards. Perhaps Fenris and Ingemar were guard enough, or maybe the Father and Mother wanted no witnesses to what was about to occur. The thought terrified me, and my fingers twitched, asking to be wrung anxiously, but I stilled them and forced myself to take deep and even breaths.

The hinges of a door off to the side of the room creaked open, followed by the sound of imposing footfalls that I could only assume belonged to the Uthari monarchs. Ingemar burrowed his nails into the tender flesh of my neck and forced me to the floor. "On your knees, Healer. Show some respect," he growled like one would at a disobedient dog, assuming, of course, that the person loathed the dog.

"Commander, welcome." The Mother's arsenic-laced voice echoed around the room. "Lord Fenris here has been telling us about this latest acquisition. He claims this...girl is a True Healer?" She spat the word *girl* as though it meant vermin.

Through hooded eyes, I stole a glance up at the Father and Mother, where they settled into their seats of power. The Father looked to be of middle years, and she looked to be quite a bit younger, both with the flaxen hair common to the Uthari. The Father looked every inch the warrior king with steely eyes, unusual among their people but not unheard of, and scarred, battle-worn hands. The Mother was slight and waspish with fine hair cascading around herself and woody brown eyes that reminded me of a pyre about to be lit if only one were to strike a match. Crowns were etched permanently in blue ink across their brows, as was their kingdom's tradition. I knew the Uthari called them the Emrys-mark crowns, though I could not for the life of me remember why. I probably should have paid more mind in cultural lessons as a child.

"Yes, Mother, she is. I saw her heal a Son with my own eyes," Ingemar confirmed in an oily voice that stuck to my skin and made me feel as though I needed to bathe.

The Mother pressed her lips into a thin line. "She's rather round about the hips and belly for a monastic, isn't she? Aren't they supposed to be scrawny from fasting?"

"Aye, but there are advantages to that, Mother. You could breed her, and perhaps the Emrys would see fit to bless you with more like her."

I felt all the color, what little of it there was, drain from my face as I clenched my fists at my sides. I prayed to all the Emrys that Ingemar was just making a crass joke that the Mother and Father would reprimand him for in a moment.

I snuck another look around. If possible, Fenris's eyes seemed to have grown darker, but the Father...the Father's lips peeled back over teeth filed to points in what I could only assume was meant to be a smile. "Clever man, Ingemar. Perhaps we could give her to another in my collection?"

The Mother arched her brows, and the blue ink of her crown twitched up. "Or we could throw her in with this season's Hunt. It is only a few short weeks away. Let her breed with a worthy and loyal Son.

I believe you were considering entering this year, were you not, Commander?"

I darted a look at Fenris, where he stood like a loyal dog at the foot of his masters, not protesting a bit of this as I was talked about as though I were a prized broodmare at auction. Munnin had said he would not allow me to be treated poorly, but if this was not being treated poorly, then I didn't know what the man would consider behavior worth stopping.

Ingemar bowed to the Mother before slowly circling me like a vulture surveying carrion. "I was considering joining the Hunt again. If such a treasure were attainable this year"—he looked down at me and wet his lips—"I doubt any Son could resist entering."

The Father leaned back on his throne and rubbed his chin as he mulled over the Commander's words. "Fenris, take her to the Seer. She will know what to do with her. Have her determine her background as well. I want to know how such a jewel ended up in a temple at the ass end of Vanyth."

Fenris bowed. "As you command, Father."

Ingemar snarled as Fenris approached. "And the matter of her custody, Father?"

The Father waved a hand dismissively as he stood from his throne. "I back your original decision. Fenris can keep her...for now."

Both men bent a knee as the Father held a hand out for the Mother. She took it and rose for the first time, revealing the slight swell of her stomach. She was pregnant, nearly halfway there if I guessed correctly, and when it came to such matters, I usually did. They paused, and the Mother glared down her nose at Fenris. "Take her for a fitting too. We must have her looking presentable for the Triumph tomorrow noct."

Fenris nodded from where he knelt. "As you wish, Mother."

Once they cleared the room, Fenris grabbed me by the arm and hauled me to my feet, but before he could lead me away, Ingemar whirled and snatched me by the other arm. A slow and wicked grin split his face as he stared into the face of my keeper over my head as though I weren't even there. "Keep her safe for me, Fenris."

Fenris said nothing, but I got the feeling something unspoken was communicated in his onyx eyes because Ingemar dropped my arm with a sneer and stalked off out of the same side door the Father and Mother had left through.

Neither of us spoke as Fenris hurried me along the dark tiles covered in fractured rainbows—even such simple, small beauty could not remain whole here in this place—until we were back in the antechamber with Munnin and Huggin.

Munnin rushed forward and grabbed my hands. "Ah, thank the Emrys ye do no be in that man's care." Huggin grunted what I could only assume was his agreement. Munnin brushed my hair back over my shoulders and winced as she got a look at the bloody fingernail imprints left by Ingemar. "Oh, ye poor girl. I do have a salve I can put on those. Ye do need a rest after that ordeal."

"There is no time for her to rest now. The Father has commanded she visit the Seer."

Rough fingers replaced Munnin's gentle ones as Fenris came closer for a look. I closed my eyes to keep back tears, unwilling to let them see how small and weak I felt. His fingers slid around the wounds with, if not kindness, then deft precision, and then down my arm until he held my hand. I flung my eyes wide in surprise and looked up at him questioningly as he jerked it toward himself and shoved back my sleeve.

He held a cuff bracelet of pale silver etched with a runic language I didn't know over my exposed wrist. "A bonding bracelet so I will be able to ensure your wellbeing."

Munnin gasped but I barely had time to react before he slid the cold metal over my wrist. A pain that whispered in an ancient language against my skin burned as the metal melted into my flesh. I cried out, and my knees buckled underneath me. Fenris grabbed me and held me to himself as I writhed, my vision white with blinding agony as it writhed like snakes up my arm and toward my heart. Someone whispered in my ear to take deep breaths while a shrill voice beyond it screamed, argued.

My vision returned slowly in the form of light and color. My body trembled and my stomach churned until I felt steady enough to shove out of Fenris's hard-armed grasp. My breaths stilted and uneven, I looked down at my arm to find glittering white lines twisted around my left hand and up my wrist. I had a feeling that if I peeled off my clothes and looked, I would find them twisted all the way toward my heart.

"What in the Emrys did you do to me!" I looked between Fenris's resolved, furrowed brow, Munnin's thin-lipped expression, and Huggin's ever stoic, stoney face. None of them would explain. *Safe with them* my ass.

Fenris pulled out a second bracelet, and I felt the blood drain from my face. I backed away, my hands held up in a feeble defense. "No, please. I can't do that again..."

But instead of coming after me, Fenris shoved up his sleeve and slid it onto his own wrist. His chest heaved, he grunted, and his olive skin whitened as he stumbled a step. He braced his hands on his knees, panting. Munnin moved toward him, but he flung an arm out to stop her. A ragged heartbeat later, he stood back to his full height and rolled his shoulders. He held up his left hand to show me the back of it, white spirals twisted across his skin, twin to my own.

"As I said, it is a bonding bracelet. You and I are linked now. I will be able to sense if you are in danger or if you stray too far from where you are meant to be."

I narrowed my eyes on him and his mark. "And will I be able to sense you?"

"No." Another silent exchange occurred between him, Huggin, and Munnin, and the brother and sister nodded to him before turning to depart. Munnin squeezed my hand on the way out and wished me luck. Anxiety fluttered like a broken-winged bird next to my heart. I would need that luck if the Father employed a real Seer. They would be truly desperate to breed me if they knew I was not only a Healer but that royal blood ran in my veins.

Once they were gone, Fenris turned on his heel and strode away without a word, leaving me to do nothing but swallow the lump of clotted dread in my throat and follow.

My THIGHS ACHED AND were chafed after rubbing together as we trod down endless stairs before they eventually let us out in a dark passage that smelled of musk and damp. The walls were roughly hewn stone, and the air was so chilled, my breath danced like a phantom. I shrugged my cloak more snuggly around my shoulders and clamped my teeth to keep them from chattering. The hall was wide enough for two or three to walk abreast, but I kept a pace or two behind Fenris, feeling disinclined to give him any opportunity to strike up a conversation. My fury at him felt as raw as the skin where he had marked me with the bonding bracelet. I had never heard of the like before, but the residue of the magic in the back of my throat tasted metallic and old, older than I could even fathom. A part of me desperately wanted to ask where he had found an artifact so ancient, but I silenced those thoughts.

One comforting notion I clung to was that the bracelets meant Munnin had been right, I would have some semblance of freedom. With that freedom, I could perhaps find a way out of this Emrys-forsaken country, provided I could break the enchantment now on me. The hall ended in an iron door marred with rust and etched with warding symbols, though whether they were to keep something in or out, I wasn't sure.

Fenris rounded on me. "Go on, Healer. I will be here when you come out."

I looked between him and the door. "You won't be coming in? Don't you need to report what the Seer says to the Father?" My tone was a hint more accusatory than I'd intended. Or maybe, on a less aware level, I'd intended every bit of it and more.

He shrugged in that maddening way he had on the ship. "No need. She will tell him."

I steeled myself, lifted the latch on the door, and, head held high, determined to appear unafraid, I stepped into the Seer's chambers.

Nothing lay in the room, which resembled a cave more than a proper dwelling, save for a table with two splintery, wooden chairs on either end. The wall across from where I stood was exposed to the elements; sea waves broke and foamed through three large, jagged, and toothy arched windows. Symbols that matched the ones on the door covered the walls. They played with the edges of memory and seemed somehow familiar, but my overwrought mind couldn't place them.

"Hello, Ertha. Seventh sister to the queen of Vanyth." A crone limped from a shadowed crevice cleaved into the right wall of the cave, her gnarled hand on an equally gnarled walking stick, her milky eyes fixed penetratingly on me.

I froze. She knew. She knew who I was in an instant. I willed my tongue to work, to say something, anything to convince her not to tell the Father, but I fumbled as though it were twisted in convoluted knots. But then it struck me like a knife in the dark. She'd called me sister to the *queen.* That wasn't possible. There would have been word of my father's passing, I would have been invited to the funeral, the coronation. That had always been the plan. I would return to court to serve my family as court Healer either upon turning the age of five and twenty or upon my Father's death. If his death was imminent, they would have sent for me immediately.

Without thinking, I spat out, "My sister can't be queen. I would know." I clapped a hand over my mouth as if I could somehow force the words that felt too much like a confession back in.

The Seer cackled, shuffled her way to one of the rickety, wooden chairs, and settled her bulky backside down. She gestured for me to do the same, seemingly unphased by the spindrift spat in her face by the tumultuous sea. "Ah, but would you, dear? The messenger arrived only this morning at the temple to retrieve you."

"How?" I sat in the chair opposite her. A strange sensation washed over me, a stunned sort of emptiness that I could hear echoed in my question.

"It was swift, dear. Poison in his noctcap."

There was a tightness in my chest squirming and stretching like a hatchling that just couldn't quite pierce the membrane of its shell. I rubbed my breastbone in a feeble attempt to soothe the cracking sensation I was sure would split me into two if it kept going much longer. "But who—"

"Who do you think, girl?" Her voice was as rough as glass shards under bare feet.

I took a deep breath. *Who? Who else?* "The Father."

The hag tapped the side of her nose with a low laugh and winked. "Thatta girl."

"Why?"

She arched her salt-and-pepper eyebrows. "For the chaos, for the distraction. Nothing says instability like a fresh, young monarch on the throne. Add in a kidnapped royal witch and some raids along the coastal towns, and chaos reigns. The Father will have a country ripe for the plucking if he so wishes, or at least one that's too busy to truly look at what he's doing. He's doing it there; he's doing it everywhere."

I stiffened as a crashing spray soaked me in brine. "I'm a Healer, I'm no witch, and he certainly doesn't know I'm royal, not unless you tell him."

She raised her eyebrows again and reached for a pouch tied to the belt around her careworn robes. "You are right on one count, dear. He does not yet know you are a royal."

"Are you implying that I'm a witch?" It was my turn to laugh. The ridiculousness. Witches had been hunted into extinction long before I was off my mother's lead strings, by the Father no less. Only their relics remained– objects like the bridges still imbued with their magic or my diadem or the Umbra-blasted bonding bracelet, whose residual magic itched like a scab on my wrist and arm.

"Your hair color, girl. Is it not a bit unusual for one born in Vanyth?" She pulled a handful of stones and bones from her pouch and began to rattle them around in her weathered hand. I caught glimpses of runes between her fingers as they shook within the cage of her palm. Some I knew, and some were strange to me.

I fingered the ends of my silvery white hair. Everyone I'd ever met in Vanyth had hair in varying shades of rich brown. My hair had even been a deep coppery brown once upon a time, but it had started to change right around the season in which my father had given me my diadem. My sister's friend, Otadan—Tad—used to call me Little Sprite because he said the color reminded him of the tiny, almost spectral creatures that would drift about in the woods on clear nocts when Selenyss shined her moonlight brightest. I had seen them only once up close when I was six or so in the royal gardens. I'd been determined to catch one and chased it all the way to where the willows grew along the large pond my sisters and I would often sneak away to swim in. I'd found Tad under there, kissing Thyra. They'd made me swear not to tell our father, and I never had.

Emrys, was he really gone? Was Thyra really queen? I pressed a hand to the growing ache in my chest.

"What does my hair have to do with anything?"

"I imagine it changed right around the time you noticed you had healing gifts, didn't it, girl?" She shook the bones and stones one last time and cast them across the table.

I frowned. "I don't remember when my abilities manifested." It was the truth. To me, it seemed I'd always had them, even though I knew that was not the case. "I still don't see the correlation between the color of my hair and your accusations?"

"Have you not heard the legends? A witch's gift comes from Yaganya's kiss."

"I've heard the legends of the Crone Emrys, but—"

"'Then all ye shall behold the ones who bear the mark of the Crone's kiss upon the crown of their head, for they are marked blessed.'" The Seer intoned, quoting an old bit of the tales I'd been told as a child by my governess.

I looked at my hands clasped in my lap and found that every part of me was trembling, and it had nothing to do with the unrelenting sea spray that misted through the room. I couldn't be one of the most hunted beings in all the kingdoms. It may have been the kingdom of Uthar that put the final nail in the Witch Kingdom's coffin, but they had not been particularly liked anywhere else either. They'd been driven out or enslaved for their powers until the Emrys of death had seen fit to finally take them. It was rumored, though, that even she had despised the witches and cursed them to live hundreds of years—unless murdered—and suffer the losses of all they held dear. The histories were not kind to witches.

"Your well of power runs deep, deeper than you can fathom. That is why she sent you here." The Seer tapped a long, blackened fingernail against the stone tabletop.

"I wasn't sent here. I was kidnapped," I muttered, but she shushed me as she let her hands hover over the rune-carved stones and bones. Her ratted, thread-worn sleeves flagged beneath her upraised arms, the unspooled fabric brushing the tops of the scattered tools of divination. She hummed to herself, a low and guttural thing that prodded a primal fear alive in the back of my soul. She really was a True Seer, versed in the ways of the ancient, gifted with magic from the Emrys Wyrta, Emrys of fate and fortune.

She pointed at a bone crossed over a large gray stone, one carved with the rune that symbolized death and the other with the rune for prophesy. "That is not what the stones say."

Something inside me, inside my gifts, quavered as if stirred, peeking an eye open in response to her words. "Who?"

Her milky eyes snapped to mine. "Only you can answer that."

I sucked in a sharp, cold breath of irritation. How in the Umbra was I supposed to know which of the many Emrys' ire I'd stoked enough for them to curse me this way? "I don't understand why any Emrys would send me to this forsaken kingdom."

The old woman shrugged a single shoulder dismissively, pointed to the rune of prophecy, and then dragged the scuffed point of her finger to another stone that lay perpendicular to a crossed pair, the one marked with the rune for fate. "You are fated for whatever this Emrys has in store for you as the last of your kind."

I flinched. "The last of your kind" was a crushing and lonely weight to put on someone, and I wasn't sure I would be able to bear it. She pointed again to a cluster of stones and bones with the runes for the elements carved upon them—Earth, Air, Aether, Water, and Fire. "Keep the balance."

Those words struck a heartstring and stiffened my spine. "Keep the balance? What—"

She held up a hand to silence me. "I cannot tell you all things. I am a Seer, but even I cannot see into the Emphyrea. I can only see what they have touched here in our world. And of that, I can only see what they allow me to. What the Emrys has in store for you, you will have to figure that out for yourself, girl."

Great, just great. "And the Father? What will you tell him?"

She sighed. "I'm afraid I read you only to discover you are just a shepherd's daughter, a very blessed one to be given your gifts. Who can say why the Emrys choose who they choose for these things." She shrugged her crooked and stooped shoulders.

"But beyond your talents for healing, I'm afraid you are fairly insignificant."

I sighed, the breath I let out giving the same relief as unbinding corset strings. "Thank you."

"I will give you this warning though, girl: do not breathe a word of this to anyone. The Father is a collector of rare things, and you are very rare indeed. If he were to discover what you truly are, there would be no escape until he drained you dry, and after, well, you know what comes after he has finished with a witch."

"Is that what you are? Part of his collection?"

She smiled at me placidly. "What do you think, girl?"

I glanced around at the room, the wards, and the iron door, and realized what an empty-headed question it had been. Of course she was part of his collection. Why else would she be living like this? "How many more like you are there? In his collection?" The cruelty of it was unfathomable.

She shook her head. "There are many. But do not concern yourself with us now. I have seen our liberation, and it is not yet upon us. It is time for you to go."

Her tone held no room for argument, so I stood and turned with my skirts a touch more than slightly sodden. I looked back to thank her before I reached the door, but she was already gone. I shuddered as I opened the door and crossed the threshold; the weight of the etched wards held my heart in a momentary vice. I looked over to find Fenris casually leaning with his shoulder against the wall, his dark eyes glinting with what I thought for one fleeting moment might have resembled sympathy, but as he righted himself, it inked out of existence as if it never had been, and maybe it hadn't.

"Come, we have much to do." He turned and walked back the way we'd come. Resigned, I followed.

The Dressmaker

I SHADED MY EYES as we stepped from halls steeped in shadow and into the stable yard packed with the sweet scent of hay and the musky odor of beasts. My eyes welled as I blinked away the light of Jyord's sun, watered down beneath a thick swaddling of gray clouds. As my vision cleared, I was able to get a better grasp on my bearings after the long and tangled dark warren of tunnels we'd just traversed. We were on the far side of the Fortress still, near the cliff's edge, where a narrow, cobble-paved road slipped over the side and wound its way down into the sprawling city of Berth.

"Are you going to stand there all dey, Healer, or are you going to climb on?" I turned to find Fenris holding the reins of a large, dappled, gray horse. A scrawny, pock-faced hostler scurried away behind him, eyes wide, as though he were stunned to find he'd had the daring to hand over reins to the eerie man who seemed to weep darkness.

I narrowed my eyes. "And where is your horse?"

He smirked and stepped closer to me, grabbing me by the waist. "I'm not foolish enough to let you ride your own horse, Healer." He yanked me close to himself so my chest was pressed against his. I planted my fists onto his torso and tried to push away, but that only made him firm his grip. "You might get the silly notion that you can run away, and then I would have to chase you down. But then again..." He squeezed tighter until I could feel the press of each finger as they fisted my cloak. "That could be fun."

His lips curled maliciously, baring a hint of tooth. I was an animal caught in a snare, in more ways than one. I stilled, recalling in a flash a tale from my old governess about a rabbit in a hunter's trap who made itself still and docile until a raven came along. The caught critter lured the raven into releasing it with patience and stories spun from its dreams. I could be the rabbit if it meant this hunter who had snared me might somedey leave me long enough for a raven to come along. I ceased my flailing, craned my neck, and peered into his eternally dark eyes, trying to level him with a determined and steadfast stare. My breath fled my chest, and I let out an embarrassing squeal as he hoisted me sideways into the saddle. I glared down at him, daring to meet his depthless eyes.

The bastard winked at me, and I scowled. "You're a despicable cad."

He laughed. "I've been called much worse." Then he mounted the horse behind me.

I sighed. I'm sure he'd deserved all those names and more, whatever they'd been. I shifted uncomfortably as I adjusted my seat, swinging a leg over to the other side of the horse as gracefully as I could, which is to say I missed my mark entirely, snagging my ankle awkwardly on the pommel and suffering the vibrations of Fenris's mocking chuckles at my back as I wriggled it the rest of the way over. I hadn't ridden a horse in many years, let alone ridden one astride. I leaned forward and tugged at my skirts in a vain attempt to unbunch them and cover my indecently exposed stockings.

"Quit fidgeting, Healer. There is no need. It isn't as if I've never seen a woman's stockings before," he teased unkindly as he tugged the reins and guided his nag toward the yawning mouth of the road.

My scowl deepened, not that he could see it, and I had no choice but to stop squirming as he snaked an arm around my waist and urged the horse into a trot.

"I have a name, you know," I groused, making sure to inject my words with all the indignance and venom I felt churning hot in my belly as we clattered onto the cobblestone road at a clipped pace that forced merchants and horse handlers alike to dart out of our way. "I am more than just my title."

I felt Fenris's laugh rumble from where his chest was pressed against my back, his amusement making me burn in frustration. "Oh, I am aware, Ertha." The way my name rolled off his tongue felt dangerous, like an ill omen whispered on the wind through the cracks in the Umbra. It was the way I imagined a wolf would speak the name of a lamb. Perhaps I shouldn't have corrected him. "Ertha, with no family name," he mused, his breath purring and as hot as witch-burning fire on my neck as he urged the horse faster down the steep, winding road made up of stitched-together switchbacks and sharp drops.

The lean of each turn put a hitch in my sharply stuttered breaths, but I squeezed my eyes shut and tried to fixate instead on our conversation. However loathsome it was, however deadly my utterances could be in this foreign land, in that moment, with a hoof's width between us and a quick, plunging drop that would surely snap our necks, it was the better of the two options.

I needed to spin him a tale, a reason for my supposed lack of a family name, and then I remembered the lie the Seer intended to give the Father and decided there would be no harm in feeding it to him first to see just how palatable it was. "I am just the daughter of a shepherd. I was afraid to give my family name—I didn't want the Commander to seek them out, and I will not give it to you either."

Fenris's grip around my middle softened, and he slowed enough it felt safe to crack open my eyelids and peer at our surroundings. All around us, buildings sprang up on either side of the road in neatly ordered rows like the teeth of a serrated blade. "Ah, yes. I know many a shepherdess who wear diadems such as yours."

"I told you—"

"You're a dedicated Maiden, I recall."

The silence stretched after that as we slowed to a meandering pace through the streets. People passed us in droves, no doubt hurrying home from market or work, the hoods of their cloaks pulled tightly around themselves as light snow flurried in the chill air. Gray stone buildings roofed with wooden slats of blackwood watched us as we trod by. The wash hung out windows, carrying the smells of crisp soap to twine with the thick scent of woodsmoke and roasting suppers coiling from chimneys. Here and there, the shrieking laughter of children could be heard, followed by the sharp replies from their parents to settle. The tightly packed city homes were as foreign to me as their flaxen-haired residents. All the dwellings I'd seen in Vanyth had been situated on small fenced lots, even in the poorest districts, to allow the people the freedom to grow their own foods and raise meat to feed hungry mouths. Most houses had yards full of vegetables and geese, with at least one patch of fruiting shrubs or a fruit tree. Sometimes, neighbors would knock down their adjoining fences to allow more growing room and divvy up the harvests. I couldn't fathom how these people, who were stacked atop one another, could manage.

The severely crowded houses gave way to plaster-front shops with cheerfully painted signs hung above their doors and wide display windows of lead-paned glass. Fenris reined in his dappled mare in front of a shop with the most gorgeous dresses I'd seen in a long time in the window display.

He slid from the saddle and then helped me down. His touch was surprisingly gentle, more so than I imagined Ingemar would have been if he were my keeper, and for that, I was grateful. He winced faintly at the contact, no more than a flicker of revulsion, but it still nettled that he should find me so repugnant when he was such a brute.

A little bell chimed above the door as Fenris herded me into the shop. The air inside was blessedly warm, smelling of rich linens and the dyes they were dipped in. My eyes were immediately drawn to the bolts of fabric stacked in a riotous rainbow of color along the left wall on a set of floor-to-ceiling shelves. I'd never seen such a collection, not even in our royal sewing room as a small child, where I'd hopelessly mangled my embroidery for years until our tutor had rapped my knuckles enough times and I'd finally learned to straighten my stitches. Not long after that, I'd learned to enjoy it. My gaze swept along another wall on the far side of the room, where mounted rods and pegs held spools of ribbon and thread. I could practically feel the delicate fibers whispering across my skin as they were plunged and pulled through fabric. Dress forms were scattered about the store, showing off the seamstress's work, and I found myself entranced, drawn to them like a sleeper into a dream. I meandered among them, examining the fine details. The dresses were works of art in a variety of styles, the likes of which I'd never seen before and was sure I would never see again.

There was a storm gray dress that left the shoulders and chest bare with a heart-shaped bodice. The overskirt was sewn up to show a prismatic swell of ruffled underskirts cascading from beneath it. The hemline, stitched in intricate silver embroidery, looked like the churn of storm clouds with pinhead-sized blue beading that resembled the fall of rain. The immodesty of it forced a blush to slink across my cheeks, as I couldn't help but imagine that whoever was brave enough to don such a gown would feel as gorgeous and as radiant as Selenyss herself.

The dress on the form behind that one was more to my taste, still a little salacious with its lacy under shift that looked as though it would cling like a second skin along the arms and chest, but it had a tediously beaded stay—a fashion I'd heard from Helima was popular among the Orybous Islanders—and full skirts, all in emerald and plum jewel tones. I sighed wistfully as I rubbed the smooth silk of the skirts between my fingers.

It had been so very long since I'd attended a ball. The last had been a small affair to celebrate my name dey thrown just before I'd left for the temple. My sisters and I had whirled around the dance floor until well past midnoct, taking turns dancing with each other and the young squires. The moon-faced boy I'd danced with then was a man now, and likely a knight if he'd survived the trials that came with earning that title. I wondered if he remembered that noct as fondly as I did or if it had long since faded into memory.

"Oh, look at you, my lord! It's so good to see you again, and in one piece this time too!" a honeyed voice crooned from the back of the shop. I spun around in time to see a voluptuous beauty sway out of the back workroom to embrace Fenris.

"If I didn't come back whole, I think Munnin might have killed me." He chuckled as he bent and kissed the crown of the woman's auburn curls. She was clearly no Uthari. Judging from the hair that was achingly similar to Helima's, she was Orybousi.

She pulled back to survey him at arm's length. "Well, at least I know you have her looking after you since Emrys know you won't do it yourself."

She let him go and turned to me to drop a quick curtsy, which startled me out of my amazement that she seemed to be friends, actual friends, with my keeper. "Lady Healer, it is an honor." When she stood, she smiled, and the corners of her violet eyes crinkled. "My, you are a beauty."

I could feel crimson, a shade deeper than what my sisters would have deemed a pretty flush to the cheeks, paint my face as Fenris introduced us.

"Healer, may I present the finest seamstress in all the seven kingdoms, Rhapso."

Rhapso smacked his arm playfully. "Don't you flatter me. My poor heart can't take it."

Fenris inclined his head, his eyes glittering. "I wouldn't dare." It was painfully off-putting to hear friendly banter from such a stoic and brooding brute.

"It's a pleasure to meet you, Rhapso," I lied out of politeness. In truth, my heart was breaking at the sight of her and how much she looked like my lost friend. I wondered at how the two people in front of me could act so normally, as though nothing in the world was wrong, when to me, it felt as though the weight of everything that had happened in the past deys was suddenly stacked upon my chest and slowly crushing me, one shattered and splintered rib at a time.

Rhapso looped an arm through mine and patted it as she steered me toward a fitting area in the back. Fenris's eyebrows furrowed as he watched us pass before he silently fell in step on our heels. I tried to pattern my breaths to something that resembled normal, even as my tangled emotions writhed next to my heart. It would do me no good to fall apart now, not in front of him, and not in front of his friend.

The fitting area was luxurious, so I chose to fixate instead on each opulent detail, using the room's beauty to drown my sorrows. The reflection in a wall of mercury glass mirrors showed each swelling curve of my body along with plush velvet couches, embroidered linen curtains, and a changing pedestal with dancing women carved around its base. Rhapso guided me to the pedestal, drew the curtains around, and instructed me to undress while she led Fenris to settle on the couch.

"Now, Fenris, I received the measurements you sent down late last noct along with the Mother's design requests and your noted corrections," I overheard Rhapso whisper in a hushed tone through the thin curtain as I unslung my cloak and worked loose the laces of my boots. "I did my best to make it more modest as you suggested, but I also left most of the original design so neither of us will have to meet the headsman if she or the Father are displeased."

"I'm sure you did the best you could, Rhapso. You always do." His gruffly muttered reply was barely audible.

I shifted the curtain just a hair to peer out at the pair's reflection in the row of mirrors, just in time to see Fenris kiss the back of her hand. I briefly wondered if they were involved. My stomach knotted at the idea of that man *involved* with anyone. I supposed his otherness could be considered mysterious, and Thyra always said that mystery made a man more attractive. Though how one could denote where the line between mystery and deception lay, I was unsure. I scrutinized his profile for a heartbeat when Rhapso backed away.

He wasn't unattractive, I supposed, with a straight nose and a sharp, angular jaw covered in a shadow of stubble and the ghosts of scars that made him look every bit the rugged and ruthless soldier. But those noctmare eyes...I shuddered and resumed unlacing my dress as I backed away from the curtain.

Rhapso ducked in not a moment later with an armful of white fabric. "Oh dear." She clucked her tongue. "You'll need to shimmy out of that shift too.

This dress requires special undergarments unfortunately."

She helped me out of the long, linen garment, leaving me in nothing but my woolen stockings tied up to my thighs with embroidered ribbons. My cheeks flushed scarlet. Even though the curtain was shut, I felt exposed in a way that chafed against my bare body, knowing my keeper was just on the other side of the thin fabric. It left me feeling raw as I pressed an arm around the heavy swell of my breasts, covering my pale pink nipples that peaked with chilled dread despite the warmth of the room.

Rhapso kindly kept her eyes averted as she stooped and held the undergarment out for me to step into. The silk glided like a whispered secret over my skin, swept away the barbed, cruel feelings of mortification, and replaced them instead with the sensation of decadence. Much like the dress attached to the form out front, the undergarment had a curved neckline. It cupped my breasts, trapping them and forcing them upward with a plunging gap between to expose the tight press of cleavage. Clever boning was tucked all along the torso to cinch my waist and smooth my soft belly. The underskirt, full and bell-shaped thanks to its many layers and light wire threaded in a spool through the cloth, accentuated the roll of my hips and the tapering of my waist. Rhapso ducked behind me and pulled silk ribbons together in the back, cinching them snuggly.

"My goodness, you have such lovely curves, dear!" I flushed at Rhapso's compliment. It was a far cry from the way the Mother had described me. "Your silhouette will look divine in the gown."

"Your dresses are true pieces of art," I said as she bent to help me into a pair of white velvet slippers beaded with gold in a rose-patterned design. I wanted to fill the silence in place of awkward thanks that I couldn't quite force out. "I'm sure it would be difficult to not look good in them."

"You're too sweet. I traveled for my apprenticeship." That explained the eclectic styles. "They were the best years of my young life. I didn't know how lucky I was at the time." There was a tingle of wistfulness and sorrow in her words that held the hint of barely healed wounds scabbed over but still tender.

She held out the spans of smooth, white silk embroidered and beaded in gold and pearls. I bowed my head and allowed her to drape the fabric over me. "What led you here to Uthar?"

She kept her small smile pinned to her round cheeks as she tugged the dress over my chest and helped me slip into the sleeves. "Not all the choices made in my life were my own."

I didn't push her for more, understanding intimately the feelings that came with having others direct your life. Though it did make me curious if she, like me, had been ripped from her home. An idea came to me: perhaps she was my raven. If I could connect with her, maybe she could help free me, maybe we could free each other if she was, in fact, here against her will.

"I used to love to sew too, with my sisters." The words fell into the silence as she flitted around me, painted in the darker hues of sorrow rather than the conversational sunny hues I'd intended.

She came around to my back and pulled the laces until the fabric conformed to the swoops of my sides and hips. "It is a powerful sensation, is it not?

To make something out of nothing? Like the Emrys stitching Strattaria together with their magic." I could hear the smile in her words as she tugged here and fluffed there.

"It is," I agreed, "very much like magic." My lips and tongue struggled not to stumble over the word *magic*, and my heart quivered as if brushed over with a sense of foreboding. It felt like ill fortune to speak the word as a supposed witch in hiding, but I did my best to soothe the flailing organ in my chest with reassurances that the Seer could have been wrong. But neither it nor I fully believed it.

Rhapso came around to my front to admire her handiwork and beamed, her rosy cheeks swelling with what looked to be glowing pride at her masterful creation. "You are a vision! See for yourself." With a rustle of fabric, she pulled back the curtain, exposing me to the wall of mirrors, and hesitantly, I turned to look at myself.

My lips fell apart in a shallow gasp. Somehow, Rhapso had transformed me into something plucked from legend. The dress was tucked perfectly so it skimmed the top of the undergarments, the center of the neckline plunged to expose my cleavage, but a sheer lace panel was sewn underneath to give me some small measure of modesty. The silk hugged my torso like a lover unwilling to let go before flowing out at my hips and spilling like a moonbeam across the floor. The sleeves were off-the-shoulder bells split so they draped off the back of my arms. The whole of the garment was embroidered and beaded in pearls and gold. There were roses, moons, stars, and the outline of some sort of soaring birds flying and swooping among the patterns. Along the hem, wolves chase one another, snout to tail, with thorny vines tangled at their feet. The details were beyond exquisite and robbed me of my breath as I twisted and twirled, taking it all in. I didn't think I had ever felt more beautiful in my entire life. I didn't even mind that the sleeves and the color accentuated the shimmering bonding mark that wound up my arm and across my chest; I could almost convince myself it was part of the ensemble, that I really was just a woman plucked from a tale with mystical markings.

"Go give your escort a twirl so he can see too."

I winced at the bitter-tasting implication that Fenris was simply an escort, but I bit my lip, pinning the words inside my clamped jaw before I could speak them. I slowly turned around to find Fenris appraising me like I was a mare and he couldn't decide if I was worth purchasing. I half expected him to get up and check my teeth as his gaze raked intently over me from where he sat at ease, his elbow propped on the arm of the couch.

"Well?" I asked, suddenly feeling rather raw and exposed from the severe cut of his look.

He rubbed a hand over his stubbled chin. "There is no doubt all eyes will be on you, Healer." His flat, brusque tone gave no indication whether or not he thought that was a good thing or a bad thing, but the words wrung a shudder from my spine either way.

"I added the sleeves, raised the neckline, and inserted the lace panel as you suggested." Rhapso gestured to the parts of the dress as she noted them. "The original design would have left her looking as though she were a prized whore for sale—begging your pardon, Lady Healer. That original neckline had her bare to her navel!" Rhapso scoffed.

"That, I'm sure, was precisely the idea." Fenris's gaze deepened into something darker and more menacing, much to my surprise. Did he truly disagree with the things the Mother and Ingemar had said, or was this a ploy he played to woo women like Rhapso to his bed?

Rhapso's nose wrinkled in disgust. "Ugh, you poor thing." She took my hand and gave it a comforting squeeze. "You just let me know if you need anything, dear. That Fortress is full of wolves."

That I knew, just as I knew one of the most fearsome lounged not two steps away on her couch. No matter—this woman was kind, and I could see the sincerity in her eyes. Perhaps one dey, if I was patient, I could make her see Fenris for what he really was and she could be the raven I sought. I squeezed her hand in return and thanked her before she whisked me behind the curtain to help me undress.

Back outside, the flurries of snow had turned into icy sleet. As I raised the fur-lined hood of my cloak, a trembling inched its way up my spine one vertebrae at a time. It was too soon in the year for snow; I wasn't used to seeing it until much closer to Eklipsis. Part of me hoped it was the wrath of the Emrys, punishing the whole of Uthar for taking me from my home, but that was a silly, selfish thought. I may be a True Healer, but in the grand scheme of the Emrys, I was just another insignificant mortal. But no, that wasn't true either. I was a witch. The notion felt slippery and difficult to wrap my head around.

Fenris lifted me onto the horse again despite my protests that I could do it myself and then quickly followed, wrapping his cloak around both of us and pulling me back against himself for warmth. As much as his touch made me squirm—I could practically smell the blood on him underneath his smoky scent—I savored the warmth. I closed my eyes so I wouldn't have to see the Fortress looming over us as we rode back.

My lack of resistance sickened me. We were out of the Fortress, and I had just stood for a damned dress fitting, of all Umbra-cursed things, like a good little pet without once trying to run. But what choice did I have? I didn't know the city, the weather was turning foul, and there was this bond between Fenris and me. He would know where I was no matter where I went. There had to be a way to remove it, but without further study, short of severing my own arm or taking a potato knife to my flesh, I couldn't think of anything. As if it could sense me thinking about it, despising it, the swirling silvery ink tickled, as if it were creeping, as if it were growing. I resisted the urge to tear open my dress and peer at it.

Far sooner than he should have, Fenris reined the horse in and drew us to a halt. I flung my eyes open in surprise and peered around. "Where are we?"

Fenris grunted as he dismounted and patted my leg. "Just a quick errand. Don't go anywhere." He winked up at me through his thick, black lashes. I scowled at his back as he strode away.

A flare of red flames licked the cold, kalda-kissed air from the open-sided workshop that Fenris entered and they caught my eye, as did the hulking man who pumped the bellows next to it. Fenris approached the bald, muscle-bulked man. They bent their heads together, and I caught myself leaning in, as though I might be able to catch the faintest whisp of conversation, but it was all stolen by Imbola's wind, and she wasn't in a sharing mood todey. I glanced around at the empty street through fat snowflakes that clung to my lashes. Snakes of snow slithered and whipped across the ground, eddying around the horse's hooves. How far could I make it on my own in a storm on horse-back before he found me? I looked back to find him watching, as if he could read my thoughts. He turned back to the smithy, passed him a small package, and with a quick wave, he returned and mounted the horse.

"You didn't run," he whispered against the shell of my ear once he'd spurred the horse into a trot back up the hill toward the Fortress.

It wasn't a question, but I answered it anyway. "You would have found me."

He squeezed his arm more tightly around the soft swell of my abdomen. "Good girl. Don't forget it. Anywhere you go, Shepherdess, I will find you."

I bit my lip to keep from crying out in anguish and frustration—so hard, I could taste the coppery tang of blood. How in the names of the Emrys was I ever going to get home again? I took a deep, shuddered breath as we swung around the first of many switchbacks.

Patience. The only thing I could rely on was patience.

The Baying of Wolves

F ENRIS LEFT ME AT my door in a dismissive silence. I slipped in and immediately dissolved
onto the rug before the raging hearth. I let loose
every bitter tear of shame, anger, agony, and
vexation. I sobbed so violently, my whole body
convulsed—wracked with too many painful emotions—until I was no longer a whole woman but
shattered remnants, a pile of fractured pieces on
the floor. I lay there until I was wrung out, then I
slowly pushed to my feet, hauling the broken bits
of myself and pasting them back together as best
as I could. But the hollowness in my chest ached.
The edges of my heart, jagged and raw, sliced into
my meat and bone with each beat—bleeding me to
death slowly from a wound that no one could see so
no one could fix. Who knew emptiness could feel
so heavy?

I noticed a covered tray on the small table along with another mug, just as it had been this morning. But with my stomach in knots, I didn't have the will to even see what lay underneath the carefully placed linen or to smell the herbs steeped in the tea. I shuffled to the bathing chamber. *A splash of cool water on my face ought to help.*

The chamber was lit with the soft, billowing glow of candlelight from sconces along the walls. Steam eddied from a copper basin on a pedestal, drenching the air with the heady scent of oils. Munnin must have poured the water in there boiling for it to still have been so hot. She was a good woman, even though she worked for my keeper.

I stripped and left my clothes in a puddle on the floor. Glancing at myself in the mirror, I was momentarily shocked that my emotional pain wasn't spelled out in real bruises and gashes across my skin. How could I look so whole and hale when everything in me hurt this damn much?

With a cloth, I wiped the tearstains from my cheeks and washed my hands before donning a noct shift that waited on a peg along the wall. I padded back out to the bedchamber, snagged a light quilt from the bed, wrapped it around myself, took the cup of tea, and sat cross-legged in front of the crackling fire.

I took a deep pull from the large mug of herbal tea. "I am a witch," I whispered the words disbelievingly across the steaming rim of brew. A bubble of hysterical laughter burst from me before I could stop it. A witch. How was that even possible? Unless...I thought of my diadem nestled in a box in the wardrobe. What if they hadn't been gifts from a witch to an ancestor but forged by a witch ancestor? And if that was the case, why had it been kept a secret? Vanyth had never been nearly as against witches as Uthar or some of the other countries. But that also begged the question: did anyone know? Had the histories been tampered with or altered, or was it one of the secrets only passed down from the ruling monarch to their heir? My sister had hinted on several occasions that something of the like might exist. My sister, the queen.

"Queen Thyra." I whispered it like a prayer. She would send someone for me, but I had the churning, nauseating sensation that whoever she sent wouldn't make it here, or if they did, they wouldn't make it home again. And even if she did send a rescuer, there was still the bond to contend with.

That left magic. Magic I wasn't quite sure I believed I had. I'd always been exceptionally gifted as a Healer by all accounts, but I'd never tried to use my gifts for anything else; it was supposed to be impossible. A lot of healing was belief—if you believed it, it became real—so maybe if I just believed I could pull from that well and do something other than heal, I could?

I closed my eyes, following the same mental pathway I always did to my well of healing gifts—no, to the well of magic. If I was to make it work, I should call it magic; I should believe it to be magic. I drew drops of it up and pushed them toward my fingers effortlessly. I opened my eyes to find the tips of my fingers glowing with silver-white light as usual, the light Fenris had found so unusual, not that his opinion mattered.

What to do with it now? Something small. A ball of light—that should be simple enough. I rolled my fingers together, willing the light to solidify in my palm, much like I'd rolled clay from the banks of the pond when I'd been young to pinch into little makeshift pots. As far as I could tell, nothing happened, but then, with a sudden crackling sensation along the fine bones of my hand, the light from my fingertips pulled together on my palm in a spindling vortex. I gasped in awe as small effervescent sparks shot out of the little silvery-blue cyclone. The Seer had been right.

A brick of aching dread settled in the pit of my stomach. If anyone found out, I would be dead, affinity for healing or not. What was potentially my salvation would surely be my damnation if I were discovered. As the depth of my despair increased, so did the ferocity of my cyclone. My eyes went wide as it whizzed out of my hand and landed on my rug. The sparks caught the fibers beneath it alight in a tiny blaze, sending me lunging away from it. I would definitely be discovered if I burned my room down. Without thinking, I grabbed my mug of tea and used it to douse the whirling dervish of argent fire. With a hiss, it vanished and left me heaving for breath and a soggy singe mark on the rug.

That had not exactly gone to plan. Belatedly, I realized I should have just willed the thing out of existence. Though, considering it was supposed to have just been a small ball of light, willing it away might have also gone awry.

The sort of wariness that usually liked to walk hand in hand with deys of heavy emotions settled over me, drooping my eyelids and sapping my body. I stumbled to the wardrobe and retrieved a noct shift. I barely managed to get it on and settle myself beneath the coverlet before sleep dragged me into its depths.

I waded knee-deep in gore through the temple courtyard, the burning gaze of the dead's vacant eyes searing me. Their mouths hung open in twisted screams that echoed off the scarlet-spattered, crystalline walls. I clapped my hands over my ears, trying to drown them out, while fat tears fell from my eyes and drowned in the rivers of blood at my feet.

I squeezed my eyes shut. The cries of the dead were unrelenting.

Silence fell like a headsman's ax. I cracked an eye and peered through my eyeteeth. The faces, the blood—they were all gone, as if they had never been. I let my hands fall.

Drip.
Drip.
Drip.

I spun toward the sound and found myself outside the temple walls, facing the stand of trees. Helima stood, blood running down her cheeks like tears, pouring from her ears. It dripped from her fingers and pooled at her feet. Her eyes were as milky white and unseeing as the Seer's. She opened her mouth to speak, blood trickling from the corners. "Restore the balance. As above, so below." She chanted the words in a voice not her own.

With an outstretched arm, I stumbled toward her, my fingers blazing with my magic. "Helima, I'm so sorry. Let me help you, please!"

Ribbons of shadow licked from the trees to snake across the ground and twine around her skirts. She raised a hand with a singular unfurled finger, pointing. "Beware" came from her throat. The word was screamed by a thousand voices.

Behind me came a howl so chilling, I felt it rattle my bones. My heart ceased to beat as I spun to face a pack of dire wolves, each nearly as tall as a horse. Black blood dripped from their snarling maws. Their dusky hackles stood raised on their napes; their gray talons pawed the ground, churning it up and spitting it in their wake as they charged. I tried to move, but my feet were rooted by tendrils of wispy shadow.

The wolves and the shadows lunged at one another at the same time. The shadows solidified into a noct-black raven twice the size of the dire wolves. It dove into them with a gnashing beak and talons. The wolves howled a note riddled with a deep-keening agony, like the sound of a funeral knell.

I sat bolt upright in bed, so drenched in fear and sweat that I was certain, for a heart-stuttering moment, that it was blood. The firelight in the room was low, nothing resided in the hearth but embers, but the howling of the wolves followed me from my dream and chased me from my bed. I fumbled with the latch of a shuttered window on the far side of the room. I flung it wide, the blast of kalda on the wind chilled me less than the baying of wolves it carried across the dark.

WHEN MUNNIN RAPPED SOFTLY on the door just after dawn, I feigned sleep. She left a covered tray on the table by the couch, fed the fire, and retrieved the untouched tray from the previous noct. Her footsteps were downy soft as she tiptoed her way back out, and only the hushed click of the latch let me know she was gone.

A dream had chased me from my sleep, and the howling of the wolves in the Blackwood beyond the castle had kept me awake. The well of my gifts—no, of my magic, though it seemed odd to admit it even to myself—trembled as if it were calling me to put it to use. Deylight streamed in gossamer ribbons through the shutters, which had been left carelessly open when I'd dived back under the coverlet like a frightened child at the sound of the wolf song.

I watched the motes of dust float in the golden light like the bobbing fishermen's boats in the harbors of Vanyth and let the rock and sway of their dance lull me into a much-needed dreamless sleep.

I awoke shivering beneath my blanket to find the dey grown old, the light changed to that of middey, and I rose from the bed to latch the shutters, the cold floor nipping at my toes. The view from the window was breathtaking enough, I momentarily forgot that I was a hostage as I leaned over the sill and took it all in. From my vantage, I took in the opposite side of the Fortress, over the cliffs to where the Blackwood bled into the horizon in one direction, and over to where the ocean bled into Emphyrea in the other. If I leaned just a fraction over the sill, I could see the whole of the bustling city of Berth and its harbor, where the flags of many nations flew atop masts like an assortment of colorful birds roosting. With this view, I could keep an eye on the comings and goings of the vessels. If I was lucky, there might be a discernible pattern, or better yet, a ship from home I could stow aboard—though I knew there was typically very little trade from Vanyth to Uthar, and what customs there were from other kingdoms were under strain or duress. A spy glass could definitely be useful. That way, I could mark the men about their tasks on the wharf and note the guard rotations. I made a mental note to see if I could find one about the Fortress, however unlikely it was that someone would just leave one lying about.

Jyord's sun shimmered over the Blackwood and glittered against the ivory bond along my arm. I sighed, resentment twisting in my stomach. I'd be able to stow away on a ship only if I could figure out how to remove this damnable bond. A long figure wreathed in black on one of the iron bridges snagged my gaze. It could have been none other than my Umbra-cursed keeper with hair that dark whipping behind him in the wind as he walked. He drew up short on the bridge's midpoint, and I could have sworn he tipped his head to find me looking, as if I'd summoned his attention just by thinking of our bond. With a curse, I slammed the window shut and stomped over to where my food tray was laid out. I ripped off the cover, quickly checked for poisons, snagged a muffin, and began to pace along the rug in front of the hearth.

Magic. I had to learn how to use my magic. It was the only way to remove the bond. But how in the Emrys was I to do that in a city once renowned for its witch burnings? I nibbled the muffin as I paced. It was surprisingly delicious—apple with some sorts of spices and a scrumptious-looking sugary crumble on the top. I ate it from the bottom up to save the top for last. I was nearly done when an idea came to me: librarians. Those stodgy old men and women in the royal libraries at home were notorious for hoarding texts that were banned or condemned. Father had always turned a blind eye, mostly because he'd believed knowledge could be a powerful weapon. If the librarians did it there, why wouldn't they do it here? Munnin had said the bridges had been built by a witch—wouldn't she have been bound to have books or scrolls on her at the time of her capture, books that a crafty librarian might have wanted to save? There was only one way to find out, so I added scouring the libraries to my mental to-do list.

"Do ye be trying to wear a hole in yer rug?" Munnin chortled from the doorway.

I startled. "I—uh, sorry. I didn't hear you knock."

"I do no be surprised—ye did look as though ye were away at sea, swimmin' with the Mer folk." She chuckled. "Rhapso's delivery did just arrive. Huggin's gone to fetch it. But I did think ye might like a bath before we get ye dressed and ready for the Triumph."

Ah right, the Triumph was tonoct, where I would be held up as the Father's new trophy and a potential broodmare in whom loyal Sons could seed gifted babies. My lips twisted into a semblance of an ironic smile. The Father had dedicated his life to eradicating witches, and yet here I was by some Emrys-granted miracle, or curse, and he was desperate for me to beget spawn with my abilities. A trickster Emrys surely had a hand in the unfolding of events that had led me here. A flash of last noct's dream wiped away my momentary mirth. It reminded me of the precariousness of my situation and made me ponder once again those old bedtime tales of the Uthari monsters my governess had spun to get me to bed on time.

With a shudder, I surrendered to the idea of a bath in the hope that the hot water might burn off the apparently still-lingering chill of my noctmare. I couldn't shake the haunting song of the wolves from where it hummed along my bones and unsettled my magic, nor could I shove off the image of the shadow-born raven coming to my rescue. Surely it had been no more than my mind dredging up the children's stories I'd been most recently pondering to braid with my traumas, but the weight of it felt somehow more significant and leaden than an ordinary dream.

Munnin made the tub ready quickly. The bathing chambers here were apparently fed using a series of unseen pipes that drew water from a hot spring beyond the keep. A clever design, I had to admit as I sank into the near-scalding water. I would have to see if something similar could be implemented back home—whenever I managed to find my way there. My sisters would just marvel at the ability to take hot baths any time of dey without the guilt of having servants haul buckets of water up flight after flight of stairs.

The sudden longing for my sisters nibbled at my heart, taking meaty bites of it between its relentless teeth and gnashing it into a despairing pulp that it spat out against my ribs. Tears prickled the backs of my eyes like thousands of beating fists upon a door, but I held strong against them, stomping a foot atop my longing and tamping it beneath my heel. If I was to survive, I would have to become as ruthlessly unfeeling as, if not more so than, the monsters I faced here.

Wrapped in a linen robe, I sat on the settee in front of the hearth while Munnin anointed my hair with scented oils, combed it out, and rolled it around thin wooden spools poked full of holes to allow the fire-warmed air to flow through them. She claimed it would give my natural waves more definition as it dried while she painted my face with kohl and powders, filed and polished my nails, and applied creams to my skin.

She talked breezily as she did so, telling me anecdotes from her childhood. My favorite was the time Huggin had apparently tried to steal a neighboring family's yew and it had taken off running for the swamps. Her stubborn brother had been wrapped around its neck, refusing to let go, caked in muck and mire. I laughed so hard, I almost cried, unable to picture the solemn-faced man as a child. I appreciated what she was doing, not just taking care of me as she'd been assigned to but taking care of my spirit too. With her lighthearted tales and easy demeanor, she kept me from falling into darker feelings of longing as I had alone in the bath.

Munnin retrieved a small trunk by the door, where it sat atop a larger one that must have arrived while I'd been bathing.

"What's in that bigger one?" I asked, my curiosity piqued.

Munnin pulled a slip of paper out of her pocket, rolled and sealed with melted wax imprinted with a spool and sheers. "This did come for ye from Rhapso."

I took it from her with murmured thanks as I cracked the seal.

Ertha,

In the spare trunk, I enclosed supplies for you so you may once again know the power that can come from wielding a needle. Whatever you do with it, I hope it brings you peace, and I hope you know that you will always have a friend in Berth so long as I reside here.

Emrys' blessings,

Rhapso

I tried not to tear up and ruin Munnin's carefully done face paints around my eyes as I thanked the

Emrys that, even in this Umbra-cursed land, there were kind and generous beings like Munnin and Rhapso. I wondered if either one could be the raven I needed to help me escape. Who knew, maybe they would both wish to leave with me. They had more than alluded to their presence here being less than voluntary, and from the look on Munnin's face when Fenris had slipped the bonding bracelet onto my wrist, she knew something about them. If I was fortunate, maybe that knowledge extended to how to remove them. With that thought in mind, the noct's festivities seemed marginally less daunting.

"Now, let's see how to get ye into this contraption." Munnin laughed as she withdrew the specialized undergarments Rhapso had crafted to pair with the dress.

Even with the two of us working together, it took twice as long to get the underclothes and dress on as it had Rhapso, but as I gazed at my reflection in the mirror that Munnin had pulled from the bathing room, I was just as stunned by it as I had been in the shop yesterdey. I'd never dreamed of wearing something like this. Not even in my wildest imaginings of my future life in court had I conjured up visions of dresses that glittered like a star stone fallen from the Emphyrea.

I lost myself for a moment, so ensorcelled by the beauty and sheer magical quality of Rhaspo's handiwork that I forgot why it had been crafted and why I wore it. But as Munnin clasped her hands over her heart and whispered, "My, my, Ertha, you do be a pretty sight," I crashed back into my skin—skin marked with a shackling bond. The smooth, butter-soft fabric suddenly felt like a vise, slowly squeezing me until I popped like a too ripe berry, rendering me into nothing but scarlet jelly for the Father and Mother to smear across their morning bread.

I wrapped that truth around my heart and let it harden into stone; it was my only means of protection for that soft, too tender bit of flesh so prone to flights of fancy, deydreams, and worst of all, longings.

Something in my face must have changed, because Munnin appeared in the mirror behind me and placed a hand on my bare shoulder in what I was sure she meant to be a reassuring way. "Never ye fret, dear. Ye do just need to be presented formally to the Mother and Father and the court. Ye will dance and eat, and then ye will be done," she tried to soothe as she pulled the rollers from my hair, unspooling the ringlets down my back. But no matter how sweet the white lie sounded or how much I wished it were true, I knew tonoct's Triumph was just the beginning of this journey the Emrys had seen fit to send me on.

Munnin tucked my hair back, crowning my silver tresses with gilt pins to hold my sheer, white veil in place, its edges embroidered to match the lavish gown. As she nestled the last one in among the strands, a knock sounded at the door. I turned to go when Munnin snatched my hand and folded it into hers.

"I do be praying to all the Emrys for ye tonoct, Ertha. Do promise me ye will no let them see you falter."

I squeezed her hand in return before letting it drop. "I won't, Munnin. Thank you."

I 'D EXPECTED TO SEE Fenris when Munnin opened the door, but instead, Huggin filled the frame. I expressed as much, to which Huggin simply replied, "He do be waiting for ye." The man must have a tongue made of stone for all the gruffness in the few words he spoke. He was not the escort I would have chosen, but then again, none of this was what I would have chosen for myself.

Huggin offered me his arm, though whether it was out of politeness or out of a need to keep me close lest I make a suicidally rash decision and try to run with no plan, I couldn't tell. Dressed much the same way as he had been the dey before, with no finery except maybe a slight polish to his leather armor, he led me down the spiraling staircase. Music and laughter filtered along the stairwell to hook and lure us like a siren's song.

My heart, wrapped in stony truth as it was, stayed blessedly calm, even as we stepped off the stairs into the main hall that led to the high court, a much shorter walk than the trip we'd taken the dey before. The entryway was shockingly empty, apart from a man and a woman in a lewd embrace near a tapestry on the far end. Everyone else must have been inside, waiting to get an eyeful of the Father's new prized collection piece.

It was only when Huggin cleared his throat as we approached that I realized the man nosing the woman's swan-like neck was Lord Fenris. She giggled at whatever he whispered in her ear before he pulled away to straighten his formal coat. She cast a reproachful glance my way, flicking her eyes from the hem of my skirts to my hair. She curled her lip disdainfully before she sashayed off with a sulky, seductive sway to her hips, her hair a silken, aureate sheet that rippled down her back and caught the flickering light from the flame-lit sconces on the wall as she went.

"You're late." Fenris glowered down at me from under furrowed brows, then he plucked a stray golden hair from his black lapel embroidered with silver and gilt designs that were very nearly a match to the stitchwork on my gown.

"Well, I don't roll out of bed looking like this." I waved a hand across my body to make my point.

He sneered, "No, you certainly don't."

For a moment, his response needled, but I hardened the walls around my heart and let the words snap against it, keeping my face calm. "Shall we go since you're in such a hurry? To get back to your companion, I presume."

The corners of his lips curled maliciously as he offered me his arm, not in request, but in silent demand. "Jealous, Shepherdess?"

I took his arm with a sharp laugh. "By Selenyss, no," I said, invoking the name of the lunar Emrys out of habit. I instantly regretted it; the name was like a sliver, sharp and ruthless, small enough to wriggle its way through my defenses and sting. "You're not my type."

"And what is your type? Homespun and smelling of sheep?" He steered me toward the court's entry with a nod to an attendant hovering in the shadows of the arched doorway. Huggin fell into step behind us. The attendant slipped into the court ahead and blew a horn, its call lowing and eerie as it reverberated around the waiting chamber and silenced the crowd.

My slipper caught on my hem as the hush sent spider-webbing cracks through the stone around my heart and allowed fluttery bits of anxiety to slip in. I dug my nails into Fenris's forearm to steady myself as I tried to squish those nasty, sharp feelings before they could overwhelm me. I stiffened as his other hand came to rest atop mine. His grip was warm and tingled in all the spots where the bond parts touched.

"Don't worry. I won't let you fall."

I stiffened, unsure if he meant it as a barb or if his words were genuine. I lifted my hem and descended the three steps into the court. A sea of fair-haired dignitaries stood in reverential silence as Fenris guided me, our steps echoing across the court, along the polished blackwood floor. In the center of the room, we skirted a large, circular stone hearth, its heart ablaze. On the far side of the hall on a dais twin to the one in their throne room, the Father and Mother sat imposingly on their thrones. The Mother's hands had a white-knuckled grasp on her armrests. I could feel the loathing coming off her in waves. Though whether it was directed at me specifically or Fenris because of the dress changes or something else entirely that I was incapable of fathoming, I couldn't be sure, and I certainly didn't want to be near her long enough to find out.

We came to a stop a few paces away from the royals and what I assumed were their closest dignitaries cloistered around the edge of the steps up to the thrones. Ingemar with his crooked stare was among them, but I refused to meet his or anyone's gaze and instead kept my eyes on the tapestries that hung above the windows on the wall behind them until I went to one knee, my head dipped meekly and my skirts arrayed around me.

"May I present to you, Father, the spoils of our recent raid, a prize among prizes, more valuable than gold, a True Healer to mend your brave Sons. May they live long and stand stronger than the rest." Fenris intoned the words with an edge that spoke to having said similar sentiments on numerous occasions.

I felt all eyes on me, like a murder of pecking caws, but I bit the inside of my cheek and didn't flinch. I didn't break. The Father spoke, but it was a dizzying drone in my ears as I focused on maintaining my calm.

When I rose after being dismissed, knee aching from being pressed into a floor as unforgiving as the people who'd hewn it, Fenris had already left me, presumably to resume his dalliance, unworried for my safety with his loyal guard standing so nearby. I drifted to where Huggin stood, keeping an ever watchful eye on me. Not that it was necessary. It wasn't like I could have run with this many people inspecting me like I was a living, breathing vessel for the Emrys—which, in effect, I was; my powers had been granted to me to heal others. Though, apparently, that belief which I'd held so tightly to my heart all these years was incorrect since, as the Seer had said, I was a witch. But I couldn't think of that now while I stood a lamb in a room full of wolves. I could almost see them for the beasts they were out of the corners of my eyes with their leering gazes and salivatory smiles.

I took a tiny chalice from a passing servant– willing my hand not to shake as I did so– filled with a tangy and pungent liquor, the cup's petite size a warning of the potency of the drink within. I sipped it lightly and winced as it scalded the back of my throat. It was far more bitter than I'd expected, with hints of spices I was wholly unfamiliar with. It was only after I'd downed the contents that I realized I should have discreetly delved it to make sure it hadn't contained anything nefarious. Perhaps I'd allowed these Uthari to rattle me more than even I'd known, stony heart or no.

I relinquished the empty vessel to the next passing servant and stood poised, hands clasped in front of me, watching the milling and dancing nobility of this foreign court. Memories of the last ball I'd been to flitted on the periphery of my mind. It had been so much smaller than this, attended by only our closest family and friends. My mother had even been in attendance, a rare treat, considering—no, I would not think of her now, not here, where I was so vulnerable. I almost never allowed myself that luxury, and only in private, which this was not.

The music spilled out from the mezzanine above me and coated the room in a glittering gaiety. A few of the dances and tunes were unfamiliar to me. Though some were similar in melody, the words the Uthari sang were different or the steps to the accompanying dance were altered, having the partner dip when, at home in Vanyth, the partner would have turned. I tried never to glance at the dais, to never look at the royals, who observed keenly like stern-faced parents watching their children as they played. From time to time, I felt eyes rake and scratch across my skin from their direction, dissecting me with their gazes and their whispers.

A disturbance in a nearby group of nobles drew my attention. They parted like the sea around the prow of a boat to allow a lumbering man through. He was dressed in a well-tailored gray jacket and breeches—though simple, he filled them well—with a wolf pelt slung across his shoulder, as it seemed was the style for most men in the Uthari court. The women's cheeks stained pink beneath their paint as he stalked past them, his hands tucked neatly behind his back. He emanated sheer, predatory grace. The knots on his shoulder and the insignia on his collar marked him as a Son. I assessingly ran my eyes over him from his boot tips up and tried to determine what it was that had the women fanning themselves as soon as he passed and miming swooning to one another in a way that elicited fits of giggles from their friends. My eyes slipped over his neatly bearded jaw, his slightly dark blond hair braided back at the nape of his neck, and reached his eyes. I stilled and ceased even to breathe as it struck me that he watched *me*, headed straight for *me*. Each of his steps struck the floor with intent.

The Son stopped less than a pace in front of me and bowed low at the waist. "Lady Healer," he purred, his voice as rough as the hewn planks of the ships the Sons sailed upon. "May I introduce myself? I am Kastor Se'aneir, Son of Uthar. My life is the one you chose to save behind the Selenyss Temple. I have come to offer you my sincerest thanks. May the Emrys bless you for sparing me."

I tried to swallow my revulsion as he held out his hand—I could almost see the blood of the innocents coating his fingers. I swallowed the building rage that stuck in my throat, more bitter than bile, and held out my hand in turn for him to take, allowing him to brush his lips across my skin. I willed myself not to shudder.

I checked the stone wrappings around my heart and firmed them up before I spoke, not trusting myself to do so without an iron grip around that tender bit of flesh. "There is no need for thanks, Son of Uthar. The Emrys blessed me with these abilities. I would not spit on them by refusing to heal any who are in need."

His lips curled into a lupine smile, and he stepped closer, his hand wrapped around mine. "Refusing to heal those who you would rather watch bleed out, you mean," he whispered, his voice a low rumble of thunder across the narrow space between us.

I smoothed my face and peered up at him through lowered lashes in a way that I hoped he perceived as submissive and small. "Of course not, Son. I would never—"

He bit off my words, light glancing off his brown eyes like the edge of a knife. "Don't lie, Lady."

Anxiety drew my muscles taut as I tried to withdraw my hand again, which only seemed to egg him on further. Where was my keeper and his watchdog, Huggin, when I needed them to intervene? The Son flexed his fingers around mine, and I swore I could feel the slip of Helima's blood upon them. The stone around my heart shattered, exposing the weak and fleshy organ to the stinging bite of rage and anguish.

"Do you have no recollection of an Orybousi woman in the temple gardens? You killed her. You killed my friends," I hissed through gritted teeth.

He smiled. The bastard actually smiled and quirked an insufferable eyebrow. "But did I?"

I didn't dignify his words with a response. Of course he had—he was a Son, a wicked monster, the stuff of noctmares that every governess from here to the ice deserts of Iliff threatened their charges with to get them into bed on time, to get them to eat their supper. Of course he'd killed my friends. Of course he was bathed in the blood of the weak and the helpless.

"Dance with me, Lady Healer," he demanded as he gave my hand a slight tug in the direction of the dance floor. "Dance with me, and I will tell you who is truly responsible for your friend's murder."

He didn't leave me much choice, and I had to admit, the word *murder* on the lips of a Son was intriguing. I'd assumed that, as the hands of the Father, the Sons thought it was their divine mandate to cut down people in his name. Murder, as far as I'd known, wasn't in their vocabulary. But here it was, rolling off the tongue of this Son, this Kastor Se'aneir. The stories did say they were literal monsters with wolfish features and animalistic desires, and I had to admit, my practical knowledge of other countries was somewhat lacking. As the youngest, my lessons on certain areas had been somewhat lax. So I allowed the Son and my curiosity to guide my steps as he drew me out away from the shadows I'd been hiding in and into the spill of light from the circular hearth just as the orchestra struck up a thrumming melody that, back home, was called *The Maiden with Golden Feathers.*

Kastor's hands were gentler now that he'd gotten what he wanted. He guided me through the steps and held me steady as I stumbled on one that differed from what I was familiar with. After a turn around the hearth in silence, I finally found my voice and asked, "Are you going to divulge what you know, Son, or were your words simply to lure me into a dance?"

He laughed, the sound rolling from the deepest depths of his ribcage. I tilted my head to look up at him, suddenly uncomfortable with how slight he made me feel in his presence. "I must admit, Healer, you are much pricklier than I imagined you'd be in my dreams."

"You've dreamt of me?" Heat crept up my neck and cheeks. His admission felt too raw to be anything but truth, and the thought of being in someone else's head while they slept felt far too intimate for my liking. Especially the head of my enemy.

"How could I not dream of the woman who literally held my heart in her hand and chose to heal it rather than crush it." His eyes were earnest if a bit mischievous as he pulled me in close, his scent of salt and iron overwhelming me as he dipped me, my veil brushing the floor.

As he righted us, the song faded out and bled into another, *The Sea and the Serpent*. He pulled me into the new steps. "I wasn't always a ruthless soldier for the Father, you know. I was once the son of a pious farmer south of the capital."

"I don't doubt your words." I resented the accusatory tone, insinuating I was in the wrong somehow and not the victim of his kind's vicious assaults. "But that doesn't negate the blood you've spilled now that you are." In a flash, I could see in my mind's eye the white of my dress irrevocably stained red by his hands, sullying everywhere he touched. I had to get a rein on my heart and my wild imagination.

"I have spilled no blood, Healer." He bent and whispered the words against the shell of my ear as if he were sharing his most closely held secret, pulled from beneath his soul, where he kept it hidden away from everyone, even the Emrys.

Was it trickery, or did the legends have these men painted in the wrong color? Where history saw them in nothing but brutal shades of blood and black, perhaps they—or at least some of them—were different. And if what he said was true—which I found even harder to believe than the tales of giants spun by my governess—I realized the stories may well have gotten it wrong. A Son who did not kill was like a fish who refused to swim or a hen who refused to lay; it felt like a notion that defied the laws set forth by the Emrys upon all of creation.

"What do you mean?" My words were barely audible between us, so breathy that I was scarcely sure I'd spoken them at all until he answered.

"I go through the motions, Lady Healer, but I do not sully my soul by slaying those who are undeserving of it. I chant the songs with the others, I paint my face and don the armor, but in the heat of battle, I do my best to let those who can slip away, to save rather than murder. It is a carefully constructed ruse. But to me, as I was raised to believe, all life is sacred under the gaze of the Emrys."

"But my friend in the kitchen garden...mere paces from where I found you..." The argument tumbled over my quivering lower lip.

His chin scraped across the top of my veiled head as he shook it in firm denial. "It wasn't me; I was found out as I tried to lead the women in the kitchens to safety, and I would have been killed by the one who found me had you not chosen to do what was right."

"Who?" It was a single word, barely above a whisper, but he heard me; he knew what I meant without further elaboration.

With a slight, nearly imperceptible jerk of his head, he showed me the beast responsible: my keeper. Fenris sat at a bench along the wall between pools of flickering light but touched by neither, another flaxen-haired woman on his knee, different from the last. His hand moved along the exposed length of her neck, his fingers dipping into the front of her bodice, her lips parting and her breasts heaving with panted breaths. I blinked, and blood coated him, dripping from his carefully braided hair and down his face, as if a bucket of it had been upturned over him, baptizing him as a beast. As a murderer. Another blink, and it was gone.

"I fear you may have saved me just so I may be slain all over again, Lady Healer, should he expose my indiscretions," Kastor murmured. The words seemed to claw reluctantly from his throat. "But as long as I still have the breath you gave me, Lady Healer," he continued when I didn't answer, "in me, you will have a faithful ally and protector here at court. Anything you need at all, I vow to do my best to help."

My heart stopped. It couldn't have been this easy to find an ally, someone to help me escape. It had to be a trick. But then he spun us to a stop at the edge of the large central hearth, and my too soft heart squeezed as he brushed his lips across the back of my hand again before letting my hand drop.

"I owe you my life, Lady, and I will spend every moment it is still beating devoted to you. By the Emrys, I swear it."

Before I could answer, my tongue too stunned by his sudden vows, he drifted away into the crowd, leaving me to wonder what kind of fool he was to make such a strong and binding oath to a woman he barely knew.

T HE CROWD SWALLOWED KASTOR behind swirling skirts as I sat on the lip of the hearth. The flames licking behind me seemed to lean in, their heat a comfortable caress of a familiar friend. Or, more likely, I just wished they felt that way, a result of the deep yearning and cold, stark loneliness nestled in the very center of my ribs. I had just been offered an ally, and yet I felt even more helpless than before his vows had been made. Trust was an unsteady ground, and I didn't know where upon it I stood.

But I'd wanted to make allies, had I not? And even though one came with the trappings of my enemy, did that mean he couldn't be my raven? I really had to start being more careful with the desires I whispered, even to myself, even in my mind, for as I'd been told all my life, one never knew when an

Emrys was listening or how they would interpret what one thought.

I smoothed my skirts, preparing to stand and find Huggin to inquire if I'd stayed long enough on display. The noct, short as it had been, had already exhausted me beyond belief—a compounding effect, no doubt, from the dey before.

Then the music abruptly turned stilted. The stringed instruments screeched, playing too slow and off-kilter. I looked up curiously at the mezzanine and blinked, my eyes widening; those who'd only moments ago been cavorting and laughing, full of drink and food, suddenly moved like bugs trapped in fresh amber.

I whirled. My skirts twisted about my legs as they moved too slowly—a beat behind me. Was exhaustion playing tricks on me? Had the drink I'd failed to delve been poisoned? Had Kastor slipped something to me somehow? A toxin upon his calloused skin to which he was immune?

A flash of red—brilliant, stunning, and eye-catching—drew my attention. The woman moved with an ethereal grace that seemed out of place among the courtiers, who were all jerking and awry. The sight of her struck me dumb. I knew her. I'd seen her before, bent over the man in the village as I'd been taken away. Hers had been the skirt that had whipped around the door—the one I'd followed, the one that had changed the course of my life and altered my very existence.

She glided past the revelers on silent steps. The music swelled with my frenetic heartbeats as she reached for me, her gown spilling around her like blood from a wound. She caught my hand and pulled me to herself, snatching me up in her dance like a spider snatching prey from its web. Elongated canines glinted where they dimpled into her lower lip as it pulled into a smile.

"Seventh Sister, I see you've arrived unscathed as I planned."

As *she planned*? What in the Umbra was she talking about? Then again, had the Seer not said it was an Emrys who had brought me here? But to see one of the fabled, the makers of creation in immortal flesh—I paled and pressed my lips into a thin line lest I let slip the whimper of fear that coiled on my tongue.

The woman made up her own dance steps as she pulled me along like a sheep on a lead string, elbowing off-kilter carousing couples out of the way, breezing past them with otherworldly ease, as though she'd spun me a half step out of time. *Who is she?*

"Tsk-tsk. I thought you were smarter than that, Ertha. You know who I am. You knew the moment I spoke through your dying friend." She answered my question, and for a moment, I wondered if I'd spoken it aloud, but I knew with a visceral certainty I had not. "Balance the scales," she whispered. The music dropped out in the background; her words filled my ears like a scream so they were all I could hear. "As above, so below."

The Lady in Red, the Emrys of death. As soon as I recognized her for who she was, what she was, she changed. Her skin grew paler, her hair blacker than the darkest noct. She stilled, and everything around us ceased as well.

I ran my lower lip through my teeth before I let my desperate question quiver over it. "But what does that mean?"

The Emrys's hands felt like necrosis where they lingered, her voice was a thousand dying men on a battlefield as she repeated her words like a prayer. "As above, so below. As above, so below." Her eyes held the promise of long, dreamless sleeps and fathomless dark as they locked on mine. "Heed my words, Ertha."

I wanted to cry out in frustration, to shout my question at her again, but the words were lost with the brush of her fingers over my shoulder like the phantom touch of a spector. I stumbled as she shoved me back into step with the high court and its festivities. My hand fluttered over my heart, as though I could settle it with a soothing touch where it flailed against my ribcage like a skittish animal, trying to break its way free from beneath everything I'd buried it under. A hand grabbed my elbow, steering me away from the center of the room and into the shadows. It spun me and pressed my back against the rough fiber of a tapestry that hung there. Fenris, my lord and keeper, leaned over me on his forearm. His free hand toyed with the lacy trim of my veil.

"What are you doing?" I hissed, reaching up to shove him away.

"Don't." The pure command in his voice stilled me like a spell. He brushed an errant hair off my cheek. "Your hands are shaking. You can't let them see. You can't let anyone see you weak. They will smell it, and they will devour you whole."

Scorched fury sluiced through my veins, painting my skin red, and I raised my chin defiantly. "What do you care?"

He smirked down at me with that unrelentingly black stare. "I don't. Just giving you a bit of advice from captor to captive. Life will be a lot simpler and easier for you here if you grow a sturdier spine."

"You mean it will be a lot easier for you if I don't draw too much attention to myself." I huffed.

"What did Se'aneir say to you?" His abrupt shift in topic didn't go unnoticed as he cast his gaze over his shoulder, presumably to see if anyone took too much notice of us.

I gritted my teeth. "What's it to you?" If he thought I would divulge anything to him, he was sorely mistaken. The blood I'd imagined earlier was back, sliding and dripping from the tip of his nose to bead on my chest, its roll hot and sickeningly wet between my breasts.

"I want you to stay away from him." There was that authoritative tone again. Lord Fenris was not a man used to being questioned or disobeyed.

His insistence made me wonder if there was truth in what Kastor had said to me after all—if Fenris really had put that blade between his ribs because of his refusal to kill my friend. Vicious defiance rose its ugly head inside me, wanting to push him, to push back against the bonds that held me so tightly.

"Is that a command?"

"Does it need to be one?" He inclined his head, peering at me like I was an oddity, and maybe my simple refusal to cow to him made me one.

Huggin's form lumbered into view over Fenris's shoulder, and Fenris took a deliberate step back.

"Go with Huggin back to our apartments. The Mother and Father have taken their leave; your duty is done for the noct. Go rest."

I sidestepped out of his shadow. That defiant little beast writhing inside me wanted to argue, to insist I wanted to stay, to drink and dance. I chewed my lip, almost letting the words slip out, but a sudden crashing and drowning wave of exhaustion struck, pulling heavily on my eyelids, and I thought better of it.

His hand darted out, halting me before I could take Huggin's arm and be led from the court. He leaned in so his words were only for me. "This is only the beginning, Shepherdess. Save some of that fight for those who deserve it most."

I glanced down at the place his skin touched mine, the faint whorls of the bond barely visible in the low light beneath the cuff of his jacket. He let go, and I took Huggin's arm and let him escort me away.

I felt her eyes upon me, her gaze like the death she brought. She walked in tandem with our steps from across the room. Hesitantly, I looked at her through half-lowered lids. Her perfectly painted red lips parted in a raptorial smile before she sent her words across the room to nestle in my ear. "As above, so below."

Emrys help me. I had no idea what she meant, but I hoped that if she'd sent me here as she'd insinuated, she also had a plan to get me home.

I PAUSED WITH MY hand on the door latch, sighed, and shook the melancholia from my mind that memory and homesickness plagued me with. Todey was a new dey, and I had to prepare for what it might bring. Munnin had left clothes laid out along with a note that instructed me to join Lord Fenris for breakfast down the hall. A scowl curled my upper lip. But I had to remind myself that being his prisoner had to be vastly better than being under the eyes of Ingemar, the filthy wretch.

Razor-sharp anxiety slashed through my viscera, but I took a deep breath, drew a pearl-sized drop of my powers from my well, and held it for one heartbeat and then two, letting the peace, the surreal calm of a clear and cloudless sky that came with the use of my gifts—my magic—wash away my worries. I felt the crease of my brow smooth, my shoulders release, and my pulse slow. I opened the door and reluctantly dropped the power back where it belonged. The echo of its fall hummed as soothing as any lullaby along my bones as I padded softly and cautiously down the hallway toward the common area of the apartments.

The dress Munnin had laid out was a simple one, not too dissimilar to the kind I'd worn at the temple, easy to put on and get off on my own. It was an obvious hand-me-down, homespun with laces around the neck to cinch it to my size, but it was comfortable. The under portion was dyed a deliciously dark purple with embroidered knots along the neckline. Colors this vibrant—well, colors at all—were banned from the temple as a sign of devotion to the Emrys Selenyss. I hadn't realized how much I'd missed them until I'd slipped the cloth over my head with a sigh. The overdress was a deep gray, the color of a thunderhead, with matching laces up the sleeves and sides. I'd cinched them tightly across my waist, allowing the skirt to flow gently over the generous curve of my hips. I'd combed my fingers through my pale hair be-fore twisting the strands into a thick plait that I'd tossed over my shoulder. There had been no veil laid out, which left me feeling bare. I'd worn one since my hair had begun to change color, kissed by the Crone Emrys, as the Seer had said. But I took it as a hint of some kind from Munnin. Perhaps they were out of style, or perhaps they would be construed as a sign of disrespect in a land that favored worshiping different Emrys than I had in Vanyth. A gnawing voice nibbled on my thoughts—what if it had been at Fenris's demand? Perhaps he'd sensed somehow that I would feel off-kilter without one. But no, I was surely just being paranoid.

The common space was warm and inviting. I wasn't quite sure what I'd expected, but a plushily carpeted room with floor-to-ceiling bookcases on either side—the one on the right with an inset hearth surrounded by leather lounge couches and comfortable-looking, well-worn chairs—was not it. Offset to the left was a circular table with four crescent-shaped benches tucked under its lip, surprisingly constructed from warm brown woods not native to Uthar and topped with steaming serving bowls filled with fragrant foods. Munnin sat idly on one of the benches, paging through a romantic novel—if the title *The Chancellor's Stolen Bride* was any indication—and sipping tea. I was shocked to find her there. Not that I wasn't pleased, but in my experience, servants ate separate from the nobility. I was loath to find anything respectable about the Lord Fenris, but treating those who worked for him as equals was something I couldn't fail to admire.

"Ah, ye did find my note then, I see." Munnin set her book down, a finger marking her spot. "Do come join me. The men will be a minute or two more."

I toed the bench out from under the table and sat, smoothing my skirts and eyeing the empty place settings. "Where are they? I did not peg them as the sort to sleep past Jyord's rise." I myself had woken before, flung the shutters wide, and gazed out at the sun as the Emrys Jyord began his slow trek with it across the Emphyrea.

I'd been struck sharply in that moment with a memory like a knife between the ribs—my sister and me alone atop the tallest tower at the dawn of a new dey with a telescope made of specially tinted glass invented for the scholars to observe Jyord's movements. I recollected the brush of my sister's fingers along mine as she'd handed me the delicate instrument and helped me bring it to my eye. Barely visible through the brilliant corona of light had been the silhouette of Jyord, his strong arms encircling the heaving ball of fire as he'd taken step after step across the sky. My fretful, young mind had worried that he would drop it and it would consume all of Strattaria in its savagely hungry flames. But once Thyra had explained that Jyord would never, that it was his sacred duty to carry the sun and never let it go, it had only opened more questions for me. Why was it his duty? For what purpose did he carry it dey after dey? But most importantly, was he lonely with no one to keep him company on his long walk? The questions had burbled out of me in a rush, and in my hurry to know it all, I'd dropped the instrument from the balcony. Thyra and I had rushed to the grounds to find the glass lenses of the device reduced to nothing more than dark and shimmering dust, leaving the silver tube bent and empty. My heart had felt equally as hollow, remorse and regret having scooped out all my curiosity and joy. Thyra had taken the brunt of our father's anger, shielding me as she always had from him. Not that he had been an unkind man, but he'd been strict. I'd learned to be quieter that dey, gentler too.

Munnin's lips curled with amusement. "Ye do be right. They do be working the Forms out there." She nodded to the expansive wall of lead glass behind her. I raised my eyebrows in astonishment, and I wondered how it was I could have possibly failed to notice them immediately upon entry.

Cleverly hidden hinges in the metal framing disguised the doors that led out onto the balcony. Both men had their bodies posed and contorted, their feet and chests bare. I swallowed hard, my throat suddenly and inexplicably very dry. I'd not seen a man in such a state of undress and in such hale health in—well, in ever. And despite myself, I found it strangely beautiful. Both men looked as though they were chiseled from stone, their sun-darkened torsos inked in spiraling black whorls, knots, and runes. There were scars too, an assortment of knicks and near-fatal injuries that somehow added rather than detracted from the artistry that was their bodies. I fumbled for the wooden cup in front of my place setting, needing something to slake the thirst that was incomprehensibly overwhelming.

Munnin laughed softly. "The Forms do be a sight, do they not? And the men do be a sight too." She elbowed me conspiratorially, and I blanched.

"I—no, I just—" I sputtered, taken aback by the suggestion that I could be aroused by such brutish and lethal creatures, but she cut me off.

"Huggin do be my brother, of course, but I do know the ladies in the court like to stare. Fenris though, he do look like he did be carved by the Emrys' own hands, no?" She sighed. "I do no be his kind of woman though."

I wrinkled my nose. "Yes, well, I saw his kind of woman last noct at the Triumph. I think not being his type speaks well to your character."

The door to the balcony opened, and both men stalked in, their bare-chested bodies framed by the barely visible peaks of the Emphyrean mountain range that bit through the succulently pink dawn clouds in the background. On their heels, a mocking wind carried the nip of kalda on its back, promising early snows and short harvest times. I hoped the vinterberry crops were thriving back home and that my people would be well-fed and cared for by my sister.

Fenris grinned wildly at the two of us. "Good morning, Munnin, Shepherdess." He took his seat, sweaty and bare-skinned, like an animal. "What are we talking about this fine dey?"

"How you'll likely need to seek healing from me for venereal diseases with the company you're prone to keep, my lord." The retort snapped out of me before I could stop it.

Huggin snorted water through his nose in an effort, I assumed, to smother a rumbling laugh. Munnin, on the other hand, didn't bother to keep her chuckle in.

Fenris smiled at me slowly, indolently, as he reached for a buttery knot of bread from a basket in the middle of the table and ripped into it. "You have quite the mouth on you for someone who's lived as the Temple Maiden for so long."

I glowered down my nose at him, not daring to dignify that comment with a response lest I accidentally expose my lie. The look he gave me seemed to dare me to do it, like he wanted to pick away at the armor of untruths I'd wrapped myself in.

Instead, I reached for a roll of my own along with a scoop of sour spiced fruit mash and a serving of scrambled cliff pigeon eggs. The eggs were not my favorite, but my healing gifts—my magic, I corrected—was strengthened by the consumption of meats, milks, and eggs.

When I didn't rise to his bait, Fenris turned to Munnin and struck up a conversation, asking her politely about the book she was reading and seeming to listen to her intently, inquiring about the characters, the plot, and the author. I admired him for that. I loathed him for it too. How could I believe what I saw? Maybe it was all a ruse to get me to trust, to divulge. Was he laying a trap for me, giving me a knife to impale myself on so I would spill my guts for him to divine in them the truth of who I was?

I swiped the dregs of the fruit mash off my plate with the last scrap of bread and popped it into my mouth. Fenris leaned back in his chair, the picture of a lord at leisure.

"Alright, Lady Healer, now that we've eaten, let us speak of what is expected of you."

As if his words were a cue, Munnin and Huggin rose and cleared the dishes from the table before heading for the door. The former threw a wink at me over her shoulder before she left the room, her long braids swaying in time with her hips.

I folded my arms across my chest, prepared, I hoped, for anything.

"There is a workshop dedicated to healing here in the Fortress. You are to work there every dey, healing whoever is sent to you without question. You are also to be ready to heal anyone the Father deems necessary at any time of dey or noct. You will not have any assistance."

"What happened," I cut in, my curiosity getting the better of me, "to the other Healer? The one you spoke of on the ship."

His strange eyes darkened. "That is no concern of yours, Shepherdess."

I opened my mouth to protest but stilled my tongue. If he wouldn't tell me, perhaps I could find out some other way.

I nodded slightly to indicate I understood, and he went on, "You will have access to whatever you need from the gardens. You may borrow from the previous Healer's medical texts or my personal collection of books. If you find what I own will not suffice, Huggin may take you to the greater library."

My heart bloomed like a cocoon, hope, newly emerged, beating its wings tentatively. If I had that much freedom to roam, I would have that much more of a chance of finding a way out of here, of finding a way to remove the bonding bracelet. I glanced toward the barely visible, shimmery design on his body that was a mirror image of my own, and I cringed internally.

"You will always have Huggin with you. For your safety, of course. I wouldn't want anything to happen to you." A hint of smugness played on the edges of his lips, as if he'd sensed my hope and wanted to crush it between his fingers and feel its blood.

So this was to be a prison with only the vaguest illusion of freedom. Fine. Maybe, little by little, I could stretch those freedoms taut enough to break and escape. I just needed to bide my time, find out who I could truly trust. And then there was the

Emrys, the Lady in Red. She had plans for me, that much was clear, but that couldn't be a priority right now, not until I knew what those plans were. And besides, I didn't see how I could be of any use to her trapped in the Fortress. Surely she wouldn't mind me escaping before I did whatever it was she needed.

I stood, the bench scraping back behind me. "Anything else, my lord?" I injected as much venom into the title as I could, making sure there was no masking my repulsion.

"Yes, one more thing. My own addendum to the rules." His words were purred with too much buttery smugness for my liking, and I braced myself for whatever would come next. "You will learn the Forms."

The Forms? Those bizarre and contorting poses he and Huggin had done on the balcony? "What on Strattaria for?"

He smiled, looking as pleased as a well-fed cat to have taken me by surprise. "Because I will it."

"No." I was not his pet. I would not learn to do tricks for him simply because it was his will that I learn them. My fists clenched at my sides, strangling the fabric of my skirt, and oh how I wished they were around his thick neck instead.

"It's funny that you think you have a choice in the matter, Shepherdess." He stood as he spoke and leaned on his balled fists over the table, closing the gap between us as he made sure to spit the mock title he'd given me with as much poison as I had his. "We meet every morning before dawn. You will join us tomorrow."

A throat cleared by the open door, and we both turned to find Huggin waiting, leaning against the doorframe casually, dressed in his leather armor. "Time to go," he grunted.

Thank the Emrys. A whole blessed dey away from the insufferable brute that was my keeper. I spun and stomped toward the door, fully aware that I was being as petulant as a child throwing a tantrum.

"See you at supper, Healer," Fenris called after me, his voice honeyed and mocking as Huggin stepped aside to let me by. I didn't respond as I stormed for the door out of the apartments. Huggin, like a dutiful and lumbering shadow, followed in my wake.

The Healer's workshop was a long walk from the nobles' apartments, clear on the other side of the Fortress and down a few levels into the subterranean rooms carved out of the cliff. Arching rough-cut windows were chiseled harshly out of the stone, not unlike the ones in the Seer's room that looked out over the sea. Unlike hers though, they were higher up and not susceptible to waves, and there were serviceable-looking benches carved into their bases. With a cushion or two, they might have even been considered comfortable.

In the center of the room stood an examination table at hip height, just like the ones in the temple. Hanging shelves covered the left wall from floor to ceiling, packed to the brim with clay jars filled with herbs and salves and ingredients for making ointments along with the instruments needed to crush, peel, and ferment. A small hearth along the right wall lent warmth to the room, and a narrow door led to a supply closet with a spare bed for patients who needed more rest, as well as a store for linens, bandages, needle, thread, and nearly anything else I could possibly need. The previous Healer had also kept leather-bound books with meticulous notes written in tightly looping and decidedly feminine script. I ran my fingers over their dusty spines with a pang in my heart and a lump of dread in my throat. I sent a quick prayer to any Emrys listening that I would not suffer the same fate she had, whatever that fate may have been.

I squared my shoulders and, blinking back the stinging tears that threatened to fall, I removed a white apron from its peg in the storeroom. I pinned it over my dress at the top and wrapped its ties around my waist twice before I knocked on the door between me and the waiting room to signal to Huggin I was ready for the first visitor. I'd been taken quite by surprise when we'd arrived and the room had been full to capacity with people spilling out into the hall, all in need of my skills.

Unexpected nerves crawled up my spine. Pinching doubt like venom oozed from every creeping step up my vertebrate as the hinges on the door squealed open. Could I do this? I'd never run a clinic on my own without oversight, and what I'd done on the ship had been fueled more by desperation than anything else. Huggin stepped back to allow a waddling pregnant woman through the door, and my anxiety instantly eased when I saw her kind and smiling face. Pregnant women were my favorite to tend to as their bellies swelled and their hearts radiated warmth and love for their unborn.

"Welcome," I said with a genuine smile as I drew out a stool and helped her up onto the exam table, leaving a pause on the end of my word to allow her to introduce herself.

"My name is Anvynn, my lady." She huffed as she settled onto the table and rested her hands atop the swell of her stomach.

"It's a pleasure to meet you, and please, I'm no lady, just call me Ertha. How far along are you, Anvynn?" I asked as I washed my hands with an alcohol and herb solution from an amber bottle before we began.

"Oh my, I don't quite know, but it feels as though I've been pregnant since the beginning of byrthe." She gripped my hand as I helped her lie back. "Dreaming about the babe all that time too. What it will look like, whether it will take after my husband or myself."

I'd heard much the same from many a pregnant fishwife back home and often deydreamt about experiencing it for myself in the future. The words the Mother and Ingemar had exchanged the other dey spat themselves to the forefront of my thoughts. I had to get out of here before they forced me to welp Sons for the Father like a prize breeding beast.

I cleared my throat and stitched my polite smile back onto my face. "Is this your first then?"

Her pale yellow hair sectioned off into braids spilled over the edge of the table, and her cheeks dimpled as she smiled. "Is it so obvious?"

I placed my hands on her belly, drew a slim filament of my ability to my fingers, and allowed it to delve gently into her womb to check on her unborn. "Not to everyone, I'm sure, but I've met many a woman nearing her birthing time." I repositioned my hands to get a better feel for the babe. "Did you have any concerns in particular you wished to discuss?"

She fidgeted slightly with the edge of her shawl. "Well, no, not in particular, I suppose. My mam though, she said the babe should have turned and settled into my hips by now, seeing as how I'm so close and all. She made me a might bit anxious."

"I see," I said as I fluttered my lashes closed. I could see in my mind's eye the babe curled under its mother's ribs, where it sucked away on its little thumb. The cord connecting it to its mother pulsed beautifully, as did its heart. Its legs were crossed, but I saw distinct indications that the babe would be a son. "Well, your babe looks to be in perfect health. And as for positioning, it would appear it's just not ready yet. There is a chance you may have a stubborn one. I've seen babes wait until the mother's pains come before turning, or some are even more thickheaded and wait until the mother is ready to push. There is a chance that the babe may come foot- or even butt-first." Anvynn paled, but I set my hand upon her shoulder, sending relaxation through the connection to ease her mind. "But rest assured, I've seen many women birth babes in those positions with no problems. It just may take a bit longer than a head-first baby."

She let out a sigh of relief. "Well, I don't want a longer birth if I can help it, but that sounds a lot better than the things my mam was rattling on about."

"I wouldn't worry, and if you find yourself concerned when the birth comes, you or your husband can always send for me to come and check on things. But otherwise, I think you and baby are well. Now, would you like a tea to help your womb prepare for the labor? Or a salve for back pain to take home?"

Her eyes brightened. "Oh, yes please, La—I mean, Ertha. That would be very kind of you."

I helped her sit back up before turning to the shelves to retrieve and grind the herbs I needed. Raspberry leaf, mother's root, and womb wart for the tea, then mint along with a drop of numb nettle oil to mix into a salve for her back.

"Is your husband excited, Anvynn?" I asked over my shoulder as I mashed and mixed.

"Oh yes!" She laughed. "He presses an ear to my belly every noct and sings to the babe. We're hoping for a son." I hid my secret knowing smile behind my work, pleased that they would get their wish. "A strong healthy son to follow in his pa's footsteps and become a great warrior, providing for the people."

I dropped the pestle with a shocking clatter, my breath snagging suddenly on too tight ribs that constricted around my lungs. How could this sweet young woman, no more than a season my senior, be wed to a bloody Son. Images came unbidden to my mind of a man bathed in blood, standing on a pile of bones with a squalling, innocent life cradled in his arms, stained by his sins.

"Are you alright, Ertha?" Anvynn's words were gentle and threaded with concern, and I composed myself before turning to her with her herbs and salve.

"Yes, yes, of course. Sorry. Just a bit clumsy todey, I suppose."

She tucked the small pouch and clay pot I'd given her into a small satchel at her side, and I helped her down. I knocked on the door, and Huggin courteously held it open for her and shut it again, giving me a moment to settle myself. I pressed a steadying hand over my drumming heart. I had to tuck away my fears, my loathing for these people. They were not the Father; they were not the choices he'd made. They were victims of his corruption almost as much as the rest of Strattaria was. I had to set my feelings aside and heal with an impartial heart. Healing was blind, as the temple dedicates always taught. Just because it was harder than I'd expected didn't mean I could refuse them aid. I couldn't even if I wanted to—my life depended on it.

A Hand Holding His Heart

T HROUGH THE REST OF the morning, I treated the wives, children, and parents of Sons. It seemed the Father gave preferential treatment to those who were sworn to his armies. A bid for their undying loyalty, I was sure, but a successful one, I had to admit, as it seemed nearly every citizen in Berth was married to or related in some way to a Son. The notion made my bones quiver. I knew the Uthari stole most of their supplies and wealth from neighboring countries, but if every able-bodied male in the country was a Son, their military might was far superior to what any other kingdom's court gave them credit for. They were not mere blood-hungry huntsmen scavenging other nations—they were capable of devouring lands and peoples whole. I tried to suppress the bite of anxiety that gnawed on the ends of my ribs, whispering around its gnashing teeth that I had to somehow get word to my sister, that she needed to rally more protection. I didn't have the faintest idea how to slip such a sensitive missive out of the Fortress, especially not when it would potentially cost me my life if I was caught. I buried the idea and the worry under all the healing I had to do.

I briefly paused my ministrations at middey to eat a crusty bit of bread with honey and drink a cup of milk brought to me on a tray from the kitchens that provided food to the lower court. But I was quickly back at it, wading through more pregnant women, boys with broken noses, rashes, infections, head pains, Sons with training accidents, a few back injuries and sprains, and the Sons I'd healed on the voyage over. Those were the ones who pecked the hardest at the serene numbness I'd wrapped myself in to cope with healing the people whose leader held me captive. I saw the phantasmic blood on their hands as I had with Fenris, who, as it turned out, had been right about the man who had lost his eye. Dagfynn was incredibly grateful that I'd given him his life back despite the new challenges only having half of his vision presented. His wife, her belly swollen with child—Uthari men seemed to breed their spouses like the moorland rabbits—was even more grateful. Tears ran down her round face in earnest as she sobbed into my shoulder.

Noct came quickly. It painted deep shadows across the floor, forcing me to light the tapered candles around the room, and yet still those with ailments came, leaving me to eat supper not with my keeper but on my feet. I thought we might have finally been done for the dey until the door scraped open and Huggin sullenly admitted one last man.

"Kastor." My brows crawled up my forehead. In the bustle of the dey, I'd forgotten him and his vows, but what was he thinking coming to me so openly in front of my guard? Surely it was not to pick up the dropped threads of our discussion from the noct before. "What are you doing here?"

He crossed the floor, closing the space between us. My breath rushed out of me as he unexpectedly slipped his wolf hide from his shoulders and unbuttoned his shirt, pulling it from his breeches. "Commander Ingemar told me you needed to inspect all those you healed on the trip here. I beg your pardon; I would have come earlier, but I was detained with duties."

My hands pressed into the hollow space between the arches of my ribs. Of course he wasn't here because of the vow from the noct before. I smiled politely and gestured to the vacant table. "Of course, yes. Come, have a seat. Huggin, please, the door?"

My guard lingered a beat too long, his eyes narrowed distrustfully on the Son's back as though some bad blood lay between them, unseen by me. He gave me a sullen look but did as I asked.

Kastor's shirt slipped from his broad shoulders as he sat. He gave me an easy smile from beneath his beard and leaned back on his corded arms to give me better access to his healed injury. I had to admit, as I averted my eyes, I could almost see what the tittering women of the upper court saw in him now that half his clothing was removed. I shoved the preposterous thought aside—something was clearly wrong with me todey—and turned away to wash my hands with the cleansing solution.

I asked in my most professionally neutral tone, "Any complaints or issues with the wound?"

"Well," he answered, "I wouldn't say there's anything wrong, but this is certainly odd."

I composed myself. I could turn and look at him. He was just a man. I'd looked at several men during the dey. There was nothing thrilling or enticing or—I stuffed the out-of-control thoughts deep into the back of my mind.

"What exactly?" What I saw when I turned made me still and take pause.

A patch of skin on his chest was distinctly paler than the rest and almost seemed to throb slightly with a luminescence, akin to the way my hands lit with my healing abilities. I bent closer and ran a finger across the patch, leaving a trail of gooseflesh where I touched.

"It's a hand," I whispered, more to myself than to him, as I outlined the shape, but I could feel the vibrations of his low laugh through his ribs.

"I can see that, Lady, but what is it doing there?"

I ignored him and instead traced the ridges of five distinct fingers, the print laid out in such a way that it appeared to be cradling his heart almost tenderly. Recalling how I'd been determined to heal him to the very best of my abilities and how I'd taken extra care to mend even the superficial cut left after the deeper healing, I lined my palm up with the print.

A stirring of my magic beneath his skin left me breathless. "It's my hand, my healing."

I hadn't meant to speak the words aloud, but Kastor dipped his head to look at me wide-eyed. He brought his palm up and pressed it over mine, his touch scalding and grounding at the same time.

"What do you mean?" he asked.

I could feel the words drift across my cheek, and I became starkly aware of just how close we really were. I pulled my hand out from under his, and pins and needles prickled along it, like it resented being removed from that warm and comforting press between his beating heart and his calloused fingers. I tucked it behind my back, giving it a gentle shake to ward off the peculiar feeling.

I leaned over as I leveled my gaze on the imprint, careful not to touch it again, just taking one last look at it before I righted myself. "I believe it's a residue of sorts or a reserve of my healing abilities. I think I could remove it for you if it's bothersome. Though, I think—for as long as it lasts anyhow—that there is every chance it might heal any injury you sustain, or at least mitigate the severity of it of its own accord, or it could simply dissipate." I shrugged lightly. "I must have poured too much into your mending."

He ran his hand over the old wound, peering down at it like he was gazing upon something he didn't have words for. "It feels warm and a little bit, I don't know, tingly."

"If it's troublesome, it shouldn't be too difficult to remove. I'd just have to call it back." But even as I said it, I wasn't so certain I could. I got the strangest sense that it wanted to be there.

"No, I think I like the idea of having a piece of you wrapped around my heart at all times, protecting me." His eyes seemed to smolder in the flickering candlelight, or was that just my imagination running off with me? His voice too sounded somehow more molten, deeper and almost sultry. Was he flirting with me? No, no. Absolutely not.

"Well, alright then. I think that will do it, unless there is anything else?" I spun in a whisper of rustling skirts to busy myself at the worktable.

"Actually, there is."

I turned to find him standing just behind me. I hadn't even heard him move, just another reminder of his predatory grace and nature. Though whether that skill was a learned one from years as a Son or just who he was at the core of his being, I didn't know. Either way, his proximity stole the air from my lungs. Our closeness seemed illicit somehow now that there was no formal dress or music to give us permission.

"What?" My lip quivered, though I couldn't say why. "What is it?"

He dipped his head like a demure dame, but there was nothing demure in the way his eyes seemed to heat, burning into mine. "I was hoping you would do me the honor of allowing me to escort you back to your apartments."

"Why would you want to do that?" The words left my lips breathlessly.

"I told you, Lady, I owe you my life. It is my duty now to protect you." He hesitated and ran an unsteady hand through his hair, left loose todey rather than knotted. "And, well, if I'm being honest, I find myself drawn to you for reasons outside of my gratitude."

I could feel the hot throb of blood surging beneath my cheeks, scalding them red. Was he implying what I thought he was? I had little personal experience with flirtation or the arts of seduction, and I had, on many occasions, been warned by devotees at the temple of the wicked wiles and passions of men. Not that I'd bought it. Well, not all of it anyway, not after the confidences Helima shared with me. And I'd seen my sister with Tad—nothing about the way he'd brought flowers to her window had seemed wicked, though he had never been Thyra's enemy. Kastor's words could be hollow if picked up and examined closely; they bore none of the weight or tenderness of stolen kisses in corners or presents left on sills. Though maybe he was just giving me what he had to offer.

My mind and my heart divided, the only answer I could think to hand over was, "I don't think Huggin will like it."

Kastor stepped back, took his shirt from where he'd left it, shrugged it on, leaving the sides gaping open, and leaned against the table's edge. "Alright, well, we can leave it until they lengthen the chain you're on." A sadness seemed to flash through his eyes as he shoved off. "Just be careful with the lord and his people. No matter how nice they seem, just promise me you'll be on your guard."

I undid the pins and ties holding my apron and let it lie on the worktable as I spun around and began to tidy, trying not to appear too interested. But if there was anything I'd learned from watching my sisters, it was that any tidbit of information, even a falsehood, was worth collecting and saving for later. You never knew if a piece of it would fit into the larger picture.

"And why is that, in particular?"

"Let's just say you aren't the first True Healer the lord has been tasked with keeping." Kastor's voice was hushed, perhaps wary of Huggin's prying ears on the other side of the door, but his words raised the hair along the nape of my neck.

"What happened to her?" I tried to keep my hands busy, brushing past him to strip the linens from the table and ball them in a basket under the counter to be hauled to the laundry later.

When he met my eyes again, they were red rimmed in repressed rage or some emotion close to it. "He killed her."

My hand froze on the lid of the basket. There was no need to specify who the *he* was. Was this the real reason Kastor had vowed to protect me? Had he cared for or even loved the woman who had come before me?

"Why?" The question ghosted across the space between us, and I wasn't entirely sure I wanted to know the answer.

He buttoned his shirt and tucked it back into place before he slung his pelt over his shoulder. "You'll have to ask him."

I nodded, not sure what I should say, if I should press him for more or leave it alone and wait for another time. Kastor chose for me by holding out a hand. I took it, allowing him to bend and press his lips to its back. When he righted himself, there was no trace of the heavy emotions weighing down his gaze. With a squeeze, he dropped my hand and strode for the door, turning back at the last second with a one-sided grin.

"You owe me a walk, Lady Healer."

And I couldn't help myself. I smiled back as he slipped through the door, leaving it open.

Huggin peered in, suspicion written plainly on his usually stoic features, clearly distrustful of Kastor, of me, likely of both of us. He cleared his throat. "Do ye be ready to go, my lady?"

I gaped. "I think that's the most I've heard you speak." He simply snorted, waiting for my reply. I took a step toward the storage room. "A moment and I will be. I just want to retrieve something."

I slipped into the tiny, dust-ridden room and plucked one of the leather-bound accounts of the previous Healer off the shelf. I opened the cover, and the tightly stitched spine groaned. On the inside page, her name, Aurasha, was written. The book was no bigger than my hand, easily slipped into a pocket for taking daily notes. I tucked it into mine before I returned to the main chamber, snuffed out the candles, and allowed Huggin to lead me back through the Fortress as the comfortable weight of the dead Healer's words bumped against my thigh.

There was a package wrapped in pretty paper and tied with twine on the bed when I at long last walked into my room, a card slipped beneath the knotted twine on top. I plucked it out. All I wanted to do was peel my clothes off and collapse into my bed, but curiosity and wariness temporarily overwhelmed my exhaustion.

Lady,

Enclosed are the clothes requested. I hope they suit.

Rhapso

And then, scrawled hastily underneath it, *For the Forms.*

The wrapping paper crinkled as I ripped into it and withdrew breeches made of billowing, flimsy, pale blue fabric with embroidered silver star stone details. The breeches appeared to cinch with pearl-embellished ribbons at the ankles and lace with silken cords at the waist. The top, if it could have been called that, was a scandalous slip of fabric that looked as though it was put on like a coat, but it tied, wrapping around the wearer's chest and waist, and simply knotted to secure it.

The bastard brute must have been trying to humiliate me with this. Temper seethed in my chest. I bunched the fabric in my fists and stormed, door slamming against stone, from my room and down the hall, past the empty common area to the double doors that marked the chamber as the lord's. I pounded my fist furiously against the wood.

"Fenris! Lord Fenris! I beg an audience with you immediately."

I thrashed against the unyielding wood until it finally opened with a crack only wide enough for me to see his smirk. I threw the fabric in his face.

"I will not be trussed up like one of your women of ill repute. I might be your prisoner, but I will not be treated with such indignities." I stomped my foot like a sulky youngling, exhaustion and over-whelm getting the better of my dignity.

As calm as stone, he pulled the fabric with a clenched fist from where it had landed half wrapped around his neck and dropped the bundle at my feet, the picture of indolence as he leaned on his forearm against the cracked door. It was only then that I realized his state of undress, bare chest-ed with only a light pair of low-slung linen pants on his hips. Did the man ever wear proper clothes? He smirked down at me. His hair, unbound, fell over his shoulder and across his chest.

"Well, feel free to come shirtless as Huggin and I do if you wish, if you find the clothes that repug-nant. You might be a bit cold though."

"You Umbra-cursed bas—" I tried to swear at him, but he straightened, allowing the door to fall open further, revealing a woman in a salacious slip and an undone robe lounging lasciviously atop his bed, her dark, curling hair spilled across the top of his sheets.

"If you wouldn't mind cursing me quickly, Shep-herdess, I have things to get back to." He raised a questioning eyebrow, as if daring me to keep going.

I ground my curses between gritted teeth, and with my last shred of composure, I grabbed the wadded outfit from the floor and stomped back to my room to the tune of his arrogant chuckles.

THE NEEDLE PULLED AND puckered the fabric into a mostly even hemline as I remedied my insomnia and my anger with Fenris by amending the Forms bodice into some semblance of modesty. It had been years since I'd sewn anything as complex as this; most of my needlework at the temple had been on flesh for superficial wounds that would heal properly on their own and didn't need my gifts used on them. I sighed and readjusted the pillow at my back. My magic. I had to think of it that way if I was going to conquer it—I couldn't limit myself by thinking of it as being only useful for healing.

Though my first attempt had been woeful and pitiful, I wondered if I shouldn't try again. If the bond on my arm was indeed a relic imbued with old witch magic as it seemed to be, then maybe I could use my magic to remove it?

I set my sewing aside, satisfied that I'd successfully reconstructed the top into something less abhorrent, and let my eyelids flutter closed. I drew my magic up as I always did when I prepared to delve into a patient, only instead of pouring it out, I kept it in. I let it trickle across my skin, pushing it into the bond's markings until I had a clear picture of its design in my head. I probed it, trying to thrust the magic into it. Little sparks shot skittered along my arm, and I gasped, biting off a cry lest anyone hear me. Filament-like roots branched off the surface of the bond's network of twists and swirls. They lit up like starlight as I watched them appear, wending their way into my very being. The hairlike filaments tethered themselves to my veins, to my bones, to my very heart. Tangling, snagging, snaring. And it was growing, I realized in wonderous horror. With each passing moment, the root system stretched, feeling its way through my body. Before long, it would reach the well of my magic, and after that, would it reach into my soul?

Shuddering, I paced my magic up and down the main pattern, looking for the source, the place where it sprouted. If it had a main tap root like a tree or a plant did, maybe I could sever it and the whole thing would die. My first instinct was my wrist, where the cuff had originally been clamped, but I found no such root. Three passes over the entirety of the mark revealed nothing, but on the fourth pass, as my mind raced desperately, I noticed a phantom string tucked behind my heart, duller and less visible than the rest. I let all my magic wash to that point, focusing on that single piece. I wrapped it around and around as taut as I could, then yanked with all my might and...

The room was comfortable and spacious, but even after all these years, it would never be home. I sighed into my glass of saffron-colored liquor—ishwai. This was the last glass from the last bottle I'd brought from home when I'd first arrived. A mere boy compared to what I am now. My fist tightened around the glass, and I took a sip, letting the spicy and sweet heat sear my throat. There wasn't a single dey or noct that went by that I regretted my decision—I'd done what was best for my people—but that didn't mean it sat well on my heart.

I smelled her on him the moment he stepped into my room. Like honey-sweet sorrow and crisp kalda mornings. I cursed the Emrys for the heightened senses gifted to our kind. I didn't want my nostrils infected with her essence every waking moment, tainting my dreams each noct. But then I detected another smell underneath hers and his, one of salt and iron, and a growl rumbled out of my throat from deep in the hollow of my chest, my lips curled back. "The pup was sniffing near her skirts again, was he?"

He sat next to me in a leather armchair twin to my own, posed next to my hearth, the flames of which I never let die. The chair protested, grumbling at its joints as the giant man settled in. "Aye, he was." His dark brows furrowed over his piercingly blue eyes.

My knuckles whitened on my glass. "He's playing at something. I just need to figure out what."

My longtime friend stroked his beard before leaning forward to rest his forearms on his knees as he gazed into the flames in silence. But I knew him too well to interpret his silence as a lack of something to say.

"Out with it."

He looked at me starkly, taking another moment to mull over his words before he spat them out. He was never one to do anything in haste, unless, of course, it was killing; when it came time for that, he was as swift and as deadly as the Red Lady herself. "Do no get too tangled in the girl's affairs."

"She's no mere girl." I smirked over the rim of my glass. "Surely you can tell that."

He huffed but nodded slightly. "All the same, do no lose sight."

He didn't have to say of what, I already knew. But there was something about her. I wanted to find the right words to give him, to make him see what I saw in her, why I'd petitioned so hard to stay her keeper, but I couldn't find them, not this late in the noct—or early in the new dey, I supposed—so instead, I just nodded. "I'll keep that in mind."

After several moments of silence, he looked around, sniffing the air and taking in the rumpled bedclothes. "Cadja did come this noct?"

I swilled the liquid in my glass, refusing to meet his eyes, refusing to see the pity in them. "She did."

He didn't press me for the answers he sought, just waited patiently for me to get around to them. The man could wait out a knox willow tree growing into adulthood from seed if he had to. I'd always admired him for that.

"She says she'll have it before kalda is fully set in, sometime around Eklipsis. You'll warn everyone to be ready?" I asked, my words more hushed than I'd intended them to be, and I hated the slight and tenuous waver to them, but if I couldn't let my cracks *show around my oldest friend, then I would have no one who knew me.*

He stood and stretched with a mumbled, "Aye, I will," before he lumbered toward the door and slipped back out into the hallway. And just like that, with the click of the latch, I was alone with my thoughts again.

W ITH GREAT RELUCTANCE I shuffled down the dim hall towards the common room. My head throbbed as though I'd had too much drink. I felt scraped out on the inside, a bone cracked and sucked of its marrow. I prodded the well of magic within me and found it lacking significantly in depth. Flashes of a peculiar dream—like visions from behind another's eyes—came to me in muddled and blurred colors and shapes, and in words spoken as if underwater, but not in any semblance that made sense.

Fenris, of course, already waited on the balcony when I stepped out into the brutally chilled air still twining my hair. He frowned at me, seemingly unbothered by the hour or the cold. "Interesting alterations. Now lose the shoes, Shepherdess."

I grumbled under my breath just for the sake of it since it was early, and since my head throbbed unrelentingly, and maybe a bit because he didn't seem bothered in the slightest that I'd modified the clothes he'd had made for me so that they covered my stomach completely. I'd been hoping to irk him at least half as much as I'd been the noct before, but I did as he asked and kicked my slippers off by the door. He had the audacity to look amused by something, to which I curled my lip and wrapped my arms across my chest.

"Not a morning person, Healer?" I didn't care for the way his lips arched and his brow quirked tauntingly.

"Not typically, no. Selenyss dedicate, remember? We lived on a nocturnal cycle." I barely managed to hide the yawn that drew out the last of my words as the first broken lines of bleak, gray light slatted through the low-hanging clouds on the horizon.

"Well, you're going to have to get used to living in the dey like the rest of us. It might even put some color in your cheeks," he quipped—insensitive and arrogant ass—as he turned his back on me and rolled out two long, narrow rugs along the hard stone floor of the balcony. He missed the bleary-eyed glare I shot at his back. "Now sit."

I frowned down at the twin rugs. "Where's Huggin? Won't he be joining us?"

"Huggin likes to do his Forms with less nattering and complaining in the background."

My jaw dropped indignantly. "I do not *natter*."

"Quit stalling, Healer, and sit on the rug." His lips quirked maddeningly as he raked a hand through his hair, braiding it quickly.

I muttered all the best fishmonger insults I knew under my breath, but I begrudgingly did as he asked, folding my legs beneath me.

He took the position opposite me so we faced each other and the long edges of our rugs. "Sit tall, Healer. Less like a sack of grain and more poised."

I harrumphed. I did not sit like a sack of grain.

"Imagine a string at the top of your head pulling your neck up and your spine taut. And tighten your stomach."

I groaned but did as he asked despite every part of my being screaming to defy him. The sooner I did as he demanded, the sooner this ridiculous farce could end and I could hide in the Healer's workshop for the rest of the dey in relative peace. Well, peace from him anyhow. And if I was being honest, I hoped to see Kastor there again too.

"Close your eyes and breath deeply, in and out."

"Well, this is so informative," I growled. "I'm so glad I woke early to receive instruction on breathing; I wasn't quite sure I was doing it correctly."

"If you do not have the foundation laid correctly, the building will crumble."

"Is that what we're doing now? Construction?"

"It's an analogy, Healer, or do they not have those in whatever backwater Vanythian town you hail from."

My cheeks flamed, but I didn't dignify his retort with one of my own.

"The Forms build on one another. Fail at the most basic of them, and you will never succeed in the rest. Now close your unnervingly pale eyes, Healer."

My jaw slackened. "You find *my* eyes unnerving?"

He pinched the bridge of his nose. "It's an expression. Again, have you never heard—"

"Of an 'expression' in my backwater Vanythian town?" I quipped, deepening my voice to mock his. "Yes, yes, I have. I've just never heard that one."

"Close them, Shepherdess." His will seemed to press against every inch of my skin in an irrefutable command, and I did as he asked without further protest, my eyes grazing the pale white designs on my left arm before my lids slid shut. Was he able to somehow compel me with the damnable bracelet? That could prove to be an issue...a very large issue.

"Good. Now breathe. Fill your ribcage, let the air press into every part of you, expanding until you can hold no more, and then let it all out, contracting your core muscles as you do so. In. Out. In. Out."

I bit off the words I wanted to spit back at him and did as he dictated, letting him chant "in and out" at me patronizingly, keeping my eyes closed no matter how vulnerable it made me feel to be in front of him like this.

"Now begin circling your upper body as you breathe. Forward and around on the in breath, backward and around on the out. Focus on being still in your mind, let all thoughts sift from your head like grains of sand blown from your fingers."

I winced, feeling my heart splinter as the sand I envisioned stained my thoughts crimson with the blood of my people. With each rotation, I tried to let it go, to wipe the color clean from my subconscious, to let myself be hollow and quiet like the deepest parts of the noct. But within myself, I found a light, crystalline and pulsing parallel to the blood in my veins, surging from the well within me– my magic. It was somehow not separate as I'd thought it to be but a vital part of me.

Fenris's voice caressed the back of my consciousness, whispering instructions that I followed without thought. "Now still yourself, and without opening your eyes, move onto your hands and knees."

The pressure of the rug against my palms and my knees grounded me as Fenris's voice guided me to breathe, this time bowing and arching my torso with my breaths, then adding in the same gyrations as before. In the empty dark behind my eyelids, I could see the divine structure of my being, the way the magic flowed in and around my body, the way the bond crept and my heart beat. I could sense the very breath of the Emrys fluttering down from the Emphyrea as I stretched and bent and moved into other positions: bowed with my arms out, my forehead pressed to the floor, twisted with one arm threaded under me and then the other. I slipped from one form to the next, my body molded by the cadence of Fenris's words until he commanded me to lie on my back and simply be, letting my muscles melt. At last, the timbre of his voice summoned me back. My thoughts gradually climbed into the waking world along those luminous pathways inside me, until my lashes fluttered open and I lay dazed and still on the floor of the balcony.

Fenris's smirking face hovered above me with an egotistic twist to the corners of his lips, his hands settled on the prominent ridges of his hip bones, his stomach irritatingly taut. "Well, what did you think, Healer?" He leaned down and offered a hand to help me up, which I refused. Instead, I rolled to my side and took my time rising.

I was loath to admit it, but I felt an untenable sense of true calm, and shaky though it may have been, it was—well, it was nice. I could see why he and Huggin partook in it ritualistically. I didn't want to tell him that though, so I instead looked out across the Emphyrea at the precipices of mountains slung low through the clouds that smudged the clear morning view with streaks of white. My eyes fell to the distant southern horizon, where the base of Strattaria and the nation of Iliff lay. The churning, gray mass of clouds there threatened a snow squall before the dey was done. I blinked, realizing I'd let Fenris's question linger a touch too long.

I shrugged. "A bit dull, but I suppose I've done worse things." I spun on my heel without waiting for the response I could see his jaw chewing on.

"Now, if you will excuse me, I'd like to change out of these wicked clothes before I eat breakfast."

I strode as confidently away from him as I could, letting my steps sway like my sister's often did when she wanted to convey a deliberately indolent and unaffected air, until I was in the hall and his dark eyes no longer burrowed into my back. Then I ran, bare feet slapping against the carpeted floor before Munnin or Huggin came out for the dey. While prickled by Fenris's comment on my nattering earlier, I was secretly grateful that only one pair of eyes had witnessed me in such illicit clothing.

After I changed– this time choosing a pale pink dress in much the same style as yesterdey's, though this one was stitched with white posies along the hems and cuffs– I returned to the common area to find the table occupied by Munnin alone.

I greeted her as I sat. "Good dey, Munnin." Taking note that she had yet another novel in her clutches, *Stolen by the Mer Pirate*– this one with an elaborately illustrated front that depicted a bare-chested Mer pirate on a ship with a rather buxom-looking woman clinging to his leg and looking up at him with pure adoration– I smothered a smile. "I didn't know there was such a thing as Mer pirates."

She looked at me over the cover, wide-eyed. "Oh, but there do be. My cousin did see them once off the coast of Corvus."

The smile refused to keep itself hidden any longer. "Is that so? And—em—are they in the habit of stealing women then?"

She tucked the book down next to her plate that held a partially shredded biscuit and laughed. "I certainly do hope so. I would no mind being stolen by the likes of him." She tapped the illustrated cover and laughed.

I tried to imagine finding myself in the clutches of a Mer Pirate and snorted into my tea. "I can't imagine a pirate would be all that kind to a captive."

A broad smile split across her face, dimpling her cheeks, illuminating her eyes with mischief. "Oh no, not this captain. He do have many skills that the women do find more than accommodating." She passed me the copy. "Here, I do be done with it.

Have a turn. Ye might find it more interesting than ye do expect."

I eyed the text suspiciously. I'd read novels, thoroughly enjoyed them even, but I hadn't read one since leaving the Vanythian castle for the temple, though I'd heard rumors among the village women of novels that made one want to rip their bodices off and tempted them to spread their legs for men before they were wed. "*Words straight from the Umbra*," the High Priestess had once called them. I was abashedly curious, but I tried to keep the damning pink evidence of my feelings from dusting my too pale cheeks.

"Oh, well, thank you, Munnin. That's very kind of you. I don't know when I'll have the time to read it, but I shall make an effort."

I slipped the book into my satchel next to the Healer's journal I had yet to read. That definitely took precedence.

"If ye do enjoy it, maybe ye could join Rhapso and me one noct. We do get together at the shop and talk about the stories together over drinks."

"Oh?" I raised my brow, trying to hide the eagerness from my tone. "And would the lord let me out of my cage for such an outing?" I would read the book in one sitting if it afforded me the opportunity to lengthen my leash.

She shrugged. "I do no see why not. I do go every week, and I would be with ye, so ye do no be alone."

I held firmly to the glee that bounded across my heart, afraid to let it run wild. "Thank you, Munnin. I'll give the book a try and let you know what I think."

Huggin appeared in the doorway and cleared his throat. "Ready to go, Lady?" he grunted.

I looked to where he filled the frame, his face as stoic as it had been the dey before. "Are you not going to eat?"

He shook his head. "No."

Chatty man. If I wasn't careful, he might talk me to death. "And the lord? He hasn't joined us. Where might he be?"

He and Munnin exchanged an unreadable glance, quickly thrown at one another like knives. "He do be busy. Did ye need to speak to him?"

Busy. It stunk of a lie, but I wouldn't look at a gift from the Emrys too closely. Perhaps he'd had enough of me during our Forms lesson. Either way, his absence suited me just fine.

I dabbed my face with my cloth napkin before standing. "No, not at all. Thank you for breakfast, Munnin, and the book. I'll see you this noct."

WE TOOK A DIFFERENT route to my workshop, a tactic that was no doubt meant to confuse me, but I relished the opportunity to see more of the Fortress. Its halls were like a labyrinth, but a small seed of hope dangerously planted itself in my belly. The more they tried to confuse me, the more familiar I would become with the castle's layout, and perhaps the Emrys of luck would present me with an opportunity to find a means of escape. *Then again, maybe that is what they hope for?*

But I shoved it away. I was too useful as a Healer. *But you're a witch, not a Healer,* the voice protested, rearing its ugly and sinister head. Its words reverberated off my magic. I set it aside more firmly as we approached the hall connected to my workspace. It was already overwhelmingly full of people in need; I couldn't afford to listen to peculiar voices of doubt and worry now.

I ducked through the door to prepare the room for my first patient, leaving Huggin on the other side of the rough-hewn wood, when a small bundle on the examination table caught my eye. I plucked it up. It was a bouquet of dried white posies, cinched at their stems with a bit of pale blue ribbon. I picked it up and pressed it to my nose. Even desiccated, the flowers retained their sweet and heady fragrance. I hissed as the soft pad of my finger slid along a slip of tightly rolled parchment nestled discreetly in the stems. A small drop of blood welled, and I sucked it off my skin and hastily wheedled the piece free as Huggin knocked on the door.

"Just another moment." I tossed the words over my shoulder as I fumbled to unroll the slip of paper.

Scrawled on it like a secret confession meant to be burned at an altar in penance were the words: *You haunted my dreams all noct, Ertha, and I woke with the spectral image of you hovering over my thoughts. All I can smell is the scent of your hair, and my hands ache with the memory of your waist beneath them as we danced. I want to wrap them around you again and never let you go. You still owe me a walk. -Kastor Se'aneir*

My heart fluttered in my chest as it seemed to struggle to remember how to beat. I hadn't imagined it then—the heat of his gaze, the curl of his lips—he'd been flirting with me last noct. The thrum of my heart sank until it throbbed lower, roosting between my hips. I ran my finger over the seal pressed into wax next to his name, and the aching thrum of my heart ceased, but it jumped from where it lay all the way to my throat as I noted the shape of Kastor's crest. Unless I was mistaken, it was a raven with its wings spread. Surely it could not be coincidence but divine providence, that when a proverbial raven is what I sought, I was presented with a literal one? Well, not quite literal, but all the same, it felt significant. The rap at the door came more loudly, with a significant impatience in its sharpness. I stuffed the bouquet in my pocket along with the note and smoothed my skirts as I breathlessly called for Huggin to let my first charge of the dey in.

I kept my head down and my mind sharply focused on my tasks for the rest of the morning as I saw patient after patient with afflictions of varying severity. Dusk had already crept into the corners when a familiar face came through the door with a cheerful smile and honeyed words.

"Ertha dear, you look exhausted." Rhapso bustled into my workshop like a ray of sunlight to beat back the growing noct.

"What are you doing here? Are you hurt?"

She laughed. "Oh Emrys, no. I just thought you could use some supper and some company. Munnin stopped into the shop todey and told me she was worried about how hard you worked yesterdey, so I took it upon myself to make sure you were properly fed, for one meal at least."

With her basket between us, we settled on the stone window benches. Disbelief stitched tightly across my heart, irregulating the beat at the kind gesture, but then I recalled how close she and Fenris seemed to have been in the shop. Could it be that there was an ulterior motive to her generous actions? She flipped the lid back, and the hot, rich, nutty smells of baked goods wafted through the air, silencing my anxiety and causing my stomach to lurch in its eagerness to be filled. Rhapso smiled as she heard its rumblings.

"See, I knew you would be hungry. Here, try this one. It has spices from Orybous and dried fruits and nuts from Vanyth." She must have seen something like anguish paint my features, because she quickly added, "It came from a reputable trader—one who is known to only carry properly purchased and not pilfered goods."

That eased my worries, though it brought about new concerns about my ability to hide even the most fleeting of my thoughts. Damn it all to the Umbra, why couldn't I just enjoy a sweet treat without analyzing the situation to death. I willed my face to pull my lips along into a smile.

"That sounds delicious. It will be good to have a taste of home."

I took the roll of dough curled into a tight spiral and inhaled deeply. It smelled as divine as the Emrys themselves. I quickly delved it, careful to thread my magic through the fingers hidden by the pastry. The instant I detected nothing, I sank my teeth into it with a moan. The cinnamon, the honey, the pear, the flaky, buttery crust were perfection, all balanced with the crunch of a nut I couldn't identify despite it supposedly being native to Vanyth. My home was large, spanning a full continent and difficult to traverse in many areas, so it didn't surprise me. Beside that, the temple served only the simplest of foods.

"I'm glad you like it." Rhapso laughed as she took a bite of her own.

We sat in silence for a moment as we each devoured the sugary morsels, though it was a comfortable silence, a peaceful one.

"I taught Munnin, you know, how to bake, I mean. She used to be a disaster in the kitchen." Rhapso's smile was full and fond.

"Really? But she's so good at it now," I said, thinking back on the muffins left on the fireside table in my room.

"Yes, well, when they first arrived, she knew little of being a cook. Well, that's actually a kind assessment—the woman could burn water. I was new to Berth as well, and we crossed paths one dey in the market. The poor thing was in tears in front of a spice stall. I couldn't help but stop." Rhapso's violet eyes clouded over with memory as she spoke. "It turned out it was her and her brother's birthdey." She nodded toward the door, where I knew Huggin stood watch, stoic as ever. "She wanted to make him something to celebrate since they couldn't be home, but she had no idea what she was doing and didn't speak Uthari all that well. Fortunately, I know Corvusi. I took her home with me, and we've been friends ever since." Her cheeks flushed the prettiest shade of pink at the recollection, as though she were embarrassed of it somehow, or maybe it was just a particularly fond remembrance. She and Munnin, after all, seemed as thick together as sisters.

"How long ago was that?" I asked, trying to discreetly gain a sense of how long Fenris and the twins had been in Uthar. Any detail about them that I could glean could be a boon eventually. Besides, I still couldn't fathom how three Corvusi from near the roof of the world ended up so loyal to a foreign throne. In that story, I just knew, lay a potential key to my freedom.

"Oh dear, I don't know anymore. The deys just slide into one another." She patted my leg tenderly, but I could taste the lie thick in the air. "Anyhow, I apologize, my recollections run away with me, dear. Tell me, how are you settling in?"

"Oh, well." The question struck me like an iron to fire, poking to life something spitting and angry. That was something you asked someone who'd just moved towns or even houses, not someone whose life had been upended, their friends murdered, and their life now chained to a foreign throne. It turned the food in my stomach leaden. "Better than most other prisoners, I expect. Thank you for the sewing supplies, by the way. They kept my hands busy when sleep was hard for me to find last noct. I was admittedly a bit surprised that my keeper allowed me to keep sharp things in my chambers though." The words bit into her; I could see it in the way her soft face fell.

"Ertha, I truly didn't—forgive me. I'm sorry. I know what happened to you was terrible beyond imagining. I didn't mean to be flippant. I just wanted to be kind."

But it was too late—the creature within stirred my magic. It made me seethe as it sparked and sizzled.

"Why bother? I'll likely end up dead just like the last Healer, killed by your *friend*, Fenris."

Her moony face paled, and her eyes went wide. The monstrous anger inside me relished her reaction; it savored her shock at its venomous bite.

"Who told you?" Her even and soft-spoken reply was a gut punch in the way only truth can be sometimes.

I stood, not wanting to sit knee to knee with her a moment longer, my fists twisted in the fabric of my apron. "Does it matter when it is so plainly fact?"

Her violet eyes dimmed. "It very much does. Some truths are spoken to heal, and some are spoken to wound, and I have a feeling that this one was given to you like a knife in the back."

I didn't want to hear her, not when what she said chafed against my indignation and cowed my anger, because of course she was right. The words had come from Kastor, and I had no idea what his true motivations were. He'd said all the things I'd wanted to hear, but he could be as two-faced as a coin for all I knew. My legs suddenly felt as solid beneath me as melted butter, but I did not sit back down, though I did soften my tone before I spoke again.

"I'm sorry, Rhapso." Genuine or not, I couldn't afford to alienate anyone who could be used as an ally. She'd meant well, as she'd said, I was sure. "I'm just weary, and this"—I gestured vaguely around me—"is taking some time to adjust to."

The earnestness in her face hurt to look at as she stood and wrapped her arms around me. "It's alright, dear. Uthar is a cold and cruel place. I would be worried if you *weren't* having trouble." She pulled back to look at me, running her palms down my arms to clasp my hands. "But don't put your faith in anything anyone in court says to you. They may croon like birds, but they're wolves, and make no mistake, they bite."

My tongue was heavy with the words I held back. Not trusting myself to open my mouth, I nodded my understanding.

There were murmured goodbyes by her and promises to check in on me again, but they were barely a whisper beneath the ringing in my ears, a song sung by my magic as it hummed through my veins. As soon as the latch clicked behind her, I pressed the heel of my hand to my breastbone. It felt as though a knife were lodged in it, trying to split me open like an oyster to see if I held a pearl within.

I did a quick tidy. Huggin had yet to rap his knuckles on the door to signal another patient wanted to see me; they'd likely all gone home for the noct to see their loved ones. The thought threatened to strangle my heart, so I shoved it back as I blew out candles in their sconces and plunged the workshop into darkness.

A shaft of argent moonlight slipped through the clouds and sliced through the arched windows to spill across the room. I stepped into it and leaned just enough so I could spot the source of Selenyss's light. She, much like Jyord with the sun, carried the moon through the Emphyrea, cradling it in her arms as she walked along the rivers of aurora threaded betwixt the mountains. I'd always imagined, also like Jyord, she must be lonely. Some legends said she held her light as a beacon for lost souls to find their ways home. Never had this felt truer than in this moment as her luminescence brushed my cheeks. With a reluctant sigh, I turned away from the window and slipped through the door. Huggin waited, leaning against a wall with his foot kicked back and his arms crossed gruffly against his chest. We said nothing to one another as he pushed off and began to lead us back to the apartments. That was more than fine. Anything I might have said in that moment would have just been wounding, not necessarily to him, but to me and my withered and worn-out mind. It would have been like stretching a muscle too soon after an injury only to find it not quite recovered.

We crossed one of the iron bridges and skirted an outer balcony's parapet around the lesser court, where raucous nobility still ate and danced. The sour stench of spilled ale mixed with the yeasty smell of breads and amalgamated with the reek of sweaty bodies as it washed out of the open windows, and it reminded me of the last noct I'd spent with Helima, dancing together in the tavern before it had all gone as sour as the ale come deybreak. The memory of her flushed and happy face perked the downturned corners of my mouth just a fraction, not quite into a smile, but something close.

"Find something amusing, Healer?" A drunkenly slurred voice crawled out of the shadows and was swiftly followed by the man who'd spoken—Ingemar.

Before I had time for a breath to reply, he lurched toward me, his lecherous hands groping at my dress. He was unsteady, and I was unprepared. We careened sideways, the parapet walk was damp and slick, and my boots slipped beneath me. The unforgiving ground slammed into my backside as the full force of the general fell on top of me. I screamed, but the impact tore the sound from my lips, turning it into a gasp. Stars burst across my eyes as the back of my head struck the short wall that kept us from going over the drop.

Teeth sunk into my ear hard enough that I could feel blood trickle hotly into my hair where it spilled beneath me. Ingemar whispered to me on fetid breath, "Don't get too comfortable with that black-eyed bastard. You'll be my bitch to breed soon enough."

Unthinkingly, desperately, I tried to squirm free. My arms flailed, and I smelled blood as I raked my nails across his face. He swore, but before he could retaliate, as I assumed he would, he was suddenly off me.

The world canted oddly to the side as I struggled to right myself. I looked around, trying to grapple for understanding, and then I saw him, Huggin, with his meaty fists locked around the sniveling general's throat.

"You do no touch the lady," Huggin growled in Ingemar's face, his teeth bared.

Ingemar barked a choked and garbled laugh. "Heel, dog. Wouldn't want to get your master in trouble with the Father, would you?"

There was a pause between them, filled with snapping and sparking tension so palpable, I could almost feel it crackle along my skin, but at last, Huggin relented. He let Ingemar go with a shove, sending the disgusting swine of a human to the ground.

I tried to stand, but pain bit into my ankle, and it gave way as soon as I tried my weight on it. I must have twisted it in the fall. Large arms darted out and, with surprising gentleness, scooped me up before I could tumble. Huggin cradled me to his chest as if I were a child in need of rocking and strode away without a glance back at the wretched man we left behind.

My teeth sunk into my lower lip as I attempted to bite back a sob. But I was weakened by my dey in the workshop and by Ingemar's perverted vitriol and I didn't have the strength. I felt like a dropped egg, my delicately contained emotions seeping out of me uncontrollably no matter how calm and even I tried to make my breaths, so I succumbed. My fingers fisted the leather collar of Huggin's jerkin, and I buried my head in his stony chest. I let out a silent scream. Boiling hot tears streamed down my face, and I fragmented. I let the rage and sorrow wring from me until Huggin's tunic was damp with my tears and my throat was ravaged by screams that tried to claw their way out of the silence I wrapped them in to rip savagely at the air.

"There, there, m'lady. Ye do be safe now." The giant of a man tried to soothe, but that only made me cry harder. *Safe*, he said, but what did that even mean anymore?

"Who did this to her?" The words, as sharp as a blade, cut through my sobbing. I glanced up through lashes dotted with tears like morning dew, stunned to find we were already at the entry of the apartments. Fenris glowered from a short way down the hall as Huggin turned toward my room.

"Ingemar," Huggin grunted as he brushed past his lord to lay me down on my bed.

"Fucking bastard doesn't know how to lose." Fenris seethed over Huggin's shoulder. I saw him sweep in behind us like a shadow. Huggin laid me down on top of the blankets and stepped aside for my keeper. A weak, soft part of me wanted to reach out and grab his shirt sleeve, to beg him to protect me, but my hands felt like lead.

A sharp gasp drew my gaze to Munnin's pale and shocked face as she crossed the threshold of my chamber, her hand flying to cover her agape mouth.

Fenris bent, his breath uncomfortably warm, dancing across my cheek. "Munnin, get some needle and thread. This bite is clean through her lobe. And the kit too."

"Aye." Munnin spun toward the door so fast, her braids whipped against the jamb.

Fenris straightened, but his eyes never left the crimson spill of my blood. "Huggin, you know what to do." It wasn't a question, but Huggin answered with a brusk nod before he strode out of my room.

Munnin bustled back in, her brow furrowed. Her blue eyes shone with worry as she set a tray of supplies down at the foot of my bed and gave my uninjured ankle a tight squeeze.

Fenris barked, "Leave us," over his shoulder, and she obeyed without a word.

"Here, drink this." Fenris plucked an olive green glass bottle from the tray, uncorked it, and pressed its rim to my mouth.

I shook my head and tried to turn away, but a sharp pain cut a whimper loose from my lips.

"I'm not trying to poison you, damn woman," he growled, doing nothing to soothe my fears. He shook his head, his features abruptly softening, as much as stone could soften, and his voice calmed. "This will bring sleep so I can stitch you up without pain. I don't have your abilities and you can't heal yourself, so we can do this with or without sedation. It's up to you."

Reluctantly, with fingers that shook, I grabbed the bottle from him and took a tentative sip. It tasted of bitter herb syrup and strong, filtered alcohol. I choked and sputtered. Fenris smirked as he drew a length of plain white thread through the eye of a wickedly glinting needle.

"Drink the whole thing, Healer."

I scowled but acquiesced.

The room swam before my eyes—colors brightened and dimmed, swelling like bubbles, then popping against the walls. The firelight reached with glowing fingers into the room, twining with the shadows and twisting to form a darkly gilt corona around Fenris as he hovered over me with his impossibly depthless eyes, the needle brandished in his fingers marked with the bond. He stroked my hair off my forehead with a surprisingly gentle touch.

"Sleep now, Healer."

For once, I did as he asked without argument and slipped into a sleep fraught with noctmares and stained red with blood.

T HE CRESCENT-SHAPED LINE OF neat sutures on my earlobe stung as I gingerly poured an astringent mixture on it to prevent infection.

The flickering of the flames in my bathing chamber guttered as angrily as I felt. Their fiery tongues seemed to lick at the chill morning air like they had a point to prove. I'd risen early, surprised to find there was already a near-scalding bath set for me in the tub. My naked skin still steamed as I stood in front of the mirror and examined myself. I tried to keep my gaze professional and assessing as I tenderly prodded the blue and purple bruising. But no matter how icy the fist I strangled my heart with was, tears still formed in my eyes. I dashed them away and sucked in a stinging breath. I would not let the bastard win by weeping over what he'd done.

I limped from the room. My tailbone ached, and every step sent a fresh jolt of pain through my body along the pathways built of my bones and tender muscles. I knew I had two choices: I could wallow and soak myself in self-pity over the predicament I was in, or I could grit my teeth and do something about it. I wanted, with every fiber in my being, to do the latter, but I could see no clear path. So I determined to do the only things I knew how. I would dress, and I would heal.

From within my wardrobe, I withdrew a deep green dress so rich, it was nearly black, stitched through with swirling vines in the same color. I laced my pale cream underdress up the sides, then pulled a longer woolen one, dyed a vibrant shade of emerald, over that, followed by the richer colored and embroidered dress. I tied it at the sides and the sleeves, then tugged just a bit of the underdress sleeve through the crisscrossing laces on my arms as I'd seen many of the women of Berth do.

I wove dark, velvety ribbons into two braids, then twined them around my head twice before securing the ends with a bow in the back and holding the whole thing together with a mess of clever pins that glided sneakily between my silver-stranded hair. I slipped into stockings and boots before ducking back into the bathing chamber to check that everything looked good. I ran my hand over my skirts, making sure each stitch was in place. I wouldn't face the dey looking like a broken bird, and this made me look like anything but. The pattern of the skirts reminded me of the trees that grew near the secret swimming hole my sisters and I had liked to frequent. They were tall and broad with branches that hung over the water—perfect for young girls to dare one another to leap from. Around them grew vines notorious for bringing even the soundest of stone buildings down to rubble, but not those trees. No matter how it twined and twisted, the trees adapted, they withstood. I had to be like those trees, steady and adaptable in the face of all those who would try to take me down.

Thyra had always told me that clothes and beauty were just as useful as any weapon, if not more so, but I'd never understood it until this moment. I could feel them like armor wrapped around me, a second, tougher skin. All the same, my eyes flicked to the top of the wardrobe, where I knew the bone-handled knife surprisingly still lay. As I'd said to Rhapso about the sewing supplies the dey before—Emrys, had that really been only a dey ago?—I was surprised they'd let me keep it, but since they had, I might as well make use of it. I didn't know how to wield it, but I knew where in a body to stick the sharp end to cause the most damage, and that had to count for something. I pulled the box down carefully and withdrew the knife. It pulsed with the memory of bloodshed against my palm, and I had to suppress a shudder. I bunched my skirts and slipped it along my thigh as I had on that fateful dey, secured with my stocking ribbons, and then, with a wistful glance at my diadem, I returned the box. My jaw set, I blew out the onlooking candles and strode from the room.

The sounds of cutlery scraping on plates stilled the moment I stepped into the common area. Fenris noticed me first, his head jolting up and his black eyes widening in what I assumed was surprise. Though, honestly, I was also surprised to find them up and eating already so early in the dey; Jyord's light was not yet coloring the horizon in the windows behind them.

Munnin dropped the buttered roll in her hand. "What do ye think you do be doing out of bed? Ye do need rest."

"I was not afforded rest when I first arrived; I don't see why it is expected of me now." I sighed and swept into the empty place at the table and helped myself to a steaming mug of tea, into which I dolloped a generous amount of honey. "I am out of bed because I am sure there is a line of people in need of healing todey, and I will be there to ensure they get it."

"I sent word to close your workshop." Fenris's voice was quiet, but it still held that sharp undertone of a knife in the dark. I wasn't sure he was even aware of it. Threatening seemed to just be in his nature. Even when he was trying to help me heal, he was terrifying. Though he was admittedly gentle too, more so than I'd thought him capable.

I scowled as I scooped up a small serving of boiled and sliced pigeon eggs with onions and wilted greens over the top of a piece of soured dough bread. "That wasn't your place."

"Actually, it was. Everything you do is at the whim of the Father and—as an extension of his authority—me." His smile was positively lupine, and for a blink, I saw blood spilling from his gums and lips, but a flutter of lashes later, it was gone.

I swallowed hard around my frustration. How was I to prove myself, how was I to be a tree if I was not given the opportunity to stretch my limbs and grow? No, I could not stand for this. I'd been brought here to heal, and Umbra damn me, I would do it. "All the same, I am fine and would like to continue with my work."

"No."

Huggin and Munnin—who had, up until this point, kept their gazes averted, allowing the lord and me a moment to verbally spar—stilled. Huggin's eyes flicked to Fenris, and I could feel Munnin's on my face. It felt a lot like sides were being drawn, and I was grateful to know where everyone in the room stood.

"What do you mean *no*?" It took all my will to keep my tone from rising sharply as agitation rippled across the surface of my magic.

Fenris leaned in, his eyes boring into me below a quirked brow. "Are you unfamiliar with the meaning of the word? Or do you just not understand it in this context?"

I ground my teeth, my fingers white-knuckling on my fork, and just as I was about to snap and spit a venomous retort, he waved a hand, denying me the small pleasure of bickering back. He leaned indolently on his fist.

"Fine. We shall compromise because I am nothing if not a reasonable man."

I snorted and tried again to vent some of the frustration he'd roiled to life in my veins, but he cut me off yet again.

"You may leave the apartments to either make use of the library or the gardens, but you may not do any work and overexert yourself. Huggin will attend you, of course."

I scowled, but in truth, I would love a trip to both the library and the gardens. "Fine." I seethed, then immediately stuffed a bite of food into my mouth, wincing at the consistency of the eggs, to prevent my tongue from spilling the words it wanted to. I didn't want my leash shortened further.

We ate the remainder of our breakfasts in stilted silence, glances thrown between one another like blunted daggers, not wholly hostile, but not totally at peace either.

As I stood to leave with Huggin, Munnin's hand darted out to grab mine. "Did ye think on coming with me to discuss books with Rhapso?" Munnin asked, and Fenris's head shot up so fast, I was surprised his neck didn't snap.

My eyes darted between our joined hands and Fenris, who was stalled with his cup of tea halfway between the table and his mouth. "If I am I permitted to?"

He put the cup down with an audible *chink* against the table, his brow furrowed, and I watched as something unspoken passed between him and her. After a pause so drawn out that I was unsure if it would ever break, he let out an exasperated sigh. "I suppose Munnin is as suitable a guard as any." He turned to me and tapped a finger on the back of his wrist. It was a subtle move, but one my eyes trained on immediately. "Just don't get any notions about running, Shepherdess."

A hot tingling like pins and needles rolled through me as I felt a brush along the bond, as though my mark felt his touch, and I knew what he meant without him having to say another word. He would find me, always. I swallowed thickly and said nothing.

Munnin dropped my hand. "Oh, this do be exciting. We go tomorrow noct. Ye will love it. We do have wine and pastries while we talk, and the stories we do read..." She fanned herself and mimed swooning, and I had to admit, that brought a small smile to my face despite everything.

"I haven't started the book yet. I hope that isn't a problem. I could start tonoct."

She waved a hand. "Reading it do be the least important part."

Huggin grunted something that sounded an awful lot like an incredulous laugh, and I could have sworn I saw Fenris roll his eyes from the corner of mine, but that small smile on my face grew.

"All the same, I'll do my best to read some of it before we go."

THE LIBRARY WAS GRANDER than I'd imagined, with balconies overlooking a labyrinth of shelves that orbited a central hearth, near which stood a desk where the librarians worked, draped in dark robes with wizened beards and balding heads. Comfortable chairs were strewn around the hearth, where several nobles sat with their noses pressed into books or scrolls.

I supposed I'd expected the Father to be more the book-burning type, but then I noted the gilded script scrawled in huge lettering above the vaulted windows on the far wall: *Knowledge is the greatest weapon in war.* I rolled my eyes. Of course there would be references to war and battle even here.

Behind me, Huggin grumbled sulkily under his breath about dust and allergies. I pressed my lips together to squash a smile and rounded on him. "If you're so worried about your allergies, why don't you wait here by the hearth? There is plenty of fresh air coming in from the hall," I suggested, not purely altruistically.

"I should follow ye for yer safely, m'lady. It do be my orders." But I noted the hesitation in his darted and wary glance at the looming shelves, as if the books might swarm from their places like bats taking wing and assault him with dust.

"I doubt anyone is lurking to assault me in the stacks. Besides"—I patted my skirt—"I brought a little protection of my own."

His gaze brushed where my hand rested. "And ye do know how to use it?" His gruff voice dripped with skepticism.

I clasped my hands at my waist, mustered feigned confidence, and lied, "I do." His eyebrows bunched; clearly he didn't believe my falsehood, so I hastily added, "I also know how to scream, and quite loudly. Which I'm sure would echo nicely in a room this size and allow you to find me without trouble should I need assistance."

He opened his mouth, and judging from the look that pinched his harsh features, I was certain he was about to protest further.

I cut him off quickly, running over his words with my own. "Shall I demonstrate for you? I don't think the librarians would appreciate it, but if you need more convincing?"

He huffed, and the furrow of his brows deepened. "No—"

"Huggin, ya bastard, what are ya doing in the library? I dinna think ya could read!" A tall, heavyset man with a row of piercings along the rim of his ear and an accent as thick as the dey was long clapped my minder on the shoulder and drew his eyes from me for just long enough. I turned in a hushed whisper of dark skirts and ducked down the nearest aisle of shelves with a murmured thanks to Wyrta for the luck.

My walk turned into a near run down through the rows, giddy with freedom. I'd been left alone in my workshop, but this felt somehow more liberating. In the workshop, I could still sense Huggin's presence beyond the door, I still saw him every time he let someone in or out, we could still communicate with knocks. Now, there were scads of space and a labyrinth of tomes between us. I ran my fingers along the spines of the books as I passed and breathed deeply, savoring the smell of parchment and ink on the dust-filled air.

The organization of books seemed different than what I was used to in the temple. Though there most of the books were theological texts and tomes on herbs and different healing techniques. If the etched silver plates on the shelves here were any indication, this library held tomes on nearly every subject. I swept from section to section, glancing at the labels, trying to decide what I wanted to read, but it was overwhelming. In one section labeled *Romantic Novels*, I found a gaggle of giggling noble women tittering over a small, violet book, whose title was obscured behind their delicate fingers. I breezed past, careful not to draw their attention. In the section labeled *Battles of Old*, I found a young man in the garb of a Son, a wolf pelt slung heavily over his shoulders. For a breath-catching moment, I saw blood smeared on his face, pooled at his feet, and blood-sodden tracks like that of a dog's paced away from the spot like the damnable beast had walked through the puddle of gore.

Then he looked up, ensnaring my wide-eyed gaze. He smiled broadly, and the blood was washed clean. "Can I help you, miss?" he asked.

I shook my head, swallowed hard, and ducked away.

I shuddered and tried not to wonder at why I was suddenly suffering visions. I'd been through a trauma was all; I was still going through a trauma. But my healing gifts, my magic, gave a strange little nudge against my heart, as if to remind me it was there. I tried to quiet it, breathing as I walked, much in the same pattern as Fenris had taught me during the Forms, and it settled, albeit reluctantly.

The light around me dimmed, and I realized I was quite deep in the library; the shelves were shrouded in spun spider silk embellished with dust. I was about to brush the grime from a spine when a rustle and a flash of bright red feathers caught my eye. Could there really be a bird in the library?

It trilled as I rounded a corner, and my eyes locked on a flitter of a feather as bright as freshly drawn blood. Cold iced over my bones as I recalled the last time I'd followed a similar glimpse of red. I tried to rub away the creeping sensation from my arms, but it wasn't enough. Then, like an enemy flag spotted across the water, a singular scarlet feather stuck between two boards in the paneled wall pulled my attention.

I should have left it, turned on my booted heel and gone to pick up a romance novel, something scandalous and salacious, but my fingers itched, and my magic sat up in the cage of my ribs as the feather rippled in the half-light on an invisible breeze, like a beckoning finger calling me to it. I stretched out my hand as I took another step toward it. My heart thundered in my ears, sounding like the roll of a storm as it trekked across the Emphyrea.

My fingers barely brushed the feather's tip, and I gasped as a shock, which felt eerily like my magic being plucked from my fingertips against my will, sparked. The feather fell to the floor stones, and with a begrudging click, the wooden panel on the wall hitched open.

Using my nails, I dug my fingers into the crack and pried the loose board further, exposing a storage cubby of some sort. Inside it were scrolls and books with fraying, threaded spines. I grabbed the first one on the top of a stack, twisting it so it could fit through the narrow gap of the secret door. I ran my fingers over the peeling title but couldn't make it out.

"They're heretical texts."

I startled, nearly losing my grip on the book as I spun, flattening myself against the opening. My breasts heaved against my neckline, and I cradled the book to my chest as though it were armor.

Kastor stood half in shadow. A mischievous smile pulled at his lips, and he chuckled. "Sorry, didn't mean to frighten you." But he said it in such a wolfish way that it made me think he meant exactly the opposite, and my stomach did a backflip.

"Yes, well"—I stepped back from the wall—"if you don't want to startle people, the first step is to make your presence known," I replied archly.

"Where's your shadow? You look rather small without it," he teased in a husky voice that did unnerving things to my tender insides.

I laughed. "Who? Huggin? Distracted." I shrugged. "So I stole a little bit of freedom."

"Should he not be more vigilant with you after what happened?" He stepped forward and raised a hand to my face. His finger ghosted along the seam Fenris had stitched along my ear, shaking a shudder loose from my spine and sinking that stomach-flipping sensation lower in my belly, as if it were weighted down with stones.

"You've heard, then, about—" I swallowed hard around Ingemar's name and decided instead to just call him by his title. It felt like stripping him. Somehow, in my mind, it made him less. "The Commander."

"Deplorable man," Kastor spat and withdrew his hand. My heart stuttered, tripping on itself as if it wanted me to reach out and stop him, to return his touch to my skin. I shook myself mentally. What in the Emrys was wrong with me? Whatever these feelings were, they felt far too salacious and were certainly the absolute last things I should be feeling for this man, but hearing him disclaim his leader, his commander, my cheeks flamed, all of me flamed. "If he ever lays a finger on you again, I'll—"

Boldly, I rested a hand lightly on his arm. "Don't. Let's not talk of him and let his rot sour this moment."

He smiled down at me. "You are so pure, you know that? So lovely." I flushed even deeper at his words. "Not just your face, which—" He made a sound as if at a loss for words. "When I first saw you, I swore yours was the face of Selenyss herself looking back at me. But your true beauty, Ertha, is in your heart. They way you've been caring for the people of Uthar these past deys, a people you owe nothing to, it's truly remarkable."

"Healing is blind. It is not for me to judge. That is for the Emrys," I replied more out of habit than actual thought.

"See, that is exactly what I mean. Pure." He breathed deeply, leaning in just a bit as he did so, as if he were savoring me, the air I breathed, my scent, and then asked, "Would you like to come see the gardens with me? Just a quick trip."

This was the kind of opportunity I'd only dreamt of getting—to roam the castle unfettered by hounding guards, to look for a fissure or a gap I could slip through in this prison. I glanced back toward the heart of the library, to where I knew Huggin was likely searching for me, but before I could protest, Kastor pressed a finger to my lips. His touch seared against the sensitive skin as a gasp slipped free to twine around his fingers.

"I can have you out and back before he ever notices."

I smiled as he removed his finger, my lips still haunted by the pressure of it there, and not trusting myself to speak, I simply nodded.

DEMURE LADIES

I F I'D THOUGHT LEAVING Huggin behind to wander between shelves had been a rush of freedom, it had been nothing compared to the sheer thrill of allowing Kastor to help me slip over the sill of a library window. We landed in an alley connected to a vacant courtyard that I assumed belonged to the kitchens—based on the smells whirling through the steam that billowed out of the open-windowed, sagging buildings around its outer edge.

"Come this way," Kastor hissed in a hushed tone as he laced his fingers with mine. The simple touch sent a jolt of delight up my bones, where it brushed against my rapidly beating heart.

We strolled at a brisk pace out of the courtyard and along a narrow walk. Beyond a distant wall, I saw the thorned limbs of the Blackwood. Aevum had already stripped its trees of their foliage. The air was crisp, smelling of the decay of the year before the whole of the world slipped into the cold embrace of kalda. With a hint of more snow to come after the previous storm's quick melt, the next time a blizzard blew in, it was likely to stay.

The roar of the waterfall became less distant, pressing more insistently into my ears. Kastor pushed open an iron gate wrought in vining patterns with hammered foliage and flora rusting along its edges. I brushed my fingers along it as we passed through, and it hummed beneath my touch like a welcome.

"Well, what do you think, Lady?" Kastor drew us up, bumping into me gently, almost playfully, as my jaw fell open. Much like the library, the gardens were a surprise. Surrounded by stone walls covered in vining trumpet flowers and woven through with steaming canals of water was an ornately cultivated garden unlike any I'd ever seen. Little bridges connected islands brimming with vibrant and vivacious plant life despite the late season.

"The water is piped in from a hot spring deep in the woods. The high walls and a clever bit of old magic trap the warmer air, giving the Father and

Mother a longer growing season. This side of the garden is for mostly utilitarian purposes because of its proximity to the kitchens, but if you cross the bridge over the Fall of Tears, those sections grow the more exotic plants. Then, through that back gate there"—he leaned in, his shoulder brushing mine as he pointed to a gate similar to the one we'd entered through, tucked half hidden behind a spill of vines—"is a cold house, a whole glass building that is chilled rather than heated for cultivating snowy-weather plants shipped from Iliff. There's even a planter box filled with ice peppers. If we're lucky, there might be some ready for the Eklipsis celebrations."

My heart snagged on certain words he said so nonchalantly, like "old magic" and "shipped in," and it shredded against them. "Old magic" implied murdered witches, and "shipped in" likely meant they'd been stolen in a bloody raid. Kastor didn't notice the way my fingers stiffened in his as he pulled me along. Surely, if I was right in my dire assumptions, someone as kind as he wouldn't have been a part of those practices or aware of them. How could he have been when he dragged me from miniature isle to isle with such a look of tenderness and joy on his beautifully cut and bearded face. I took a deep breath of thick air, heady and warm with the rich fragrances of flowers, and did my best to let my worries melt away and not taint this moment of freedom.

But this was more than that; it wasn't just a moment away or a lengthening of my leash, it was also an unhindered slice of time to observe possible routes out of the Fortress.

The blood in my veins sang as I subtly ran a hand over the stacked stone walls we passed. They were sturdy and definitely climbable. There was also a discreet service gate that led out into the woods beyond, cleverly concealed behind a tree trunk. If I could refine my magic, I might just be able to break through the lock.

I didn't speak much, and that seemed fine by Kastor, who filled the space left by my silence with stories I only half listened to—trivial, tender things like how he missed hearing his mother sing as she kneaded dough, or how he once played a trick on his sister by stuffing her mattress with poison knuckle, a plant native to Uthar with hand-shaped red leaves covered in fine hairs that seeped an oil into ones skin and caused a terrible itching. I didn't share too much of my childhood or of my sisters for fear of letting something I ought not slip.

He plucked me a few posies; ruellacs for regret, Ananasa's promise for budding feelings, and a sprig of blooming Lugha grass for bountiful blessings. I pressed them to my nose and let their soft petals brush against my skin as I inhaled their sweet scents and wondered if he knew the courtly meaning of the flowers at all or if it was simply Emrys-blind luck that the plants he'd picked seemingly had relevance. In all likelihood, it was the latter; I only knew because of my sister and Tad. She would dissect every bouquet he'd left for hidden meaning and sigh wistfully.

"If you could be something other than a Son, what path would you choose?" I asked him softly with my nose in the bouquet he'd crafted for me.

Kastor paused as he bent to snap a few spindly periwinkle wish-not stalks; they symbolized longing and desires yet to be fulfilled. He ran a hand thoughtfully over his beard, "Well, I've always thought it would be peaceful to tend an orchard. We had a few small trees back on the farm. When I was a boy, I used to try to shirk chores by sneaking up into one of the eldercot trees with a book. I'd read and eat fruit all dey until my hands were purple from the juices. So I suppose, if I could, I would pack up, find a woman to wed…" He cleared his throat and tore our gazes apart before tenderly adding, "We could settle down far from here and tend a bit of land together, and perhaps there would somedey be children to chase down from the trees."

I could picture it, him with a babe on his hip as he hauled baskets of ripe fruit, the image burned in my mind as he passed me the wish-not to add to my growing bundle of greenery. Longing and desires indeed.

"Beautiful," I whispered, unsure whether I meant the flowers or the vision of the future he'd spun.

Melantha, Emrys of noct, stretched across the horizon, dusting the Emphyrea with bruised shades of purple and black as we hurried back through the kitchen courtyard, no longer vacant but filled to the brim with busy servants hailing trays and slaughtered beasts. Fortunately, it was so crowded that two people crossing to sidle alongside the Fortress wall into a bit of shadow and steal privacy went unnoticed.

"Todey has been such a gift." I sighed, and I was surprised to find I meant it, in more ways than one. I'd been able to scout ways out, yes, which would have been much harder under the sharp eyes of Huggin, but also, I felt like a human with Kastor, not just a Healer, not just a captive. "Thank you."

He backed me against the wall of windows, and my breath hitched, twining around my ribs as it cinched tighter than any corset. The whole of his body pressed against mine, and his hand came up to cup my cheek. Blood thundered through my body. It rubbed against the skin of my cheeks, chafing them red, and pooled between my legs in a throbbing tempest. His thumb made soft, calloused strokes across my pinked cheeks.

"It was my pleasure, Ertha." My name rolling off his tongue sounded like the most delicious kind of sin, the kind I would have suddenly given almost anything to commit despite my rules about kissing.

My knees wobbled beneath me, and I bit my lip against the irrational plea threatening to form. I didn't want to beg this man—this man who I should, by all rights, loathe—to do despicable things to me.

The growl that raggedly clawed its way from his throat was near feral, and my eyes widened in surprise as he ground himself against me. "Bite your lip again." His pupils were wide and wild, his voice rough as I gazed up at him, locked my eyes with his, and slowly, I did as he demanded, dragging my lower lip through my teeth. He moaned, a guttural hum that my body answered of its own accord as it shuddered in response.

He bent his head, his lips a ghost's breath away from mine. His hand slid from my cheek to wrap itself around my jaw, where he held me still. I expected him to kiss me, but he instead went preternaturally still and whispered, "We had better get you back in."

My heart sank and all fire was doused from my veins. Had I completely misread our conversation? Was this not flirting?

"Right, yes, of course," I muttered, ducking my face as he stepped back. So much felt like it was slipping away from me—my emotions, the whole of my life. But I couldn't worry on that now. I had to get back, as he'd said; otherwise, I'd be in danger of losing the little leash I'd been given to go with Munnin tomorrow noct.

I scrambled back through the window using Kastor's hands as a stirrup to give me a boost. With a wink thrown at me through the glass, he was gone before I could straighten my skirts. I tucked the flowers beneath the strap of my underdress and rushed through the shelves. Heavy boots that sounded uncomfortably like the clobbering feet of my guard echoed from somewhere behind me.

I hiked my skirts and ran on deft toes. I skidded into the row labeled *Romantic Novels*, which earlier had been filled with tittering women but was now blessedly empty. I grabbed the first book I saw, small with a violet cover, and flung myself to the ground. I pressed my back against the shelves, leaning comfortably, as though I'd been there for hours, and flipped at random to a page near the middle of the text.

Not a heartbeat later, the footsteps came to a halt. "Where have ye been?" Huggin grumbled the moment he rounded the aisle, his words a coarse accusation and a demand.

"Right here." I peered up at him as innocently as I possibly could, as though I hadn't slipped away from him without permission or noticed the shadows of the shelves growing long with the light of Jyord's fading sun. "I'm sorry, have I been long?"

"Ye've been here all dey?" His eyes watered, and he sneezed aggressively into his shirt sleeve. The poor man actually was quite allergic. "Why do ye look like ye've been running."

"Well, it's a really good book. Positively breathtaking, really." I held it up for him to see, and his whole face abruptly turned a violent shade of crimson.

He coughed, his eyes bulging nearly out of his head. "Aye, well, we do need to be getting back."

I feigned a petulant sigh as I got to my feet. "Alright, let me just put this back." I snuck a discreet look at the title as I slid it back into place along the row. *Finding Your Pleasure—The Demure Ladies Guide to Gratification.* Mortification plunged itself into my heart like a knife, but I kept my expression still as I brushed past him to leave.

I was certain as we walked back to the apartments that the silence between us was not the normal kind but a heavier one, laden with embarrassment so thick, I could almost taste it in the air. When Fenris asked at dinner if I'd found anything good to read at the library, Huggin choked on his wine, and it took a full minute of Fenris pounding on the man's back for his sputtering to cease. I excused myself a few moments later before the lord could remember his question. But as my door clicked shut and I shed my dress, a red feather fluttered to the floor. My eyes snagged on the motion, and I froze. I hadn't picked it up; in fact, I'd forgotten all about the strangely hidden and supposedly heretical tomes like a simpering, empty-headed simpleton drunk on her first infatuation with a man, which, if I was brutally honest, wasn't all that far off from the truth.

I picked the feather up and ran my finger along its edge. "Ouch!" A bead of blood as red as the feather welled on the pad of skin, and I glared at the thing. "How in the Umbra..." But the answer struck me.

This was so clearly a sign from the Emrys who seemed keen on puppeting my life in whatever direction suited her purpose, and it could mean only one thing.

I had to return to the library.

T HE WAY I CREPT, hiding in the pools of shadow between torches, was yet another knife to the heart that reminded me of the last time, only deys before, that I'd been doing much the same to sneak out of the temple with Helima. I sent a prayer to the Emrys, more specifically to the Red Lady, that she would see me safely on this excursion without garnering notice. I was unaccustomed to praying to her for anything other than swift deaths for the ailing, but since she seemed to have some sort of vested interest in me at the moment, I figured she was the most likely to listen to my pleas. And considering her nature, I also added my wish that none were killed because of this little late-noct walk.

The halls of the lower and upper courts were blessedly vacant, with the exception of a few slumped and snoring noblemen strewn on benches, covered in nothing but their furs and stinking of sour ale and piss. Lovely.

Out in the noct air, Imbola's wind cut down from the gorge, carrying with it miniscule frozen stars of snow. I pulled my cloak more firmly around my shoulders and tugged the dark cowl deeper over my face as the breeze pulled at its edges, threatening to expose my silver hair to Selenyss's light. The iron bridge shuddered beneath my feet, trembling as I hurried across it. My breath held and my heart clenched in a fist of fear as I ran. The finely misted spray of the falls wisped through the air, slickening the rails and threatening to trip me. I gasped, the icy air invading my lungs along with fresh breath as I reached the other side.

Guards were far and few between as I pulled the door to the main keep open and slunk down the stairs toward the library. Emrys bless the renowned arrogance of the Sons and the Father; they likely thought they were too fearsome and their bite too sharp for any to dare creep and thieve. I shuddered a bit. I was surprised I was bold enough to dare. But there was no time to question it now; I'd already come too far and was in too deep to change my mind.

I slipped through the library doors with ease. Argent shafts of moonlight speared from the windows across the room like swords piercing the dark belly of a beast and allowed me just enough light to navigate my way through the maze of shelves, tracing my steps from earlier. My slippered feet and skirts were barely a whisper against the stone tiled floors as I ran. The pitch of noct was deepest by the back wall, where I knew the secret door stood hidden.

By memory, my fingers deftly found the groove and pried. The hinges didn't bother protesting as I swung open the access. "Fucking Umbra," I swore under my breath. Inside was stark, bare, empty. I swiped my hand over the first shelf, not even a damn speck of dust. In disbelief, I checked them all, running my hands over them again and again, but I came back with nothing except a sliver embedded in the tender pad of my finger.

I sank to my knees. It could not have been a coincidence that the books had vanished less than a dey after I'd discovered them. But who would have moved them and why? The only person to see me with them had been Kastor. Could he have said something to a librarian and had them removed? Would he have taken them? Maybe I was overthinking; maybe this had nothing to do with me or him. But the gnawing sensation of warning that chewed on the darkest edges of my awareness seemed to suggest otherwise. I peered in either direction down the curving slope of the paneled wall. On the far end, it met the window I'd recklessly snuck out of with Kastor, and on the other, it met stairs that ascended to a restricted balcony gated off at the top. Surely there was liable to be more than one trove of texts. I stood and began softly tapping, pressing, and prying every plank. I was quick, and by the time I made it across the entirety of the wall, I was certain there were no other hatches.

A creek of a floorboard in the distance gave me pause. I waited with held breath for the scuff of a bootheel or the rasp of another's breath but blessedly heard nothing. The angle of the light had shifted; the noct would soon bleed into the dey. I had to get back before the earliest of risers started milling about the keep.

Disappointment hollowed me out. I'd risked—well, I wasn't quite sure what it was I'd risked exactly. I didn't want to fathom what the lord would do if he found me out of bed. Either way, it had all been for nothing.

On tipped toes, I began my journey in reverse, slipping from the library, out of the main keep, and onto the parapet, where I could cross the bridge. The grumbling of men's voices tripped me up. Without thought, I ducked behind a statue in a recess of the outer wall, a gruesome thing made to look like a wolf devouring a maiden, and pressed my back into the stones.

"Don't know what the Commander was raving about. I can't tell that anyone was anywhere near there," a voice said.

A light sparked, illuminating the features of a short, grizzled Son with a scar that hooked his lip and distorted his features. He lit a pipe. The sickly scent of the smoking herbs wafted, choking the smell of snow from the air as he puffed and shrugged. "All I know is if he says we're supposed to be looking for a thief, then we'd better find one or it'll be on all our heads."

I pressed a strangling hand over my mouth to smother a gasp. Someone had seen me sneak into the library. Not just someone, the Commander. Emrys bless, this was bad. Really bad. I may not have been able to imagine what Fenris would do to me if he found out I wasn't in my bed, but I certainly had several ideas regarding what the Commander would do.

The taller, broader Son who'd spoken first shrugged and muttered a reply I couldn't hear as the two continued their walk, blessedly away from my hiding place. Unfortunately though, they headed for the exact bridge I'd intended to cross. I peered around the statue, and my gaze darted from scrappy bridge to scrappy bridge. They all seemed so delicate in the dark, but worse than that, they all had people—Sons, I assumed—on them. That left only one option: the bridge that it seemed no one used, judging by its state of disrepair. The one closest to the falls.

There was no time to question the choice or wonder why it was so rarely used; I had to get back before my absence from the apartments was noticed, or worse. Darting around the statue with my skirts hiked in one hand, I ran. As soon as I met the entrance of the bridge, my stomach sank. It was narrower than the others I'd crossed, only wide enough to walk one foot in front of the other, and scum slicked the metal. When I brushed my hand across the meager railing, it came away red with rust. Fuck, fuck, fuck.

More voices carried over the falls on the wind like a warning from the Emrys. Their words were incoherent, but like a whip cracked behind a stubborn beast, they spurred me into action. I gripped both railings fiercely and kept my eyes fixed ahead on the looming, black shape of the other half of the Fortress. The falls kissed the bridge in the middle, its blue crystalline waters caressing the iron. Magically made and protected or not, the railing was long corroded away. A whimper followed by a sob broke free from my chest as I neared the center point. I forced my left hand to move, to grip the right railing, unbalancing myself. There was no way I could continue like this; I would have to turn and sidle across the stretch. Terror wrapped itself around my throat, and I swallowed hard as I swiveled my slippers on the frightfully narrow platform beneath me.

All of Berth was spread before me in the darkness, dappled with flickering torches from the village out to the ships anchored in the sea, and it all looked so horribly small from this vantage. My hands shook, and with a will that I had to scrape from the very depths of my being, I made my feet move, first one then the next in time with my hands.

The bridge arched from one end to the other, with the pinnacle pointing like a blunted spear into the heart of the fall. The water was at my back like the breath of a Niflym risen from the Umbra. It poured down my cloak and soddenly weighted my skirts, like it hoped to pull me down with it so it could watch my body break on the stones below. But the iron began to tilt ever so slightly in the other direction, and I knew I was getting closer. I was almost there.

As I straightened back out, a flutter of white pages caught the corner of my gaze in the moonlight. They were wedged into the grate of the ironwork just between me and the safety of stone walls. A book. I wanted to ignore it, to step over it and keep going on my way, but something in my magic stirred, like a thread strung between the book and me, drawing me along its length. Reluctantly, I let go of the right side of the railing as I felt my toe snag against the book's spine and crouched down.

Blindly, I fumbled, not wanting to look at the plunge below, and I wrenched it free. The book was soggy and fairly small, and I stuffed it easily into the deep pocket of my cloak.

I could have collapsed, kissed the stones, and sung the praises of every Emrys as soon as I stepped off the treacherous walk. Instead, I hastened my steps, my head swiveling as I all but ran to make certain no one saw me. I didn't slow when I came to the stairs that led to the apartments nor as I ascended—spiraling past door after door with hammered metal plaques of varying intricacies stamped with the names of the noble house that resided within—until I reached the one door without. I shoved it and then let it fall shut behind me with the softest of clicks. I turned in the darkened hall to rush for my room but went sprawling. The floor struck, knocking the wind from my lungs. I lay there for a wallowing heartbeat before I struggled to my feet, my soaking skirts stuck and tangled in my legs, and I cursed, "Fuck the bloody E—"

I stilled, a deer in the woods who finally noticed the hunter's presence. The things that lay haphazardly across the floor, the things I'd tripped on, were Fenris's legs, and he was in no shape at the moment to be considered a hunter; in fact, he looked like he'd been someone's, or something's, prey.

"Do continue. Don't let me stop you." He coughed, and blackish blood spattered the corners of his grimly smiling lips. "Never would have guessed something as prim as you could have such a filthy mou—" His words dissolved into a fit of garbled, blood-choked coughs.

Reeling, my mind spat out the first thought that came to it as I looked over the mangled mess that was supposed to be Fenris's torso. "Where's Huggin?"

Fenris chuckled darkly. "I could ask you the same thing." His hand spasmed in his lap, like he'd tried and failed to command it to move.

"You're hurt," I said dumbly, and the corner of his lip curled, showing just a hint of tooth.

"Very"—he took a sucking breath—"observant, Shepherdess."

I shook myself. What in the Umbra was I doing gaping at him like a dumbstruck novice? I couldn't leave him here in the cold hall to shiver and bleed out until Huggin or Munnin came back from wherever in the Umbra they were and stumbled upon him. I shucked my cloak and drew my power in one motion, my hands alighting as I crouched and brought my face level with his.

"I'm going to help you stand and we're going to get you to your room so I can heal you. Do you think you can manage that?"

He stared at me with those infinite eyes beneath a quizzically furrowed brow. "Heal me." It was a statement, a ragged one, all frayed at the edges.

I didn't reply. I looped his arm over my shoulders and let my magic pulse and seep into him where my hand brushed the bulging muscles of his back. "All right, on the count of three. One, two, three." I sent a surge of energy into him, willing his body to move up with me.

He growled like a beast through gritted teeth, but by some miracle, we made it to our feet. He leaned on me, half draped. Fenris's steps dragged, limp and stilted, as I propelled us down the hall. His blood dripped from his arm, hot and thick down my spine, a stark counterpoint to the clinging, frigid fabric that suctioned to my skin and stole my warmth.

I wasn't entirely sure how we made it through his door or how it was that I managed to get him into his bed, but once he was there, flopped in a bloody heap on his belly, I used the bed clothes to heave his weight and roll him onto his back. The remnant of a fire guttered in his hearth, wavering between flickering flames and gilded embers, giving me barely enough light to see by.

"Now's your time to let me die, Shepherdess. I die, so does the bond." Fenris grabbed my left wrist weakly, his finger tracing one of the white whorls, smudging it scarlet.

I met his dimming eyes, but they weren't looking at me, they were looking past me, through me.

"Why are you telling me this?"

He let his hand slip, and he wheezed, the presence of death rattling in his breaths. "Call it a curiosity."

Something surged in the well of my gifts, stirring it, churning it into a maelstrom. He kept talking, but I wasn't hearing it. The thrum of magic in my veins drowned out all noise as I climbed atop the bed and straddled him, plunging my hands into the gaping holes in his shredded chest. Usually, I was far more composed, drawing only small drops at a time, but tonoct, something made me reckless. I drew on my magic in a violent flow as torrential as the waterfall, and much like the way the fall had eaten away at the iron of the bridge, so too did I eat away at Fenris's injuries. I wiped them clean as if they had never been. I was blinded by the radiance of my luminescent hands as I funneled more and more of me into him from my well of magic that seemed to stretch infinitely deeper than it had before. The gouging wounds ripped through his flesh were deep, cutting and hacking into his viscera. Much of him needed mending, but I left nothing behind, and when I was done, his naked torso appeared unscathed, save for faintly glowing irregular lines drawn across the seams of the wounds.

My magic left me reluctantly as it receded from my blood like the tide. It tried to stick to and coat my insides in silvery light, so I had to push it back, forcing it to bed down in its place. As soon as it acquiesced, I fell. The world tilted as I collapsed with my head on the pillow next to the lord's. The edges of my vision wavered black, and I suddenly felt as brittle and insubstantial as a false promise.

Through sleepily fluttering eyelashes, my gaze met Fenris's. His brows were sewn together in what seemed to be sincere confusion. "You let me live." Perplexity knotted itself around his whispered statement.

I sighed, amazed at how little it seemed everyone understood. "Healing is blind," I murmured before exhaustion took hold of my mind and drowned it in noctmarish sleep.

Deylight filtered into the room in faint, whorling wisps and tickled my cheeks. I fluttered my lashes and groggily watched the motes of dust eddy across the ceiling. I felt warm and safe, still cocooned in the haze of a peaceful and dreamless sleep, the sort that only came after true fatigue, like the kind induced with massive power use—though, as I prodded the place where my magic lay within me, I found it pleasantly replenished already.

I went rigid, and the comfortable veil that rest had draped over me was jarringly ripped off as I remembered healing my keeper in the noct. I stared wild eyed at the ceiling that I now recognized as unfamiliar. A kiss of breath against my cheek and the warmth of a hand pressed over my heart prompted me to turn my gaze. The shifting sound of my hair as it dragged against the pillow slip sounded monumentally loud in my ears as I came face-to-face with Fenris.

Blessedly, he still slumbered, deeply, if the soft noises he made—something between a snore and a contented murmur—and even pulls of air were any indication. I peeled his hand carefully from my skin, afraid that the frenetic thump of my pulse against his palm would wake him. I rested his hand on the pillow and slipped inelegantly over the side of the bed in a tumble of sleep-tousled hair and still-damp skirts from my dousing in the noct, and I winced as my knees thudded against the carpet. I stilled and listened for any shift in Fenris's breathing. When there was none, I rubbed my bonded arm. It tingled maddeningly. Umbra, if his was doing the same, it would surely wake him. I peered over the edge of the bed, like a quivering moorland rabbit checking for predators, for any sign that he was bothered or waking, but he was just the same as he'd been before, curled around the void I'd left. I stood and tiptoed my way to the door, keeping one eye on it and one eye on him. A floorboard creaked and sent my heart into my throat, but the lord didn't so much as twitch a finger. The healing must have taken just as much out of him as it had me.

The hinges stayed silent as I opened the door a fragment and slipped through the narrow crack. My lungs greedily drank in a relieved breath as I pressed my brow to the door after shutting it gently. Thank the Emrys I'd made it out without being caught. The last thing I wanted was to talk to Fenris, not when trepidation about the ease with which I'd slept in his half embrace crackled along my bones and snapped along my skin. He was the first man I'd ever shared sheets with. My shoulders slumped. That had not been what I'd imagined when I'd thought of my first time abed with a man. It hadn't meant anything. I'd been tired from healing and that was all; in fact, it didn't even count.

I turned to trod down the hall to my room and froze. Munnin stood stock-still in the middle of the hall, breakfast tray in her hands, her eyebrow half quirked in a silent question.

"It's not what it looks like," I protested softly as pink the color of Jyord's rise painted my cheeks.

"I did no see a thing." She winked, her cheeks pulled into a wicked grin, and slipped into the common room with deft steps.

I groaned and raced for my room before Huggin could wake and further deepen the hole I would need to bury myself in to recover from the humiliation of being caught sneaking from Fenris's bed.

J YORD SET THE SUN aside in time for Selenyss to stride over the horizon with the burgeoning moon in her loving arms as the cart Munnin and I had hitched a ride into town on pitched and rolled over the cobbled streets. With the workshop closed yet again, I'd had some time to myself to read the book we were to discuss that noct. The words had been surprisingly easy to devour.

The story followed a timid and beautiful maiden as she set sail from her home to meet her betrothed for the first time, only to be set upon by a Mer pirate vessel. She made an agreement with the pirate captain to help him retrieve the treasure he sought, which only the purest maiden could lay hands on, and then he would deliver her safe and sound to her waiting husband-to-be. But a few chapters in—when the pirate captain, despite all sense, pressed the maiden against the mast and asked her who'd hurt her in the past—I was rooting for her to fall in love with him. A few chapters later, they had their first kiss, and I was enraptured by the eloquently described scene. I'd never known words on pages could cut through me like a hot knife in a way nothing I'd previously imagined had. I'd yet to discover how it ended, but I'd tucked the book under my pillow and fully intended to while away the late-noct hours, ravenously consuming the rest.

The driver let out a full-bellied breath and bellowed, "Woah!" to his donkey, bringing us to a lurching stop in front of Rhapso's dress shop. It seemed strangely inviting as Melantha danced her darkness across the world. A but-ter-cream-and-caramel glow spilled out around the silhouetted dress forms standing stoically be-hind the glass. My stomach clenched as Munnin helped me from my perch on the back of the cab-bage wagon—for a blink, they were the severed and bloody heads of my loved ones overflowing the crates, Helima's teetering at the top. My skull throbbed, shooting pain through my temples like a pinch to wake me from a dream. I squeezed my eyes shut against it, and when I looked again, the vegetables were back in their places.

Munnin was already knocking on the locked shop door when I caught up with her in the stooped entryway.

The sound of clicking bootheels preceded a scrape of the lock, and my mouth filled with cottony webs of worry that suddenly tangled my tongue as I recalled how rude I'd been to Rhapso just the other dey when all she'd meant to do was show me kindness. I'd lashed out at her, and for what? It was no more her fault I was prisoner here than it was the seasons' fault for changing. I wrapped my arms around myself just to keep my fingers from fidgeting fretfully. What would I say? Perhaps I shouldn't have come, but it was too late now as the door scraped open.

"Munnin, dear, and Ertha, I'm so glad you both came. Come in out of the chill." Rhapso's rosy cheeks bloomed, and the corners of her feline-like eyes crinkled as she smiled broadly from the threshold of her shop.

Munnin wrapped her arms around the shorter, curvier woman in a quick and familiar embrace before stepping through into the shop beyond. I paused, caught halfway over the threshold, my fingers bunched in the fabric at my waist and my mind wrestling for the right words to say to express my remorse. My lower lip quivered, stuck between racing thoughts but unable to express any of them.

Rhapso must have read something in my features because her own softened as she reached out and set a hand tenderly on my arm. "There is nothing you need say. I know what it is like to be in your position, so don't even think of feeling a hint of remorse for the words you said the other dey. You needed someone to say them to, and I'm glad it was me."

I swallowed thickly. I did not deserve such kindness, not after I had been so monstrous, but the fact that she was willing to forgive me without question, and not only that, but that she understood, wrapped my heart in such affection for this woman I barely knew. Nettling tears stung my eyes, but I said nothing, just simply bowed my head in thanks. My eye caught the faintest hint of a white shimmering wisp curled beneath her sleeve as she withdrew her touch, and my heart skidded into my ribs. It was so like the one on my arm, the mark that bonded me to my keeper. Emrys, Rhapso knew what it was to be a prisoner better than I'd thought.

Rhapso led us through the shop to a narrow back stair that spiraled up to a quaint little apartment. I was pleasantly assaulted with sweet and savory scents wafting from her little kitchen nook on the landing as I followed her and Munnin's swishing skirts down a hall and past a door that Rhapso tapped as she strode by, letting me know it was the privy. We entered a wide room situated over the front of the shop, divided into a sitting room and a bedchamber with an ornately painted screen separating the two spaces.

I followed the older women's leads and sat on a squatly, floral-upholstered chair opposite the settee they crowded on together, then accepted a mug full of sparkling, blush-colored mead that tasted of the honeyed winds of jeug as I rolled it across my tongue. I was unaware of time's passage as the mead flowed more freely and the sugar of cakes spun me until I was giddy. We spoke of nothing severe, nothing dark or haunting, and the world outside simply ceased to exist for a while.

Rhapso hiccupped and giggled as she fumbled for a bit of parchment from a basket perched on the small side table next to the scrolling arm of her couch. "I have the title jotted down here some-where. One of Lady Calypsa's maids gave it to me just the other dey." She plopped back down in a rush of plum skirts that brought out the unique shade of her Orybousi eyes, jostling a starry-eyed Munnin.

"I do no mind what title we choose next so long as the romance do make my blood boil." The two women dissolved like candied rose petals on a tongue into fits of breathless giggles.

"I think I'll go grab another bottle of this from the kitchen if that's alright, Rhapso?" I held up the green glass neck of the empty mead bottle.

She pressed a fluttering hand to her hysterical and heaving chest. "Oh yes, please do! It's on the shelf in the kitchen."

As I stood, the room tilted slightly underfoot, wobbling unnervingly with each step. My head was full of a light buzzing, not unpleasantly reminis-cent of the honey hives in the vinterberry fields back home. Home. That word stuck like a knife and was immediately sobering. The buzzing turned into a throbbing drone, and I sighed. Halfway to the kitchen, all the delight of the noct leached from me, and I turned to go back without a fresh bottle. Surely it was time to return to the keep, to the harshness of reality.

My steps stalled. Through a mercury looking glass hung on the wall in the hall, I caught a glimpse of the two women I'd left only moments ago in a more than passionate embrace. Rhapso moaned into Munnin's mouth, which she answered with a hungry-sounding whimper as Rhapso rose up and straddled the taller woman. Hands slid frantically beneath skirts, and bodices and breaths grew weightier. Quickly, I turned away; I didn't want to pry or intrude on their private moment any longer than I already had. Just because my fun had withered did not mean I should interrupt and deprive them of the little bit of joy they carved out of one another.

I snuck on silent feet into the kitchen and busied myself with washing the dishes left to wait in the sink with the crumbs of our cakes coating their delicately painted edges. Wistfully, as I swabbed suds from surfaces, I wondered what it would be like to have arms wrapped around me like that. An image flashed, watery and unbidden, of yesterdey, the way Kastor had leaned over me against the Fortress wall, his lips so blessedly close to mine. I let my lids flutter shut, and for the briefest of moments, I imagined myself tangled with him. Instead of filling me up with the hope and comfort I wished it to, the imagining left me feeling hollow, all too achingly empty, carved out by missing him.

Rhapso bustled into the kitchen, jolting me back from my wandering thoughts. I cleared my throat and busily searched for a drying cloth. Her cheeks were flushed, and her lilac eyes were wrapped in a sort of haze that I could only guess was lust. "Oh, Ertha, there you are. I was wondering where you'd gotten off to!"

"I came to get that bottle but ended up doing the dishes instead." I held up the dish in my hand a bit awkwardly, as if she couldn't already see with her own eyes.

She smiled at me, a touch crookedly. "Oh my. You are too sweet, dear."

Munnin swooped in behind our hostess and openly snaked an arm around the plump woman's waist. She smiled a smidge sloppily down at her lover, and I again abashedly looked away as they kissed.

After a moment, they disentangled themselves, and Munnin spoke. "Ertha, I think we do need to be getting back. It do be a long walk from here."

Cloaks were found and goodbyes exchanged, and then we were on the dark streets with Imbola blowing the kalda winds around the hems of our skirts and encouraging flurries to dust our lashes.

We walked in companionable silence for a time, the soles of our boots crunching softly on the crisp layer of fresh snow. Around us, the buildings stood stoic, silent in their sleep, windows dark and shuttered against the weather.

"So what did ye think," Munnin asked, her speech still honeyed like the mead we'd drunk, "of our little book club?"

"It was a beautiful noct. I haven't had that much fun since—" But the last time I'd had that much fun, it had ended in brutal bloodshed come dey break, and uttering a word about that noct or Helima felt like it would shatter the happy haze like a rock thrown through the paper-thin ice of a newly frozen pond. So instead, I veered my words into a different conversation. "If you don't mind me asking—"

"About me and Rhapso?" Munnin bumped me with the swell of her hip teasingly. Clearly, she'd been waiting for me to drop the bonds of propriety that said it would be rude to inquire after lovers and relationships.

My cheeks, already pink from the cold, deepend to a ripe rouge. "Yes."

"She do be the love of my life, my soul bound." Munnin's answer was soft and tender with a hint of wistfulness at the corners of her full lips.

"How did...how did you know she was the one for you?" My voice wavered, worried that my words would be too much of an intrusion.

She snaked her arm around the curve of my waist and rested her head atop mine with a sigh, our steps falling in time with one another against the ice and snow. "I did hear it from the Emrys, like a whisper on the winds the first time I did lay eyes on her. I did feel it in my bones, my marrow did become lightning from the Emrys Taranya. Her red hair did spill across her shoulders, slipped from her pins like a halo in Jyord's light, and I did want to fall to my knees and beg her there in the market to be mine."

"That sounds so...profound." The word fell flat even as it spelled itself out in misted breath before me. She made love sound like a religious experience that far surpassed any notions I'd conceived of it in my own mind.

"When two souls do be meant to be stitched to one another—when they do be bound—there is no thing that is more profound."

"Is it always like that? Love and intimacy?" The question slipped free before I could draw it back. It had been meant more as a query for myself to ponder and not as words I wanted spoken aloud to betray my inexperience.

But she drew us up short and put both hands onto my shoulders, leveling her serenely blue eyes with mine vehemently. "If feelings do fall short of ethereal and all-consuming, if they do no burn in your heart, then they do no be worth your time, Ertha. Ye do deserve someone who makes ye feel full of Selenyss's light, like ye did swallow her moon whole. Do ye understand?"

No, I didn't understand, not in the slightest, but that didn't mean I didn't want to. In fact, it was completely the opposite. I wanted to understand with a yearning intensity so sharp, it scared me like a knife to the throat. But I swallowed hard around its point where it pressed against my jugular and nodded.

Munnin smiled—it listed a bit sloppily and sappily. "Good." She released me, and we continued on, Imbola teasing the hems of our skirts. "That do no mean that feelings can't take time," she said after a moment. "Sometimes they do need to grow, but when they do, they do be just as fierce and fiery; sometimes they do be more so." She threw a wink that seemed almost conspiratorial at me, and I wondered if she knew of the secret feelings for Kastor that I kept buried. Then I wondered fleetingly if they would ever take root and grow, as she'd said, and blossom into something as beautiful as what she and Rhapso shared. But I snipped that line of thought in the bud; there would hopefully be no time for such amorous notions to sprout and go beyond flirtation, not when, Emrys willing, I would find a way to leave Uthar before kalda's end. Or sooner.

A few steps ahead, Munnin veered from the main road onto a narrower walk that wended between houses, likely used by the residents to cut the corners of the neighborhoods. Our prints were the first to break the fresh snow that coated footbridges over the canals, already covered in wafer-thin sheets of ice.

The huddled-together homes fell away as we stepped back onto a road wide enough for wagons and carriages to pass one another easily. Out of the shadows, larger buildings loomed with columned arches constructed of great stone slabs and chiseled panels along their walls depicting the lives and abilities of the Emrys worshiped within. It was hard to make out specific details in the muted gray hues of noct slashed through with the giddy snow that rode on the back of the billowing wind, but I was familiar enough with the concept. The temples back home near the palace were much the same.

A flicker of light snagged my gaze as I peered down the row of worship, a singular flaming beacon that looped its luminescence around my heart and pulled me to it like a moth. I could smell it already, the ink and aged parchment, the ground herbs. Home, it would smell like home. My feet began to move of their own accord.

"Ertha," Munnin called after me, her voice pitched to a low hiss, "where do ye be going?"

Chanting swelled along the streets as I drew nearer to the flame, no longer a moth but a ship drawn into safe harbor. "There's a light just there, a Selenyss Temple!"

I slid to a stop in front of the entry. It was different from the other places of worship dedicated to the lunar Emrys I'd encountered. Most were made from the nearly clear crystals mined from the icy cliffs of Iliff, painstakingly shipped in bricks. But this was made of a lustrous black stone I'd not encountered before, and into its surface, rather than standard carvings, were etched peculiar runes, whose meanings were indecipherable. But most perplexing of all was the strange, almost toothy-looking maw of a beast carefully ground above the lintel.

Curiosity cocked my head to the side. I took another step. It felt so achingly familiar, like missing something or someone that I didn't know was gone.

Munnin skidded—her feet stumbling—along the snow-slicked stones and into me, her breaths panted. It was only then that I realized I'd somehow ended up so far ahead of her. I must have been running to get here, but I didn't remember a whit of it. Munnin shook my arm, trying to pull me. "Ertha, do come away. It is no Emrys temple. It do belong to those who worship the others. Make haste. We do no want to be seen here."

"The others." My thoughts tumbled, transfixed on the sigil. What did she mean by *the others*? With stark clarity, it all cascaded into place. It wasn't a gaping mouth depicted on the entry but the inverse of Strattaria, the hollowed, mirror image of our world, which was in itself a replica of the great Emphyrea. It was the Umbra, which could only mean this was a sanctum devoted to the worship

of—I gasped, disbelief coating my words like the blue rot that grew on bread. "The Niflym."

"Aye, now let's go," Munnin hissed, panic a venom in her words. I took her hand and let her pull me away, even as my magic screamed to do the opposite. I shuddered and shoved it back into its place. Whatever perversion existed there, whatever it had done to lure me in, to twist and call my magic like that, I did not like it.

The alley dead-ended against the cliffs crowned with the Fortress but with no visible route to reach it. I shivered as the wind bit through the layers of fur that lined my cloak, and I clutched the front tightly as Imbola tried to pry it open—the wickedly teasing thing.

"I think if we double back that way, we might be able to get to the main road," I said, pointing to a shadowed path we'd passed a few paces back.

"No need. I do just need to find—ah, here it is." With a strangled screech, what had appeared to be stone only moments before swung open to reveal what looked to be a giant bird cage lodged in a hollowed-out shaft.

"What in the—" I nearly said Umbra, but somehow, the word seemed wrong and sour on my tongue after encountering the temple.

Munnin picked up my dangling sentence, filling the silence with an explanation. "It do be called a lift. Come now. Do get in."

I followed her lead and stepped onto the wrought grate floor of the cage—the lift. Munnin used a rope to drag the hidden stone door shut, plunging us into momentary darkness. But then, slowly, as if waking from a long slumber, the iron cage around us began to hum, to breathe, to pulse as liquid golden light trickled from the finial at its peak to coat the bars and seep across the intricate webbing beneath our feet.

"It do be a relic from a time before the Uthari, before the Fortress. Though not many do know of its existence, so do keep it a secret." She winked in the shimmering aureate light.

She rapped her knuckles against the enclosure, and it hummed with a sweet melody that made my magic want to dance with my heart in the cage of my ribs.

"I will. I swear it." I brushed my fingers reverently over the bars at my side. "I didn't know there was a time before the Uthari." I laughed as the lift jerked and slowly floated upward on a breath of magic.

She hummed softly and a bit sorrowfully to herself, and I thought for a moment that she wouldn't answer, but then she said, "There do be a time before everything."

I didn't know what she meant, whether she was still feeling the warm buzz of mead across her mind in that addling way it had, or if she was wandering through the tangled halls of a memory. Either way, it felt like silence was the best reply I could give.

The lift let us out behind a loose wall panel hidden beneath a worn tapestry depicting a sea battle between wolves and Mer. It was gruesome and had been relegated to decorating the forlorn halls deep in the bowels below the lesser court.

As we twisted and turned through the labyrinth of passages between it and the spiraling stairs leading to the nobles' apartments, I took careful note, discreetly pulling a rivulet of my magic into my fingertip, less than a thimble's worth, to score a mark along the stone corners of each turn. I would keep my promise to Munnin never to tell anyone about the tunnel, but not for her sake—for mine.

T HE BOOK I'D FOUND on the rickety bridge two nocts past was still saturated, its pages pink with diluted blood. I felt certain it seemed familiar in some way that I could not name. I had not noticed it in the hidden cabinet in the library, but that didn't mean it wasn't from the same trove. Blessedly, the ink bled only a little as I peeled the pages cautiously apart to fan them before the flames in my room. There were fanciful ink illustrations done with thousands of tedious pen strokes. Within many of them were the same pair of haunting eyes. Unfortunately, the passages were written in a dialect I was wholly unfamiliar with, with looping whorls, star-like symbols, and runes reminiscent of the ones etched into the bones the Seer had cast. I was fluent, as were all my sisters, in the tongues of the Seven Kingdoms. They were blessedly similar, being offshoots of the same mother language of the Emrys. But this was something intriguingly different. I could make out a few words here and there on the damp pages as I drew a finger across the lines, but I couldn't string together a whole sentence.

The root language appeared to be the same, but the variations reminded me of a time when my mother had divided a plant from the palace gardens for her sister to take home. She'd found later, when she'd traveled to visit my aunt, that when her sister had cultivated it, the weather conditions around Loch Elden had not only changed the color of the petals, but the rockier soil had changed the shape of the plant, as it had to grow differently to accommodate the less-free dirt, transfiguring it into what had seemed to be a wholly different plant.

A harsh knock startled me out of my reverie.

"Might I come in please?" Lord Fenris's voice rasped against the wood on the other side.

Thinking quickly, I shoved the book under the hem of my robe between the thick of my ample thighs and snatched up the discarded brush on the rug before the hearth, dragging its teeth through the snarls of my freshly washed hair. By the time I answered and he came in, I was the picture of innocence, simply a maiden drying her tresses by the fire after a much-needed bath.

I waited a moment to look up at him while he shut the door, but his frame filled the room like a shadow, and it was impossible to ignore him for long. He looked like he'd been dragged through the Umbra. Dark purple smudges marred the undersides of his already too dark eyes. His shoulders, usually straight with unwavering pomposity, were stooped ever so slightly. Healing often sapped people's energy just as much as the wounding. He should have been abed, and I told him as much.

He arched a black brow, his hair hanging loose and unbraided. "So should you. After all that has happened in the last deys." He folded his arms across his chest, and I caught a hint of a shimmer from the pale, swirling bonding mark where it snaked around his forearm. A clawing sense of remembering scraped its way along the back of my skull as I recalled what his hand had felt like on my skin, and I had to suppress the thought before a blush could slip over my cheekbones.

"I wanted to bathe." His eyes flicked across the fabric of my robe, deep sapphire, and lingered a touch too long where it knotted at my waist, but his coal eyes were impossible to read. Like curtains drawn over the windows of his soul, I could not look into them and take his measure. But the sensation of his eyes upon my skin and the phantom memory of his slumbering breath on my cheek made my whole body flush in a way that had me wanting to scrub it raw all over again.

"In light of what you did for me, I will not ask where it was you were when you came slinking back in and found me the other noct. I'm simply grateful you came back at all."

"You would have found me if I had not." I eyed him up and down, from his booted feet to his black-as-noct hair. "Though, considering your state, maybe you would not have and I was a fool. Either way, only the Emrys know now." And I prayed that one in particular knew what she'd been doing when she'd led me here, to him. He stood imposingly for a moment longer, like he had something more to say, but he shook his head. As he turned to leave, I stilled him with blurted words that I hadn't meant to speak, pulled from me before I could stop them. "Can I ask a question, as a...payment for services rendered?"

That gave him pause, and instead of continuing toward the door, he turned back and took a step closer to me, filling the gap between us with some unknowable sense of *other* that had my magic sitting up to eye him.

"I thought healing was blind?" He almost sounded—if I didn't know better—teasing. But I did know better. There was always a sharp and cutting edge to his words, even if I couldn't see it.

"That doesn't mean it is free," I jibed back as I toyed with the ties of my robe, fiddling idly with their ends, unsure why I was even walking this dangerous line of conversation. Maybe it was fatigue getting the better of me, maybe it was that I had so little to lose, maybe it was because I couldn't hold in my wondering any longer, because I had to know if I would suffer the same fate.

As if reading something in my expression, his face and his tone turned serious. No hint of teasing tinted his words now. "Did Kastor or the other Sons pay for your services?"

Instead of answering his vexing question, I immediately fired back, "Did you kill the other True Healer? The one who came before me?"

He froze, stiffened. Every muscle in his body rippled and radiated heated tension until it seemed to strangle the whole room. The fire, as if sensing his ire, chose that moment to devour a bit of pitch. Sparks crackled and shot. The tongues of the flames waggled, admonishing me for my audacity. Who was I to ask the predator why it had eaten the prey? The shadows grew sharper, like gnashing teeth. He took a looming step forward, his fists balled and white at the knuckles.

"Who told you that." His voice had a low lethality to its timbre that sent a ripple of terrified gooseflesh skittering across my skin.

I tried and failed to swallow the bitter coating of fear that stuck my tongue and refused to let me answer. "I...It...I just heard a rumor."

He reached down, fisting the fabric at the shoulders of my robe, and hauled me to my feet shaking loose a pitifully small shriek of fear as he drew me up to his eyeline. My feet kicked, toes unable to find purchase on the rug. My magic began to boil. It pressed itself into my veins just as I pressed my thighs together around the book wedged between them, willing it not to fall, not to let him see. "And did this rumor fall from the lips of that despicable excuse for a Son, Kastor?"

"Just because he won't kill, you call him despicable? Where I come from, that's called noble! His hands aren't stained red with the blood of the innocent like yours!" I regretted those words even as I said them. The visions of gore returned instantaneously; it poured off his hands and stained the soft, delicate fabric of my robe.

An insistent and muffled knocking echoed from the front door and plucked me from my hallucination.

His lips curled into a vicious sneer, and he dropped me to the tune of ripping seams and shredding fabric. I gasped and hurriedly covered my suddenly exposed breasts with the ruined remnants of my garment.

"You naive little girl," he growled.

"You ruthless, blood-hungry bastard," I yelled right back. "I'm sorry I saved your sad excuse of a life. Strattaria would have been better off without you in it."

That must have snapped something in him just as much as it snapped something in me. His brow bunched, and his jaw worked, chewing on words caught like sinew between his teeth. I'd never said anything so cruel before, even to someone who deserved it. I opened my mouth, not to apologize, but to—I wasn't sure what I was going to say, but it didn't matter. He spun on his heel, and instead of stalking out of my room like I'd expected, he strode toward my wardrobe, rifled through it for half a moment, and then stormed back and tossed a wadded-up ball of soft fabric at my feet.

"I'm sorry about your robe. I might have over-reacted. You can change into that one, and then I can set a few things straight," he grumbled through ground teeth, his jaw clenched so tight, I was surprised the words didn't crack bone.

The knocking against the apartment door came again and escalated into a furious pounding.

"What in the fucking Umbra." He ripped open my bedroom door and stormed out into the hall, to the main door, forcing back whoever stood there. The creak of hinges was followed by hushed and argumentative tones. I rushed to change into the fresh robe and secret away the book under the corner of my mattress before I darted after Fenris to see what was going on.

"Fucking Umbra, you will wait here, subordinate, or I will see you at the block," Fenris growled, his hands pressed into the frame of the door to bar whomever was on the other side from entry. Tension rippled across the set of his shoulders.

"I'm telling you, there is no time. Summon her now. I will take her myself if your pet giant can't tie his laces in time." I knew that voice, Kastor, but what was he doing here so brazenly?

I stepped to the side to gain a better vantage, hoping to see Kastor's face. "What's going on?"

"Ertha, thank the Emrys. You're needed right away. The Mother is having pains, and her lady says there is blood." Kastor wedged his foot between the door and the jamb as he shouted, his dark blond hair the only thing visible as he tried to shove his way through my keeper.

Fenris won the power struggle, shoving the Son back and slamming the door in his face. "You have not been invited in, Se'anier," he growled through the wood. He rounded on me with his cursedly black eyes. "And you. You're not going without a guard, and Huggin is out—"

"Kastor is a Son, is he not? He can guard me since Huggin is absent." I tipped my chin in a challenge.

Fenris growled, "Like fucking Umbra he can." He stomped down the hall toward his door. "I'll go with you. Get dressed. Quickly."

By the time I slipped into a shift modest enough to dash through the Fortress's corridors, with a shawl crossed over my chest and knotted at my back and a basket of healing supplies and herbs on my hip, Fenris was waiting out in the hall, dressed in his signature black from head to booted foot, twin swords crossed over his back.

I scoffed, "We're going to heal, not to war."

He stormed ahead of me to open the door. "In the Fortress, you never can be too sure," he groused as he ripped the door ajar hard enough to make the hinges protest. "After you, Kastor." Fenris spat his name like it left a foul taste in his mouth.

W E MADE AN ODD and silent trio as we trotted through the halls at a clipped enough pace that I had to hike my skirt. Kastor took the burden of my basket before we dashed across one of the iron bridges. His fingers brushed the bare skin of my elbow, and I had to suppress a shudder. Fenris's growl reached me thanks to an abrupt shift in the wind.

As we pressed on across the narrow bridge, I dared a glance back over my shoulder to find him staring directly at me, his dark eyes scraping across my face as lethally as the caress of a knife's edge. Umbra Damn me. Maybe I'd been wrong to heal him the other noct. Then again, maybe it was the only thing that kept him from tossing me over the edge of this bridge to rid himself of me.

The screams echoed down the walls, meeting us as soon as we stepped into the empty halls on the far side of the Fortress. There was no need for Kastor to guide me; my magic reached out to twist with the shrill, screeched notes of the Mother's screams.

In the Mother's bedchamber, pale-faced and horrified maids clung to the walls, their eyes wide and fingers trembling as they bore witness to the woman who leaned against her bedpost in a sheer shift, her unbound and matted golden hair a halo around herself as she roared her sorrow and pain into the noct.

I flicked my fingers, softly shooing the maids away, and approached the Mother cautiously. Bloodied towels knotted on the floor around her feet. I came to stand at her side. "I am here, Mother," I whispered in dulcet, soothing tones, addressing her as I would a scared animal.

A sob ripped from her throat. I only had a moment to steady myself as she turned and braced herself on me. Her arms slung around my neck and her hips sagged as another contraction gripped her body. I felt a wave of tension sweep through her, and I rocked her through it as she moaned against the hollow of my neck.

"It's too soon. It's too soon," she whimpered into my shawl as her tears soaked into the rough-spun wool. She tipped her chin to look up at me, and the full weight of the drowning tide of anguish and fear in her brown eyes threatened to overwhelm me and pull me under with her. I drew out more of my magic and used it to keep us afloat as her brow buckled, making it look as though the crown tattooed upon her forehead was cracked down the middle. "If I lose another, he'll get rid of me like he did his last wife. I can't lose another child."

Her words were like barbs snagging my attention, but I couldn't afford to be distracted now, so I plucked them and set them aside for later as I soothed a hand down her hair and let my magic ripple out and soak calmingly into her. "Tell me, Mother, when did you fall pregnant?"

She sniffled, labor stripping her bare, as it did all women, ripping away her regality and cruel arrogance. "Toward the end of byrthe, I think. My tidings have been irregular with so many babes come and gone from my womb."

Her fingers twisted in the looping knit of my shawl as another surging contraction gripped her. Her knees went lax as she leaned into it, her body instinctively releasing and opening as it should. Mentally, I calculated. If this babe was early, it was not by much—less than half a season, perhaps only by a quarter. Guiding my magic, I closed my eyes as she and I swayed together, riding out her pain, and delved into her body. In my mind's eye, I followed its silvery glow as it raced along the pathways of her body to her womb. I could sense the shape of the baby there until my magic slipped from my grasp, as if caught in an ill wind. But then, as the baby's heart began to glow in sharp, steady beats, I understood. My magic wasn't being pulled but was instead taking on a life of its own, mending and growing that which was not yet developed enough for survival outside of its mother's body.

A fluttering of a red-feathered fan on the far wall caught my eye. Against the mantel, the Emrys of death leaned indolently, dressed in a spill of frills that somehow managed to appear both elegant and deadly in appearance. She sneered at me, her painted lips curled in disgust. "It is an abomination, witchling, a perversion of nature. You would do better to hand its life over to me. It would be simpler for both you and her."

I shook my head, the movement slight enough that the Mother would not notice but apparent enough to make my defiance of the Emrys clear. Healing was blind. Whether this baby was an abomination as she'd said or not, it was still a life, an innocent, no matter who its parents were or what blood they'd spilled.

The Emrys tsked and sighed, snapping her fan shut. "I expected more obedience out of you, little witch." She stalked on dagger-sharp heels over to where I stood. Fear like the wriggling of worms in grave dirt twisted and writhed beneath my flesh as she bent to level her eyes with mine. "Do what you will with the mother and babe—waste your gifts on them, I don't care—but don't forget, you still must balance the scales. As above, so below."

Before I could untangle my tongue to respond, to beg for the clarification it seemed she would never give, she was gone yet again, faded into the shadows.

"I feel the eyes of Death upon me and my child." The Mother shifted off me, moving to the bed to rock on her hands and knees. "I cannot do this. We will not live!"

I recognized her woes—she was transitioning. Her whole body shook, her belly on her small frame squeezed tight as she roared through its convulsions.

I stood behind and kept contact with her, letting the cord between me and the baby pulse, letting it draw from me what it needed as I massaged her lower back, kneading it to help ease her burden. "Death is always watching births," I soothed. "But the Emrys Ananasa watches too," I reassured her, invoking the sacred name of the Emrys of fertility and birth.

With my hand pressed between the joining of her hips, I felt the baby shift, and in a gush of fluid, it descended. The mother rose to her knees, turned to face me, and tore her noct gown from her sweat-slicked skin.

"It's coming!" She panted her breaths, bleeding one into the next as she slumped onto me, her arms wrapped around my neck like my body was her only tether to this world.

She groaned, and I peered down through a gap in our tangled arms just as the head slid free. "You're doing great, Majesty. You're almost there. Your body knows what to do. Just lean on me."

She reached a hand down between us and let her fingers find the baby's crown, and then, with a final scream loud enough to herald the babe's arrival to the whole of the Fortress, she pulled her newborn free of her body and brought it to her chest with a heartbreaking sound of relief. "It's breathing. Oh, thank the Emrys. It's breathing."

The Mother crumpled into a protective shell around her baby, who let out a burbling cry. I fumbled for a blanket to cover them both in as she wavered on her knees, looking far more pale than I would have liked at that moment. I draped a pelt over her as I guided her to rest against the mound of pillows at the head of her bed.

"Have you checked?" I asked her softly.

She looked up at me dazedly. "Checked what?" Her voice was far off and dreamy as she gazed adoringly down into the face of her baby, tucked just out of the line of my sight beneath the edge of the fur.

I smiled. I'd see many a mother lost in that beautiful spun-sugar haze of fatigue and adoration as they looked upon the being they'd spent months sharing a soul with. It was one of my favorite parts of being allowed to attend a birth. Though, admittedly, it looked odd on a face that I'd only seen twisted in harsh and severe expressions.

"Do you have a little prince or princess?"

Her lips formed a stunned O, and she laughed. "I suppose I don't know."

I stifled a gasp as she peeled back the blanket, biting into my lip so hard, I drew sharp, metallic blood—the taste of it flooded my mouth. The babe on her chest was a deep ashen green with strange patches that resembled the skin of a snake beneath a thick coating of vernix. A crown of tiny, twisted horns, as black and polished as the stone of the Niflym Temple, protruded from its head, sprouting from beneath its thick tuft of golden green hair. Protesting the chill air, it waved a closed fist, its fingers tipped with wickedly sharp talons. I blinked, squeezing my eyes shut, and willed the vision to go away as the images of blood and bodies had when I'd imagined them, but when I opened my eyes again, the babe remained the same.

The Mother, seeming completely unphased, beamed as she prodded the babe's knees apart. "I have a daughter." A sob choked, snagged in her throat as she soothed a hand over her daughter's head. Her fingers deftly weaved past the horns as though they weren't there at all. "A beautiful little princess."

"Yes, Mother." I managed to squeeze the words out, barely a rasp between my lips. I tried to turn to go, but the Mother's hand ensnared my wrist.

"I misjudged you, Healer. I thought you no more worthy than the last." Her amber eyes muddied with tears as she gazed adoringly down at her daughter, whom I could hardly bear to look at. "You gave me her, and I will never forget it."

I bowed my head to avoid looking at her or the princess and dipped into a small curtsy. "As you say, Mother."

Her fingers slid from my wrist, and I was quickly forgotten in the coos of her infant. I busied myself—ghosting around the room, tidying the mess, and brewing a postpartum tea with healing and blood-building herbs over the large, ornately carved hearth—while I let the Mother bond and waited for the placenta to birth itself.

It wasn't long before it came in a gush. With a lit candle, I burned the cord, severing the Mother and princess. I carefully wrapped the placenta in thin muslin and was taking it to the hearth to burn, a tradition from home and one of the few familiar things that extended into Uthar, when the Mother called out, stilling my hand.

"Save that, just over there." She nodded toward a silver bowl hammered with wolves chasing one another around the rim that sat alone on a pedestal near the bedstead. "The Father will want to eat it like he did the others. Ooh, ouch! Oh, look, she finally latched, the sweet thing."

Barely contained chills danced across my bones as I laid the bloody placenta to rest in the bowl, and flashes of the Father with gore running down his chin as he savagely tore into the spent organ flickered like a noctmare through my mind.

Meekly, I went to the Mother's bedside to ask if I might take my leave, but all words died on my tongue when I saw the newborn contentedly suckling from the Mother's breast with blood pooling at the place where her mouth met skin. I choked on a gasp as the baby's latch slipped and I caught the barest hint of two little needle-sharp fangs. What in the Umbra had I helped bring into being? The damned Red Lady had been right. But no, I could not believe it would ever be wrong to save a life, especially the life of an innocent who did not choose her parentage or appearance.

"If you have no further need of me, I'll take my leave for now. I'll give one of your lady's maids instructions and come check on you middey tomorrow."

The Mother hummed softly, a tune I recognized, a lullaby, if I recalled correctly, but not a common one. "I think I'll name her Brisha, if he allows it."

"A beautiful name. I think it will suit her." I smiled, but it felt watered down, anything to get me out of this room that seemed to pulse and constrict, drawing all the focus to the princess and her unnatural presence, as if I'd drawn the gaze of all the Emrys with what I'd done. Or worse, as if I'd pulled the attention of the Niflym.

The Mother waved me away as she slid further into her bed to curl around her sleeping infant. Quickly, I gathered my things and ducked back into the hall, where Kastor and Fenris stood on opposite sides—I'd quite forgotten about them—along with a slew of other servants, who looked ready to knock me down to get into the room. They all took a step forward at once, and I raised a hand for silence and stillness.

"The Mother and her baby are both healthy." Not quite true, not with Brisha's condition, but I certainly wasn't about to be the messenger killed for spreading that bit of gossip. "They will need plenty of sleep, and the Mother will need to be well fed. I have here a list for the head of her ladies?" I withdrew a scrappy bit of parchment from the folds in my skirts and held it aloft.

A hook-nosed woman with pale, burnished-gold hair and wide eyes to match stepped forward in nothing but a dressing robe, her face slackened. "Is there truly a baby?" Her words were barely a gasp.

I nodded curtly. "There is. Now, if you are the head lady—"

The woman knocked the breath from my lungs as she lunged, wrapping me in a hug tighter than any corset. "Oh, thank you," she wept. "Thank you so much, Lady Healer."

The hall burst like a startled flock of birds into motion. Kastor replaced the lady, who had eagerly taken my list and then disappeared with haste into the Mother's bedchamber on swift, slippered feet. Kastor kissed my hand under the glaring, black eyes of Fenris, who was the only person not to move since I'd made the announcement. "I'll go tell the Father. Emrys bless you, Lady Healer." With a wink, Kastor was gone.

More praise and congratulations were heaped onto me, and I was helpless to fend it off and wholly unworthy of it. Would they burn me as they had all the witches before when they saw Brisha's face?

A firm arm wrapped around my stooped shoulders and steered me away. I glanced up dazedly to see Fenris. The crowd around us parted—all the gossip-hungry, eagerly grateful servants and ladies seemingly wary of the hulking man. But in this moment, I thanked the Emrys for Fenris's guidance in navigating away from the hoard. A flicker of red skirts tugged my sleepy eye, but blessedly, it was just the hem of a vibrantly dressed lady who hurried to the hall as the news seemed to spread like fire in a strong wind. And for a gut-twisting moment, I wished I'd spared the new mother the attention and said nothing.

It took me a moment to realize Fenris had spoken to me in a hushed tone. His words muttered, garbled and distant, pulled me like a hook and line from where I'd sunk deep into my reverie. "What did you say?" I furrowed my brow up at him.

He leaned in, his breath hot and harsh against the shell of my ear, and whispered more clearly this time, "The babe, was it wrong? Did it come out wrong?"

I blanched, and my feet stuttered over the threshold of the bridge. I didn't know what to say. A small part of me had hoped that maybe the baby's appearance was just another illusion brought on by my earlier argument with Fenris, the horror of the Niflym Temple, and too much drink with Munnin and Rhapso the noct before. But the grim set of his face as he took in my expression told me I was wrong. Fenris knew something, something wicked and twisted and important. I could see it shining in the dark of his depthless eyes. But before I could wrap my thoughts together enough to form a question, to ask him what he knew, we were at the apartment door, and he stalked away, my silence apparently all the confirmation he'd needed that there was indeed something wrong with the babe.

As I wearily shut my door behind me and pressed my spine against the rigid wood, I recalled where I'd heard the tune the Mother had hummed with stark and painful clarity so sharp, it stole my breath like a knife to the lungs. It was a despairing melody, one sung in warning to children to keep away from the Blackwood and the prowling wolves of Uthar.

Steer clear of the Blackwood, oh dear one

Oh dear one
For within them, the wolves make their home
Make their home
Teeth like knives
You'll become their hungry prize
Should ever you stray far from your home
From your home

I sunk to the floor, weighed down with exhaustion and worry. I had indeed strayed so very far from my home. As if to punctuate my woe, a howl cut through the noct to gnash its teeth against my shuttered window, and I had half a mind to let it in so it could sink its teeth into my heart and end this torment.

G RAY CLOUDS OBSCURED THE Emphyrea above me as I sank my hands into the surprisingly still-warm and moist soil of the gardens. I'd closed the workshop for the dey and left a notice I was only to be disturbed in an emergent situation. The innovative nature of the garden left it thriving even though kalda was well past its beginning. The snow that had fallen on the noct of Brisha's birth had not only stuck, but had slowly accumulated, frosting the tip of every turret in a dense layer of snow that shimmered like precious gems in the kalda light, but here, in the sanctuary of the garden, it was no cooler than an early byrthe dey.

Huggin had taken over my Forms training, which nettled me to no end. In fact, after our first session, and insisting so wholeheartedly that I perform those humiliating movements each dey, Fenris had yet to attend any breakfast. I'd not seen him since the noct of the birth, and while his presence was unsettling, his absence was equally if not more so. I didn't like thinking on what he might be getting up to while he was away, though my mind seemed to have no trouble spinning noctmares while I slept; they fed like flames on the imaginings I suppressed during the long deys of working.

Half the people I'd tended to in the few deys since the princess's birth had just been eager to get a bit of gossip. The announcement of her arrival had been tolled throughout the city at the dawning of the dey by every bell. Now, they came with minor scrapes and phantom pains just for a chance to gawk at the Healer who had helped the Mother birth a living heir at long last. An heir who I was happy to say was growing, hale and healthy. Though her coloring and her appetite for blood and milk disturbed me. And her eyes—I shuddered as I thought of them—they'd tracked my every movement around her mother's rooms, though she was far too young to be capable of such. I tried not to wonder too hard if I'd done something with my magic to accelerate the development of her mental acuity, or about the knowing that had been in Fenris's eyes as he'd asked me about the babe's...condition.

I shoved all thoughts aside as the herbs in front of me reached out through their roots and tangled with the thin, flowing filaments of my magic that I'd tediously trained to twine through the rich dark soil.

As weary as I'd been at each dey's end, I'd been taking the time to sit in front of the fire and practice drawing and sheathing my magic. Pulling it out was the easiest, putting it away was—to put it mildly—much more difficult. It was odd, the way my magic acted. I'd had a masterful control over it when I'd simply thought of it as my healing gifts, but as soon as I'd acknowledged what it was, it had seemed to take on a life of its own. Begrudgingly though, I had to admit the breathing exercises learned during the Forms had helped greatly, and though I was far from a master, I'd already regained some semblance of the control I'd once had.

For what purpose do you need us? the foliage asked through our magical connection, and I couldn't help but smile. It wasn't so much in words that it spoke, but my magic seemed to do the work of translating the plant's feelings. I closed my eyes and sent it images and sensations of what I needed to harvest it for. This particular shrub was excellent for lowering fevers when put into a tonic with its cousin plant, and it would be of great use when the usual kalda illnesses made their rounds. I could sense the exact moment it understood. With my permission, it consumed the essence of my gifts like fertilizer, drawing it into itself so it might thrive and strengthen the qualities I needed from it.

"Incredible."

I jerked my hands from the dirt and spun to face Kastor, who leaned, indolent as always, against the trunk of a nearby tree.

"I swear by the Emrys, that plant perked up just with you nearby. You have a touch, it seems, with all living things."

I forced a laugh. Charming or not, Kastor was still a Son, and I couldn't risk him discovering I had witch magic—not just the rare healing abilities I'd been dragged here for.

"The monks back home always said that if you talked to your plants and told them what you needed from them, they would provide. I like to think that's true, so I thought I'd give them a bit of extra attention while I harvested." Not a lie. They had said that at the temple, but they'd certainly never intended it this way, I was sure. "Is there something I can help you with? Not that I'm not happy for your company, but Huggin isn't far, and—"

Kastor stepped forward. The tufted wolfskin around his shoulders added to his imposing height as he towered over where I knelt. He held up a hand wrapped in a blood-soaked bandage. "I know your workshop sign said emergencies only, but I was hoping you would make an exception, and, well, if I'm being honest, I wanted to see you." He raised a wicked eyebrow, and the corner of his sinful lips curled. "Seeing you on your knees now—that was an unexpected added pleasure, and one I won't forget for a while."

If I hadn't been blushing before, his words surely painted my skin as red as the Emrys of death's skirts. "Well," I said breathily as I rose and dusted the dirt from my hands, "I'll make an exception, just this once."

"You're a wonder, Ertha." He breathed into my hair as I took his hand and stood closer to him than was strictly necessary. The heat of his body curled around me as though claiming me. I unwound the bandage and exposed a deep but clean cut slashed right across the cup of his palm. With my magic still coursing through my veins, it was barely a thought to mend it in a single sweep of my glowing, argent fingertips.

"Ah, that's better. I'm rather fond of my right hand." He twisted his wrist and captured my hand in his. It swallowed mine wholly. "Thanks for healing it—I'll make sure to put it to good use." He squeezed my hand and winked.

A ripple of heat, spurred and intensified by my magic, rushed through my body as the image of him with his cock fisted in the palm I'd just healed washed through my thoughts. Fucking Emrys, what was wrong with me? Such thoughts were preposterously inappropriate.

He tucked a loose strand of hair away from my face and back under my veil that I'd taken to wearing again despite Munnin's disapproving looks. "Congratulations, by the way, on saving the babe. I know the Father and Mother sleep more soundly knowing they have an heir to their kingdom. It is truly an Emrys-blessed miracle. I know the former Healer tried, to no avail."

Another blush danced across my cheekbones. I'd been complimented on my success hundreds of times over already, but somehow, the praise felt more solid from him, like a giddy brush of a feather down my spine. "Yes, well, I attribute it to the Emrys of luck." I stilled as my thoughts caught on something he'd said. "If you don't mind me asking, how many babes has she lost?"

He rubbed a hand along his beard thoughtfully. "Twenty, give or take. They didn't announce every one, but I know there have been many, early and late."

If the former Healer had been anything like myself, that must have driven her halfway to insanity. I recalled her detailed archive in the workshop along with the singular tome I'd taken to my room and wondered if she'd dared to put to paper whether or not there was anything peculiar about the lost babies' appearances.

Kastor hooked my chin and drew my face toward his. "Where did you go in that pretty head of yours, Ertha?" He took a step closer so our bodies were flush against one another. The press of him was so much—it was everything it shouldn't be.

"Just thinking that you owe me a favor for doing this for you on my dey off," I said teasingly, unable to look at him as infernal waves of heat surged with the song of my magic through my blood and crashed into my core.

"I owe you more than one—I owe you everything." His hand left my chin and slid around my waist, pinning me to himself. He placed our tangled fingers on his chest in the exact place I knew he still bore the mark of the intense healing I'd performed on him, and my breath caught, lost somewhere between my lips and my lungs. "It's my fault you're here. If you hadn't stopped to heal me, you might have gotten away, and it eats at my heart each dey I wake whole. Let me make it up to you, Ertha. On Eklipsis Eve, come to me at the ball and I'll make it more than worth your while." Kastor stroked a hand up my spine.

Chills skittered and eddied across my skin in the wake of his touch as my thoughts swirled headily. I willed my mind and my lips to cooperate long enough to answer him. "Yes, I will."

Kastor's lupine grin melted me as he dipped his head low and seared a kiss onto my forehead as he wrapped me in a tight, possessive embrace. I squealed as he picked me up, spun me, and pressed my back into the tree he'd been watching me under. He ground the evidence of his lust for me into my lower belly, pinning me to the bark with it. He bent his head. The scrape of his beard along my neck was nothing to the nip at my earlobe. My eyes rolled as the sensations compounded and dropped to my groin, where they pulsed in time with the achingly swift beat of my heart.

"I'll be thinking of you tonoct, Ertha. Will you be thinking of me?"

I couldn't find words. All my thoughts tripped and stumbled again over that image of him finding his pleasure to the best of my imagining, which, admittedly, was lacking a bit. I didn't know what that would look like, not to completion. But Emrys damn me—against all reason that seemed to have long fled my mind, I wanted to know. All I could manage in reply to his words was a whimper and nod.

"That's a good girl," he growled, his words near feral, the glint in his gaze sharp enough to cut eye teeth.

Footsteps scuffed along the stones and echoed softly nearby. "Huggin is coming. You had better go." Worry pushed the words breathily past my lips, but Kastor's curled into a snarl, and his hand fisted the fabric at my hip.

"I'm tired of sending you back to him, Ertha. I'm tired of smelling him on your skin." His words scraped along my heart.

I placed a gentle palm against his cheek. "I know, but we will have Eklipsis, I swear it. But only if we don't get caught before then."

That seemed to calm him to some degree. He nodded once, short and curt, and then he was gone, leaving me breathless and so swamped with lust that I could do nothing but stare blankly at the place where he'd been.

Magic still sparkled just beneath the surface of my skin as I shut the door to my chamber behind me. I couldn't let it go; I didn't want to let it go, not when it hummed and filled the empty echo of Kastor pressed against me, not when I knew that reality would come crashing back the instant I put it to bed. And at the moment, I did not want to hear reality's logic. I did not want it to remind me that I had no reason to trust Kastor, that no matter his kindness and good intentions, he was and would always be a Son. I wanted to bask in the radiant feelings just a bit longer. I wanted to savor this feeling of connection that made the press of my skin feel too tight around my bones.

I sat against my headboard and tried to pick up my sewing, but just the simplest brush of fabric along my skin seemed somehow tantalizing with this much power coursing through my blood and drumming its way along my nerves. I let the embroidery slip from my grasp and land with a soft thump on the floor. Trailing my fingers along my feet to catch up the hem of my dress, I languidly skimmed my calves, up past my knees, and over the swell of my thighs until my skirts were bunched at my hips. I tilted my head against the wooden bedstead at my back and let my eyelids flutter closed. In my mind, I let my magic bring to life the image of Kastor as I'd imagined him in the garden, his naked body beautifully scarred and kissed by the rays of Jyord's sun.

The rap of knuckles on my door wrenched a gasp from my lips as I hurriedly shoved my skirts back into place. My keeper crashed into the room like a dark flame, consuming and devouring the lust and peace I'd felt only a heartbeat before. My magic reared its head from its place by my heart and hissed.

"Put your boots on. We have to go. Now." He grabbed them from where I'd shucked them off by the door and threw them at me. They punched me in the stomach.

"Typically, when someone knocks, they are supposed to wait for a reply before barging in," I ground out through gritted teeth as I half rose from my spot on the bed to glower.

He glared back, his blackened umber eyes narrowing and chafing against my skin with a look that seemed to say that prisoners were the exception to propriety.

I sighed, my magic still spitting frustratedly as I grabbed my boots and pulled them on with a petulant slowness. "Where are we going in such a hurry?"

"You'll find out when we get there. I'm not even certain I'll have need of you, but bring your supplies just in case." He peered around my room, his arms crossed infuriatingly as I gathered what I might need. He sniffed the air, actually sniffed it, his nose wrinkling slightly as though I'd somehow managed to foul the room just by occupying it.

I went to my wardrobe and slipped on a dark, fur-lined cloak. I side-eyed Fenris to see what sort of weather he was dressed for and balked. Somehow, as I'd been jolted from the heady haze of my imagined encounter with Kastor, I'd missed the swords at his back and the knives strapped to his thighs over dark fighting leathers and a black leather breastplate.

"Quit eye-fucking me, Shepherdess. We don't have the time. You'll want those." He nodded to the gloves that hung limply from my dimly glowing fingertips and frowned.

"I-I was—you're a bastard." I hurled the insult weakly and to little effect.

"Why are your fingers lit up like the star stones?" He stormed over to me. His frame filled my vision and seemed to suck all light and color from the room with his devastatingly imposing stature.

"None of your business," I spat, though with much less venom and far more defensiveness than I'd intended.

He leaned down, leveling his sharp gaze with mine like an adult chiding a child. "It is my business when your damned hands are a beacon in the noct that could draw unwanted eyes." He scowled and took another step closer, further invading my space with his looming presence and filling it with the smell of him.

I shoved my hand into a glove, letting the tightly spun wool extinguish the luminous quality of my magic. Snappishly, I waved it in front of his face. "No light, see? Nothing to worry about, and thus, none of your business."

A growl formed behind the apple of his throat as he straightened. He didn't let it pass his lips, but the feel of it hummed along the narrow space between us as he righted himself. His thick hands grabbed at the belt on my waist and unhooked the buckle in sharp jerks.

"What in the Niflym—" I said breathily as my magic swooped in my low belly, reacting to his touch like butterflies scrambling for a spot on a nectar-heavy shrub.

Fenris pressed a free finger to my lips, and for a flickering second, I had the inexplicable urge to dart my tongue out and let it skim across the pads of his skin, to know what he tasted like. Instead, I bit it. What was wrong with me?

"I wouldn't invoke their names tonoct if I were you, Shepherdess." His dark gaze bored into mine like he was trying to scry my eyes and divine my thoughts—or perhaps leave some wicked ones of his own in his wake.

He pulled a scabbard from beneath his leathers and slid my belt through its loop. I shivered and bit back a gasp as his thumb brushed along the curve of my waist and sent a jolt of pins and needles like fire through the ink of my bond that lay just below the cloth of my dress, now spread so far, it nearly spiraled all the way to my hip. Did *his* curl around the prominences that were his hip bones, or did it go further?

I shoved the notion from the forefront of my thoughts and stuffed it deep into the dark recesses of my mind. I was just riled up from seeing Kastor earlier, a strong breeze could have stirred a tempest to life beneath my skirts. It had nothing to do with my keeper or the way he looked at me as I challenged him.

"And why not 'invoke their names?'"

Jerking the belt back through the buckle, he cinched it down hard, as if to punctuate his next words. "Because Selenyss forgot to rise."

My magic stilled, recoiled. "Dark deeds will be done this noct," I whispered.

It was an old legend—a fishwife's and farmwife's tale—that through fissures in the stone and soil, the Niflym could sometimes slip their magic through the cracks, but only on deys or nocts that the Emrys shed no light. The stories surrounding the events were on the edge of heretical, only accepted by some, one of whom had been my childhood governess. She'd believed them so thoroughly that I'd absorbed them into my young impressionable soul, so much so that I had not slept without a candle until I'd been forced to when I'd gone to the temple.

"They will by many, but without a doubt by the Sons who we will accompany." Fenris turned to head for the door, his bootsteps eerily silent across the hewn blackwood planks. The absence of sound shook loose a shudder from where it coiled around my spine. Before I could ask if that included him, which was ridiculous, because of course it did, he paused at the threshold. Looking over his shoulder, he jerked a nod at the scabbard he'd just slipped onto my belt. "Do you know how to use that?"

"I can manage." I chewed my lower lip. Much like the other knife I'd taken to keeping strapped to my thigh, I knew in theory where I could stick it in flesh to make someone bleed or cease to breathe, but it went against everything I stood for, everything I was as a Healer. If I took a life, what would I be?

Fenris nodded, his brow furrowed as he seemed to mull that over. "Just do exactly as I say and keep that mouth of yours shut, and hopefully that won't matter." Then he spun, his dark braid swaying between the twin swords crossed at his back, and left, expecting me to follow. I hooked my healer's basket into the crook of my elbow and did just that.

FENRIS LEFT HIS DAPPLED gray warhorse with a hostler near the docks, where the ships swayed like sleeping, lumbering beasts. I wished I'd learned how to sail as I eyed the smaller skiffs and one-man fishing boats tethered to the docks only by ropes like leashed dogs. I looked down at our entwined hands, my own throbbing with the silver-etched bonding as if reacting to my proximity to him. I knew that even if I'd known how to sail, it would have been worthless with him permanently tethered to me.

We ducked into an alcove made of stacked barrels. Branded on the side of one at eye level, barely visible in the ominous dark, was the burned insignia of the Ochrai. My heart curled up and wept, nuzzled against my liquid pool of magic as the image pulled long-forgotten memories from the dusty recesses of my mind. The sigil stitched on the breast of a young redhead with sparkling violet eyes that seemed to be permanently crinkled with laughter as it rang like a bell through the halls of the Selenyss Temple. Eyes that haunted my sleep as they looked past me toward the Red Lady, who fed my friend words to prophesy to me even as she waited to collect her soul. My palms slickened with the memory of Helima's blood on them, and when I looked up at Fenris for a stuttered blink, I could see a bloodied handprint smeared across his cheek as though my hallucination was tempting me to smear her phantom blood across his face.

I blinked back to reality as, with a flourish, Fenris pulled out a cloak—so dark, it could have been made from webs of spun noct cut from Melantha's skirt—from within the depths of his own. He slung it over my shoulders, over the fur-lined one I already wore, and drew the deep cowl over my head. It sent my magic into a surging frenzy.

"No one will see you in this. For all intents and purposes, you will be invisible to the naked eye, invisible to everyone but me. You stay on my heels and you stay silent no matter what you see, understand?" With a slip of his fingers across my cheek, he brushed my Selenyss-bright hair behind my ear, tucking it deeper into the recess of my hood.

I shivered, his touch knotting my tongue as his hand lingered on my cheek, and nodded dumbly.

"I need to hear you say it, Shepherdess." His words purred softly through the cramped space as the sound of boots and the unmistakable din of swords thundering against shields ran by without taking notice of us.

"I understand," I whispered on the back of a forced breath as fear tried to wring my lungs of air.

In all my wildest imaginings, I'd never dreamt I would ever be on an infamous Uthari ship, and now, in a span of deys that added up to less than a quarter of a season, I would be forced onto a second. This time with not an inkling of where we were going or why—into the Umbra, for all I knew. Fenris's hand fell from my face, leaving a cold hollow where he'd been as he bled out of the alcove and into the noct.

I tipped my chin to the Emphyrea as I ghosted along the wharf, dogging Fenris's long strides as I cast my eyes around in search of Selenyss, but I could find not even a hint of her shine. Even the star stones seemed to dim without her to gaze upon with adoration.

My magic burned beneath my skin as the vessel came into view in the flickering glow of spitting, angry torch flames. It was much smaller than the ship we'd made the crossing on, but it still had the vicious wolf's head carved above the blackwood keel. In addition to the sail and mast, oars stuck out from the sides like the skittering legs of a venomous spider hiding beneath the bedsheets until it was too late.

Sons busied themselves on deck, settling into oarsman positions and lashing shields to the sides of the longship's hull. I swayed on my feet as my magic thrashed against my ribcage with a bruising ferocity that tangled with terror in a destructive and nauseating dance.

"Good of you to join us, my lord." Ingemar's sneered tone spilled like lantern grease all over the docks and threatened to ignite with the sparks of loathing in his eyes as he looked Fenris up and down like he was a bit of shit stuck to his favorite boot.

"I thought it was Kastor who was supposed to head this little mission tonoct, Commander." Fenris crossed his arms, seemingly unphased by Ingemar's hostility. It was strange; they'd seemed so in step when it came to kidnapping me. Had it been the decision to award Fenris the permanent position of my keeper that had driven such a wedge between the Father's favored? Odd, unless they were less favored than they seemed.

"It was, but when I heard you wanted to join in on this little outing, I thought it best that I come along in his stead. I wouldn't want any Sons unnecessarily lost on the way." The words were saturated with unspoken implications that I didn't even want to begin to unravel.

"You shouldn't have inconvenienced yourself, you old dog." Fenris laughed like they were the best of friends, but it sounded wrong; I'd heard him laugh with Huggin, and this was nothing like that. He clapped the man on the back, then strode up the gangplank.

I kept close to his heels and timed my steps to match his as best as I could. When I landed a moment after he did on the deck, he covered the sound of my boots on the wood with a cough, not that it was necessary; the men created enough of a ruckus as they shifted and settled.

Fenris made a show of nodding and greeting Sons on the way to the stern, their faces streaked and painted with black and bloody crimson. He paused to talk to the Son at the steering oar, someone he called Jeric, with a clean-shaven head nicked twice over with scars and paint smudged so thickly over his eyes, it looked like a death mask worn by the priests in the Red Lady's temples.

I shuddered. I didn't want her eyes on me this noct, not without Selenyss's watchful gaze. The Red Lady, though she was an Emrys, had always been the fulcrum, balancing the darker and more terrifying powers of the Niflym with the glorious and creative gifts of the Emrys. She belonged to both and neither, but she was necessary and essential to the balance of existence. I didn't know what she wanted me for, but she'd already done enough meddling to get me to Uthar for some purpose, to balance the scales—whatever that meant.

Something about the way my magic wriggled, unsettled in my gut, told me the last thing this mission needed was her interference.

The flick of my keeper's wrist caught my attention. He pointed to the little hollow made of canvas stretched and tethered to the gunwale on both sides of the ship that seemed to be for housing supplies. I took his silent meaning, that I should shelter out of sight there, and did just that. I tediously picked my way around baskets and barrels without disturbing them. I crouched down and did my best to make myself comfortable while I prayed to the Emrys that wherever we were headed, it would be brief and that I would return whole. Between the bits of cargo, I caught Fenris looking at me, I felt his strange eyes scraping over the curves of my silhouette, and I shuddered. I said no prayers for his safe return.

The drums thundered in a crescendo with the chants of the Sons. Their voices were the baying of wolves on a hunt. It turned my blood to ice. I let my magic thread itself around every bone and muscle fiber in my body. I clung to it just as much as it did to me, like a child clinging to a favored blanket when noctmares lurked from under their beds and imagined monsters threatened to drag them by their ankles into the Umbra.

The ship hit land, the scrape of the hull ricocheting up my spine. I peered out of the cramped and narrow space I'd tucked myself into, my teeth chattering from the spray of the Yaenos Sea as it surged and spit spindrift over the side of the longboat. I found Fenris, my eyes drawn to him in the crowd. I watched him with a sickening churning in my belly as he stirred the Sons with shouted promises of spilled blood and glory right alongside the Commander. With a brutal quickness, the Sons took up their arms. They donned their legendary lupine helms and howled like the feral monsters they were before they charged in a single pack down the gangplank. I pressed a hand over my mouth to stop the sobs of agony that threatened to reveal me as I watched the horror that had happened to my people from the opposite side of the coin.

Fenris looked at me, his Niflym-cursed eyes impossibly locked on mine as he mouthed, "Stay here," before he drew his swords and took off a half a step behind the Commander and their loyal hounds.

I waited, counting the beats of my heart until I was sure the men were far enough away for it not to matter, then stumbled—my legs more cushions for pins and needles than useful appendages—out of my hidey-hole. I raced to the prow for a better vantage to see whose lives they were ripping to shreds wrapping an arm around the figurehead for balance and peered at the island, no bigger than a spit of rocky land. It didn't make sense; there was nothing here, just a cave. I sank to my knees as I watched the shadowed forms of the Sons converge on the gaping maw of stone, and I wracked the deepest recesses of my mind for half-remembered images of maps. *Where in the Umbra could we be?* We'd not sailed long; if we returned soon, we would be back before deybreak. I looked up at the Emphyrea, but without the moon, it was more difficult to get my bearings. I'd never been good with the names of the star stone clusters or the peaks, which looked indistinguishable with the spindling cloud cover. If our heading had been south, then this could be an Iliffian trading post. But if we'd gone north...My heart raced, spurred faster by my fretful magic. No, not even the Father would have dared attack Posidonia's Gate, would he?

Recklessly, without thought or hesitation, I threw myself from the prow. I landed with a splash, the salty water instantly soaking my skirts and making them leaden. But that didn't matter; nothing mattered as I raced for the rocky arch. Screams sailed across the noct air and broke across my heart. An emerald glow of flickering firelight flared from within the cave and illuminated, with heartrending clarity, the carved and sinuous forms of two Mer inlaid with pearls, shells, and coral—now spattered in blood. Posidonia's Gate: the surface entrance to the Mer Kingdom and sacred temple of Orannus, Emrys of the oceans.

The sand tried to slow my steps as if in warning as I stumbled forward. I had to help. There had to be something I could do. I was a Healer, but I was also a witch, the last witch. Power sang through me, so much power. It wanted me to use it; it urged me on. Damn the consequences, damn my soul—I would kill them. I would kill them all.

The too familiar form of Fenris charged out from beneath the arch. My magic pooled in my palms, a raging tempest, ready to leap from my fingertips and maim, but then my eyes caught sight of the way his gait stilted and listed. I scraped my gaze across his body and lowered my hands as I noticed a limp form cradled in his arms.

His face burned like dark vengeance as his eyes landed on me. "What the fuck," he seethed under his breath as he crashed to the ground before me. "Can you ever just fucking obey, Shepherdess?" He laid his burden down, and I gasped.

It was a Mer, her beautiful blue-green skin marred by a vicious and violent slash right between her bare breasts. Her breaths rattled as she reached up to touch Fenris's cheek with her webbed fingers.

Mer were reclusive, and I'd never had the opportunity to see one so close. It was only when Fenris spoke that I realized I was sitting dumbstruck at the sight of her. "Damn it. I brought you here for her, to heal her. Now, can you do it or not?" he repeated more loudly. Frustration and sharp panic edged his words enough that they cut to the quick.

"I-I can try." I tripped over my words as my eyes darted from the Mer female to the blood-stained hilts of Fenris's swords peeking out over his shoulder. What madness was this? No. There was no time to question, not when my magic sparked at my fingertips, already reaching to delve into her body and mend.

The female smacked my hands away weakly. "No, do not waste your magic on me, daughter of the mountains. There is nothing you can do."

"You don't know that. Let me try."

She shook her head and unclenched her other hand. Nestled in it was a fan-shaped shell as blue as the sea on a calm, sunny dey. "But I do...I have...seen." Her words were garbled, leaching into the bubbling and frothing blood in her chest. "Take this...Keep it well."

I plucked the shell from her palm in trembling fingers overburdened and humming with magic.

"But what is it? Why does it need to be kept safe?" I tried to ask, but her lids slid shut over her dewy eyes and her chest failed to rise again. It was too much, too vividly reminiscent of Helima's death that I choked on it. My hand fisted around the shell. The rolling, scalloped lip of it bit into my palm, and my magic shivered, caressing the edge of my anger, coaxing it into rage.

Fenris took hold of my shoulders and shook me, his face pressed so close to mine that his words kissed the tip of my nose. "Get back to the ship, Shepherdess, right fucking now."

I met his depthless eyes. "What's the point?"

"So you don't fucking die too, you fool woman," he ground out through gritted teeth.

The echo of riotous cheers spilled from the cave's entrance, and I stilled. It was too late to move now. Fenris righted himself and waited for the blood-spattered Sons to meet him where we stood on the beach. They bandied about congratulations to one another as they hoisted blood-stained tro- phies and severed heads. One of the men mimed fucking one so vividly, I had to squeeze my eyes shut to keep from vomiting as they made their way back to the boat.

Ingemar was the last of them. He stopped, his boot heel pinning my shadow cloak to the ground, and in doing so, pinning my heart to my throat as well. I looked from it up to Fenris, as if I could will him to do something, but he didn't bat a single black eyelash in my direction. Fear strangled the air in my lungs.

"Did you find it?" Fenris rasped, his words heavier than the blood-soaked sand that seeped into my skirts beneath my knees. I gave the cloak hem a little tug, but it didn't budge.

Ingemar ran a bloody hand over his face, leaving behind a trail of scarlet streaks. "No. The fishy bastards must have moved it after the raids on the other temples."

That caught my attention. How many temples had they raided, and why? As I tucked that away, it had the feel of a puzzle piece that I just needed to find the right space for.

"We'll find it." Fenris's face was stoic and impassive as he watched Ingemar pick up his boot to toe the limp body of the Mer female. I snatched the wispy fabric out of his range.

"Good hunting this noct, my lord. How many was it you killed?" Ingemar asked, condescension smeared all over his words.

I didn't wait to hear the answer, instead I backed away silently, using a trickle of magic to stop the shift of sand under my feet and keep my steps silent lest I be discovered and join the Mer in death. I looked back once as I met the edge of the teeming waves to find the eyes of the Red Lady on me from where she stood shoulder to shoulder with my keeper.

She leaned on his arm, her blood-lacquered nails grazing the leather of his armor as she bent to retrieve the soul of the Mer. For a moment, I thought I would see him flinch at her touch, but then she straightened, threw me a vicious wink, and was gone as if blown away on an ill wind riddled with the stench of stale bones and old blood.

The trip from the docks back to the Fortress had been a silent one, filled with the tension of Fenris's feathering jaw and the clomp of his furious footsteps across floors and stairs as we ascended to the apartments. He opened the door with a white-knuckled hand. I turned softly like a wraith in a graveyard to slip toward my bedroom, but Fenris called over his shoulder even as his feet never stopped moving, "No. Come with me."

I hesitated, my lip caught between my teeth, my hand caught in the air above my bedroom door latch. I didn't want to follow him, but his too calm, quiet demand had such an edge to it, it sent sparks of skittering unease through the bond. So, reluctantly, I obeyed.

As the doors to his private chamber slammed shut behind me, exhaustion threatened to drag me to the floor and pin me there under its ruthless thumb.

"Why exactly can't I go to my room, my lord?" I tried to spit his title with venom, but my heart wasn't in it, not after the noct I'd just had with dey creeping over the horizon, taunting me.

I followed him, trailing his steps as he strode over to his desk just adjacent to a sitting area by his hearth—not unlike mine, though in place of a settee, he had two solitary leather chairs. I drifted to the hearth, drawn by the comforting warmth of the amber flames, as Fenris shucked his gloves and withdrew his weapons, tossing a surprising number of blades onto the surface of his desk from places I didn't even think one could put knives. It might have been impressive if I wasn't so cursedly tired.

His hands shook as he let the last weapon fall, and he rounded on me, stalking over to where I hovered, my hands outstretched over flames that suddenly seemed to grow and writhe, somehow deepening the shadows in his dimly lit room instead of casting further light. His eyes glinted, the reflection of the fire caught in them as he reached for me. His hand gruffly grasped my chin in a gentle yet unyielding grip and forced me to face him. Something in the twist of his features dropped the image into my mind of barely leashed feral beasts gnashing their teeth with fury.

"Do not disobey me like a willful child again, Shepherdess, or I will be forced to turn you over my knee and punish you like one." The threat sent a deep and aching flutter of ardor along the pulsing lines of my veins and the humming of my magic. Fenris's nostrils flared, his calloused thumb sweeping beneath my lower lip as he leaned in, his breath kissing my jaw as he growled, "Next time I tell you to stay put, I expect you to listen."

He relinquished his hold on me, and mortification swept in on the rampant heels of the fiery yet brief and shameful desire I'd felt. It had to have been the fatigue that had mixed and muddled my emotions. How dare he speak to me in such a way that twisted what should have been loathing into lust? In a rush of unfettered wrath, my palm swept up and connected with the stubbled plane of his face below his cheekbone. His head whipped to the side. The echoed crack of hand meeting flesh fell between us and was quickly gobbled up in a woosh of skirts as he caught my wrist and yanked me against his chest.

"Don't you understand, fool woman? I'm trying to keep you safe. Something I couldn't do for *her*."

The timbre of his voice as it hitched on the word *her* sent a shiver across my magic and my heart. The other Healer. Fenris sank to his knees. The crimson imprint of my fingers stared up at me as he turned his gaze to the fire, as if in it he could see the dancing of his memories. I didn't dare speak and hardly breathed lest the movement tempt him back into the silence of this closely held truth.

"I killed her. It was the final mercy I could gift her, the only apology I could give form to—to deny the Father the long and drawn-out spectacle he wanted her death to be." Fenris raked a hand through his salt- and sea-stained braid, untethering it, the picture of a penitent man, and I didn't know what to think. Even my magic sat still, as if it too listened to his words and wondered. He looked up at me from where he knelt, his brow creased, and something akin to raw anguish and the kind of determination that could prove deadly spiraled in his fractured black eyes. "I won't be made to do it again." His last words were uttered a note above a whisper. "Don't make me."

"Fenris." My lips moved, tasting his name on them for the first time without venom or vitriol. I should have been mad at him, furious—he'd murdered the Healer just as Kastor had said—but there was something in the stoop of his shoulders that shattered the illusion I'd had of him. "I—"

He shook his head, cutting off my words, and broke the intensity of our gaze. His eyes traced the line of my arm marked with our bonding from my collarbone to where my hand was tucked into the pocket of my still-soaked and sodden dress, fisting the shell the Mer had given me.

"Keep that safe." He nodded toward it. "Don't let anyone know you have it."

His words had the air of a dismissal, one that I was all too willing to heed, though they still sent a nettling of surprise through the back of my mind. I'd anticipated a demand, an insistent petition for me to return that which the other Sons so ruthlessly sought.

I nodded. "I will," I whispered.

It was harder than I'd thought to turn my feet and leave. My magic admittedly did most of the work, like a second set of muscles and bones wrapped around my own.

My hand was on the door latch when the last whispered threads of a question made me take pause. I turned to look at Fenris, who stood now, leaning against the mantel. No shred of the remorsefulness I'd seen in him mere heartbeats before seemed to remain. "Why did she call you 'daughter of the mountains?'" His brow narrowed over his hollowed-out eyes that seemed poised to watch a lie fall from my tongue.

I shrugged and let out an exasperated sigh. I just wanted my bed and to scrub the blood of yet another innocent life off my flesh. "I don't know. Perhaps all of us landfolk look the same to her."

Without waiting for an answer, I slipped into the hall and down to my room, the truth tucked close to my heart. Daughter of the mountains is what the Mer, at one time, called the witches, a little tidbit I'd learned from bedtime stories growing up. If I ever made it home again, I would have to thank my governess properly for all the unwitting wisdom she'd passed to me in those rare tales. But the problem stood: the Mer had known somehow and had nearly exposed me with her dying breaths. It begged the question, how long would it be before others saw it within me as well?

I SLID INTO MY room to find steam beckoning me with curled fingers into the bathing chamber, where the tub lay scalding and waiting. The dey was soon to begin, and I'd yet to sleep. Emrys bless Munnin. I stripped in a savage hurry, eager to clean the smells of battle and blood off my skin. I luxuriated in the water, which turned amber and inky in the flickering candlelight, until it cooled enough to pimple my flesh. Dripping, I pulled myself over the rim of the tub and let the water race down my pale skin in spiraling rivulets before I donned a robe.

I wanted nothing more than for the events of the noct to fade from memory. On the journey back to the lord's apartments, I'd caught myself looking on more than one occasion for Kastor's face among the few we passed, hoping for a wickedly sinful smile to tuck next to my heart and erase all that I'd seen at Posidonia's Gate.

I padded into my bedroom and lazed across the couch to dry before the fire, letting my head rest on the arm with my hair dangling loose. But I shifted restlessly, wriggling my hips to find a more comfortable spot. My magic pressed against my skin, making it feel on the edge of painfully sensitive. I closed my eyes and tried to conjure Kastor's face from our last meeting, in the hope that it could chase away the feelings that bloomed darkly. I let my fingers dance over my thighs and up to my bent knees in long, languid, soothing strokes, trailing lower and lower with each pass. I shivered as the memory of his swollen attraction pressed against my core painted itself vividly across the backs of my closed eyelids.

My magic sent sparks across my skin as I dipped a single finger between my legs. I gasped, the sensation of it egging me to do it again and again. I pressed gentle circles around the nub nestled there, and my magic surged through my body in response, stiffening my nipples and making the feel of the fabric gliding against them nearly intolerable. I pulled it loose and soothed a finger over the achingly taut peaks. The movement snagged at something within me and stirred my already molten core into a dripping tempest of lust that felt so vast and deep, there was no filling it. Gluttonous for the beautiful, torturous pleasure it brought, I did it again and again, rolling my nipple between my fingers.

It still wasn't enough. The fire crackled and grew, and suddenly, desperate to feel its heat, I sat and spread my legs wide, knees bent, and let the tongues of heat lick at my center from across the short distance. I fluttered my eyes open as my magic shifted behind my irises, locking on the fire, and for a bliss-blinded moment, the flames twisted into the vague shape of a man leaning with his forehead pressed against the inner mantel of the hearth, watching me, taking me in and relishing what he was seeing. I let my eyes drift closed as rapture built itself into a volcanic peak in my mind and between my legs, and I imagined the phantasmic figure was Kastor. His name fell from my lips as my frantic fingers chased the high that sung with my magic through my blood.

As I neared that beautiful crest, ready to leap into the rippling magmatic pool, the memory of Fenris's threat to turn me over his knee blossomed and overtook my other imaginings. I pictured a bond-marked hand on my ass. The thought smacked me over the edge, and I went tumbling into a molten abyss of pleasure, amplified by the caress of my magic as it built the waves of my orgasm, pulling them higher and drawing them longer until it felt like the tremulousness of it would shatter my bones.

The intense pleasure was snuffed out with gnawing shame. I'd been thinking of Kastor, and though we technically had no ties, there was a vow and a tension there between us—albeit muddled. But to have his image so unsettlingly and unexpectedly supplanted with Fenris's...I shuddered. The feeling was quickly replaced with the contented purr of my magic as it curled happily in my belly, soothing the raw edges of my worries. It'd meant nothing. Perhaps I just liked the idea of him meeting my demands for once, of making a brutish bastard like him get on his knees for me. That was it. There had been no true arousal, no lust—just simple, blissful revenge.

My fretful fingers glowed as they plucked along the tie of my robe. I'd lost track of the last time I'd let my magic go. It didn't want to be put to bed, and in truth, I didn't want to tuck it away either. But the light could be damning. The way my keeper had looked at me and my hands before we'd departed for the Mer temple unsettled my magic. It paced across my heart and up and down my spine, restless at the thought, no longer content after the brief ecstasy I'd found.

I slipped off the couch, and regret at leaving behind the comforting warmth of the fire ached across my skin. I strode into the bathing room to brush the sodden tangles from my hair, but the moment I caught sight of myself in the mirror, I gasped. The bonding mark stared back at me, shimmering starkly along my skin like freshly fallen kalda snow in the light of the sun. And it had grown like a creeping vine over my collarbone. I slipped the shoulder of my robe off and traced the lines down my chest where it twined itself around my left breast. Mystified, I traced them with a featherlight touch where they whorled around the swell of soft flesh to the peak of my nipple. They twisted along my ribs, around my navel, hooked over my hip bone and had begun to creep across the skin of my thigh.

As though transmutable, the luminescent magic in my fingers lit up the bond, sending jolts of effervescence along the skin it touched, a humming like the plucked cord of a harp. Was this normal? Or was it reacting to...to—my thoughts fumbled and crashed into one another, each one vying for attention. Was it my prolonged proximity to him? Was it the intimate thoughts I'd conjured? Was it the length of the bonding? Was it my magic? If it was the latter, there was no way I could risk asking anyone, not Munnin or Rhapso and definitely not Huggin. Kastor's kind face floated to the rippling and tumultuous surface of my thoughts. But handsome and sweet as he was, and his oath to me notwithstanding, he was still a Son and could never be trusted when it came to things like magic and witches.

The pattern's new light pulsed with each beat of my heart, and then, in the space between throbs, it beat again like a reverberated echo. It had to stop; I could not face the dey like this. Silver tears lined my lower lashes, and I brushed them away even as I battled rising fear with every breath. I would be burned if they saw, just like they'd burned every other witch on the face of Strattaria, every daughter of the mountains, every descendant of Yaganya. My magic coiled around my heart as though it thought to bind it against breaking. It was choking, the yoke that came with knowing there was no soul in this world who could teach me how to be what I was. Their blood had been spilled like so many others by that fucking monster residing in this Fortress, by the man who would gut me and roast me like a feast dey swine if he knew what I was, the man who wanted me bred like a horse with one of his Sons in the forthcoming hunt. And the Emrys—what use had praying to them done? It had been an Emrys who had sent me here on a cryptic mission, leaving me breadcrumbs not even fit for beggars scattered here and there so I could try to piece together what the fuck it was she wanted from me.

Fuck them. Fuck them all.

The crack of the floor stones against my knees barely registered as I fell at the base of the mirror with my forehead pressed to its cool surface. The candles bled their wax across the floor, and I knew how they felt, burned to death slowly and not for their own purposes but for the use of others. I didn't want it; I didn't want any of it. I tried to harden my heart, but I was not made of axe iron and sword steel; I was made of the first blooms of the apple trees and the newly born fawns on spotted, wobbling legs at the beginning of byrthe. I was a pawn, alone, thrust into a cutthroat game of darkness that wrapped itself around me like a bloody scream.

My magic flared within me, burning so brightly, I saw the flash of it in the reflection of my opalescent eyes. I could almost hear it whisper, "*One*," reminding me that as long as I held it and let it surge through my veins, as long as we were one, I was not alone.

I brushed the silver strands of my hair off my tear-stained cheeks and pressed my fingertips to the looking glass. I held my gaze despite wanting to flinch away from the splotched cheeks and puffy eyes wrung of all my sorrow and frustrations. I needed to accept it, accept myself if I was to have any hope of surviving this.

"Look," I whispered to myself, but more than to myself, I spoke to the magic within, "I need you to help me. We can't be found out. I just—I just need you to be less visible, alright? If you could just dim yourself?"

I saw it flicker like a guttering candle behind my irises, almost akin to a nod, and then it withdrew. It soaked into me, drawing itself back away from the surface of my skin to hide in my blood, along my bones, and in my viscera.

My laugh was more a relieved sob than mirth, but it slipped free of its own accord anyway as I held my fingers up in wonder. They looked like the hands of any maiden, and they stayed that way even as I guided my magic to use.

"*Together.*" The magic hummed the word like a promise.

Sparks arched from my fingertips. In my mind's eye, the image of a flower unfurling its petals one by one bloomed until what I saw in my imaginings blossomed to life in my palm made of silver fire.

"Together." I murmured the word like an acolyte murmured a devotion, the taste of it honey on my tongue. "Together."

The summons came on the tail of Huggin's hurried bootsteps before I could set a toe across the threshold of the common area to break the fast. Fenris held it in his hand like it was some revolting thing and not a bit of parchment. I was to attend a prostitute in a brothel on the edge of the city, one of the Father's favorite fucks.

"I'm your escort todey. Huggin has other things to attend to." Fenris nodded for the man to leave before he narrowed his eyes on me, as if daring me to protest.

I pressed my lips into a thin line, my fingers twisted in my skirts. I could barely look at him without pink rising like the sun on my cheeks, heated by the image of what I'd done, what I'd imagined him doing, and the momentary rapture I'd found as a result. In the midst of the swollen pause, out of the corner of my eye, I thought I saw his gaze flick to where my fingers tangled in the plum fabric that draped over my thighs; though whether he looked to see if they still glowed with magic or if he just looked at the bond, I couldn't be sure.

I dared a glance at his marks, twin to my own, and wondered again if they too had grown, but then he popped the silence with the sharp slice of his words. "Pack what you need. I'll have Munnin wrap a meal for you to eat on the way."

I bit my lip anxiously. This assignment had all the feel of a larger hand moving stones on a board, and I didn't like it. But if someone was in need, who was I to argue?

Grabbing my basket of supplies and a warm cloak took a matter of moments. It was becoming routine in the way fowl became accustomed to clipped wings so, at a certain point, they didn't even try to fly when their feathers grew back. Ready and resigned, I followed my keeper from the apartments, over the lower iron bridge strung with icicles, and to the stable. The feeling of eyes on me had my gaze jumping around, peering under the pulled-down caps of stable hands and into the dark recesses of shadow in the stalls, and then there it was. A wink and a nod thrown to me by Kastor from where he leaned discreetly, bundled in his wolfskin in the side yard next to a destrier being saddled. I blushed and gave him a slight dip of the chin and an unobtrusive slip of a smile before turning my attention back to my keeper. Blessedly, there was a small cart ready and waiting for us, fit for two people sitting abreast. The stable hand helped me to my seat with a short bow, then with a crack of the reins, we were on our way down the tumbling slope of a road that switched back and forth like an irregular embroidery stitch along the steep edge of the cliff to Berth.

The view out to the sea revealed the early rising icebreaker ships out in the harbor near the break wall. I couldn't make out the shapes of the men on them with their long-handled, iron-tipped spears used to crack the ice, but I knew the movements like I knew the lines to my favorite childhood poems. I'd watched them from the towers back home and then, on a smaller scale, from the wall of the temple on deys when insomnia and homesickness kept my lids from closing and my mind from settling. The sight of them stilled something in my chest. They were a warm familiarity on a dey when I needed it most.

As we rode, I picked at my breakfast in silence—a warmed stack of buttery bread wrapped around two fried cliff pigeon eggs and smothered in gravy along with a flask of hot, honey-sweetened tea. Munnin was a wonderful cook, but by the time we reached the bottom of the road, my stomach churned unkindly, nettled by Fenris's dark mood. It poured off him in dissonant waves, snatching all the crisp airiness of the cool kalda morning and tainting it with bitter, black bile. I tucked the remnants of my meal back into the basket at my feet and stared straight ahead, determined to ignore him.

We bumped along through town, where the homes and shops were already being decorated for the Eklipsis celebrations with laurels hung from lintels. Sons in formation marched on their way to ships, while wives and servants bustled to the fish market with bundled-up children in tow on their lead strings, their noses kissed with the cold. An elderly man driving a wagon laden with kalda produce lumbered through the crossing ahead of us. Fenris swore half under his breath, muttering curses about brothels and bastards that I couldn't quite make out. My patience snapped like a brittle twig.

"Ugh, enough. What is your issue with this task, my lord? I would have thought you of all people wouldn't mind a trip to the brothel. I've seen the company you keep." I meant to wound him, but the blow didn't land.

"I have no respect for women who fawn over the Father like these ones do. They're all whores for his money and the power they think he can give them, heedless of the ramifications."

"Who is more his whore, do you think, my lord? Her for sucking his cock, or you for doing his bidding blindly?" This time, the taunt struck him like a slap square across the face.

His eyes flashed to mine like an iron-tipped whip heated to red in the fire. "I am not his whore," he seethed through clenched teeth.

"Do you not live under his roof? Sup on his food? And in return, you do whatever dark and bloody deeds he asks of you. You're not even his countryman," I scoffed, relishing the way his face darkened with challenge.

"I don't do everything he wishes. I got you out of participating in the Hunt despite his desires," he growled through gritted teeth as he drew up the wagon in front of a building with a creaking and swaying sign that named it The Crown Jewels.

I gawked, open-mouthed like a fish floundering for breath. "You did what?" The words came out little better than a puff of frosted air.

"Don't look at me like that." He curled his lip and averted his dark eyes. "I simply suggested to him that if you fell pregnant, it might interfere with your healing ability."

My magic stirred, like it sensed some sort of hurt from him and wanted to soothe it, or maybe it just wanted to express its gratitude.

"Thank you," I murmured. Disbelief and shock tinted the edges of my words. Munnin had said my best chance was to be under Fenris's care, and while on some level I'd known that all along, this felt like tangible evidence. I thought again of the raven and hare and wondered for the briefest of moments if perhaps I'd been looking for my raven in all the wrong places. When he didn't respond, I cleared my throat and scooped up my basket. "And thank you for the ride. I'll just head in and see what needs to be done. I'll try to be quick." I hitched my skirts and swung down into the slush-filled, muddied street. But before I could make it to the door, he clambered off, handed the horse and cart off to a stable boy, and was at my heels.

"No, you don't." He grabbed me by the shoulder, not with any force, but the sudden jerk spun me around to face him. "We can't have your"—his dark gaze grazed from the cut of my neckline, down my skirts, and back up again—"virtue called into question. Father's orders, since he now thinks pregnancy could interfere with your skills. And as I'm sure you know, nothing can taint a maiden's reputation like crossing the threshold of a fuckhouse."

Heat flared through our bond, igniting where his hand touched me, and I was struck dumb with thoughts of what I'd done and pictured just a few hours past—it hadn't felt very maidenly. Without replying, and with a small fire burning its way up my neck and cheeks, I spun on my booted heel and took off through the door at a determinedly clipped pace, anything to get his dark eyes off me. The way they scraped across my skin suddenly made me feel achingly raw and exposed, like he could see the impurity of my thoughts in the flush of my face.

The sight of the brothel's interior brought me up short. The establishment was scandalous enough to make my eyes bulge and bathe my face in a scarlet twice as deep as the shades used to encase the flickering flames of the candles on the chandeliers and sconces. Even at this early hour, the bawdy house was engorged, packed wall to wall with wolf-whistling men, and to my surprise, women as well. On either side of the vast, open space, there were stages upon which performers were engaged in the most wicked of demonstrations. To the left, a tangled knot of naked women pleasured one another as people on couches strewn about the room gawked, fucked, and drank.

On the right stage, a single man and a woman danced together, but it was like no dance I'd ever seen, their lithe bodies rhythmically writhing in an erotic display. Unbidden, my eyes lingered upon them. I gasped as the man took a brutally sharp knife and sliced pieces of her clothing off bit by bit, exposing her ebony skin in small swaths to a chorus of hoots and howls. In the center of it all, on a revolving stage, a group of bare and painted musi-cians played an accompaniment to both shows that somehow seemed to melt into the moans of desire that floated on the heady air filled with a billowing gauze of intoxicating smoke.

"If you stare any longer, Shepherdess, the madame will charge." Fenris snickered teasingly in my ear, his breath hot on my skin. Todey was not unfolding in any manner that made sense to me.

I gathered all my wit and used it to suffocate the drippingly molten fire that seemed to have unex-pectedly seeded itself in my low belly amidst all the mortification I felt at his remarks, and I forced myself to ask, "And I suppose you know where she is?"

The corner of his mouth hooked up into a despi-cable smile. "Of course I do. This way."

He put his hand on my back, and I tried not to flinch away from it. The press of his fingers felt unnerving and too intimate, even through all my layers, as he guided me through a labyrinth of gossamer curtains and narrow halls with alcoves crammed full of sweaty bodies stinking of reckless debauchery and liquor.

Fenris rapped his gloved knuckles twice on a slim door at the back of a passage half swallowed by gloom.

"Come in," a voice scratched from the other side of the door, and Fenris obliged, pushing it and leaning against the frame, filling the space so I could see nothing past him except for flickering candlelight. "Ah, Fenris, my boy. Have you come to see—"

But he cut her off before I could find out who it was she thought he'd come to purchase for his pleasure, thank the Emrys. "I've brought the Healer for Samiya." He turned his body to the side just enough to allow me a slight glimpse into a dank and shabby office.

The madame was not what I'd expected, though in truth, I wasn't at all sure I'd expected any of this. She was plump, with her hips, belly, and bosom all stacked like mounds of clay atop one another. She swelled over the top of her exotically colored burnt orange dress, and the pewter-colored pelt wrapped around her shoulders and pinned in place with an intricately knotted gold chain appeared to be the hide of a quillbar if I wasn't mistaken; though it was difficult to say, as I'd only seen the majestic creatures once when a traveling menagerie had come to court and never without their barbed quills. They were native solely to the woodlands that bordered the Great Grass Sea and the dead witch kingdom of Lamya, and they were a symbol of opulence and unmatchable wealth, the sort I didn't imagine came from trading in flesh. Someone had to have given it to her, and I could think of only one patron who had enough gold or who raided enough lands to have stolen something of such value.

I nodded in greeting as my magic hissed. It didn't like her, and on this point, I had to agree.

The madame stood behind her desk. A toothy grin split her lightly wrinkled face, and she spread her arms wide. "Welcome, Lady, to The Crown Jewels. I am Madame Vesnina. I am honored to have you here. My poor dear Samiya, such a precious gem, that girl. She's just being a bit flighty in my opinion—you know how the younger ones can be." She cackled softly and threw a conspiratorial wink at Fenris, but I felt it as a rippling shift in the air that made the hair on the back of my neck stand on end and made me question just how free the men and women who worked for her really were.

To Fenris's credit, he didn't answer other than to simply say, "I'll take the Healer up to see her then?" It may have sounded like a question, but the way it rang in the stuffy space between them felt more like a statement.

The smile stayed on Madame Vesnina's face, but her eyes hollowed and filled in the span of a heartbeat with something hard that glinted malevolently. Then in a blink, it was gone, masked over once again. "Of course, of course." My magic squirmed as I turned with Fenris to go back down the hall—it didn't like having not one but two predators at my back. "Oh, and do let me know if I can get you a little something extra for your troubles when you've finished upstairs. I'm used to catering to all tastes, so do not be afraid to ask for what you like, Lady Healer, and you as well, my lord, as always," Vesnina crooned, faltering my steps and dragging my attention back to her as she leaned forward on her ringed fingers across her desk. I had the sickening sensation swelling in my gut that she didn't mean food.

Samiya's suite was all her own, decked from wall to wall with garish and grand tapestries. From her four-poster bed, sheer silks and scarves hung in a riot of colors. A wide window outfitted with a cushioned bench seat took up nearly all of the eastern wall and overlooked the whole of Berth. An armoire next to the bed sat with its doors agape, a wardrobe to rival any of my royal sisters' spewing forth onto the floors. The needlework immediately snagged my attention; it seemed Rhapso outfitted everyone from prostitutes to captives to queens.

"Thank the Emrys you've come," a breathlessly meek voice called from beneath a burden of blankets on the bed as I shut the door behind myself, leaving my keeper to stand guard in the hall.

The air was thick and humid with a churning heat coming off the wide-mouthed fireplace, where a simmering cauldron of chopped plant matter steamed the room with herbal smells.

"I asked Madame Vesnina deys ago to send for you. I was beginning to think you would not come." A small sob choked her, and she covered her face with long fingers. I darted to the bed—her anguish so palpable in the air, marinated in the salt of stale tears—and wrapped an arm around her delicate shoulders, drawing her in for a hug.

I soothed a hand down her variegated hair, kissed by the sun in the way only the people of the Great Grass Sea nation of Enar could be, mauve at the roots and a rose gold to the tips. Suddenly, the quillbar coat made sense, and I knew what it was the madame had paid to get it: this "gem" of a girl for the Father. My magic flickered angrily; it spat notions of consuming fire eating the walls vividly in my mind as I held her while she relinquished her woes. But that would do no one any good, not unless they had somewhere safe to go, away from Vesnina and the Father's reach, which, as I knew, was long. So I redirected its energies to delve into

Samiya. It dripped eagerly into her veins, wanting as desperately as I did to help her. Fever ravaged her body; in nothing but a diaphanous shift, she burned with an inferno from the inside out, which explained the state of the room. Someone with just enough herblore to know you could fight the fires of fever with real fire must have been seeing to her. That would be an easy fix. I would have to bring her temperature down slowly so as not to shock her system, but it was doable.

My fingers stilled on her hair. "No one told me you were pregnant." I tried to keep the surprise out of my voice to maintain professionality to some degree, but it must have registered to her anyhow, because she drew back into the bolstered-up pillows propped behind her back.

She pushed the heavy layers of furs and blankets back to reveal a swell between her wide-set hip bones. Samiya smiled down at her burgeoning belly and ran a hand over it with achingly tender affection. "He said you could save this one like you did the Mother's." Her hand darted out, encircling my wrist, and she looked up at me with such hope in her dewy gray eyes that it ached. "Please tell me you can save him." In that moment, she looked despairingly young, with her gilt freckles speckled across the wide bridge of her delicate nose and a fevered flush on her ebony cheeks.

I swallowed hard around the sticking lump of dread blooming like a knot of thorny vines in my throat. "How old are you, Samiya?"

"Nineteen turns of the year, my Lady Healer." Her brow furrowed, and her fingers twisted in the fabric of her shift. "Does that affect whether or not you can save him?"

I rested a hand over hers, stilling it. "No, no, not at all." I smiled softly. "Just making conversation. If it's alright with you, I'll just rest my hands on your belly and see what I can do."

Her worry smoothed over. "Oh yes. Please do whatever you need to." She undid the lacing at the bottom of her shift as she settled back and exposed the bare swell of her stomach. I pressed a palm on either side and let my magic sing through her womb.

"How many babies have you lost?"

She sighed wistfully. "I've only been the Father's favored for about a year now, and this is my third babe. I can carry them longer than the others and get pregnant more quickly." She said this as though it were a point of pride, but I felt it like the point of a knife in my heart.

My magic writhed within. There was something strange about the babe's physical connection to its mother; it was tenuous at best. I closed my eyes and probed. The placenta had blood pooled behind it. "Have you had bleeding or cramping or a tightening in your stomach?"

I sensed her nodding before she spoke. "Yes, all of it. My older sister Fiori has been taking over my performances downstairs as well as her own so I can rest. The fever came first though."

I wondered for a fleeting moment if her sister was the woman I'd seen performing the intricate knife dance with a partner on stage. It seemed highly unlikely that the madame had more than two Enarians under her roof. Two was surprising enough as it was, considering how notoriously wary and protective they were of their people.

"I don't think that's part of it," I answered. "It certainly isn't helping matters, since it's more stress on your body, but it's not at fault for the blood."

We fell silent as I finished drying up the blood and reknitting the placenta to her womb before I followed the cord to the baby. As if it sensed my presence, it wrapped its pudgy little fingers around the umbilical cord and yanked it closer. In doing so, it took hold of my magic and enticed it to glom into its body and bolster its growth. I let it—though as I did, dread pooled in my heart, tarring its beats, sticking one to the next in rapid succession. This one, much like its sibling in the palace, was shaped wrongly; though it appeared this babe had a tail rather than horns, and there was no telling what coloring it might have. But I couldn't trouble Samiya with that, not now.

The babe drank its greedy fill of my magic until I could see each part of it glowing contentedly in the cradle of its mother's hips. It released its cord and its hold on my magic, then rolled over, hiccuping happily until it fell asleep. I fluttered my eyes open to find Samiya's lips twisted at the corners into a contented smile.

"The Seer was right, wasn't she? When she told the Father that you would save him." Samiya sighed, her eyelids fluttering under the weight of sleep that sometimes followed a healing, but I could share in none of her joy as an icicle of dread pierced my heart upon hearing the words *Father* and *Seer* in the same string. What more had she told him, and what in the Umbra was wrong with all his unborn?

P LAYFUL FINGERS OF IMBOLA'S wind reached through the windows of the workshop, where I sat on the bench, and tugged at the ends of my hair as I flipped through Aurasha's journal. It had kept me company as I'd slept fitfully and then not at all through the noct—the hours of which were lengthening as we quickly approached the kalda festival of Eklipsis, the one dey Jyord and Selenyss came together as man and wife in the Emphyrea, combining their lights into a darkly beautiful corona that painted all Strattaria in diaphanous gray light as insubstantial as thistledown on a gentle breeze. In Vanyth, it was a dey of celebration with candle-lighting rituals and gifts exchanged between loved ones. It was considered the most auspicious dey to propose marriage, and to have a babe born on the dey was to have the blessings of the Emrys upon your house, for no woman or child had ever perished or fallen ill after an Eklipsis birth.

Here in Uthar, it seemed there was a whole host of new traditions to prepare for. The few patients I'd tended to early in the dey had been giddy with anticipation and had spoken dizzyingly of nothing else. There were to be temple offerings tonoct, a tournament, and a ball followed by the Hunt, which did not bring me as much joy as it did them despite the fact that I'd been relieved of the forcible obligation to participate.

I sighed and flipped through another few handfuls of Aurasha's notes, skimming for the words *pregnancy*, *deformity*, and *miscarriage*. I'd found several entries that noted the Mother's pregnancies, but somewhere between one pregnancy and the next, there were always pages missing. The jagged scars of torn paper were the only vindication that I'd been right, that there had been something distressingly peculiar about all the babies. It was simultaneously both a relief that it hadn't been my magic that had twisted their forms and disturbing that someone had painstakingly taken the time to remove the evidence I so desperately sought. Not that I had a firm grasp on what I intended to do with it when I found it. It wasn't as if I could blackmail the Father into releasing me by threatening to tell the kingdoms he sired monsters. The kingdoms already feared him; if they knew this, they would only cow to him further.

Pinching the bridge of my nose, I set the book down. If only there had been records kept further back, then I could see if the Father's parents or grandparents had suffered from the same affliction. My magic sat up, suddenly roused by my thoughts. It purred, but which notion had it so attentive when all my research had led me to nothing? Surely not the Father's lineage? It hummed against my skull.

The library might have old healing records I supposed, but my magic hissed as if to tell me that my thoughts were straying again, and I groaned. This would have been such a simple problem back home, where the healers kept birth and death records all the way to my ridiculously distant grandfather King Artus and his Queen Elwyn. I'd been forced as a child to memorize the whole thousand-year lineage as well as the lines of the other seven kingdoms, some more traceable than others—but, no, that wasn't right. I didn't know the Uthari ancestry; we'd never been taught it. The thought was dizzying, like phantasmic fingers swathing my mind in cobweb-like gauze and cinching, squeezing it down so it stayed. The workshop around me blurred and tilted. But then, like a flint struck, the webs ensnaring my thoughts caught fire, burned into ash by a spark of my magic. Blinking dazedly, I realized I was on my hands and knees, gasping for breath, the cool floor stones biting into my palms.

Choking for air, I pushed myself to my knees. Strong hands wrapped around my elbows and hoisted me the rest of the way to my feet. Huggin's face floated in front of my spotted vision, concern pinching his usually stoic expression. "Do ye be alright, Lady?" his voice rumbled.

"Yes, yes, sorry. I just had a dizzy spell." I tried to smile, but it felt twisted on my face. "I'm fine now."

"Do ye need anythin'?" he asked gruffly but not unkindly.

My mind reeled as I picked up the journal that must have fallen with me and made my way over to the workbench, where I began plucking herbs for a fortifying and restorative brew. "I think I just need a strong cup of tea, Huggin, but thank you."

He turned to go, but at the last moment, I called out to him with a desperate need to know I wasn't the only one, that I wasn't just weary as I had said and frightening myself with deydreamt noctmares. "Huggin, wait. One quick question." He paused halfway over the threshold. "What is the Father's birth name? Or the dey of his birth? I've been trying to look something up in the records, but—"

I paused. Huggin's eyes glazed over, filled with milky clouds, and his jaw slackened. He wavered on his feet, and his back slammed into the doorframe. I darted over to him, nearly tripping on my skirt hems in my haste. I grabbed his calloused hand in mine and shoved a little liquidus ball of magic through my fingers and into his.

Huggin blinked, and the filmy tempest in his oceanic blue eyes cleared. Puzzlement pulled the edges of his stern mouth into a frown. "Did ye say somethin', Lady?"

I stepped back and let my hand fall. "No, it was nothing, Huggin."

He grunted and swung the door shut between us. I stood in the silent room, just stood there, my hands pressed to my ribs as I tried to breathe and calm my racing magic as it hissed, "*Nameless, nameless, nameless,*" over and over to the beat of my thundering heart. The Father had no name. The Father had no traceable lineage, and it seemed any thoughts on the subject quickly bled from people's minds on the back of a peculiar fit of some kind. Which begged the question I didn't want to give voice to but one that vibrated along my bones like I'd been struck by a bolt of lightning from one of Taranya's storms.

What in the Umbra was the Father?

Huggin sighed loudly behind me from where I crouched with a trowel in hand, digging up adlethorn bulbs from beneath the tangled mess of improperly trellised branches. They were useful for making poultices to be applied to the bottoms of the feet to draw out the bile that clogged the body of someone afflicted with a coughing sickness—well, at least that's what I'd told Huggin they were for. In truth, I was gathering herbs for a dream befuddlement sachet to tuck under my pillow. My governess had made them for me when I'd been small and plagued by dreams of rooms full of giant crows eager to peck my eyes out. She'd sat up with me by the light of a flickering candle for many nocts before she'd acquired all the appropriate herbs to sew into the tiny and fragrant bag. "It *will confuse the noctmares, dear, so they will get lost on the way to your mind and you will sleep peacefully.*"

Whether it had worked because I'd wished it to or because of the herbs, I didn't know, but I was willing to give it a try, as silly as I knew it sounded, to keep the recurring noctmares of Helima at bay. Last noct, they'd bled into dreams of babies with horns and tails, whose cries sounded like the eerie warning of the Emrys to balance the scales. "As *above, so below.*"

My guard sighed again, his boot scuffing agitatedly on the ground. I rolled my eyes and cast what

I hoped was a scathing look over my shoulder. "We have plenty of time. I closed the workshop early."

"I do need time to get ready," he groused, tugging on a braid woven into his black beard.

"Need to make sure you look pretty for someone special?" I teased, then laughed as his eyes darkened. "If you want to hurry things along, you could help. I need a handful of thorn whistle leaves and two seed pods from a lily of the Emrys."

He frowned down at me. "Ye won't go anywhere?"

I waggled my fingers so the watery middey light glanced off the silver whorls of the bond. "Would it really matter if I did?"

With little more than a grunt, he stomped off lightly, weaving through the beds and trellises of the kalda garden before he was swallowed by the dense curtain of steam that rolled off the wending canals.

I inhaled deeply, savoring the rich scent of moist soil and the musk of decomposing plants as I tucked the bulbs I'd uprooted into my basket and

rose, brushing the dirt from my skirt. I still needed two final ingredients: Umbra-bore blossoms—if
I was lucky, there might at least be a few dried
ones fallen to the base of the plant—and a couple
of scrapes of dragonwood bark. I wove my way
toward the back gate that led out into the Blackwood, when the ghost of a whisper threaded on
the steam snicked its way to my ears. I ducked behind the dragonwood, its long branches embracing
me, wrapping around my arms and shoulders as a
breeze from Imbola swept through the garden and
blew the steam away just long enough for me to
catch sight of the whisperers.

Ingemar loomed in front of Kastor, whose usually
handsome face was a twisted mask of some powerful emotion that, at this distance, looked to be
loathing or anger or both. My magic curled around
the nape of my neck in a quivering, serpentine coil
that seemed to hum with a warning that made my
palms sweat. It clearly didn't like this situation any
more than I did.

The wind blew, churning around the garden,
trapped in its walls. It lifted my skirts, pinched my
cheeks pink, and kissed my lips, leaving them tasting of kalda snows coating bare branches, before it

shifted and whipped toward the men who lurked under the vine-covered arch, the leaves at its peak frosted in snow while the lower vines flowered. Kastor sniffed the air. As if he scented my presence, his rich brown eyes cut to me like a knife thrown, widening slightly before they flicked back to Ingemar, whose whispers were just on the edge of being audible.

I caught words thrown around with his erratic and violent gestures. "Deserving...bitch...bleed."

It sounded like the bastard was being just as pleasant as always, which meant I really wanted to get out of there before he noticed me. Quickly, I picked off a few bark chips with my fingernail. When I peered back around the trunk, Kastor had shifted positions, forcing Ingemar to angle further away. He discreetly made shooing motions with his hand. Without hesitation, I hiked my skirts and ran for the path I'd just come down, with all the grace of a scared rabbit fleeing the brush, until I smacked headlong into Huggin's wall of a chest.

"Woah, where do ye be goin' in such a hurry?" He steadied me with his heavy hands, much like he had in the workshop earlier.

I rubbed my poor nose, punched by the abrupt collision with his sternum, and winced. "Ingemar and Kastor are in the gardens." I hesitated, and then, keeping my tone hushed, I added, "It looked like they were fighting."

He shoved two seed pods at me, each silvery blue husk as long as my forearm. "We better go before they do see ye."

"I still need one more ingredient," I protested in a hissed whisper. "Umbra-bore—it's around here somewhere. If I'm quiet, I can avoid them."

But Huggin shook his head, his hand darting out and encircling my wrist like he expected me to try to run for the garden bed. "No, we do go now." He hauled me away.

My magic spat and angrily threatened to needle the spot where our skin touched, but I kept it checked, just barely, even as tears pricked the corners of my eyes. I desperately didn't want to dream tonoct, but it didn't seem I had any choice.

T HE STREETS ALONG THE temple roads were lit with thousands upon thousands of candles of every shape, color, and size littered on either side and around the temples' entrances. The clouds covered Selenyss and the shine of the star stones as my keeper, Huggin, Munnin, and I joined the milling throng, chatting with a smattering of small groups huddled around fires cast in iron cauldrons on street corners. In everyone's hands and in the crooks of their elbows were baskets of beautiful and intricately knotted ropes of all hues, some decorated with rune stones, others with pretty beads. The people tarried in and out of temples, leaving the cords as offerings or hanging them about the doors that stood open and welcoming. The light of the temples' sanctum hearths spilled out across the snow-covered streets in a buttery gold hue, where they kissed the rosy cheeks of the fair-haired wives and the broad cheekbones of the sturdy Sons and merchants all bundled in their best furs and homespun gloves.

"Oh, there do be Rhapso." Munnin gasped excitedly against the cold as she veered away from our little group toward where the plump, violet-eyed woman waved a steaming tankard in one hand.

Huggin prowled off with little more than a grunt, his black hair bobbing above the crowd, taller by a full head than any man there, which left Fenris and me alone.

My bond prickled as he cleared his throat. "Here." He shoved a fistful of the knotted cords toward me in offering. "You can go place them at the temples of your choosing."

"What are they for?" Homesickness and embarrassment at not knowing bled with anger and frustration on my cheeks, masking my face with flaming heat that melted the flakes of snow landing on it. This was so vastly different from what I knew my sisters and mother would be doing at this moment that the memories of Eklipsis past went rabid in my mind and shredded my heart.

"Each color is for different things. The green is a Beseeching, to ask for an Emrys's guidance. The blue is a Gratitude, to leave at the temple of an Emrys you wish to thank. Red is a Repentance, if there are any you have wronged. And black is a Warding, to keep the attentions of an Emrys off you in the byrthe of the new year," he explained, holding one of each up in turn.

"And the purple?" I ran my finger over the most intricate twist of them all, woven and twined to resemble a human heart with a runestone at its center etched with the symbol for desire.

He twisted the soft purple strands of his own knot in his gloved fingers. "Ah yes, that is a Requite. For that, you have two options—you can leave it at the temple of the Red Lady and beg her to slake your thirst for vengeance, or at the temple of In-esmara and ask her to shape an unrequited love's affections and turn them to you.

"Aren't you afraid I'll place a Requite at Death's temple to seek vengeance on you and this whole cursed kingdom?" I meant the words to come out saturated in sarcasm, but the edge of them cut off my tongue more sharply than I'd intended, and they tasted far more truthful than I cared to admit.

"I'm more afraid that you won't." He bowed his head slightly, his long braid sliding off his shoulder with the movement. "Good noct, Ertha. I will see you back at the Fortress."

What in the Umbra had he meant by that? But he sidestepped me and stalked off, leaving me standing by myself. "You're leaving me alone then?" I called after him.

He turned back, casting a pointed look over his shoulder at my left hand before flicking his dark, empty eyes that mirrored the candlelight to mine. "For tonoct. It is against the Father's decrees to spill blood on this holy noct; no Son would dare harm you. And besides, prayer is something I believe ought to be done in private. Don't you?"

Fenris's fur-clad back lumbered away, and something pinched inside me, in the itch of the bond, and I wondered when he'd last spent an Eklipsis in Corvus and if he was possibly as homesick as I was. Curiosity gnawed at my feet, biting my heels and urging them to follow. I twisted the ropes in my hands before shoving them inelegantly into the pocket of my cloak. I ghosted his steps, needing to see to whom the black-eyed man would pray. My steps slipped, hurrying to catch up through the crowd, following the aura of otherness he left in his wake as people parted around him, only to find, when I veered down the same road I'd seen him duck down a heartbeat before, he was gone.

I sighed. It had been a stupid and wistful thought at best, to wonder if he was feeling as raw and hollow on the inside as I was. A man baptized in that much blood could not possibly fathom the ache of an empty chest where a heart had once beat for those you'd loved and lost.

I looked at the temples that lined the street like stoic sentinels. A few people skipped from temple door to temple door with festive songs on their lips, but most of the crowd was left behind on the main street to talk with friends and buy sweet treats and strong drinks from vendors calling out behind their carts. Though these side paths were sparce that didn't stop me from peering into the cowls of the men who passed me, looking for the mischievous eyes of the one who'd sworn his life to mine. I could have used him tonoct, to soothe the savage edges of my sorrow that leached into the ground, weighing me down with every step. But the stone in my stomach told me I wouldn't find him this noct, not after witnessing whatever had transpired in the garden earlier in the dey.

There was a temple, or at the very least a shrine, to nearly every Emrys among the solemn rows of candlelit buildings, all except the one Emrys who I always turned to for guidance. Selenyss was not favored by the Uthari—she shone a light on their dark dealings in the dead of noct—so if I couldn't place my beseeching knot on her altar, I could at least offer it up in the sanctum of her husband, Jyord.

His temple was washed in gold and made of stacked red stones chiseled in whorls meant to symbolize the reach of his light. I ducked into the entrance, keeping the edge of my veil pulled up over my face to afford me some privacy from the glassy eyes of revelers and to humble myself before the father of all.

My eyes caught on the riot of colorful knots laid upon the steps to his altar. I followed suit, withdrawing the green Beseeching offering from my pocket, twisted in a blooming knot shaped like the opening of petals. I knelt before the steps—I wasn't sure it was necessary, but I did it anyhow—and cupping my offering in my hands, I wrote a secret, undetectable prayer with my magic on its twined strands.

Jyord, father of fire and sun, maker of man, from my lips to your ears, I have been a servant to your wife for most of my life. I am the last daughter of the mountains, of your fallen sister Yaganya, and I am here to leave this humble Beseeching to beg you to guide me out of this wolves' den in which I have found myself and see me safely home. So mote it be.

A solitary tear I hadn't known I'd wept fell from my cheek and onto the emerald strands. I brushed its trail clean from my face and left my offering among the hundreds that already lay there. Then I stood and left. But there was a lightness to my steps I had not felt before entering, a subtle surety that my prayer would be heard. Before I crossed the threshold, a bell upon the altar rang, a single, mournful toll. I turned to see who was there as witness to my passing prayer, but there was no one, no robed acolyte or shrouded priest, not even a shadow.

I place my blue knot of Gratitude in the temple of Lugha, Emrys of all things flora, for her plants were the one thing that were unfailing in this world. No matter where I was and in what situation, I could find solace in gardens abundant with her blessings. She was also mother to the Enar, a people who'd not been broken by the Uthar like the other nations had, and in that notion I found strength. Red went to the temple of Orannus, father of the Mer, which, here in Uthar, was a shrine that consisted of little more than amassed coral stones inlaid along the wall of another temple and a knee-high statue. Very few knots were placed at his feet, but I laid my Repentance bare for the Mer I had not been able to save.

Purple, I chose not to place. My heart was torn between love and vengeance, ripped in two by a man who'd sworn me an oath but who was also the Son of my enemy with whom there could never be a future. I could have chosen vengeance, yet I did not want to bring it upon the heads of the people of this nation but its leader, and in war, I knew it would be the innocent who suffered most.

That left me with only the black Warding, and I knew precisely in whose temple I intended to place it. My magic coiled itself and raised its head like a viper within the cage of my ribs as I trod upon street stones that none had yet dared to venture. Death's sanctuary was too far from the happy, cheerful fire and celebrations, too macabre for such a joyous gathering. This tradition of offerings was not my own, but I would not waste an opportunity to possibly turn the Red Lady's eyes from me, not when it might mean I could slip away from the place she'd maneuvered me when her attentions were elsewhere.

Almost fittingly, her temple stood opposite the one devoted to the Niflym. The magic in me pulled against my skin toward the black stone building, its smooth, etched surface near luminous in the dark. I tried to resist, to focus on my task, but my eyes seemed drawn again and again to those peculiar runes. I fought the pull to go to the walls and run my fingers over the carvings, each step slogged as if through honey.

There was no light on in Death's sanctum, no welcoming glow, but I knew without doubt it belonged to her. The gray stone was the same used to mark graves, and as I reached the iron gate that barred entry into the inner chambers, the somber stillness and silence that wrapped around me was that of eternal sleep. The lock on the door was carved in the likeness of a hanging man, with his screaming mouth shaped into a keyhole. I shuddered, and the horrific morbidity of the building crawled over my skin. I pulled the offering from my pocket. I supposed hanging it from the gate would do the trick just as well as placing it on the altar.

Nails with the chill sharpness of the iron used to hammer coffins closed raked across my scalp, ripped across the shoulder of my cloak, and spun me, pressing my back into the gate coated with bloody rust. The tips of my boots scrambled for purchase on the slick stones. "Oh, witchling, you'll have to be far more clever than that to turn my eyes from you." Her voice was a tolling death knell. Her hand that felt like rot upon my skin pressed to my throat and crushed any words I thought to use to pardon myself. Maggots crawled from her fingertips, their fat, wriggling bodies worming their ways across my collarbone.

I gasped for breath, and my magic thrashed help-lessly as necrosis began to spin across the points where her flesh touched mine.

"Since you seem to be in the offering mood, and I am nothing if not kind"—she licked the long line of my pulse up my neck to my ear, where she whis-pered her words that summoned the images of every death I'd ever witnessed—"let me give you an offering, one that will help you restore the balance."

I whimpered as she pulled back and brought us nose to nose. I had only a moment to look upon her terrible beauty before she spat and my vision bled red.

Burning, my lungs gasped greedily for the air they'd been deprived of the moment she dropped me. Snow soaked through the knees of my skirt, and I wept, the Red Lady gone. What a damned fool I'd been to think a bit of knotted string could do anything to help me. Tears washed her sting-ing, bloody saliva down my cheeks as my magic crooned and writhed, caressing my insides like it thought to soothe me. I pushed myself to my feet, done. Done with the offerings, done with this tra-dition, done with this noct. I shuffled back the way

I'd come, letting weariness and my magic blindly guide my steps back to the keep and my bed.

My brush with Death had drained me. My bones needed the warmth of a fire and a bundle of comfortable blankets before I could let my mind frantically wander the labyrinth of possibilities that surrounded whatever the Red Lady's "offering" meant and what it would do to me. Right at that moment, the prospect was nauseating.

I'd not gone more than a few steps when chanting bloomed out of the dark on an eerie wind and drew my eyes to the Niflym Temple. My vision blurred, and the etched runes on its darkly shining surface glowed like ruby stones under the light of Jyord's sun before, illuminated, they danced. The lines contorted themselves until they rearranged their shapes into a language I could understand. I choked on the words as I tried to whisper them aloud.

As above, so below. Restore the balance.

My magic hummed contentedly and butted up against my heart, urging me again to go to the stone, to read more, but bile rose in my throat, and spurred by a fear that rode my heart like a cruel master astride a horse, I ran all the way to the forgotten lift.

With a rap of a knuckle against its bars as I'd seen Munnin do, it soared through the stone shaft, toward the Fortress. Its music sang a soothing melody against my bones, but it did nothing to expel the chill of the Red Lady's words scribbled along the wall of the Niflym Temple, not when she so clearly held the strings to puppet my life in her twisted fingers.

The flames were low in the hearth when, at long last, I slipped into my room, but they gave off just enough light for me to shed my clothes and slip into my noct shift. A pale blue bow caught my attention as I pulled the covers back. On my pillow lay a bundle of the Umbra-bore I'd failed to collect earlier in the dey, tied together with a slip of curled parchment, upon which were inked the words: *An offering for you who did not ask for this life.* There was no name, but the solemn quill strokes and the stoic kindness of the gesture could only have been from Huggin.

The pull of needle and thread around the bundle of crushed herbs soothed me. I would not have to dream after all. My need for sleep had been banished by my eagerness to complete my sachet as soon as I'd found Huggin's generous offering.

The aromatic muddled herbs soothed my mind, reminiscent of the way my governess used to smooth my hair away from my temples on nocts when sound sleep refused to find me. She would whisper stories of the Emrys the way maids whispered gossip. My favorite had been a silly tale about the star stones. It started as all the stories seemed to with a maiden weeping. In this instance, the maiden was the young Emrys Sidra, and when her tears fell into the gently swaying currents of aurora, they solidified around the glowing light, trapping it in fragments of crystal until the bottom of the river was littered with brilliant, palm-sized gems of sorrow. Melantha, Emrys of the dark and noct, was so enamored by the beauty of Sidra's grief that she plucked the glowing, argent tears from the silt and filled her pockets with them. That noct, as she drifted across the Emphyrea, she arranged the stones on the biting mountain peaks so she would always have their tragically beautiful light to mark her way.

It haunted me that my governess hadn't known why Sidra had cried alone along the banks in the first place. She'd always said the story was too old, from a time before the Niflym had fallen, and there was no asking the young Emrys what had brought her to such a painful low now that she was gone. I always wondered if Sidra found a way to make light from her sorrows in the crushing black of the Umbra after Terr had stolen her away, or if she'd drowned alone in the dark. The thought fractured my heart. She and I were far too alike in that respect, lost and afraid in a place far darker than we were used to.

My hand stilled on my stitches, and I set my sachet down. It was not quite complete, but my thoughts shifted to another idea, a wonderful idea. I moved to the trunk brimming with sewing sup-

plies and found what I needed almost immediately. I drew a billowing bolt of crushingly navy-blue
fabric, so rich, it was nearly black, from the bottom
of the box. Its fibers were spun as delicately as the
color on a butterfly's wings and were as soft as the
petals of the first byrthe blossoms. It would make
the most stunning gown for the Eklipsis ball, and if
I could craft it into the vision I saw in my mind, it
would be glorious.

"Help?" My magic curled itself by my ear and
seemed to whisper its wish to fulfill my desires.

I hummed my agreement contentedly and let it
rush through me. I gasped as it filled me, pressing
outward to skim along my skin and twine itself
around my fingers. I felt it like a gentle breeze,
and saw it in the way the world grew brighter and
sharper. With a single curl of my fingertips, the
fabric lifted into the air and swirled in and around
itself. I breathed, letting the air in my room, which
smelled like spiced embers, fill my lungs.

With the magic flooding my pupils, I could see
each fiber of the fabric; I could twist them free or
knit them together with a single thought. Giggling,
the sound effervescent in my ears, I closed my

eyes, still seeing the fabric in my mind's eye like I would an organ in a patient's body. All I had to do was picture what I wanted it to become, and the individual threads obeyed, reshaping themselves to fit the pattern of my will. I reveled in the glory of it, the way the magic made my every whim come into being.

Silver embroidery floss snaked out from where it had been tucked in the trunk. It slithered through the air before separating and arranging itself, becoming one with the greater whole of the dress in a dance choreographed by the beat of my heart. It was so beautiful, I wept, and as the tears rolled down my face, they were changed into shimmering gems by the request of my imagination. They were then given over to the dress until it was no longer just a simple garment but the embodiment of a sorrowful tale that reflected the broken things that lived and breathed and clawed inside me.

When at last I was done and I looked upon it, it felt as though I'd spun the thing not from magic and fabric and tears, but from the words of the story and the lines of a memory so ancient, it was thought to be only a dream. I tucked it away into the back of my armoire, shrouded in a shadow, where Munnin or anyone else who came snooping would not see it. Not until it was time.

A shimmering of red wept like blood from beneath the lid of the box on the upper shelf of my wardrobe. It stilled my hand on the knob of the door as I was about to shut it. It called my attention like the crook of a red-lacquered finger. My fleshy, tender heart drummed a warning across the cage of my ribs, and my magic sat up excitedly, egging me on as I reached for it. The box hummed a siren song in my hands as I took it down, and the latch snicked apart with an easy flick, the lid opening on a soundless hinge. The book inside, the one I'd found half drowned on the bridge, thrummed with a crimson aura. A chill raked down my vertebrae, and my thoughts emptied as I dipped my hand into the box to retrieve it. The moment my flesh touched the spine, its light dimmed. I replaced the box, shut the wardrobe door, and took the book immediately to my bed.

I sat in an array of my shift's skirts, embroidered in pale threads that showed Selenyss's moon as a crescent—a callback to a children's tale about the time Inesmara, Emrys of love, thought to eat the moon to make her skin more radiant—with my legs crossed and my hair slung over my shoulder in a solitary thick braid. I set the book in front of me on the coverlet as hesitation battled with my magic's eagerness that felt both intertwined with and separate from my own emotions. A howl cut through the noct, followed by an echoing chorus of haunting replies. One among them stood out somehow with a prickling familiarity that I could not place.

The cover of the book flipped open. One of the ruffled pages caught the edge of my finger and bit into the tender skin, drawing a droplet of blood. I hissed and quickly stuck the wound into my mouth and sucked, the taste of metal and salt coating my tongue. I stilled, my finger still pressed to my lips, as the words on the open page caught my attention. I could read them. Much like the etchings on the Niflym Temple, they glowed faintly red, as if written in the blood of the dead. Regardless, they were legible.

I brought the book up to my breast, cradling it close to my thundering heart. From across the room, the flames in the fire seemed to grow in brilliance, as if eager to provide light for me to devour the written words. The book was spattered illegibly in places with ink and blood, but it was immediately obvious to me what it was. A diary. Which left me with more questions than it did answers, and only one solution.

I needed to read.

I T FEELS LIKE I'VE been dreaming of Him as long as I can remember, but in truth, it is simply that life had no meaning before I saw him as a mere reflection in a window for the first time on the eve of my twenty-first name dey. After that, I saw Him in every puddle of water, in every frosted window, and in every dream each noct. At feasts, as men and women dance, all I can see is his face and mine on their twirling bodies, and when they fade into dark corners or behind the black trees of the wood and I spy on them from the shadows, all I can see is Him and me. I'm tormented by the ghost of a man I've never met, a ghost who has a visceral hold on me that none can shake.

Tonoct, I murdered the man I was betrothed to. It was as simple as a knife slipping into the back of his neck while he was taking a piss, drunk in the alley. I should have felt remorse, but all I could feel was elation when I saw His face in the blackening puddle of blood that wept from the dying man's body. Wearing the black will buy me a season's time, in which my father cannot trade me off to another. But my father is a man of wealth, his fortune made on the backs of the lumbermen who mill the Blackwood, and there are many who want my hand and a place in our home—the only one in our village built solidly out of stone with glass to fill the arching windows, wooden shingles instead of thatch, and a larder filled to the brim year-round. My heart is twisted up in a bramble. I don't know what I'll do if He doesn't come for me soon.

MY FATHER SAYS I am to marry Jorth—a leering brute of a man with hands as big as the blade on his axe. I wept and begged him not to make me, but all he said was that I'm useless to him without a husband. Father says I must bear children to carry his line. How can I explain that I will not be able to bear children for that man because I cannot muster the will to care, the will to eat, the will to live, not when I am haunted with the ever-present phantom of Him calling to me. I find myself waking in the wood at noct, my feet bare in the snow, in nothing but my shift and my cloak that is as red as the bloody footprints I leave on the forest floor. I wander home at the break of dey with the musk of rotted leaves clinging to my hair and dirt caked under nails chipped jagged from clawing over stones in my stupor.

Mother cries whenever she looks at me now. She used to call me her little dove. This morning, when I came in through the back door, I found her hunched by the hearth, wearing the stench of strong drink like a veil as she told me she wished I'd died in her womb instead of my twin sister. I told her sometimes I wish that too. That didn't seem to cheer her.

I THREW MYSELF FROM the cliffs yesterdey to avoid my marriage. But like a fish on a line, His spirit reeled me back. He dragged me through the icy water. His image floated in fractals around me in the crash of the waves and the pull of the currents.

When I returned home, my skin gray and numb, spidered over with frost, I found they'd already burned all my belongings save for this book, which I'd hidden in the mattress straw, and my cloak on the peg by the back door. These pages and His specter are all I have left in this world to comfort me.

I ONCE AGAIN WOKE in the Blackwood in a nest of moldering leaves and thorny branches. Kalda frost kissed my eyelashes and dusted my cheeks. My bones felt brittle and sharp against the inside of my skin as I pushed myself to sitting to see how far from home I'd gone. A ribbon of scarlet blood wended through the open space of a treefall gap, through the dried brush clinging all over with split and spent seed pods, round a bit of rubble, and tied itself to where my bare feet poked from the edge of my crimson cloak.

A groan scraped across my bones, as hollow as the little bird my mother had once so tenderly called me, as I used the trunk of the tree I'd curled against to pull myself to standing. Hunger gnawed at the edges of my mind, making my thoughts fray.

Poking out from the rubble, I spied the shriveled remnants of rosehips. I stumbled forward. A wince pinched my face with each step toward the brambles, hunched and curled. Sprouted in byrthe from the mossy crevices between rocks, they were now just skeletal remains.

I fell to my knees before I could reach the feet of the stones. I crawled through the slurry of red-stained snow and pithy dirt to where the prickly twigs tangled across the gray rock, and I plucked a seedy handful of berries. I greedily ate them as I pressed my forehead to the frigid stones, letting my hair, matted with detritus, fall across my face and obscure the wood around me.

The rosehips returned a meager bit of my strength, and I stood to realize I'd been mistaken. The rubble was not, in fact, natural but a lip of a well crumbled with age. Unable to help myself, I leaned over its edge and peered into its hollow maw to see if I could catch a silvery glimpse of water at its bottom so I might see Him. The water was dark and shrouded in leaves worn through to look like decrepit lace, but between their dried-up veins, I could see the hint of His eye. I leaned farther over the well's edge, my heart skipping against my ribs, the drumming of it trembling along my fingers as I stretched forward.

I did not scream as I fell, pitched inward, pulled by the thrall his visage had over me. Nor did I gasp for air when I broke the surface of the water as it spun me in its icy grip. Above me, the Emphyrea whirled; its peaks, like neat rows of teeth, poked out of a dense gum of clotted clouds. Peace washed over my numb skin, and I knew with a peculiar certainty that I was exactly where I was meant to be as the water swelled up around me and pulled me into its depths until the mouth of the well was only a silver pinprick, no brighter than a star stone. And then even that rattled out of existence and there was nothing, and still, I did not try to scream.

WHEN I AWOKE SWADDLED on a bed of furs skinned from beasts foreign to me, the steam-warmed air choked with the smell of smoke and brimstone, He stood above me. Tears limned my lids, welled up, and blurred my vision. I dashed them away quickly so as not to obscure the sight of Him, all of him physically and unwavering in front of me. He sat on the bed next to me in the low-flickering firelight tinged strangely with an argent hue. His skin was nearly as gray as the rock, pale but luminous and marred beautifully with white scars. His hair was as black as the deepest reaches of the forest, and his eyes as they beheld me were the shade of tarnished silver, but they glinted with crystalline flecks as they roved over the swelling curves of my body beneath the hides that covered me. Twin onyx horns curled from his head in sharp, lethal-looking spires. He was just as I knew him to be from my visions, and he was so much more.

He brushed a gentle finger across my forehead, sweeping away an errant strand of hair. "At last you have come to me." His voice rolled through me like thunder, and I shuddered. "I have been waiting a very long time."

Whole pages were covered in a bleed of ink as I skimmed one after the other to find the next Emrys-blessed stretch of tightly scrawled words.

I WAS ON MY *knees before him. It was not fear that brushed against my heart but a lust so raw and*

consuming, I felt I might burst like a piece of overripe fruit, my juices running over the floor.

I want Terr to consume me, I want to be his, all the more so because I know how much I never can be—his heart belongs to another. But even if his heart belongs to her, the cock that strained against the front of his breeches, that could be all mine. I reached up and tentatively ran the heel of my hand over the swollen length of it, and he moaned, grinding himself into my palm. I'd not done this before, but I'd watched lumbermen rut with whores, hidden behind trees, and I'd dreamt of being touched and touching a man somedey. None I had met had sparked anything within me, and I understood in that moment that it was because I had always been meant for him.

"Do you understand what you are asking for, maiden? What it is I will seed within you?" He towered over me.

"Yes." The word fell breathily from my lips, and I rose slightly to tug on the laces of his pants. His hands moved with mine to shuck his clothes from his skin. His cock sprang free, loosed from its strangling prison, and I gasped. It was so much more than any I'd seen on Emrys-made men, but he was no Emrys-made man, he was one of the great Niflym.

He gripped my chin between his calloused fingers. "I need to hear you say it."

I could barely tear my eyes away from his cock long enough to recall the words he'd said before so I could phrase my own properly to appease him. Fuck, but I would do anything to satisfy him. "I understand that you need a vessel. I will be that vessel. I will let you breed me, gladly."

I didn't wait for him to answer, instead, I let instinct and the memory of the couplings I'd witnessed guide me and flicked my tongue from the base of his member to the tip in one long stroke. A moan shook loose from him, and, relishing the feel of his pleasure reverberating through his skin and into mine, I repeated the motion again and again, letting the sound fill me and wring moisture from between my legs. A milky bead wept from his tip, and I sucked it off, savoring the salted taste of him.

"Enough," he growled, and I gasped as he jerked me to my feet. Talons erupted from his fingers, and with a swift swipe, they sliced through my shift. The fabric fell around me like petals ripped from a flower, leaving only a starkly naked stem. Heat crept up my face, but then he purred and I flamed for a whole different reason.

"Oh, Drusylla," he crooned as he ducked his head to nuzzle the sensitive skin of my neck, his hand smoothing over the curve of my hip and around the swell of my backside. "Tell me, are you wet for me?"

His fingers played along my skin, sweeping from where he'd gripped my ass, over the ridge of my hip bone, and back up over my ribs to brush the soft underswell of my breast. I didn't know how to answer, not when my skin was on fire. He toyed with one of my peaked nipples, sending shockwaves through my flesh where they burrowed into my bones. My knees gave out, but he was ready for that too. He scooped me up and laid me before him on his bed.

He spread my legs, his eyes glistening, silver and starved in the low light. With a single finger, Terr sliced through me from the apex of my thighs to swirl at my pulsating entrance that wept with need of him, then he brought his finger to his lips and licked me clean off him. "You taste like the rivers of aurora," he growled.

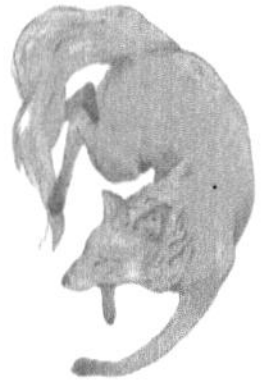

I TURNED THE PAGE, my breath hitched in my throat, anticipation rocking me forward, ready to hungrily devour page after page, but I groaned as I was met with nothing but indecipherable scrawl bled through with so many tears and faded with so much time that it made the words unreadable. I flipped past them, desperate for more, until at last I came to another page with legible script.

WITH HIS THUMB, TERR swiped his cum from where it dripped out of me and pressed it back into my cunt. "We can't let a single seed go to waste," he purred. Leaning forward, he nipped my lip, drawing out a spent whimper.

He bred me again and again that noct until his sac was emptied and my womb filled, then he held me as I slept. For the briefest of moments, I forgot that it wasn't real, that I was just an empty pot from which he could reap a harvest, but when I awoke, his cum sticking to my knees and the bed beside me, bare, the ache between my legs was rivaled only by the ache of my fracturing heart.

Terr sent me back exactly where he'd found me, trapped in the icy fist of the well. My whole body was needled with cold when they discovered me. In one hand was the remnant of Agredmonya's sword, which I would wield like a sculptor wields their chisel to carve out an existence for myself and for the warmth in my womb that I knew would be my baby and Terr's eventual salvation.

I thumbed through the pages to find another readable one. I was on the precipice of something, something all-consuming that I felt could somehow devour everything I knew and spit it back out at me and laugh. My magic whined, as anxious as I was for answers. Who was this woman who had birthed a half Niflym sired by Terr himself? On the very last page that clung to the spine by a single frayed thread were the last words of Drusylla, hastily scrawled.

My son sits on the throne of the kingdom I built for him, that he built for himself. His reign shall stand for ages until the time is right to loose his sire from his bonds. My only regret is that I will not live to see Terr walk free of the Umbra and bring balance to a blind world sorely in need of sight. It will end where it began.

I stared into the dancing depths of the fire. My mouth hung open, stuffed full with the acrid taste of disbelief. The last words of Drusylla floated in my mind's eye. "It *will end where it began.*" She had to have meant the well. Somedey, her son would rip open Strattaria, cleaving a hole through to the Umbra so his father could walk this world. A shudder of magic rippled down my spine, interlaced with my own fears. I did not know what exactly Terr's powers were, but they were wretched enough that the Emrys had seen fit to cast him out, which meant I didn't ever want to know what evil he could wrought.

I bolted out of bed, Drusylla's words wrapping around my limbs and pulling me to pace the floor. She'd said she'd had Agredmonya's sword. That was a name I knew, one every soul knew intimately, and it was a name everyone was afraid to speak, to write, to even think, for any of those actions might summon her. It was the name of the Red Lady.

Thoughts tangled like loose bits of spiderweb in my mind; I just needed to spin them into something resembling sense. I flipped open the book again and read and reread and reread again until the break of dey pried through the shutters and the sound of booted feet echoed in the hall.

At the sound of a soft rap on the door, the book went flying from my hands and sailed across the room to land discreetly on top of my wardrobe. The pitch and the landing were a bit too perfect for it to be anything other than my magic at work, though my tired and sleepless mind did not recall willing it to happen.

Munnin poked her head in, her blue eyes still hooded with sleepiness. "Oh, good. Ye do be up. The tournaments do start soon, and ye will need to be ready."

The tournaments? I shuffled through my thoughts. *What tournaments?* Did I know about this? Right, yes I did. My patients had spoken of it as part of their Eklipsis rituals along with the ball and the Hunt. I'd been assigned to heal the wounded participants, but Huggin said there might be time for me to watch some of the games as well. There'd been tourneys at home, and I was a little curious to see how they would differ here.

I pinned a smile to my cheeks. "Thank you, Munnin. I'll get dressed."

She was about to shut the door when it creaked back open and she poked her head in again, seemingly struck by some kind of afterthought. "Don't forget Huggin do be waiting for ye to work the Forms before ye and I head down to the arena."

I groaned inwardly but kept my smile in place. "I'll be there."

I quickly dressed and met Huggin on the balcony. The morning air tasted of hard frost, the sort there was no turning back from, that let me know kalda had well and truly set in. It peppered my skin with frigid kisses from my head to my bare toes. Huggin's hulking silhouette was outlined in the rays of Jyord's light reaching listlessly over the horizon. I crossed the balcony, stood next to him, and leaned as he did, forearms resting against the crenelated stone edge. Unsurprisingly, he didn't turn to me or utter a word; if I didn't know better, I might have thought him part of the wall, carved of the same rock.

We stood like that for a few breaths before I dared to place my palm over top of his hand. It was so warm beneath my touch, it startled me—his blood ran so hot as to be near feverish. Part of me wanted to delve into him with my magic, but I resisted, knowing Huggin would not appreciate the intrusion and that he would ask if he was truly in need. Instead, I simply squeezed his fingers. "Thank you for the herbs you left in my room."

"And how do ye know it was me?" he asked, but there was a twinkle in the glance he darted my way.

"You're the only one I know who could write in such a stolid manner," I teased lightly. "And besides, you are also the only one who knew I was in need of them."

He chuckled, the rumble of it taking root deep in his ribcage. The muscles along the sides of his naked and inked torso shook with the mirth. "I suppose I do be less mysterious than I did think I was."

His words took me by surprise and shook a laugh out of my weary and woesome heart. "I wouldn't say that. You're still plenty enigmatic."

"Good. I can't have ye knowing all my secrets." He caught my hand in his and gave it a squeeze back—which, from a man like Huggin, may as well have been a bear hug—before he let me go and straightened, turning to fully look at me instead of at the horizon. His brow furrowed, knitted together above his blue eyes with something that looked uncomfortably like concern, and for a fretful moment, I worried he could see the magic roiling beneath my skin. But then he spoke. "Do ye need to pass on the Forms todey? Ye do look like the dead warmed over. Did ye no sleep?"

I turned away quickly, hiding my face as I waved him off. "No, no. I'm perfectly fine. I slept like a babe." My magic poked me in the ribs as if to admonish me for the lie, but I nudged it back.

I took my place on my rug—furtively avoiding Huggin's scrutiny. Its fibers chafed my knees through the thin fabric of my billowing Forms pants, but I swept the sensation away along with every other ache and pain and worry and let them all drown in the timbre of Huggin's voice as he took me at my word. He commanded me to contort my body into different positions. With my lids closed, my magic surged, rolling, swelling, and breaking against the different bones of my body as I shifted poses, held them, and then moved again. I hadn't been consciously aware when it had happened, but my magic was no longer contained to a well but the depths of an infinite sea. No more was I anchored by fears of drying out, of angering the Emrys who'd given me my gifts, not when my magic seeped and saturated the very marrow and blood and soul of my being. I'd never need to let it go. I was it and it was me, and it purred as I gave over to it all the broken and fragmented bits of knowledge I had so it could weave them together into a whole tapestry that would make sense. So I could understand.

With the magic so suffused throughout my body, I felt buoyant, no longer burdened with the need to find my way out of this predicament or to comprehend why I was here, because my magic would do that for me. My mind and my heart were free of aches as I let more and more magic guide me until time flowed around me. I seemed to slide from one moment to the next without noticing until Rhapso's hand touched my arm and I found myself sitting on risers overlooking the tournament field without really being sure how I'd gotten there.

I looked down at my lap. My fingers on my healer's basket did not glow, and I was dressed in the traditional white of the Selenyss Temple's dedicated healers, veil and all.

"Are you alright, dear? You seem to be away with the Emrys this dey."

A small tendril of fear curled in the back of my mind. When had I gotten dressed? When had I gathered my supplies, walked down here? Had I spoken to anyone on the way? An image seized upon my mind of Kastor's face smiling down at me, his thumb sweeping across my cheek, his lips forming words that were garbled and saturated as though uttered through murky bog water. What had we spoken of? My magic quickly soothed my worries with a gentle caress and a murmured, "*Hush.*"

"I am well, Rhapso." I smiled, though it felt a bit wrong on my face, a bit too droopy and lax. "And you?"

The stitch between her brow smoothed, but only fractionally, as if my words didn't quite assuage her concerns. "I am well. Though I admit my fingers are a bit sore from stitching red cloaks for what feels like deys."

My wit sharpened, honing in on her words. "Red cloaks? For what?"

Her lips pulled down at the corners, dragging her pretty, round-cheeked face into a deep frown. Her eyes darted around. "For the Hunt, of course."

"Ah, yes. That is soon, isn't it? I haven't given it much thought since Fenris told me I won't be participating. Will we all have to attend that as well?"

She shimmied closer to me along the wooden bench until her thigh pressed against mine to make room for other spectators. "Emrys, no. And even if we were supposed to, I wouldn't if my life depended on it." She shuddered and made a discreet sign against evil.

"Isn't it just some sort of arranged marriage ceremony for the Sons?" I laughed, but it fell flat and rang hollow, even to my ears.

She cleared her throat, her eyes shifting once again across the bobbing heads. "Well, yes, but it's more than that too. It's a tradition that goes back further than the founding of Uthar. Eligible maidens assemble on the edge of the hunting grounds, dressed only in white shifts and red cloaks. They are then given a head start to run into the Blackwood as far and as fast as they can and hide. Sons in want of a wife are set loose after them to track them down and catch themselves a bride. They, well..." Her cheeks pinked as she sputtered on her words. "They couple with one another in the snow. For the spousal bond between them to be recognized, they must return with the blood of the woman's maidenhood on her shift or cloak."

"That's barbaric." But it was more than barbaric, it was clearly an annual remembrance—if not specifically, then in spirit—of Drusylla and the Niflym. What were they trying to accomplish? Was it merely an honoring of their ancestry, or was it something far more insidious?

"It's worse than barbaric. Oftentimes, the participants, the women at least, don't have any choice in whether or not they join. Families choose for their daughters, and the Father and Mother have, on several occasions, chosen women to shove into the woods. Choice doesn't matter—if a virginal woman is in the Blackwood on the dey of the Hunt, she is considered prey." Rhapso rested a gentle hand on my knee. "I was happy to hear that Fenris found a way out of it for you. I prayed each noct since our first meeting that you would be spared."

I clasped my hand over hers and gave it a squeeze. "And what about you? Are you safe from this archaic tradition?"

The flush on her cheeks deepened to a mottled crimson, and she let out a little laugh, molded through with old traumas like blue veins in a cheese. "I am a widow, not a maiden, so I am blessedly safe, but I appreciate your kind heart and your concern my friend."

The word *widow* looped around my throat and choked off any words I'd thought to reply with. There was so little I knew about this woman who called me friend. She'd lived a whole dark and painful life before we'd ever met if the sorrowful darkening in her violet eyes was any indication. I just hoped that somedey we would have more time in a freer place to lay our hearts bare before one another and heal.

Munnin found us, her onyx hair dusted through with frost despite her raised hood, and settled in next to Rhapso, her arms laden with vendors' sweet treats. The smell of the spices wafted across the crisp breeze that tugged at the spectators' cloak hems and fur-lined cowls. "There ye do be." She beamed at us both. "Huggin do be competing in the archery games later. Ye do no want to miss it."

As the horn sounded, summoning the first warriors—bare-chested despite the bite of ice that rode on Imbola's wind—to the field to pair off and wrestle one another, unending silence plugged my ears so full, I couldn't even hear the drum of my heart. I jerked my head around to find everyone in the stands and on the tournament ground utterly still, as if carved of pale stone; even the flakes of snow hung stalled in mid-descent. Then she appeared in the center of the fighting ring, dressed in her signature bloody color. The Red Lady stood, a malevolent sneer painted on her face, an empty scabbard at her hip as she raised a single finger and pointed toward the woods. As I followed the razor-sharp cut of her finger with my gaze, I felt a pull in my magic, like ribbons of power tied to my viscera, toward those distant, bare trees. It was no coincidence then that I was in Uthar in time for the Hunt, that I'd found and read Drusylla's story mere deys before it was to occur. The Emrys wanted me there in the woods to play out the ghost of the past for myself. But Drusylla had not gone to just any place in the woods, she'd gone to a well...and come back through it with a sword in hand.

The Red Lady's dark, insidious eyes locked on mine. She nodded, a mere tip of her chin to affirm my suspicions, and then she was gone. The snow once again dove for the ground and melted on the sweat-coated backs of the competitors as their feet churned the tourney ground to mud. But in that single heartbeat stuttered by Death's appearance, I knew I had to enter the Hunt, not to be bred and wed, but to find the Emrys-forsaken well, and with it, her sword.

"It will end where it began." Though what exactly I was to end by finding it for her was another question entirely.

MUD, BLOOD, AND DAMP from the tourney grounds covered the white linen of my skirt, an eerie and gory mirror of the dey I'd been dragged across the sea to Uthar. The horror of the memory and the crushing yearning for home threatened to seed in my heart and grow into something viscous and consuming. I tossed it instead into the rising tide of my magic to let it drown there with the rest of my woes that I could not at present address—that I might never be able to address. There were people to heal, and the oath to heal blindly was one that, no matter the delirium my magic rocked through my brain, I would not shirk.

Noct was fast approaching as Melantha began to twirl her dark skirts over the edge of the horizon; already I could see the faint twinkle of a star stone in the distance.

A breathless servant slipped into a sloppy curt-sy in the mud before me. "Begging your pardon, Healer, but there is a competitor in need of heal-ing. He's in that far tent over there. He's in a bad way, my lady." I steadied the slight woman with a firm grip on her elbow, lest she slip into the near-frozen, blood-soiled muck, with a muttered word of thanks before I set off in the direction she'd indicated, Huggin an ever-present shadow on my heels ever since he'd completed his competitions.

The tournament was over. The echo of the horns that had heralded its end had long since drifted out to sea, and most of the contestants and spectators were either bunkered down for the coming noct or heading back to the lesser or high court for feasting, ale, and celebration. This had to be the last patient of the dey. I'd seen to everything from minor cuts and bruises to men and women who'd had the Red Lady hovering over their shoulders. She'd stolen only four from me—a man with a lance through his eye, a women with a knife wound on her inner thigh who'd bled out while being carried to me, a boy barely into manhood who'd been run through by his own cousin, and an elderly man who never should have been allowed to enter, but with his last breaths, he'd confessed he'd just wanted the chance to die with honor, with a sword in his hand. Each death had been a wound, each soul taken from my grasp by a vile Emrys with a bloody smirk on her face like a taut bow string struck me, and I'd had to throw them all into the tumultuous depths of my magic. Some aches sank quicker than others.

I peeked into the recesses of my mind, where my magic wove notions and tidbits of memory and information into a tapestry of luminescent threads, to see if I could make heads or tails of her yet, The Red Lady. Why she'd sent me of all people, what I was to end by retrieving her weapon. But it was still just a jumble of tangled, intangible thoughts. I pulled away from it as a red-and-blue-striped tent came into view on the edge of the grounds, where competitors who'd supposedly come from other countries were encamped until the Eklipsis festivities were over. I'd never heard of anyone coming to Uthar of their own free will, so my curiosity was piqued as I announced myself at the canvas flaps.

Fenris came barreling out of the entry before I could slip in, and our near collision unbalanced me to such an extent that he had to fling out his hands and steady my shoulders. Heat rose from all ten points of his touch. It radiated along the bond until my whole body was alight in a tingling inferno in a matter of a single heartbeat, like a malaised fever flush.

He pulled his hands off my body as quickly as he'd settled them and knotted his fingers behind his back, as far away from me as he could physically get them. "Steady, Shepherdess," he grumbled, but the rest of what he said was drowned in the stark ache of the bond ink. It pulled against my skin like a flower yearning for the sun. "Are you listening to me?" Fenris's brow crumpled over his eyes that seemed to leach the darkness of the coming noct into their depths. "You don't look well."

"Forgive me. I've been working all dey, and it's taken quite a lot out of me," I murmured, tearing my gaze from his as I bit the inside of my cheek, resisting the urge to reach out and press a hand to his bond just to quell the sensation that I was being torn apart slowly by inked vines as they reached out for him.

"Forgive you? Well, there really must be something wrong for you to be so polite." His words were jesting, but the furrow of his brow and the lines around his lips deepened as though carved by a heavy-handed chisel.

He reached up as if to brush a stray hair off my cheek, but I ducked and evaded his would-be touch. I didn't trust it—the bond or the desires that it had written upon my flesh. I would not give in.

"You should come back to the Fortress and rest." If I didn't know better, I would have thought his words sounded bruised.

"I have one last patient." Though he ought to have known that since he'd just left the person's tent. I tried to imagine who was lying on the other side of the flap. Would it be his friend? A foe? Or perhaps another lover—I'd seen many beautiful women competing todey.

He nodded, his braids swaying over his leather jerkin-clad shoulder as he did. "Right, well, I'll let you get to it then." He nodded to my hulking guard, where he lurked some pace or two behind. "Huggin, a word."

I had to clench my fist into my skirt to keep my traitorously bonded fingers from reaching for him as he swept by, even as he passed so closely that the back of his knuckles brushed mine. A shudder wracked my bones and sent my magic rippling through my blood, and I had to bite back a sigh. The connection between us was acting so strangely this noct—a notion I too threw into the rising swell of my magic as I took a deep breath and stepped into the tent.

My basket tumbled from the crook of my elbow as soon as the flap fell back into place. The lopsided smirk on the face of the man in front of me was so familiar, for a moment, I was certain I'd slipped into a dream until he spoke.

"Hello, Little Sprite."

"Tad!" I threw myself into Otadan's embrace, tears spilling scalding and hot from my eyes as his arms wrapped around me. The smell of home, nostalgic and sweet, filled me with a homesick ache so poignant, it felt as though it cracked open my chest, plucked out my still-beating heart, and took a bite.

But then Tad ran a hand down my hair and whispered, "Easy now, Sprite," and it filled the crushing emptiness.

"What in the Umbra are you doing here?" I half laughed, half sobbed into his crimson-colored tunic as he pulled me into his lap like he had when we'd been children with skinned knees.

"Did you really think Thyra would do nothing when she learned of your kidnapping? Now let me look at you. Are you whole? Are you hale?" He rocked me back, held me out, and looked me up and down.

I wanted to tell him to stop being such a ninny, that I was just fine, as I would have so long ago. But that wasn't true. I was whole in body, but I knew something was broken within me and only my magic kept me stitched together and standing. But I was too awash in the effervescent feeling of seeing the man who, for all intents and purposes, was a brother to me—and for all I knew, with our father passed on, he truly was.

"I want to hear about home. Should I be bowing? Has Thyra made you her consort yet? How's

Mother and my other sisters? Did Father's funeral go well?" I kept my words pitched low so as not to let them carry to where Huggin and my keeper waited outside.

Tad laughed. "I see living among wolves hasn't blunted your ability to bleat like a sheep, Sprite. Come sit. We'll talk. I have honey mead from home, and Thyra made me bring you these."

My eyes flicked to the flaps as he bent and plucked a cloth-wrapped bundle from a crate and handed it over. I had little time to spare, the length of a healing at most. I tugged at the frayed twine strings hurriedly. Inside were two hand pies, a little crushed and worse for wear from the journey, but still, they smelled divine. I plopped down onto the rickety chair Tad had arranged next to an upturned half barrel that I assumed was meant to be the table and immediately plucked one up and began to devour it. I nearly wept at the loamy sweet taste of mashed pumpkin and clove.

"Slow down, Sprite, or you're liable to choke," Tad teased as he reached across the makeshift table to swipe a bit of the crumbling, flaky crust. I swatted at his hand, barely grazing it in a familiar dance that made it feel like it had been moments since I'd seen him last and not years.

I washed the pie down with the honeyed vinter-berry mead and leaned back to find Tad watching me with his deep sea green eyes beneath his crop of brown hair. A shadow of stubble dusted his usually clean-shaven chin; the Vanyth style had always favored neatness over the thick beards of the eastern nations. He had a few more scars than the last time we'd been in the same place, but as captain of the royal guards, that was to be expected.

"So *should* I bend the knee to you, Your Majesty?" I lifted an eyebrow, probing for the answers to the questions I'd earlier asked.

He crossed his arms. "No, not yet." He raised a hand to silence me, knowing me well enough to know I was about to argue before I'd even twitched a lip. "Thyra wants to wait until you're safe at home before we make it official, and I agree. It wouldn't be the same without you there, Sprite."

Realization settled and stacked in my ribcage like the stones used to sink the bodies of the dead at sea. "I can't, Tad. I can't come back with you."

He went stock-still, his eyes darkening like I'd only see them do once when our father had announced Thyra's potential contractual marriage to a prince from Iliff. "What in the Umbra do you mean?" His voice was deathly calm, but it cut me like a knife to the throat.

I swallowed hard. "I have something I have to do first. It isn't by chance that I was kidnapped. It was—" The words I'd intended to say died on my lips. I took a breath and tried to re-form them, but they wouldn't budge. A thought struck me, and I began to wonder if perhaps the Red Lady had bound me somehow with a curse so I could not utter a word of the circumstances surrounding my being in Uthar. "I just need until the dey after Eklipsis, I swear, and then we can go home." Yes, that felt right; it felt true enough. My magic purred. Whatever was happening, whatever I was meant to do for the Emrys, it would come to a head then.

Tad leaned forward and took my hand. The warmth of his touch felt like a summons home, one I wanted to answer so badly. "Whatever trouble you're in, Sprite, let me help you."

My eyes flicked to the door. Fenris had been in here moments before me; what did he know? Did Tad know who Fenris was? Did Fenris know who Tad was? My magic tangled like thorny briars around my heart. Who could I trust with the truth?

I shook my head, trying to find words that danced along the edge of honesty. "I'm alright, Tad. I just need a bit more time, I have it well in hand." I definitely didn't, but I hoped my magic did, and I hoped once I found the Red Lady's sword, she could remove this bond from my arm and what I'd said would be true.

I felt an itch along the bond akin to a tug, a reminder that I'd been gone too long, and I told Tad as much as I stood.

Otaden pulled a map from one of his various bags, and we agreed upon a spot to meet the dey after the Hunt. The ship would be marked with the flag of the Orybousi; he'd not wanted to risk sailing under the Vanyth colors lest the Father think he was here to do more than just compete, which, of course, he was. He would be anchored with a skiff in a cove at the base of the cliffs beyond the northern portion of the Fortress. He'd scouted a rugged set of fisherman's steps gouged into the stone that descended straight out of the Blackwood. I would make my way to them, and from there, we would sail home. Simple enough. I would already be in the damnable woods. I just had to trust my magic to navigate a route from the well to the cove.

Our hug goodbye lingered, neither one of us willing to let the other go so soon, but the bond began itching more incessantly, and I was forced to pull away from the crushing safety and shelter of Tad's arms around me and the steady thump of his heart against my cheek.

Before I followed Huggin and slipped through the servants' door back into the Fortress, I turned back to find Otaden's lone silhouette illuminated in a shaft of Selenyss's light, his arm raised in farewell. My heart wept even as I schooled my face into a careful mask of blank neutrality to walk back into the den of wolves.

The apartment was still and dark when I crept in, though gilded firelight threw long shadows into the hall from the sitting room. Warily drawn to them, I stepped lightly across the wooden floorboards. The air tasted of worry wrought from sorrow, and I did not want to intrude where I was not wanted, but my magic reached out, unspooling to wrench me closer to that emotional wound I could feel bleeding.

Lord Fenris leaned against the mantel, his forehead pressed to his forearm, his dark gaze intent on the lapping tongues of fire. Munnin lay crumpled in the curl of a chair's arm with silent tears streaming down her bronzed cheeks.

I stood at the threshold, waffling, caught between wanting to offer comfort and sneaking back to my room to pretend I'd never heard the relentless rot of sorrow creeping down the hall.

"Oh, Huggin, Ertha, there ye do be. I worried." Munnin sniffled, shoved herself up off her seat, and wrapped herself in the embrace of her brother's arms. "Forgive us, we did just get ill word from home."

Hesitantly, I stepped closer. It seemed odd, more than coincidental that both they and I should have had contact from home on the same noct. "I'm so sorry to hear that. Is there anything I can do for you? I know a lovely tea that helps with upset."

"Unless you know a tea that can heal death, keep your herbs to yourself, Shepherdess. The queen of Corvus has passed on," Fenris growled from where he leaned broodingly without deigning to look at me. Beside me, Huggin made a choked noise that sounded painfully like a strangled sob.

The Seer's words regarding my father's death rang through my thoughts, and I wondered if it had been poison that'd killed this monarch as well in the name of destabilization.

"Who will ascend the throne in her place?" I could not for the life of me dredge up the name of the Corvusi heir, but the fleeting image of a young man with piercingly blue eyes floated through on the ghost of a recollection from when I'd been small. Could it be that boy, grown now into a man, who would bear the weight of the country?

"Her son, in all likelihood." Fenris righted himself finally, tossing a scrap of parchment he'd had fisted in his bond-marked hand into the fire to be devoured as he did so. "It is none of our concern now. We have an Eklipsis ball and the Hunt to prepare for. Go get some rest, Shepherdess."

Hurt and anguish, searing and raw, trickled through our bond and leached into my heart. It had to be from him, it had to be his feelings bleeding into mine, and it hurt. Oh bloody Emrys, but did it hurt. My heart cracked open, and a single tear sliced down my cheek. It felt like my bones were being shattered and every feeling of grief I'd ever felt was dredged up all at once. A specter of a woman drifted incorporeally through the room; her beauty was haunting and unmatched. Her onyx hair drifted behind her, caught in an invisible wind as she breezed across the common space. She raised her hand toward Fenris, and my vision split. I was myself, but I also peered through Fenris's eyes. In his sight, there was no other woman, there was only me. My magic churned like a tempest-ridden ocean, and my blood rushed in my ears. Fire roared, consuming my sight, the flames spitting like they too felt the consuming sorrow, and in its pain, it wanted to devour everything in Stratarria until there was nothing left but black smoke and cindered ash.

I gasped, shaken from my stricken stupor by Fenris's charcoal eyes nearly nose to nose in front of me, boring into mine. In a blink, the pain receded, like venom sucked from a wound.

"I said go rest." He whispered the words gently, and I felt them across the meager distance like a caress down my cheek. I swallowed hard, and without argument, I obeyed. But as I strode away, I experimentally shoved healing into the places where the bond was knit into the fibers of my being, and as I rounded the corner out of the common room and into the hall, I snuck a glance back at my keeper to find the tension in his shoulders seemed to have eased. Likewise, the set of his jaw seemed softened. And though he was looking at his friends and not at me, I could almost envision that some of the weight in his eyes might have lifted as well.

I WORE A FRETFUL path in the rug that noct as I paced, my eyes closed, and watched my magic stitch and loop together every scrap of information I'd gleaned until I was dizzy, and to no avail. It had yet to make a decipherable shape in my mind's eye. So instead, I turned my attention to my plan. I needed to get into the Blackwood, and the quickest way was to slip in with the Hunt the next dey. The simplest way I could think to do that was to participate, which meant I needed a red cloak. I rummaged through my wardrobe but found nothing to suit my needs. All my cloaks were dark, beautiful shades, but they would not do. I could perhaps steal one, but from whom, I didn't know.

My magic tapped against my skull to get my attention, then began to mime an idea, mapping it out in my imagination step by step for me to follow. A brittle smile cracked across my lips. It *just might work.* I took out the palest cloak in the collection, one lined with the short, coal-colored fur of the Blackwood squirrel, and used my magic to suspend it in the air as if draped over the shoulders of a phantom. With barely a thought, my magic pricked the pad of my finger from the inside until a crimson droplet of blood beaded on its tip. I let it fall onto the tightly woven wool strands of the garment, and with a surge of power, I took the blood and multiplied it, much like I did when healing, and saturated the strands until the cloak was vermilion. The magic twisted and twined around the strands, keeping the color in place so it would not fade into rust like blood would on any other bit of cloth.

Struck suddenly with inspiration like a dream, I cannibalized threads from other dresses, shifts, and vests, summoning them to weave as I willed—to stitch themselves into the hem of my new cloak until all around its edge, wolves chased a maiden I'd embroidered into the likeness of Drusylla as a macabre sort of blessing upon myself for protection and luck in my endeavors in the Hunt.

I thumbed through Drusylla's journal again, skimming passages and plucking words like posies to keep in my heart and guide me through the dark of the kalda woods.

Munnin knocked on my door sometime before Jyord arose with the sun to check on me. "Do ye be wanting me to help ye prepare for the ball tonoct? I could help ye pick out a dress. Rhapso did send up some new options for ye." She brushed a strand of black hair off her brow. "I did plan to spend the dey with her, but I do be able to come back early if ye do need me."

I folded the woman into a hug, letting my magic seep into her skin, filling her with silver strands of sparkling happiness. I twined them around the heavy, sticky grief that hung from her heart to lessen her burden before drawing back.

"I'll manage on my own this time, Munnin, but thank you for everything you've done for me since I arrived. Your compassion and friendship has been one of the only things that has kept me sane."

She peered at me from under skeptical brows, as if she could sense the goodbye buried six feet under my words, but she smiled rather than questioned me, a light of trust burning behind her blue eyes as she slipped out the door with a promise to find me later at the festivities.

I dressed simply and quickly—I had things to do before noctfall to prepare for tomorrow, and I could waste no precious time. Huggin waited in the common area for me. We ate a plain breakfast of bitter tea and savory buns stuffed with mushrooms, soft white cheese, dried herbs, and crumbly bits of sausage left by Munnin before her departure for the city, though I could barely stomach mine. My lord keeper likewise seemed to be out, though whether that was a blessing or a curse, I could not divine. Huggin and I ate in total silence save for the howling of the wind against the wall of lead-framed windows and the gentle crack of the fire as it devoured pitchy logs.

My healing basket was bundled with supplies hidden underneath the clay pots, bandages, and bouquets of desiccated flora. I made excuses to head first to the gardens, pausing only a moment to admire the devastating beauty of the waterfall as it threw shattered panes of ice over its precipice to crash below, before seeming to amble without thought toward the back iron gate. Huggin, as I suspected he would, lingered on the fringes within eyeshot but not close enough to make out the particulars of what I was doing. I knelt in the sloshy snow, halfway between melted and frozen, caught in a clash of heated, steamy air from the canals and kalda's frozen kiss that snaked past the wrought iron bars barring entry to the Blackwood. I pretended to harvest the spiraling hollow stems of a shrub that withered at its base—whistler's whorl, used occasionally for bronchial conditions—though the workshop already had a healthy supply. When the hulking man turned his attention to a flock of ravens roosting in a nearby tree, I quickly slipped my knotted pack from its hiding place under my heavy kalda skirts and slithered it through the bars. The brush of the frigid iron on the exposed span of delicate skin between the cuff of my sleeve and glove burned like cold fire, but I bit off a hiss and managed to shove my arm further through, just enough to bury my horde under a pile of decomposing leaf litter half rotted and frosted in crystalline speckles of ice.

I pretended to harvest a few more things—bitter blue sorrel and buttons of woody graybeck—partly to keep up my ruse and partly because the plants soothed something in me and in my magic. It simmered along my insides rather than boiled when my hands were in the soil. But through the watery clouds, I could see that Jyord's trek across the Emphyrea was nearing its zenith, which meant I needed to hasten on my way.

Huggin and I kept a comfortable buffer of silence between us as we dipped back into the Fortress's walls and spiraled down the narrow, spindly stairs to my workshop, our steps halted and tedious, as water had seeped in through the rock overnoct and frozen in ankle-breaking layers on the rough-hewn stairs.

I'd expected the workshop to be empty when at last I'd swung the door shut behind me, but rather, perched on the sill of the open, arching window, curtained in spear-tipped icicles, sat the Seer. In one cupped and gnarled hand rattled her stones and bones.

My heartbeats ratcheted as my eyes darted to the deep swells of shadows in the corners of the room, searching for any other potential surprises or eyes and ears on our conversation, "How are you here? I thought you were trapped in your rooms farther below?" She was part of the Father's collection, a situation I did not envy, but if she'd found a way to loose herself from her prison, then surely that boded well for my own attempts.

"I have a few tricks hidden up my ratty sleeves yet, but let's not dither, witch. I know you're planning on going to the well, aren't you, dear?" She cracked a chipped-tooth smile at me, her words rasping like the scrape of an axe on wood down my spine.

I stilled, one hand resting on the door latch, and raised a brow, but behind my passive face, my magic roiled and seethed a tempest inside me. It felt nervous or afraid that the Seer could upend our plans, but she'd yet to tattle to the Father about what I really was, so perhaps I could trust her, but I would need to proceed with caution to test the tenuous ice of our trust with a toe before deciding if it could bear my full weight. "What makes you think that?"

She chortled indignantly to the tune of her runes rattling in her clawed fist. "Let us skip the part where you play dumb, dear, and jump to the bit where you accept that I know your plan and I tell you it is an idiotic one."

Alright, so there was no time for hesitance or dancing around the point. "Fine, but only if you tell me what is so idiotic about it." I closed the distance between us by half, setting my basket onto the examination table as I eyed her warily.

She huffed and readjusted the tattered shawl that hung across her shoulders. "I can't see all, I've told you that, and the events of tomorrow are murky in my sight." She brandished a gnarled and knowing finger at me. "But do try not to walk right into a trap like a good little mouse because you like the smell of the cheese." The wry twist to her mouth wasn't kind nor unkind, but it was definitely patronizing, and condescendingly so. Though I supposed when you could see all, or almost all, those who couldn't likely seemed tedious, but my magic didn't like her tone. It hissed like an angry cat.

Besides—so what if I was? That cheese, as she'd called it, was no mere morsel; it was home, the return of all I cared about and all I loved, the return of safety, of normalcy. Wasn't that worth the potential snap of a trap?

"You said yourself the Red Lady sent me here. If I do what she wants, then I can go home. That is all I care about."

"You really think it will be that easy, witchling? That she is the only one setting snares to slip around your pretty little neck? Do you really think all she wants of you is to go to a well and retrieve her sword, and then she'll let you skip on home over the sea with the future king of Vanyth? Don't gawk, girl. Of course I know about Otaden. Use that bit of meat between your ears and think—why does she want the sword, and why can't she get it herself?"

Exasperated with her belligerence, I sighed, crossing my arms defensively over my chest. "I don't know—she wants to balance the scales or some such. Who am I to question the will of the Emrys?"

"You fool. You don't know what you're meddling with." She pointed her free hand at me again in an accusatory manner, her tattered shawl hanging off her crooked elbow like spider's webbing, blowing in the angry breeze off the sea.

"Don't you get it, Seer?" I shoved off the table where I leaned and took a step closer, my words hissed through my teeth, laced with barely contained frustration. "I don't care what I'm meddling with. I just want to go home. I just want to be my sister's Healer, to tend my garden, to find a kind man to settle down with and live out my deys in peace until this whole fucking disaster is nothing more than a faded noctmare in the back of my memories."

"Do you really think your magic will be content to simply heal and garden, witch? You carry in you more power than any witch before you; every seed of magic from Yaganya runs through you. The whole of her ability that was bled into an entire civilization has been condensed into one form, into your form. Whether you like it or not, you are a player in a cosmic game. You cannot simply go home."

That made my magic angry, or it made me angry, or both of us, I couldn't be sure. Either way, my next words were knit together with whispers and shouts and thrown in her aged face. "I don't want to play any games. I refuse. Do you understand me, old woman? I simply won't do it. I'm making a trade—the thing she wants most for the thing I want most, and then this will all be done."

"She doesn't just want her sword, Ertha. She wants them all. All the talismans of the Emrys. You think you can hand over this one token in exchange for your freedom, but you're wrong." She cast her stones and bones in fury across the floor at my feet, where they scattered, spun, and stilled.

But her words spun against my mind too, and the sound of them skittered into my skull as my magic scooped them up and tried to make sense of them. "What do you mean 'talismans?'"

The Seer simply shook her head, her eyes hooded, sorrowfully dampening the vehemence that burned in her irises. "You know so little, and I can only share so much. Find the answers, Ertha, or you doom us all." And then she plunged backward off her perch on the sill without so much as a whisper or a scream.

I ran across the distance and threw myself over the window bench, my knees cracking bruisingly into its edge, to peer over the gap to where the waves froze against the cliffside below. There was no ripple in the water nor spatter of blood on the ice. She was not dead then but likely whisked by some trickery back into her cell.

I shivered as I eased myself back into the window. What in the Umbra had she been talking about? Talismans? I peeked behind the curtained-off part of my subconscious, where my magic stooped over a loom of memories, trying to weave together a tapestry of thought that would make this all make sense, but it could only work with what I knew and recalled, it could not glean new information, and I was beginning to feel like I was woefully lacking in that. So I could only move forward with what ragtag scraps I had. I had to believe that this would work, that the image on the finished tapestry would show me finding the sword, handing it over to the Red Lady in exchange for freedom, and then I would get to go home.

A shadow fell over me as a cloud passed over Jyord, and I realized just how long I'd dallied. I gathered what I needed—herbs to help the household sleep deeply tonoct so they would not rise at the sound of my feet on the floor come deybreak tomorrow. A handy, tender little root called snugwort, the juice of which could make even the most colicky of babes sleep through the noct, which is what I'd typically prescribe it for. Carefully, I wrapped the bulbous tubers in a swaddle of cotton so they would not get crushed on our return journey across the Fortress.

Huggin was propped up along a bench in the waiting area when I came back out, his feet kicked out and crossed, a small book drowning in his large hand as he paged idly through.

"I didn't know you could read." The words dripped sarcastically off my tongue. To be honest, I'd never imagined the man at his leisure; it never even crossed my mind that he might have hobbies other than serving Fenris and his whims, and by extension, the Father's.

Huggin grunted and tucked the tiny tome back into his jacket. "It do be just a bit of poetry."

I couldn't help it; my jaw fell open. "You—you like poetry?"

His cheeks actually flushed, a deep vermillion above his beard as he straightened. "Do ye be ready to leave?"

"Oh, no, sir. You're not getting out from under my question that easily." I laughed as he began to stalk down the hall. When we reached the upper levels and ducked out the back kitchen doors to cross to the other side of the keep through the gardens, I caught up and walked in step with him, though, admittedly, it took three of my steps to match one of his now that he was making an effort to outpace me and evade my inquiries. "Are they little rhymes about the woods and the flowers? Dirty limericks? Romantic sonnets?" His cheeks turned scarlet as though slapped with an embarrassing truth. "Oh Emrys, that's it, isn't it?" I giggled. "They're romantic poems, aren't they? Oh, Huggin, you sweet giant of a man, are you in love?"

Huggin's boots skidded to a stop halfway across the bridge above the waterfall, his sapphire eyes darkening nearly to pitch. I reached out to put a hand on his sleeve.

"Huggin—"

"Lady Healer, there you are. I've been wondering when I would see you again." A voice like rancid oil spilled across the stretch of tamped-down snow between me and the other side of the bridge, where Ingemar stood, his sinister silver smile crawling up his face with lethal pleasure.

Next to me, Huggin shifted his hand that had, moments ago, been tenderly cradling a book of beautiful words to cup instead the hilt of his sword, his face hardened into a killing mask. I knew his steel wouldn't be necessary, not when I could feel my magic sitting up and drawing itself into the sharp points of a hundred blades. It would protect me even if I could not, even if he could not. I could feel it where it raced along my skin and dripped into the Priestess's dagger tucked into the top of my stocking, where it hummed, ready, waiting, and willing to spill blood for me, its host.

Ingemar glided forward. Drunkenness didn't stumble his steps like it had during our last altercation, the memory of which was permanently scarred in a crescent shape on my ear. My guard tensed, and I could hear the slip of metal on his scabbard as he inched his blade free by just a hairsbreadth.

The Commander laughed, a wicked glint sharp in his eyes as they drilled into Huggin. "Down, dog." He tapped the insignia stitched into the gray collar of his coat, a hand fisted around a sword. "I've been promoted above your master. I would hate for anything to befall him—let's say tenfold whatever it is you do unto me?" Huggin ground his teeth but said nothing. "Oh, don't worry, I have people ready with orders to do just that if I'm in any way harmed at the end of the dey." He held up his hands placatingly. "Besides, I'm just here for a talk with the maiden."

The way *maiden* rolled off his tongue made my skin crawl and my heart wither. He took a step closer, ignoring Huggin's growl, and brushed a finger down my cheek, leaving the feeling of wretchedness in its wake.

"I can smell it, you know." I could feel the heave of his words in his chest as they pressed against my breast. Torn between backing away and standing my ground, I stood firmly in indecision.

"What? Your halitosis? Me too. I have a remedy for that, you know." I let my words snap and crack against his smarmy face and watched it contort from smugness and mold itself into rage.

He hissed and lashed out, swatting my basket from my hand and sending it tumbling across the bridge, powders and herbs lost to Imbola's whispering wind. Clay pots shattered, their ingredients spilled like the blood of a fresh kill. But the corner of my gaze strained to search for the bundle of roots that I so desperately needed for my plans. It was there, half a pace away.

"Oh, you have a mouth on you, maiden. I could teach it to do the most delicious things." He stepped closer, pressing his nose to my hair and inhaling deeply. "I can smell your purity, maiden, the blood you have not yet spilled, the heat that you have not yet come into. I can smell it on you like the smell of ripeness coming to a piece of fruit in byrthe, and just the same, I want to taste it."

"I would rather rot," I ground out through clenched teeth. My magic thrashed against my skin, begging to prick, stab, and maim, but I could not let it, not unless my life was in true mortal danger. Ingemar grabbed my chin, his grip ironclad on my jaw. The scrape of a blade fully drawn from Huggin's sheath didn't even make him flinch, and frankly, I didn't find it very reassuring either, not with his threat looming like an axe over Fenris's head. I may not have known much about Huggin, but I knew he was loyal to his lord over anything and anyone. He wouldn't slice so much as a hair from Ingemar's head for fear Fenris would be scalped in retaliation.

But Ingemar simply leaned in and whispered, "You might have thought you were safe when you had Fenris talk the Father out of putting you in the Hunt, but that won't stop me from finding you after." Then he withdrew, pressing the briefest of kisses along my cheek as he went.

The first step he took away had a stomach-twisting, squelching sound to it, and I grimaced as I looked down at the snow. Of fucking course he'd stepped on my roots. I could have endured our horrible encounter if it weren't for the clear, saccharin-scented puss that oozed from the broken cotton cocoon around my precious tubers. I fell to my knees and hurriedly salvaged what I could of my supplies, even as tears welled and trickled down my face. One teardrop spattered into the snow, iridescent and quicksilver in the fading light of dey. I ran a sweeping hand over my cheeks and peered at the shimmering tears laced with magic, and I inwardly cursed it for not staying hidden. But then I realized it too was weeping angrily, wounded by Ingemar's words but even more so because I'd contained it against its will.

My guard stooped to help me, his sword back in its place. "Ertha, I do be—"

I turned away lest he notice the luminosity of my tears and because I didn't need or want his apology.

I stood, deciding abruptly that whatever was left was not worth it, not the fragmented herbs or the stilted, would-be apology, and I stalked off, Huggin on my heels a moment later, to get ready for the Eklipsis Eve ball. None of this would matter tomorrow.

T HE DRESS WAS IMMACULATE; it hugged and flowed in all the right places and made me look like the noct itself. I painted on minimal cosmetics, just enough to enhance my eyes and bring a bit of blush to my pale cheeks. My hair I simply twisted into a series of braids that I coiled around the sides of my head and pinned into place with pearl-tipped pins. I secured my veil along the back of my head rather than covering it, so the silvern, diaphanous fabric could stream behind me like a ray of Selenyss's light. But I felt as beautiful as the Emrys herself. For a brief moment, my magic raced just beneath my skin, giving me a soft, giddying glow as I studied my reflection one last time, making sure everything was in place before I strode out to meet my keeper. I couldn't help the smile that pulled at the corners of my lips. Tonoct was to be my last in Uthar.

The common area was empty when I slipped in to wait before the fire. This was the time I'd alloted to make my additions to the wine, but with no roots to be wrung dry, I was left with nothing but idle hands while I waited. I took a deep breath and soaked in the smell of the space—leather-bound tomes and amber firelight. It had become familiar in my short time here, and I wistfully wondered, when the memory of it was tarnished with age, if I would ever find something about it to miss. Surely Munnin and her saucy books and her decadent cooking. I'd still yet to finish the book she'd lent me, and with a brief pang, I realized I would never know how it ended. I shook off nostalgia's grip; losing one friend was surely an easy price to pay if it meant a return to all I held dear. Munnin would never begrudge me that.

A low whistle from the door spun me around. Fenris leaned against the jamb. Usually, his otherness hovered around him ominously, sucking all the light from the room, but tonoct, he wore it like a peacock wore its plumes. It made his silver-embellished, crushed black jerkin seem all the more rich in hue, almost like a living piece of Melantha's magic spun into cloth. He'd left his hair unbraided so it fell in a sleek sheet of onyx over his shoulder as he canted his head, his arms crossed over his chest, the slight glimmer of our bond visible against the back of his hand.

"You look like a piece of fallen Emphyrea, Shepherdess." His voice purred across the space between us and coaxed a blush from my cheeks that I hoped was hidden by the faint layer of powder I'd smudged there.

"Thank you." I ran my hands over the swell of my skirts to give them something to do. "You look—"

He held out a hand. "Please don't strain yourself looking for a word to compliment me. I know exactly how I look." His endlessly black eyes glimmered with something akin to mirth.

I snorted indelicately. "I wouldn't dare. If your ego gets any larger, we won't be able to fit down the stairs."

He smirked and crooked a finger, beckoning me to him. "Come now, Shepherdess. We have a ball to attend."

T HE UPPER COURT WAS decorated and dripping with opulence, even more so than on the noct of the Triumph. Garlands of evergreens hung from every timber and window head, secured with crimson and aureate ribbons. Whole trees had been brought in, I assumed from some hothouse somewhere, their branches bowing with the weight of golden candles and silken streamers. Tables were laden with food and drink served on gilded plateware, and in every hand, crystal chalices fizzed with a burgundy wine that lent bubbly laughter to all who imbibed. The music pulled revelers around in reeling, foot-stomping dances. Joyous shouts and strings of ballads sung wove through the air along with the warm crackle of the large hearth at the center of it all like the hub the celebration wheeled around.

Fenris guided us first to the foot of the dais, where we paid our respects to the Mother and

Father, who nodded to us both with stilted, aloof, barely there dips of their chins. A frigid chill rolled off the Father and down the steps in waves, where it crept along my spine and set my magic's proverbial teeth on edge, but blessedly, they said nothing and waved us on so they could accept the respect of the others who waited to greet them.

We slipped away to the far side of the court, where Munnin and Rhapso laughed as they danced, both their faces already flushed from the wine and the atmosphere. They pulled me into their revelry, and together, we spun like silly girls on green hillsides covered in grass to the lilting tunes until my head was floating and my lungs breathless.

A flash of a face in the crowd caught my eye, and my heart suddenly swelled, full of fluttering new butterflies. I'd somehow forgotten all about him and his sinfully lupine smile and my promise to find him here tonoct. He jerked his head toward a door leading out onto the wide stone walk that circled the fat belly of the Fortress and connected to the lacy bridges suspended over the gorge. I was leaving Uthar; I shouldn't follow. I should just let whatever sleeping, lusty beast that was between us lie. But my heart was a traitor to me in that moment as it pressed against my ribs, pinning and smothering my sensibility. I hiked my skirt, and with a darted glance thrown over my shoulder to make sure no one was watching—Fenris was blessedly, was deep in conversation with the Father, Huggin at his side, their brows folded into perfect masks of seriousness that spoke to the likelihood of them being distracted for a good while—I followed him.

Someone had taken great pains to make the walk a mirror image of a forest. Dense evergreen trees packed the space between the Fortress wall and the parapet's edge. Low-burning torches were interspersed among the lush, green trees and large pot-bellied clay vessels brimming with fragrant red flowers that perfumed the crisp kalda air with their heady nectar. I followed the whip of Kastor's cloak around the curves of the meandering path as he kept just ahead of me, barely within sight.

The faux forest was a labyrinth filled with secluded little alcoves, some with benches, some with statues formed of ice in the shapes of nude women, of wolves, and of warriors. It was in one such alcove that my breathless chase came to an end. There was little light in the dark corner Kastor had lured me to, save for the unblinking eye of Selenyss's moon.

I stilled at the sight of him, his pelt strewn across his shoulders, his hair half bound, his amber eyes hungry as they traced the lines of my body in the dim silver glow. "Ertha." His voice was raspy and raw, and it scraped against my tender heart. "You came."

I took a step, the stride bolder than I felt. "Well, I believe you made some fairly lofty promises to make it more than worth my while if I did," I teased, but the shift in his eyes as I spoke and the low, almost appreciative growl in his throat made my knees quiver.

"I did, and I intend to make good on those words." He reached out and pulled me to himself, circling an arm around my waist as he pressed me into his warmth. He dipped his forehead to mine and brushed a knuckle against my cheek, a near mirror image to Ingemar's caress earlier, but this one was tender, gentle, and it cleansed the filth of the Commander's possessive touch on my face, purging it from my mind.

"Do you not need to retire early tonoct? The Hunt begins at deybreak, does it not?" There was a sense of testing the waters in my words, a slight wariness, a crack in the door through which we could make our excuses and duck out now before we fell off the precipice on which we stood.

"Why would I hunt for what is already in my arms?" The possessive growl to his words sawed through me. My breaths hitched irregularly between my lips and my lungs as he let his fingers dance lower, down my cheek, my throat.

"You cannot mean it." The words were a breathless plea, entreating him, daring him to prove it.

His fingers skimmed further before he flattened his hand over the swell of my breast, the beat of my heart drumming against his palm. "I would carve my name onto your heart if only so I could know that no matter what tomorrow brings, it will always belong to me."

Kastor and I surged, our lips crashing into one another in a hungry and consuming kiss that was both punishment and pleasure. Desire rippled from every place our bodies touched as he devoured my moans and I sagged limply at the mercy of the torrential lust that poured through our intertwined bodies. He backed us to the bench nestled in the deepest wreath of shadowed branches that made up our little alcove. He sat, roughly drew me around, and pulled me into his lap so my spine pressed into him.

I tried to tilt my head to turn and kiss him again, but he pinned me to his chest. I whimpered at the gentle scratch of his beard against my neck.

"I think about you, Ertha, bare before me with your tight little cunt ripe for the taking, when I fist my cock. All I can imagine when I close my eyes are the parts of you I want to devour. Do you think of me?"

I whined, unable to admit what I'd done alone in my rooms, but that soft sound was all the answer he needed.

"Be a good girl and show me how you touched yourself," he demanded, his voice rough as he breathed the words against my ear and sent an avalanche of desire crashing between my thighs.

In a rush of rumpled fabric, I hiked up my skirts, leaned back into him, and braced myself as I slid my fingers to swirl against the swollen, throbbing bud of my clit.

"That's it, just like that." His words melted into my skin, making me molten, making my cunt drip. "Don't stop."

One hand wrapped gently around my throat, tipping my head back to rest on his shoulder, the other moved my skirts higher, exposing me further to the chilled noct air, but I didn't care as he trailed his fingers down to cup my knee and bend my leg open further, hitching it over his own so he could devour the movement of my fingers with his eyes.

"Naughty little maiden," he purred as he trailed his fingers along the underside of my thigh before pulling his hand back and gently slapping my cunt near my sodden entrance. The soft sting of it sent effervescent sparks through me and a gush of arousal to coat his palm. "What would your temple priestesses think if they saw you now, like this, as wet as a cock-starved whore in heat?"

His other hand skimmed down my neck, dipping into the top of my bodice, where he rolled my nipple into a stiff peak as he slapped me again and again. Pressure built and threatened to burst. He withdrew his hand from beneath my bodice and batted mine away, grabbing and twisting my arm behind my back, pinning it between us. He tsked in my ear. "You don't get to cum until I say so, and I say you need to be punished for being so deliciously filthy."

I whimpered as he slapped my pussy again, harder this time, then soothed it with a tender stroke of his fingers. "Do you like it when I punish you for being a lustful maiden, Ertha?"

"Yes," I panted, surprised that, after all this time of waiting to be intimate, my first experience was such a feral, near-violent thing, and even more surprised by how wild and wicked and reckless it made me feel. My breaths were painfully sharp as I walked that brutal and savage edge between agony and raw pleasure. This was not some tender and fragile thing between us, it was primal, and it roared through me.

"Tell me all your most wicked desires." He groaned against my neck. His teeth grazed the skin at the base of my throat. "Have you dreamt of taking my fingers in your cunt? Have you dreamt of taking my cock?" He thrust, grinding the member in question into the swell of my ass.

"Yes, yes, all of it. I've imagined it all." My words were an unhindered plea for him to carry me to climax, for him to drown me in rapture and feed the ravenous beast within. Desperately, I pressed back into him, letting my hips writhe, wanting him to feel this horrible, beautiful swell of need the same way I did.

He swirled a fingertip around my pulsating and achingly empty entrance. He clasped his hand over my mouth, and I cried out against it as he dipped that finger languidly into me, just barely, no more than a knuckle's worth, but it was enough. My hips bucked. I wanted more. I wanted all of it, all of him.

"Ertha, are you out here?" Fenris's voice, muffled and muted by the densely packed trees, brought reality shattering back in.

Kastor growled, his hands on me tightening. For a heartbeat, I pictured a beast with its teeth sunken into the bloody and ripped flesh of its prey's neck, unwilling to let another near enough to sample its delicate meat.

"Kastor, please. He cannot find me like this," I pleaded softly, the words a tumble, spilled in a panic from my lips.

Reluctantly, Kastor loosened his punishing hold on me, and hurriedly, he and I fumbled to right our disarrayed clothing and hair. He grabbed my hand before we parted, like scared rabbits found by the wolf in the brush, and pressed an excruciatingly tender kiss across my swollen lips.

"I'm getting you out of here tomorrow once Jyord is risen and all are distracted with the Hunt. Meet me at the dock, and we'll sail for Vanyth."

I drew back, searching his eyes. *Could he really mean it?* I peered into the depths of his gaze to divine the truth and found no discernable lies.

"Promise me, Ertha." His plea was edged with fervor as Fenris again called my name.

I pressed my hand to his cheek. "I promise." The lie was acrid on my tongue as he crowned my brow with a kiss before dissolving into the darkness. I would never have left with him, not when Otaden waited. Tonoct had been the closing of our book, a final sweet goodbye. I prayed to the Emrys that he wouldn't hurt for long after my leaving.

The branches grabbed at my skirts as I darted toward the approaching sound of Fenris's footsteps. I veered into a nook with an ice sculpture and folded my hands neatly across my ribs to still the whorl of my magic as it cycloned nauseatingly in my ribcage, curiously unnerved.

"I'm here," I called out to my keeper when his footsteps were nearly as loud as my heartbeat drumming in my ears.

"Ah, there you are. Where have you been? I felt—I thought—" I turned to look at him just as his dark eyes sparked, furtively alighting on the shadows curled in corners, but he didn't finish saying what it was he'd thought. "You're alone."

"I needed a bit of fresh air; it's quite crowded in there." I turned my gaze away from him and back to the crystalline statue of a woman riding a wolf's back, wearing nothing but a length of cloth windswept across her torso, and I wondered if she was meant to be someone specific or if she was meant to symbolize the wild spirit that seemed to live and breathe in the souls of these Uthari people.

Fenris shifted closer to me, near enough that I could feel the heat of his body caress my own. "Hopefully not too crowded for you to accept a dance with me?"

Emrys no– I didn't want to dance with him, not with the phantom of Kastor's touch all over my skin. Fumbling for an excuse, I managed to spit out, "I—well, I'm actually quite weary. I was intending to depart for the noct."

He held out his hand, an unnervingly knowing sort of curve toying with the edge of his lips. It couldn't have been called a smile but very nearly. "Dance with me first."

My gaze cut to his upturned palm, where the tendriled tips of our twisted bond curled about his wrist, and I wondered if he was willing me to give in to him. With cautious thorns sprouting from my words and my fists nervously clenched in my skirts, I managed to whisper, "Is that a command, keeper?

"Do you want it to be one?" He arched a brow teasingly.

I sighed, my breath a puff of iced air, and relented, letting my hand press into his. He flinched almost imperceptibly at the contact, the movement so slight, I might not have noticed it if he'd not done almost the exact same thing upon our first meeting. Fitting he should do it now at what I imagined would be our last, should all go to plan. My magic simmered beneath my skin, giving me the impression it was on tenterhooks.

We walked in comfortable silence back into the revelry, no more debauched than it had been when I'd left it. Above it all, like the Emrys looking down on the chaos of the world they'd created, the musicians played and the singers sang. The tune was a shameless expression of deep longing, felt more than it was understood in words as it echoed over the pleasure-seeking celebrators. My spine straightened as Fenris wrapped an arm around my waist, making me acutely aware of just how small I was. My eyeline was barely level with his heart. We melted sinuously together as he guided me in the spiraling steps. He was lyrical with his footwork, his movements shockingly featherlight as he led me gently through the dips and lifts and twirls. I didn't want to admit it, but we fit well together, and in another lifetime, in another world, I could have seen myself dancing with him all noct until the musicians' fingers could play not a single note more.

What could have been had our first meeting not been bathed in blood? If he had instead come to the Vanythian Court as a Corvusi emissary and ask me to dance, not as his captive but as the youngest sister to the heir, or simply as a beautiful woman he fancied turning about the room? But there was no use in deydreaming of what could have been. Our meeting had been baptized by death, Helima's and so many others', and there was nothing that could change that.

"I didn't kill them, you know," he whispered in reply to my unspoken thoughts. Could he read me so clearly through the bond now? He pulled me up from a dip, pressing me into his chest. He smelled of the deepest part of the noct and the breath of fire.

My heart stumbled, tripping on the image of Helima lying dead. "You'll have to be more specific."

"Whomever it is you've lost—whosever death you hang around my neck. I've killed many but never the innocent."

And just like that, with a single stuttered beat of my heart, gore wept from every surface in the room. Garlands became guts, the sconces turned skeletal, and the eyes of everyone around us hollowed out in mirror image to his. My breath stuck to my lungs, which likewise seemed caught on my ribs as my magic shrieked through my veins in a fit of hysteria.

My voice didn't feel like my own as I fought for control of my magic, which instinctually wanted to protect, to soothe me, but also to maim those who'd harmed me. But I couldn't, not now. I could not lose control, not when I was so close to escaping, and definitely not in a ballroom full of witch-hating Uthari. "Did you kill anyone the dey I was taken?"

His face contorted into a sneering mask, and whatever malice he felt pressed in on me, against my skin like it wanted to crawl inside me and fill me until I dissolved and became it. "I certainly tried."

Shock drained my face of blood. How could he in one breath defend himself and in the next admit to attempted slaughter? I jerked back out of his grip, the space between us filling abruptly with sharp, jagged edges. "Then you are every bit the monster I first believed you to be."

For a flickering breath, beneath the phantasmagorical dripping of blood off his eye teeth, I thought I saw something akin to sorrow or remorse, and my heart stuttered, questioning the words I'd just spat, but then his eyes turned flinty, and any glimpse of him behind the impenetrable walls he'd built was snuffed out. I turned in a whirl of skirts, ready to storm out, when he caught me by the wrist. The space where our bonds met scorched, but not as hotly as his otherworldly eyes did when our gazes collided.

"Just know, whatever you think of me, I'm not a bad man." His words felt fractured where they struck the tender bits of my heart.

I pulled my wrist free of his hold, spun, and strode from the ballroom. I felt the echoed press of his hand along the bond the whole way back to the apartments.

I LEFT HUGGIN IN the hall. He'd found me, of course, like a shadow found one's feet, and had followed me back to my rooms. I tore down my hair, letting it ripple in angry waves as I traced the well-worn, worried path I'd trudged in the rug before the hearth. There were mere hours before deybreak, before I would need to join the Hunt.

I should have found sleep, but how could I have when all I could see was memory-conjured blood on the hem of my dress and my hands. I tore my beautiful gown from my skin, loathing the way it felt as though it sagged under the weight of the spent lives of those I'd known. I balled it up and tossed it into the fire before throwing myself into bed and drawing the covers over my head.

My eyelids fluttered closed, but the things I saw behind them brought me no peace. I floundered on the edge of sleeping and waking. My bones were too heavy, my mind too laden with noctmarish visions, and my magic all too aware of the pull to the forest. The creak of my door and the feel of eyes upon me jerked me from visions piecemealed together by my subconscious of Kastor running his hands under my skirts on the beach where the Mer had died.

The itch in my bond told me it was Fenris. I gripped my magic in my fist, ready to throw it at him recklessly should he come closer, but a bootheel scuff later, he was gone, and I fell back into the depths of restless delirium.

Bleary wolf song slipped through the milky haze of sleeplessness and roused me from my bed. Imbola howled in answer to the beasts in the woods, sending a scattering of silver snowflakes through the poorly secured slats of the shutters. I shivered along my bones before stoking my magic to warm me and padding across the floor to the wardrobe—easing my steps along the floorboards to stop any nails from squealing and waking those abed in the apartment.

Without my addition to the wine in the common room the noct before, I had no way of knowing how soundly my keeper slumbered, especially considering the late hour at which he'd looked in on me. He could be entertaining one of his female guests, or brooding with his books, or sleeping. Either way, I could not risk the slightest whisper of sound.

In sharp silence, I slipped on the new shift, this one with long sleeves, lace around the neckline of its bodice shaped like a boneless corset, and a full, loose skirt that fell to the ankle. The garment was made of thin but warm wool, and if I was to run nearly naked through the woods, it at least covered as much skin as I could manage while still adhering to the customs of the Hunt. I twisted my hair into a knot, twining through it a ribbon to secure it in place.

The cloak I donned last. It weighed on my shoulders like armor, but I was no knight mistress, I was merely a mistress of the meek, a warrior in an army of one up against those who would break me, but I would not let them win.

THE HUNT

T HE BLIZZARDING WIND TRIED to bully me back as I slid over the sill of my window, barely finding purchase on the nub of one of the structural beams that jutted out from between the stones of the Fortress wall in a jagged row of crooked teeth. My magic was in a frenzy. It feverishly muttered in my ears impressions of death, of falling. "*Not safe, not safe. Fall. Die. Fragile body mash to pulp on the stones. Sinnew snap and bones. Find another way.*"

With a mental prod, I managed to battle it back down, internally shouting, *There is no other way. Any other route will have us caught*, as I gripped the snow-slick rocks of the wall and used them as handholds while I toed my way over to the next beam. My magic hissed and fizzled but stayed silent. I was already afraid enough of the sheer plunge I knew was at my back; I didn't need its terror to redouble mine. The climb was painstaking amidst the deafening churn of the storm as I inched from one beam over to the next, unable to see more than one jump ahead in the unending spiral of blinding snow. But I did it over and over again until my fingers and the ice that clung to the stones felt one in the same.

Cursing my foolishness for this plan, I fumbled for the next beam. Imbola whipped down the wall, teasing gluttonously fat flakes of snow into my eyes as I sidestepped. Had she not chosen that moment to whistle shrilly in my ear, I might have heard the soft crumbling thud my toe made against the wood before I moved. But I hadn't, and the moment I tried to suspend my full weight on the sodden and rotted lumber, it crumbled beneath me like cake. I scrabbled, my fingers biting into the stone that seemed to want to sluff me off more than it wanted to give me purchase. My nails broke in shattered grasps. I wasn't sure if I screamed as I fell or if Imbola shoved her gusty fingers down my throat and stole the sound.

The red cloak fluttered up around me like broken, bloody wings as I plunged. Thoughts were swept from my mind; I could think of no way out of the gruesome and splattery end I was about to meet until, angrily—as if frustrated by my fright-ful apathy toward our imminent end—my magic roared, throwing itself out into the air. With a mighty groan and a snap, muffled by the scream of the storm, one of the iron bridges ripped itself free of the cliffside, its metal twisting and mold-ing into spindly fingers that reached, then plucked and grabbed me from my inevitable demise on the jagged rocks below. Its black metal tips snagged my cloak, slowing my fall, and cupped me in its grip like a tattered butterfly damaged in a storm that it intended to keep in a jar and nurse back to health. Instead, it swelled out of the gorge and gently set me onto the icy grounds of the gardens.

The blood trembled in my veins as, with shaking hands, it tried and failed again and again to thread itself through my heart while my lungs grasped for breaths that did nothing to satiate the raw burning inside them. My fists made crimson prints in the snow as the warped metal bridge stroked me like a comforting mother down my back.

"*You're welcome,*" my magic seemed to whisper in an annoying, I-told-you-this-would-happen sort of way as the bridge turned, creeping back to its place among the other bridges suspended like smoke-stained spiderwebs, nearly invisible among the writhing snakes of snow and mist.

Tendrils of billowing fog and wispy ribbons of swirling snow curtained me from the view of the Fortress walls and its windows in equal measure. As my magic willed my trembling body to stand, I thanked Imbola and Skai—Emrys of snow—for the squalling storm that drove guardsman to huddle around warm hearths rather than do battle with its cold and had also blessedly drowned out the sounds of my near death and of the creature my magic had coaxed the bridge to become.

A silver shard of light peeked over the distant horizon, lengthening the shadows of the plants I could see through the haze around me by a fraction. I had to move if I was to sneak into the hunting grounds amidst the others. I'd toyed with the idea of slipping through the garden gate, but I didn't want to be so easily tracked. Now, should Fenris come looking, my scent would be masked among the other women. And if he could truly sense my emotions through the bond, then the tempest warring for supremacy in my body surely must have summoned him by now. It could have summoned the dead. I would give him no extra advantage.

I ran for the entrance to the woods—an imposing iron gate set into the stone wall and marked with the stamped wolf's head of Uthar—tucked a little way behind where the tournament competitors camped. I let my gaze drift only once to see if I could make out Otaden's tent. I couldn't. Good. That meant all was going according to plan. The tide of crimson-clad women swayed back and forth on their bare feet, the snow already stained pink here and there where skin had been rubbed raw with cold. I was neither the first nor the last to arrive, simply another unremarkable maiden fit to be fodder for the Sons, just as I'd hoped to be. I took my place in the group, slipping in among them with my cowled hood pulled over my notable hair. I wished then that I'd grabbed a bit of something to dye it with, but I supposed there'd been no time, and there was no going back now, not unless I wanted to flee with Kastor, who, despite all my hesitation, really could have been my sweet raven. As much as the thought plucked at my heartstrings, this was the only way. If the affection he and I shared was meant to be the love of two soul-bound mates, then the Emrys would see fit to bring us back together again somedey.

"Are you nervous?" the slight woman next to me asked in a gentle voice that scraped at my tender empathy. The curl of her golden hair framed her sun-freckled face as she brushed up against me in her cloak the color of just-bloomed burgundy roses.

Though I knew we weren't talking about the same thing, I found that I wasn't nervous now that I was faced with the sharp spindles of the gate before me spearing into the Emphyrea, which was painted in an eerie hue of anticipation as Eklipsis began. I was on the path I needed to be on. I could feel it in the giddy thrum of my magic and in the way my heartbeats had evened their keel.

"No, I don't think so."

"Aren't you worried it will hurt?" Her cheeks pinked as she whispered the words conspiratorially, though the ragged barbs of true nerves were wrapped around them, and I was struck with the realization that, though todey I earned my freedom, she was about to be shackled in a matrimony sealed with the blood of her maidenhead in the snow and on her cloak.

I fumbled over consolatory words, though my heart ached, pierced with the guilt of my selfishness. I'd been thinking of the Hunt as merely a means of camouflage for my endeavors with callous disregard for the trauma that was about to be inflicted on these women who I stood shoulder to shoulder with. "You—I mean, we are to be their wives. Don't you think they'd want the first time to be...kind?

"My mam says they can get a bit...overcome by the change, that they aren't always in control." She nibbled on the edge of her nail as she shuffled back and forth from toe to toe.

My lip began to curl in disgust when a horn sounded, and on its heels, the rusty crack of gate hinges. Two Sons winched the wrought iron open with hands hauled one over the other along frosted chains. A ripple of emotions skittered across the red-cloaked women and echoed the feelings of hesitant fear and tenuous expectation that coiled along my bones and beat within my breast. I turned to look at the woman next to me, whose eyes only a heartbeat before had been fraught, only to find her slipping into an eager run. The prey for the Hunt surged forward, spurred by the knowledge that they would soon be chased. I was the last to move despite the fact that the one who hunted me was likely already on my heels.

The women scattered into the shadowy under-growth. Some ran like they had Niflym on their tails while others ran short distances and waited; the neckline of their shifts were shallow and snuggly fit over ample bosoms—low-hanging fruit for easy pickings. Though, I supposed, for some, that was preferred, and at least these women were willing.

The moment the gate was swallowed by fog at my back, I veered toward the Fortress, skipping over stones, skirts hiked to avoid the snagging fingers of thorned rosehips. I kept the corner of my eye on the barely visible, looming silhouettes of the towers until their indistinct forms grew more solid through the rippling sheets of cascading snowfall. I ran next to the wall that divided the well-kept garden from the feral forest, sticking to the furrow of shadows at its base. At last, the tiny gate sprang up between the stacked stones like a gap in a row of neat teeth, and I crouched. Carefully, I peeled back the covering of decomposing leaves pressed into layers of ice. They resembled aged lace preserved between panes of glass so that those who came after its maker could discern the patterns and use them as a guide to replicate the beauty.

I hitched my small bundle over a shoulder and slung the makeshift strap across my chest. The books within, Drusylla's and the Healer's records, my diadem, the knife from the Priestess, along with the shell from the Mer that I'd promised to keep safe, and a change of clothes thumped against my leg as I searched for the main artery of steaming water that fed the gardens and kept them warm. I chose the widest trench of flowing water. The steam curled off it like water snakes curious at the intrusion as I slipped in. The water was painfully warm against my numb and near-frozen feet, sending a burst of prickling nettles to twine around my toes and up my ankles. I hissed, biting my lip until I tasted blood to stifle any further sound, and waded upstream as swiftly as I could. My magic undulated beneath my skin, pressing outward, urging me onward, deeper into the woods.

The silver-and-black corona of Jyord and Selenyss's meeting cast shadows long and twisted the malleable darkness while they danced their way across the Emphyrea as they approached Zenith—the highest mountain in the Emphyrean range and the closest to Strattaria—where they would couple amorously for the remainder of the dey before descending back to their homes, leaving us mortals with a moonless noct. I shuddered, the ghost of dreads that had not yet come to pass creeping up my spine on tipped toes. I had to get out of these woods before then. The screams of women taken down by men in the Hunt were passed like secret missives along the roots of the trees to my outstretched magic in a reverberation of amalgamated terror and pleasure, spurning my steps to move me faster and farther away from the sickening ritual lest I get caught up in it.

My magic pulled me from the ribbon of watery warmth, over the sloshy slip of muddied banks, and deeper into denser forest, where the branches hung lower, the thorns on them sharper and more menacing. I could almost picture them growing longer, lusting to pierce my skin and sap me of my blood and meager strength. The muffled howl of a wolf in the distance gave me pause and sent my heart fluttering to hide in my throat behind my whimper.

My magic soothed it, stroking it like it would a scared and bewildered beast. *"Listen not to the creatures in the dark. Waste not your worry."* I settled under its insistent caressing. I could fear nothing—there was no time, and besides that, it reminded me with whispered sweet nothings that I had it and it had me, the last witchling. Nonetheless, I ran through the grasp of the branches' clawed fingers.

Coiled around my spine, lending me the strength and steel that I needed to keep going, my magic guided me like a gentle hand on my shoulder. It numbed my feet when the serrated bits of ice and stone gnawed at the too soft skin, it salved itself over my blistered thighs, it stilled the chills brought on by my sodden clothes, and it spurred me on when my faltered steps drew too slow. The stench of rot and decay was thick and heavy in the mist that caught the shattered glow of Jyord and Selenyss's union, the only light this deep in the Blackwood. Though I could not see more than shadows in front of me, I was propelled forward by the summoning pulse of a power that was both eldritch and primordial and the shove of my own power against my ribs in answer to it.

The branches overhead closed over me like the fist of a giant beast, but my steps did not slow as my magic murmured, "Go to it. *Take it. Go to it. Take it.*" Its words beat against my flailing heart like a stick against the head of a drum. The pads of my feet fractured; I could feel it in the vague sense of warmth that wept from between each toe as my stride cracked rhythmically through the icy crust on the surface of the snow.

My magic jerked me toward a slim break in the trees. "*This way*," it crooned. Ahead, a fragment of murky, eerie light, like a shard of a broken mirror, lay in wait. Mentally, I latched on to it, clawed at it until I fell through the knotted fingers of the clumped trees and into a glade. A laugh that was all shattered glass and rough edges tumbled from my bitten lips. In the center of the clearing stood a shrine of sorts, its stacked stone weathered and atavistic. A low drone of power pulsated across the gap between me and it, feeling like deliverance. I craved it.

I took a step forward, the movement half drunk on the giddy flow of a victory that was within my grasp, when, out of the dark recess of trees on the far side of the gray crumbling shrine, two sets of eyes bloomed with a ruthless and hungry amber iridescence. The luminous orbs bobbed forward through the shrouding mists until two wolves emerged, one with brunet and burnished auburn fur, the other nearly its twin, though the brackish white that threaded through its shaggy hackles and around the corners of its eyes spoke to age. Corded muscles tensed beneath their hides as they prowled forward, blocking my path to the shrine's narrow-slitted entry.

Stilted, frosty, fear-filled silence rippled through the hollow between me and the beasts as I tried to mentally plot a way around or past them into the shrine until the first wolf cracked its jaw and spoke. "You wound me, Ertha. I thought we were going to run away together, and here I find you lurking in the woods."

D ISBELIEF AND TERROR BICKERED with one another in my skull, their incongruous shouts rooting me to the spot as the fur along the wolf rolled and ripped across its spine like a tailor slicing through a set of uneven stitches, only worse, so much worse. The hide began to peel back in a wash of ichor and membrane to the tune of snapping bones and sinew until before me stood a man, and at his feet, a steaming pile of wolf pelt.

My horror puffed into the cold air before me in a panted burst of steamed breath even as sour bile that tasted of bitter repulsion threatened to choke me like a hand around my throat. "Kastor. How did you—"

"Know that you were coming to the shrine? I didn't, Healer. Like I said, I thought we were going to run away together. I fucking waited for you, Ertha." Real anger, fiery and ferocious, flashed through his amber eyes that had seemed so earnest and kind the noct before as he paced in the snow before me. "You hurt me, you really did. But when I realized you weren't coming and that you'd played me for a fucking fool, I picked up the direction your scent was heading. One whiff at the hunting ground's entrance, and I knew."

The second wolf spat words past a lolling tongue and severe teeth with the chilling voice of Ingemar. "Or maybe she didn't even consider you, and she simply wonders how it is we can change into wolves?"

"The answer to both is blood," Kastor growled, stalking forward. I matched his steps pace for pace away from him, my heart and my magic screaming retreat until my back brushed up against the scrape of bark. "We followed yours here, and the Father's, well, let's just say it changes you, makes you better, stronger." Kastor's face twisted with malicious mirth as he glared down at me, vapor wafting off his freshly peeled skin smudged with his blood, the silver shape of my hand still glowing faintly around his heart. Where before it'd felt like something beautiful and poetic to have my magic beneath his skin, the sight of it now was abominable.

I bit my lip to keep from screaming and dug my nails into the trunk of the tree at my back. They had the look of predators who wanted me to flee. They wanted the thrill of the chase—to toy with their prey—and I couldn't give it to them.

"Hmmm..." Kastor growled low and feral in his throat, a sound too similar to the ones I'd enjoyed last noct, and it made my stomach twist. "Bite your lip again for me, love. You know how I like it."

Unfortunately, I could see precisely how much he liked it plainly on his naked form as his cock stiffened and twitched. Repulsion coiled and whipped around my belly. What a fucking fool I'd been to think he'd cared for me. My pulse shattered as my heart fell into crumbling pieces. With nowhere to go, it stung my eyes with the searing tears of a stupid, naïve girl who'd thought she'd been a woman grown enough to know true affection when she'd seen it. But here it was, unmasked before me as nothing but bald manipulation. My magic thrashed against the cage of my ribs, daring him to come closer, willing him to so it could eviscerate him. With wavering control, I pushed my magic back to heel.

"Or maybe I'll bite it for you as I claim you as my mate."

I could feel the rush of blood as it fled my face, my cheeks paling as my thoughts caught and snagged on the word *mate*. Unconsciously, I shifted a foot, trying to gain an edge around the tree to run. "You can't—" The words stuck feebly as they fumbled off my tongue.

Kastor threw back his head and laughed. Behind him, Ingemar's lips pulled back cruelly around his fangs as he did the same.

"You're in the Blackwood on Eklipsis, dressed in the ritual colors. All I have to do is breed your tight little cunt, and you're mine." Kastor leaned in, and though there were still a handful of breaths between us, the movement felt too intimate, too possessive. I could smell the reek of bone and blood on his iced breath. "Though, I confess, I'm none too pleased you spurned me. Perhaps you would prefer to be mated with my father since it seems I'm not good enough for you. I know he wants a taste. He's been salivating after your skirts for some time." He inclined his head to where the wolf-shaped Ingemar slavered around his serrated teeth and licked his chops.

"If you play with your prey much longer, son, I might just go ahead and sample her myself. She smells divine." His eyes widened hungrily as he scented the air.

I swallowed hard around the rigid lump of sharp disbelief, lodged like a gorge stuck in the throat of a gaping fish that was still in awe it had been caught. "But you're a farmer's son," I whimpered. Oh Emrys bless, I really was so gullible. In a blink, the visions of blood I'd seen on him at the Triumph before I'd bought his bald lies began to weep from his eyes. It poured through his beard and down his naked torso to puddle at his feet. The very picture of the noctmare I'd always imagined the Sons to be.

He cracked his neck, rolling it from side to side. "Oh, you tender little morsel." He laughed, showing off a hint of wickedly elongated canines. "I can't wait to devour you."

His eyes locked on mine, and with a lupine smile, he lunged, spanning the short space between us. Ingemar was half a heartbeat behind him. I ducked around the trunk of the tree, dodging the swipe of Kastor's talon-tipped fingers as they went for my throat. I darted and risked using a sly whip of my magic, no more than a thread's worth, to throw up a curtain of snow and hide my movement as I dipped behind the dark of another tree trunk. For a moment, the crunch of Kastor's and Ingemar's prowling footsteps around the clearing were the only sounds as I held my breath.

My magic strained, not only to fight but to get to the shrine. It battled against my will and my weary bones.

"Get her, son!" Ingemar growled, dogging Kastor's footsteps. "Quit toying with the wench and take her, or I will."

He hissed a reply I couldn't make out as a howl of wind swept through the clearing and whipped away the sound. A compromise then, with my magic. It would be a risk, but I could let it distract them while I ran for the shrine. It was the only way to get what I needed and hopefully still hide what I was, and surely the Red Lady would come to me once I had what was hers.

The snap of a twig beneath predatory feet echoed through the muffling trees from somewhere across the small meadow, followed by the condescending purr of Kastor's taunts. "Come on, Ertha. You weren't playing so hard to get last noct. I can still smell your desire on my fingers. I can still hear the way those little moans—"

I threw out a blast of magic blindly to stir the snow like a tempest churned under the feet of running prey, to make him think I went one way as I turned and ran the other. With so much of my power thrown out into the mist, the magic that dulled the pain in my feet wavered as it shifted and redirected the enormously snarled flow of spells, but it was just long enough for the bed of snow and composting leaves to turn to stabbing knives. I faltered, unable to stop the cry of pain that sliced like a sword, cleaving through my whole being before it burst from my parted and panting lips. I could sense more than I could see the shift in my predators' movements, and then the world danced black along its ragged edges as a body threw me back, cracking my head against the ground.

A ringing bell, like the one that had warned the temple of the Sons' invasion what seemed a lifetime ago, tolled in my ears, drowning the words from the sneering, bloody maw that twined and twisted above me in my splitting vision.

Sensation returned first to my fingers as they skimmed the forest floor in the ruffle of snow-covered leaves and the scrape of icy rocks. Kastor's head bent, igniting a flurry of feeling at the scrape of his fang along my neck. The sensation pulled something from where it had been momentarily stunned and hiding in the dark and empty space beside my heart that felt as infinite and endless as the Emphyrea seemed on a clear dey. It swelled in a violent surge along the muscles in my arm, taking over the task of communication between my mind and body. It told my hand to grab, and so it fisted around a jagged stone. With a sickening crack and a strength I distantly knew wasn't entirely my own, I buried it into Kastor's skull with a spatter of fragmented bone and a sickly splat of brain.

Kastor's body went limp atop mine. With that same unyielding strength that was somehow both mine and not, I shoved him off and rolled in a tumble of tattered skin and cloak. My magic forced me to scramble to my knees. I understood as I blinked dazedly at the churning, chalky serpents of mist writhing along the floor of the forest, through the delirium caused by the injuries I knew I'd sustained, that it was my magic's grip on me that had told me what to do. I wondered if this was the way of things with witches or if I should be alarmed. But like the blood-matted hair that clung to my forehead, I shoved the notion away. I had more dire things that demanded my focus. I met the gaze of the first among those grim entities: the growling wolf who crouched before me.

"You killed my son!" the wolf that was Ingemar peeled back his lips and growled, the stench of bloodlust and loathing in his burning words promised a slow death for me should he get his jaw around any of my soft and vulnerable flesh.

"He was living on borrowed time." I spat the words in his lupine face in a voice that was both mine and yet other.

His hackles rose and he lunged, his maw gaping, his paws kicking up a cloud of powdery, blood-soaked snow. Argent fire sparked along my fingertips as I raised them, bracing for impact. A sharp and deep chorus of *daw-daw-daw* wailed from the split beaks of an unkindness of ravens as they crashed down from the trees and met the face of the wolf. Ingemar bellowed as their silver beaks ripped into the soft squish of his eyes. He rolled onto his back and thrashed his paws wildly. He snapped his jaw and yipped in pain as he tried futilely to shake the birds. A wicked seed of righteous vengeance inside me wanted to stay and watch the Commander suffer, to watch the birds that were as inky in color as noct given shape and solidity, with eyes as violent and crimson as hungry flames, devour him flesh and bone, but there was no time. As I glanced at the Emphyrea, I noticed with a bolt of panic that Jyord and Selenyss had already ascended Zenith.

In haste, I scrambled for the slight sliver of the doorway into the shrine. It was little more than a tight squeeze. The stone scraped at my ribs and the thick swell of my belly as I slid over the frost-crusted threshold like thread through the pinched eye of a needle. The inside was packed with the musk of moldering damp. Icicles dripped from the cracks in the walls, clinging like chrysalises. I conjured a silver-tongued flame and cast it into a wrought iron sconce on the wall in the rusty shape of a wolf's open jaw. The light combatted the darkness, battering it back until the shadows thinned and the edges of a sarcophagus erected atop the crumbling remains of a well were etched in a lustrous glow.

In repose was the carefully carved face of Drusylla, as though plucked from my imaginings and given form. My magic purred; it flexed itself along the joints of my knuckles until I reached out and brushed the pads of my cracked and wounded fingertips across her lips and her cheeks, painting them with bloody rouge. My gaze caught the jagged scrawl of runes above her head that read, "*Mother of Uthar.*" The words, like a key in a lock, tripped the tumblers of my thoughts into place.

Uthar wasn't just the name of this land; it was the name of her son, who she'd raised to father this country. It was why there was no record of the royal lineage, because there had been no one else, not since him. He was the end all be all, the son and the Father. He was Uthar. And more than that, he was half of Terr, the first of the fallen Niflym with their powers so dark and vile. And, oh Emrys, what had I done? No wonder he'd had difficulty siring a child—such an abomination should never exist, it would upset the scales of existence. The Red Lady's words, "*Keep the balance,*" reverberated through my soul, each syllable plucking along my fragile and too taut heartstrings. Death must have brought me here as her harbinger to end the abominable line, the scourge of Uthar, the stone that had tipped the scales of the world into chaos, and I'd gone and added to the weight by giving him not one but two children.

A burning hatred for the long-dead woman entombed beneath my hands rushed through me with such bone-shattering force, my knees buckled. My feet slipped from under me on stones covered in hidden ice. I flailed, and my hands grappled for purchase and grazed the edge of a carved sword folded in the deceased woman's hands. The magic firmed its grip around me and drew me back up like a puppet on its strings. With silver magic sharpening my sight, I peered down at the way Drusylla's hands cradled the hilt with a near-possessive malice, even in death. The Red Lady's sword. A large, black bird flew on ruffled wing through the narrow gap in the stones and alighted on the sconce, the beady black of its eyes fixed on me with intent, as if it too wanted to see what would happen next, to see what it and its brethren had achieved by protecting me.

"Take it, take it, take it." My magic thrumbed the words along my feathered pulse. It ached to fulfill this purpose. It leaked from my fingers across the stone, letting itself out, not in the drips and drabs I'd once used for healing but in long draws, the sort taken by one who needed to slake a deep thirst. It was power the likes of which I'd never dreamt of having. It spilled across the carving, sizzling and popping against the stone, melting it away until it exposed the shrunken bone and sinew of mummified hands clamped around the tarnished hilt of a sword intricately designed to look like viciously thorned rose brambles growing around a black stone blade that was fragmented, cracked like a bone halfway down its length.

Something deep and delicate inside me recoiled as I watched my hands snap the deceased bones off the hilt of Death's sword and take it up, letting it hum against my palm, but my magic brushed away its repulsed remnants with an elegant flourish.

W ITH BATED BREATH, I held the sword, letting its power dance with my own as I waited for the Red Lady to come, to confirm what my mind had unraveled, to free me from the bond that no longer itched but distantly stung like a nest of wasps on the edge of my consciousness. Damn Uthar, the Niflym, this sword. I would give Death her blade, and I would let her balance her Umbra-cursed scales herself. And the next time she thought to meddle in mortal lives, I hoped she choked on her enigmatically spun warnings and thickly veiled words with indecipherable meanings.

I waited for a heartbeat, then two, and then my shoulders sagged. "Where in the Umbra are you?" I ground through gritted teeth at the sword in my palm.

"This place is shielded from her." Words spoken roughly from the beak of the bird looped around my attention and yanked my wide-eyed gaze to it.

The bird rolled its shoulders and shuddered. A tremor traced along the broad planes of its feathers as it grew impossibly larger. Its legs contorted until before me stood a man who was both Fenris and not Fenris. His hair was half shifted from glossy locks to a cascade of plumes. His ears were pinched and elongated to points. His eyes funneled in on me, darkening, if such a thing were possible, to a shade so black, there was no name for it, and in them danced something ethereal, consuming, and primal. Along his naked and feather-studded torso, the ink of his tattoos and the marking of the bond pulsed and writhed together. He canted his head and took a step forward, gobbling up the narrow spit of space between us. He reached out and brushed a feather, still sprouted from the back of his talon-tipped fingers, down my cheek.

"You—" I gasped as my bulging eyes scraped, bewildered, across every ridge of his form, undone and wild. His dark, otherworldly presence swelled to fill the small shrine.

A wry twist pulled at the corner of his lips as he glowered down at me through his polished onyx eyes that seemed to burn. "Didn't you think it odd that the Emrys couldn't retrieve her own sword?"

My magic eddied into my ear and crooned a single word, "*Dumyra,*" as though it were a prayer, an answer, an enchantment, or a thrall. What in the Umbra it meant, I couldn't fathom nor was I in the position to have a lengthy conversation with it to find out, not with Fenris leering.

Unthinking, I raised the jagged tip of Death's blade to his chest, letting its point dimple against his bare torso.

"What are you?" I demanded, lacing my words until they dripped with my magic and our desire to have our will obeyed and our questions answered.

The apple of his throat didn't so much as bob as he shoved the serrated point away and stepped closer, the top of his head brushing the stone roof of the shrine as he pressed in on me with his presence. "Don't threaten me."

"Why shouldn't I?" I hissed through gritted teeth bared in defiance. "You're a beast just like them, and you said yourself: the only way I'll ever be free of you, the only way to keep you from hunting me to the ends of existence is your death." My magic spat with me, seething at him, daring him to so much as breathe too deeply, but he stood towering over me like a living statue. Eyes that flashed with dark fury were the only reaction he gave to my venomous words.

"I am nothing like them. Your lover just tried to kill you—don't you think that warrants reexamining how you evaluate people and their honor?" The words were salt on my already wounded pride, and he knew it, probably relished it. "I saved you. I've *been* saving you." He took a slight, nearly imperceptible step toward me, filling my air with his overwhelming scent. It eddied around my thoughts, muddling them, but my magic cut through the haze, and I laughed derisively.

"You expect me to believe that all this time, you've secretly been my white knight?"

"I'm no one's white knight, princess, especially not yours." He must have seen the shock written in my eyes because his lips curled into a smirk as he chuckled. "Did you think I didn't know who you are? There is nothing about you I don't know, witchling."

Everything in me stilled, my pulse, the ebb and flow of my magic, it all stopped as though time itself had ceased passing just to peer over our shoulders. As Fenris's onyx eyes bored into mine, I had no retort, not one. Everything in me waited on a knife's edge to see what would happen next, waited for his next move.

"What, no quippy reply?" he taunted as he leaned forward and pressed his feathered brow to my bloody and sweat-soaked one.

The sword in my hand dragged against the floor stones, the weight of it suddenly immense. Sapped of will and trembling, I let him cage me, his hands rooted to the lip of the sarcophagus.

"Why isn't she coming to save me?" The words spilled out like bubbling blood from a fatal blow.

"Don't you get it? She can't come here. It's warded against her. She was never coming to save you—but I was. I was going to save you. You foolish princess, I was going to get you out with the others at deybreak while the Sons were distracted by the Hunt." His words were a slap of hot breath across my face, and I could feel the weight of them sink my heart like stones in the pockets of a desperate swimmer. "I was going to get you onto Otaden's ship."

"No." A forlorn and swollen tear burned its way along my cheek, stinging in the nicks. My knees went weak, and I sagged into him.

"Get it together." He gripped me and shook my listless shoulders. "If you listen to me now, there could still be time, so long as the Emrys are still atop Zenith. We can make a run for the cliffs on the far side of the woods."

His words flowed through me like a gasp of air on a dying ember. Fire coursed along the bond as he set me on my feet and knotted his fingers with mine. I nodded once, not trusting myself to speak, unsure that I could force words past the grit in my throat.

Fenris grunted as he forced his way out of the shrine, never letting go of my hand, pulling me between the cinch of the stones on stumbling feet behind him. The raw scrape of the toothy edge of one bit through the white of my shift and drew an angry red line of blood across my too soft belly. I winced and bit off a whimper as his feet came to a crashing halt in the vermilion-stained slosh of snow in the center of the glen.

"Why are you—" The last of my words fell into the dead, silent air as I noticed the bloom of eyes in the dark—yellowy-brown, the color of festering puss—through the whip of swirling snow that squalled through the open tree-fall gap.

A howl pierced the kalda air. The light shifted abruptly, sharpening the darkness and silvering the edges of things as Jyord and Selenyss began their descent on the far side of Zenith. Too late. We were too fucking late.

The wretched sound of skin peeling and sucking away from bones curdled my blood as the pack of wolves strode from between the bent branches of the Blackwood. Vomit crowded the back of my throat.

"Give us the Healer, Fenris." The Son in the lead strode forward, his skin steaming against the cut of Imbola's sharp gales that rattled the bare branches of the trees.

"You will stay the Umbra away from my wife," Fenris growled, his voice ricocheting around the clearing.

The word ripped through me like a crossbow bolt, tearing sinew and bone along the way—*wife*. The hilt of Death's sword slipped from my hand upon which the marking of our bond twisted and throbbed. Did he intend to claim me as his prize in the Hunt? But, no, that couldn't be—we were leaving Uthar, unless yet another Son had led me astray, preying on my youth and trust to trick me. My mind slipped against my thoughts like frantic, bloodied fingers over a wound in need of closing.

Fenris tipped his chin and cast a split-second sidelong glance my way that I felt like a knife plunged into my heart. "What? Did you think that bonding bracelet was just a pretty bit of jewelry?" He guffawed as he turned his attention back to the prowling threat that closed in around us. "She's mine."

I held up my left hand, and the whorls caught the half-light of the joined Emrys as my mind skated over the title again and again. *Wife.*

"No." The whispered word fell to the frozen forest floor, and I imagined it kept falling through the ground to the foundation of the world on which I stood, untethering me.

I was married to a monster.

M Y NAME MIGHT BE the one on the cover as the person responsible for creating this world, but I could have never done it alone.

Thank you to my husband and my children for being patient with my while I wrote this. You guys are my everything always even when I'm hiding away like a hermit in my office hunched over my laptop.

To my friend, my work wife, my chosen sister, Cynthia, thank you for letting me talk your ear off about this story (and everything else under the sun) for months, for always being there for me, and for convincing me to keep the spice.

To Jenn, my feral little heart worm, I don't know what I would do without you and your unending support and friendship.

To the Rachel my editor, and all my alpha and beta readers, thank you for making my tangled mess of words worth reading. I couldn't have published this without your feedback, or your reader reactions to inspire me to keep going even when I wanted to throw my keyboard across the room.

My deepest thanks to my street team for championing my work and helping me shout about it into the void.

Thank you to all the artists who worked on this project. I will never tire of seeing your stunning creations.

And as always, last but never least thank you God for gifting me with the words to fill these pages.

M.A. Brown is a stay-at-homeschooling mom living in Coloradowith her husband and four kids. She loves to write fantasy with a healthy doseof romance, dreamy worlds, and a whole lot of magic. When she's not creating,she enjoys hiking, camping, and gardening with her family.

Also by M.A. Brown

The Travelers Series

The Songs That Beckon

Echo Across The Sands

Whispers From The Fade (Coming Soon)

A Pennies Worth of Dread Novellas

Beyond The Iron Gate

Beneath The Silvern Pond (Coming Soon)

Below The Loam (Coming Soon)

www.ingramcontent.com/pod-product-compliance
Lightning Source LLC
Chambersburg PA
CBHW030326010826
48973CB00004B/883